KEEPING A LOW PROFILE

Merrick's mission depended on him surviving the next thirty seconds. The razorarm's forearm quills were already fanning outward, the first indication that it was preparing to attack. Without his lasers or arcthrower, he didn't have a chance in hell.

Suddenly, he remembered the stick gripped in his hand.

It was an insane plan, really. But unless he wanted to simply give up and proclaim to the world that he was a Cobra, it was the only plan he had.

Merrick leaped forward and slammed the thorny end of the stick squarely across the razorarm's face. Continuing his lunge forward, he shifted the angle of his stick and slapped it across the predator's right foreleg.

As the angry howling abruptly turned into a labored snarl, he pressed the little finger of his left hand deep into the fur over one of the animal's kill points and fired his laser.

The razorarm went limp. Careful of the still-protruding quills, Merrick released his grip and pushed himself away.

Only then did he notice that the sounds from behind him had stopped.

To his relief, Anya and the two men were still standing. Merrick took a quick look at the downed fafirs, wondering if any of them might still be a danger, then raised his eyes to Anya.

She was staring back at him, her face suddenly carved from stone.

Ville was staring, too. So was Dyre.

So much for his attempt to keep a low profile.

BAEN BOOKS by TIMOTHY ZAHN

Blackcollar: The Judas Solution

Blackcollar
(contains *The Blackcollar* and
Blackcollar: The Backlash Mission)

The Cobra Trilogy
(contains *Cobra, Cobra Strike,*
and *Cobra Bargain*)

THE COBRA WAR TRILOGY
Cobra Alliance
Cobra Guardian
Cobra Gamble

THE COBRA REBELLION TRILOGY
Cobra Slave

To purchase these and all Baen Books titles in
e-book format, please go to www.baen.com.

COBRA
SLAVE
COBRA REBELLION, BOOK ONE

TIMOTHY ZAHN

Cobra Slave

This is a work of fiction. All the characters and events portrayed in this book are fictional, and any resemblance to real people or incidents is purely coincidental.

A Baen Books Original

Baen Publishing Enterprises
P.O. Box 1403
Riverdale, NY 10471
www.baen.com

ISBN: 978-1-4767-3653-2

Cover art by Dave Seeley

First Baen paperback printing, July 2014

Library of Congress Control Number: 2013005977

Distributed by Simon & Schuster
1230 Avenue of the Americas
New York, NY 10020

Pages by Joy Freeman (www.pagesbyjoy.com)
Printed in the United States of America

COBRA
SLAVE

CHAPTER ONE

There was no reason, Captain Barrington Jame Moreau thought moodily as he gazed out the twist-glass canopy of the Dominion of Man War Cruiser *Dorian*'s flying bridge, for a spaceship to even *have* a flying bridge. None at all.

There'd been a reason once, he knew, hundreds of years ago. Flying bridges had been created for ocean-going vessels to provide the pilot with a three-quarter-view visibility when coming in to dock.

But visibility and visual docking procedures had long since become irrelevant. Spacecraft had a wide array of active and passive sensor systems, and docking was handled by radar, laser-burst, and computerized transponders, without any need for human involvement. On top of that, a vehicle designed for the vacuum of space obviously couldn't have anything that was actually *open*. Especially not a warship.

And yet, in defiance of all apparent logic, the *Dorian* did indeed have a flying bridge. It wasn't much, little

1

more than a five-meter-long half-dome nestled snugly against the upper side above the main hull and just in front of the rising bulk of the Number 326 water storage tank. It even had its own piloting console, a helm repeater that the *Dorian*'s records showed had been checked out during the warship's shakedown cruise fifteen years ago and never used again. The flying bridge was still manned during battle stations, but it was never used.

So why, his fellow midshipmen back at the academy had asked, was it still here?

Barrington snorted under his breath as he gazed out at the planet turning lazily below. For that matter, why and how were Aventine and the rest of the so-called Cobra Worlds still here?

By all rights, they shouldn't be. It had been a hundred years since these colonies had been founded out in the middle of nowhere, a long and weary three months' journey from the Dominion through the very center of the Troft Assemblage. It had been nearly seventy-five years since that safe-passage corridor had been forcibly closed, leaving the colonists to struggle on alone. The general consensus of the *Dorian*'s officers throughout the voyage had been that the colonies must surely have died off by now, and that the mission they'd been sent on was so much wasted time and effort.

Yet, here they were, strong and vibrant and even reasonably populous. And not only had they survived seven decades of being cut off from the rest of humanity, but they'd apparently even made it through their own brief war against the Trofts.

Barrington scowled. He'd seen some of Aventine, and he'd seen a lot of the capital city of Capitalia, and he'd read a great deal about the Troft incursions into Silvern and Adirondack back in the Dominion of Man a century ago. Cobra Worlds Governor-General Michaelo Chintawa claimed that Aventine had been invaded, but in Barrington's view the virtual lack of damage to their cities made that claim suspicious. The fuzziness of Chintawa's testimony, and that of the other governmental and patroller officials, didn't help their credibility any.

Still, *something* had happened here. And if it hadn't been dramatic in Capitalia, it had more than made up for that elsewhere. There were places in Aventine's so-called expansion regions that had taken more serious damage, and the courier ship that had visited Palatine had reported similar evidence of brief occupation.

On Caelian, the world no one seemed to like to talk about, there was not only serious damage to the human settlements, but the wreckage of no fewer than three Troft warships. Whether or not the incident had been an actual war, it had clearly been more than just a heavily armed trade dispute. *Some* group of Trofts had moved on the Cobra Worlds, and those same Trofts had been kicked right back off again.

The question was who exactly had done the kicking. The even more crucial question was whether that situation could be recreated.

Had the Cobra Worlds' saviors been some other group of Trofts? There was testimony and evidence that at least two Troft demesnes had been here peaceably since the invaders pulled out. If there was some Troft infighting going on, and if that rivalry could be encouraged, the Dominion's mission would be a whole lot easier.

Or had it been the mysterious people who called themselves the Qasamans? Chintawa and the other

Aventinian leaders disliked talking about Qasama even more than they disliked talking about Caelian, and all the records the techs had been able to find were vague and thirty years out of date. But the testimony of the Cobra Paul Broom and his family indicated that the Qasamans had overcome even worse Troft oppression than the Cobra Worlds themselves had. If they could be found, they might prove useful allies.

Or had the key to victory been the Cobras?

Barrington's comm toned with his first officer's ident. Double-twitching his left eyelid, Barrington brought up the projector in his cornea.

The hazy image of Commander Ling Garrett appeared. "Captain, a Troft ship has just entered the system," Garrett said, his voice stiff with the formality he always reserved for the times when someone on the *Megalith* was listening in. "Our sector. He identifies himself as a merchant from the Hoibe'ryi'sarai demesne with a cargo of food and musical equipment."

"*Musical* equipment?" Barrington echoed, frowning.

"So he says," Garrett said. "He's given us the names of his buyers in Capitalia, Rosecliff, and Pindar. We're attempting to make contact with them."

Barrington peered out at the blaze of stars stretched out behind Aventine and the three Dominion ships. *Musical equipment*? "Is he armed?"

"Meteor point-defense lasers only," Garrett said. "We've got them tagged, just in case. Team Seven is prepped and loaded if you want a closer look at his cargo holds."

"Hold, but keep them prepped," Barrington told him. "Keep trying the buyers. I'll be right down."

The Command Nexus/Coordination Hub was six decks below the flying bridge, sealed behind multiple layers of steel, twist-carfibe, and compressed neutcap. Barrington's aide, Lieutenant Cottros Meekan, was waiting by the elevator when the doors opened. "Captain in CoNCH," he called formally, stiffening to full attention as Barrington stepped out onto the upper level of the complex's two decks. Apparently, whoever on the *Megalith* was eavesdropping on the *Dorian*'s CoNCH had the visual going, too.

"As you were," Barrington called, striding past Meekan and heading for the command chair. Garrett was currently seated there, his eyes on the forward status displays; without even looking up, he stood and stepped aside just in time for Barrington to take his place.

"Status?" Barrington asked, permitting himself a small, cold smile as he settled himself in the chair. If whoever was watching from the *Megalith* was hoping to find some breach in procedure or protocol that the *Dorian*'s officers or crew could be disciplined for, he was going to have a long wait. Barrington had been trained in the fine art of politics by the very best, and he'd been playing the game for a long, long time.

"No response yet from Rosecliff or Pindar, but we've reached the Capitalia buyers," Garrett reported. "All four confirm that they're awaiting shipments, and they've sent us copies of their invoice orders." He pointed to one of the displays. "They match the relevant sections of the merchant's inventory list."

"So they do," Barrington agreed, running his eye briefly down the items and numbers and then focusing on the musical equipment section. There wasn't a single word on that particular list that he recognized. "Did you ask the music buyer what his shipment consisted of?"

"He said they were performance instruments," Garrett said. "Wind class, mainly—he called them *copper-zincs*."

"What's wrong with standard Dominion performance instruments?" Barrington asked.

Garrett's shoulders hunched microscopically. "I don't know, sir. I didn't ask."

Barrington looked back at the displays, half inclined to get on the radio to the buyer and ask the question himself. But it really wasn't the kind of detail a Dominion ship captain should personally get involved with.

Meekan might have sensed his indecision. "May I remind the Captain that the next set of hearings are scheduled to begin in ninety minutes," he murmured.

Barrington felt his lip twist. Yes—Cobra Lorne Broom's final day of testimony. And it wouldn't do for the *Dorian*'s captain to arrive at the hearings after Commodore Santores made his appearance. "Is my launch prepped?"

"Prepped and awaiting your orders."

"Have the pilot begin the final checklist," Barrington said, standing up and stepping away from the chair. "Commander, you have CoNCH."

"Yes, sir," Garrett said, sitting down again. "Do you want Team Seven to check out the Troft's cargo?"

Barrington looked over at the long-range display and the Troft spacecraft centered there. In theory, any Troft action or presence posed a potential threat. Certainly many of the *Dorian*'s officers and crewers believed that. So did the majority of the military leaders on Asgard and their political masters in the Dome.

But Asgard and the Dome were a long ways away, and the situation here on the far side of the Travis Assemblage appeared to be very different from the one at the Dominion's borders.

And if the Trofts out here really did fight among themselves… "Secure Team Seven and let the merchant pass," he told Garrett. "But keep its lasers tagged."

"Yes, sir," Garrett said.

"And alert Colonel Reivaro to their approach," he added as he headed toward the elevator. "Suggest to him that he might want a couple of his men standing by at the spaceport when those copper-zincs are unloaded."

A minute later he was back in the elevator car, glowering at the universe as he headed for the tender bay. Over the past five days he and the other investigators had had to wade through more evasion and self-serving doublespeak than he'd heard in a long, long time. Most of that fog was coming from Aventine's government officials and patroller chiefs, all of whom seemed to have something to hide about their roles in the recent Troft invasion.

But at least today there should be little or none of that. The Broom family---Paul, Jasmine, and Lorne— seemed far more forthright and honest about what the Cobras and the leaders had done during the invasion.

Or, in some cases, what they hadn't done.

Barrington turned his eyes upward. Back at the academy, the prevailing theory had been that flying bridges were simply vestiges of days gone by, places that served no purpose but were a fond memory of the distant past. From the bits of conversation he'd overheard, it appeared that most of his officers were ready to put Aventine's Cobras into the same category.

But unlike his fellows, Barrington hadn't simply accepted the common wisdom on flying bridges. He'd hunted down their history and reasoning, digging until he uncovered the cold-edged logic behind their existence.

He had every intention of doing the same with the Cobras.

For nearly a century, the Cobras had been the Cobra Worlds' primary defenders, policemen, and hunters. At one time or another, they'd also been political powers, political liabilities, and political pawns. Their prestige had fluctuated from decade to decade, from region to region, and from social class to social class. Those who depended most on Cobra protection, whether in Aventine's expansion regions or on the ecological hell world of Caelian, tended to be their strongest supporters. Those who lived in the relative safety of the big cities, particularly those who paid the lion's share of the taxes, were usually the loudest in their clamoring for a better, cheaper way.

But even the Cobras' detractors conceded that they were the visible symbol of the five Cobra Worlds. As such, their dress uniforms were the finest that successive generations of designers and lovers of pomp and ceremony had been able to create.

Next to the military uniforms of the Dominion of Man, those dress uniforms looked positively shabby.

The Dominion uniforms were the first thing Lorne Broom had noticed on his initial visit to Governor-General Chintawa's private conference room. That wasn't all that surprising, really, given the blaze of royal blue shimmer, gold braid and rank epaulets, and neat rows of intricately detailed medal triangles across the officers' upper chests. They were outfits that were clearly designed to be impressive, intimidating, and more than a little arrogant.

Or maybe it was just the uniforms' wearers who were intimidating and arrogant, and not the uniforms themselves. After yesterday's long hours of testimony, Lorne still wasn't certain which it was.

Hopefully, by the end of today he would either know for sure or would never have to concern himself with it again.

"Welcome back, Cobra Broom," Commodore Rubo Santores greeted him as two of the uniformed Cobras ushered Lorne to the witness chair in front of the long table and the five Dominion officers seated behind it. "We appreciate your willingness to give us another day of your time."

"Thank you, Commodore," Lorne said politely. Like he'd actually had a choice in the matter.

"I trust you had a good night's rest?" one of the others asked blandly.

Lorne focused on him. Most of the Dominion officers had just sat there during his previous day of testimony, listening closely but otherwise keeping silent. Even Santores seemed to prefer asking short, simple questions and then letting Lorne ramble on at his own pace.

Not so Colonel Milorad Reivaro. He was the whistling image of the stereotypical courtroom bully lawyer, questioning every little nittery error, misstatement, or perceived contradiction. His attitude had quickly turned the room's atmosphere from that of a simple debriefing into something more akin to an enemy interrogation.

And if there weren't any errors Reivaro could find to jump on, the man seemed to enjoy being simply and straightforwardly annoying.

Like he was being right now. "As a matter of fact, last night was very unrestful," Lorne told him, working hard to keep his tone civil. His father, mother, and Great-Uncle Corwin had all warned him—repeatedly— not to let Reivaro's barbs get under his skin. "For some reason Ms. Gendreves thought midnight would be the perfect time to serve a search order and have my temporary quarters turned upside down."

"Really," Reivaro said. He didn't sound perturbed or surprised by the news. "What precisely was the Governor-General's office looking for?"

Lorne resisted the urge to look over at Governor-General Chintawa, sitting quiet and alone behind the clerk's desk at the side of the room. "I really can't say," he told Reivaro. "You'd have to ask Ms. Gendreves."

"She didn't bother to specify?"

"I didn't bother to listen."

"I'm sure anything of interest will be sent to us along proper channels," Santores said. His voice was casual enough, but Lorne had seen this happen a couple of times yesterday. Reivaro had apparently been granted a long leash, but play period was over and it was time to get back to work.

Sure enough, Reivaro leaned back in his seat. "Of course, sir," he said. "I'm sure Cobra Broom is anxious to get back to his hunting duties out in Donyang province."

"DeVegas province," Lorne corrected mildly. On an impulse, he keyed in the infrared part of his optical enhancers. "I'm stationed in DeVegas, not Donyang."

On the infrared view, Reivaro's face changed color slightly as his skin flushed with extra blood. Lorne's generation of Cobra enhancements had the fine-tuning necessary to watch for the subtle signs of anger or embarrassment, and he had the satisfaction of seeing both emotions flick across the colonel's face.

It was childish, he knew, to correct the man's error in front of his fellow officers and the Cobra Worlds' governor-general. But he had to admit it felt good.

And at least he didn't follow up the spike with a bland smile. Reivaro, he felt sure, would have done that.

"Correction noted," Santores said.

Lorne shifted his attention to the commodore. The other's voice was suddenly very formal. He wasn't smiling, either, blandly or otherwise.

"I thought the record should be kept straight," Lorne said, matching the other's tone.

"So it should," Santores said. "Perhaps we can move on to actual testimony now?"

"Of course," Lorne said, feeling his face flush with belated annoyance at himself. He would probably hear about this later from his parents and Uncle Corwin. "I believe we were in the middle of the battle of Azras."

"Let's go back a bit to your trip from Caelian to Qasama," Santores said, twitching his left eyelid once. From what Lorne had been able to glean from bits of conversation, that was how Dominion people accessed their communications and data-search systems. "You said you traveled aboard a ship of the Tlos'khin'fahi demesne?"

"That's correct," Lorne said, frowning. Yesterday's testimony had progressed far beyond that particular point. Why in the Worlds was Santores going all the way back to Caelian now? "The Tlossie second heir, Ingidi-inhiliziyo, took us aboard his ship at Caelian—"

"You and the Isis equipment," Reivaro put in.

"Yes," Lorne said, suppressing a sigh. Inevitably, it seemed, the conversation somehow always came back to Isis. The Integrated Structural Implantation System that Dr. Glas Croi and the Troft demesne-heir Ingidi-inhiliziyo had created—the automated surgical machinery that the Aventine press had unimaginatively labeled the Cobra Factory—had become a virtual obsession with Reivaro.

And it didn't take a genius to see that dragging up Isis every chance he got didn't bode well for the treason charges looming over the whole Broom family. Nissa Gendreves was pushing hard to turn her formal charges into a formal trial, and though Chintawa had so far been able to sidetrack her with procedural tricks, those delaying tactics had to be close to bottoming out. Santores had made it clear that if the Cobra Worlds weren't prepared to deal with the charges quickly and efficiently, the commodore himself was.

On the other hand...

Lorne stole a quick look at the man to Santores's left. Sitting straight and tall, his face composed and unreadable, was Captain Barrington Moreau, commander of the *Dorian* and decorated member of the Dominion Fleet.

And, perhaps more significantly, Lorne's mother Jin's second cousin.

Why was he here? That was the question the family had been pondering ever since their first polite but somewhat strained meeting with Barrington a few days ago. Their conversation had been hurried, sandwiched between the parade of official testimonies, and they hadn't gotten very far past the pleasantries and what Lorne's father Paul called reception-room chatter. To Lorne, the formal tone of the meeting had made it feel almost like an afterthought, as if Barrington had been idly reading up on family history during the long voyage and suddenly discovered he was related to some of the original Cobra Worlds' colonists.

Which was absurd, of course. According to Santores, the three warships had taken eight months to circle around the Troft and Minthisti-controlled sections of space on their voyage here. The Dominion Military Command would hardly have plucked Barrington and his ship from whatever duty they'd been on and sent them along just on some random whim.

Unless it hadn't been the military's idea at all.

Lorne's great-grandfather Jonny Moreau had died relatively young, suffering from anemia, arthritis, and all the rest of the physical ailments that still plagued the men who volunteered their lives to become Cobras. It was a foreshortened future Lorne himself was facing, and one he tried very hard not to think about. But Jonny's brother Jame had been a few years younger than he was, and hadn't carried the handicap of Cobra gear inside his body. Moreover, at the time the Dominion and Cobra Worlds lost contact, Jame had been on the fast track to becoming a member of the Dominion's Central Committee.

Could Jame Moreau still be alive? He would be somewhere around a hundred and twenty by now, a decade or two beyond the best lifespan anyone on the Cobra Worlds had yet been able to manage. But Lorne had no idea what the current state of Dominion medicine was; and whatever that state was, Dominion Committés would certainly have the benefits of the very best of it.

And if Jame was alive, could he still be in power? Or at least have the ear of the people in power?

Could it have been Jame Moreau himself who'd pulled strings so that his grandson Barrington could come and see what had become of this branch of his family?

"While you were aboard the Tlos'khin'fahi ship," Santores continued, "did you ever have occasion to enter the command or navigational areas?"

Lorne snapped his attention back from his musings. The *command* area? What kind of question was that? "I was on the bridge a couple of times, yes," he said.

"Were you close enough to get a look at any of the navigational readouts?"

"I don't know," Lorne said.

"It's a simple question," Reivaro put in impatiently. "Did you get close enough to the navigational displays to read them, or didn't you?"

"And I said I don't know," Lorne repeated. "Even if I was, I certainly wasn't paying any attention to them."

"Because you were focusing on how to get Isis down and into Qasaman hands?"

"Because we were focusing on how to win the damn war," Lorne shot back.

"Which you did," Santores said, inclining his head slightly. "And our sincerest congratulations on that."

He twitched his eyelid again. "As you said a moment ago, yesterday's session ended with your attack on the

Troft warship outside Azras. Let's go ahead and pick it up from there."

Captain Joshti Lij Tulu of the *Algonquin* muttered a curse. "Unbelievable," he said, twitching his eyelid to close off the data stream. "*One* world, against a combined invasion force of at least three Troft demesnes?"

"And without any modern weapons," Barrington added.

"No, I literally *mean* unbelievable," Lij Tulu growled. "Broom is lying. There has to be more to this."

"Like what?" Barrington asked.

"Like maybe the Qasamans had a lot more help than Broom says they did," Lij Tulu said. "These three demesnes—the Tlos'khin'fahi, Hoibe'ryi'sarai and—what's the other one?—the Chrii'pra'pfwoi. Maybe *they're* the ones who intervened and kicked the invaders off the planet."

"Why would he lie?" Barrington asked.

"Please," Lij Tulu said scornfully. "Can't you hear it in his voice? He's madly in love with these Qasamans—the whole damn Broom family is. He'd say anything—he'd *believe* anything—that made them look superhuman."

"If they're so superhuman, why did they need the Isis equipment?" Barrington countered.

At the head of the table, Santores stirred. "It doesn't matter how they threw the invaders off Qasama," he said quietly. "Whether they did it themselves or had strong enough ties with the Tlos'khin'fahi and others to get them to do it for them, the point remains that they *did* drive the invaders away. And not just from Qasama, either, but apparently from the Cobra Worlds, as well."

"With a lot of help from Caelian, if Nissa Gendreves's testimony is to be believed," Barrington reminded him.

"Yes," Santores murmured. "I'm thinking that we've found exactly what we're looking for." His lips compressed. "Except that we *haven't* really found it, have we?"

For a moment the room was silent. "We could, though," Lij Tulu said.

Barrington twitched up the data stream and ran it down the transcript of Lorne Broom's testimony, feeling a swirl of conflict churning through his stomach. It was necessary, he knew.

But necessary or not, the boy was kin, his second cousin once removed. What Lij Tulu was suggesting... "What if we tried the parents again?" he suggested. "They were all in the Troft control room together, and they may be able to see the big picture better than their son."

"Are you serious?" Lij Tulu scoffed. "Paul Broom owes the Qasamans his leg. Jasmine Broom owes them her life. I'd rank those beside hero worship any day of the month." He looked back at Santores. "Commodore, we've asked for cooperation. We haven't gotten it. In my opinion, it's time to bring in the MindsEye."

"Your intent being to use it on the Brooms?" Barrington shook his head. "My patron would strongly oppose any such suggestion."

"Your patron's not here," Lij Tulu countered tartly. "And we have a job to do." He raised his eyebrows. "Commodore?"

"I agree the MindsEye is our best hope at this point," Santores said. "But there's a problem. I'd hoped

Colonel Reivaro's public focus on the Isis project would pressure Chintawa to back down to the point where we could take custody of the Brooms. Unfortunately, it's also motivated Nissa Gendreves to push that much harder to have the family tried by the Cobra Worlds government. It looks to me like that Chintawa is starting to lean that direction, and once any such trial begins the family will be off-limits to us."

"Why do we care what Chintawa and Gendreves want or don't want?" Lij Tulu growled. "We're the Dominion of Man. If we want the Brooms, why can't we just take them?"

"Because we also want to maintain good relations with the local leadership," Santores said firmly. "Until we know everything about this place, including how the various Troft demesnes fit into the picture, we need their cooperation."

"But the Brooms are charged with treason," Lij Tulu said. "The locals *have* to grant authority to us, don't they?"

"In theory, yes," Santores said. "But there are two problems. I've looked through the statutes, including the original Cobra Worlds charter. It appears there's no provision for an accredited Dominion force to assume power."

Lij Tulu stared. "That's insane," he said. "That provision's *always* in planetary charters."

"It is now; it apparently wasn't back then," Santores said. "Don't forget, the whole purpose behind the Cobra Worlds was to have a place where Dome could get rid of the Cobra war veterans before their presence became a danger to the Dominion as a whole. I can see some short-sighted Committé rationalizing that no one was ever going to come out here again and therefore not bothering to add it to their charter."

"Then simply tell them charges of treason supersede their charter."

"I would," Santores agreed. "Except for one small problem. I asked Captain Moreau to look into it, and it appears that by Dominion law what the Brooms have done *isn't* treason."

Lij Tulu turned to Barrington. "You're joking."

"Isis is Cobra, and Cobra is hundred-year-old technology," Barrington pointed out. "They might as well have given the Qasamans the secret to making iron cannon."

"But—" Lij Tulu sputtered. "All right, fine. Maybe we can't grab Lorne Broom and lock him up aboard the *Algonquin* for a week. But what about six hours? Can I have him for six hours?"

Barrington felt his stomach tighten. There it was: the end game he'd known Lij Tulu would eventually get to. "You're not serious," he said.

"Why not?" Lij Tulu shot back. "I can have MindsEye disassembled and brought down here by twenty-two-hundred tonight. We make sure Lorne sticks around overnight, maybe tell him we need another round of hearings tomorrow. If we work through the night we can have everything reassembled and recalibrated by oh-six-hundred. We take him from his quarters, plug him in, and see what we get."

"What we'll probably get is a dead Cobra and a furious local government," Barrington said darkly. "Commodore, you can't seriously consider such an action."

"Because your patron wouldn't approve?" Lij Tulu countered.

"Because it isn't necessary," Barrington said. "Not yet. We're not ready to move yet anyway. There's time to explore other avenues."

"Such as?" Lij Tulu demanded. "Don't misunderstand, Captain, I'm all for doing this the easy way if possible. But you can count on one hand the number of people on Aventine who've ever been to Qasama, or have traveled to Qazadi aboard a Troft ship. They're all the same fingers, and they're all in the Broom family."

"Maybe there's something we haven't thought of," Barrington persisted. "Regardless, it wouldn't hurt to wait a little longer before doing something that drastic."

"In theory, I agree," Santores said. "But if and when Gendreves is able to force Chintawa into putting the Brooms on trial, we'll lose even short-term access. The family will be put into detention under Capitalia's control, and we won't be able to borrow one of them even for six hours."

"We will once the trial's over," Barrington persisted.

"Only if they're acquitted," Lij Tulu countered. "Even if they are, a trial could take months. We can't afford to wait that long."

For another moment the room was silent. Barrington forced himself to take deep, slow breaths, thinking furiously. The thought of bringing his patron a report of the deliberate destruction of one of the Moreau family...

But Lij Tulu was right. Santores wanted Qasama, and the only people who might be able to get him there were the Brooms.

And Barrington was sworn to obey his commander's orders, and the laws and statutes of the Dominion of Man. He could try to talk Santores into a different course of action. But if that failed, there was nothing else he could do.

"You say you can have MindsEye ready by morning?" Santores asked.

"Yes, sir," Lij Tulu confirmed. "Provided I give the order within the next hour."

"Then do so," Santores said.

"My patron would object strenuously," Barrington said, trying one last time.

"Were he here," Lij Tulu said pointedly.

"Were he here," Barrington conceded. "In his absence, I wish to go on record as protesting this course of action."

"So noted," Santores said. "I presume, Captain, you'll want to start with Lorne?"

"Yes, sir," Lij Tulu said. "As I said earlier, his parents are in deeper emotional debt to the Qasamans and will therefore have more resistance." He looked at Barrington. "And, of course, his younger age will give him a better chance of surviving the procedure."

"We know where he is?" Santores asked.

"At his great-uncle Corwin Moreau's house, that little estate thing they call the Island," Lij Tulu said. "Colonel Reivaro has a car watching him. Shall I have them go in and bring him out?"

"No," Santores said. There was some reluctance behind his eyes, Barrington could see. But his voice was the rock-solidness of a man who's made his decision. "No, we'll let him have a final good meal with his family. Just have the car follow him back to the Dome—" He broke off, shaking his head. "I can't believe they had the gall to actually name this place *the Dome*. As if it could ever actually compare. At any rate, have the colonel's men follow him back here and make sure he settles in."

"He will," Lij Tulu promised, his fingers twitching as he made notes into the *Algonquin*'s data stream. "He certainly has no reason not to. He's not scheduled to head back to DeVegas until tomorrow."

"Good," Santores said. "Once he's settled back into his quarters, have the colonel inform him that we'll want him at a closed session tomorrow at oh-six-hundred."

"Yes, sir," Lij Tulu said, making a final note. "I'll arrange for an escort to meet him then and walk him over."

"Good." Santores looked at Barrington. "Hopefully, by this time tomorrow we'll have Qasama's location."

"Or else Lorne Broom will be dead," Barrington said stiffly.

Santores's lip twitched. "Yes," he said. "Or else he'll be dead."

CHAPTER TWO

"But the weirdest part," Lorne said around a mouthful of roast sudeer, "was the out-of-the-sky question about the command area on Warrior's ship."

"Don't talk with your mouth full," Jin's Aunt Thena admonished him mildly.

"Especially when you're working on your aunt's cuisine," Uncle Corwin seconded from the head of the table. "Such works of art deserve your full attention."

"Right," Lorne said. "Sorry." He finished chewing the bite and swallowed. "It really *is* delicious, Aunt Thena."

A chorus of agreeing murmurs ran around the table. "Thank you," Thena said, inclining her head.

Jin blinked back sudden tears. Yes, the roast was good. But it wasn't like the roasts her eldest son Merrick used to make.

The son she'd left behind on Qasama.

War meant casualties. It meant people dying. She'd known that from the start, from the minute she and Merrick had first seen the shock front of Troft warships skimming across the early-morning Qasaman sky.

Some of those deaths had been quick. Others had been slower, more lingering, more painful. Many more Qasamans had been injured or maimed, some beyond even the ability of the Qasaman doctors to heal. Those victims would carry pain or disability to their graves. For some, their injuries meant those graves would arrive far sooner than they should.

Jin had been prepared for those possibilities, at least as well as anyone ever could be. She'd also been prepared, though not nearly as well, for such a fate to befall herself or Merrick.

What she hadn't been prepared for was for her son to be taken prisoner by the Trofts, and then to simply disappear.

And the true hell of it was that she had no idea of where he'd been taken. Or, indeed, why.

Her husband Paul was speaking. With an effort, Jin forced her mind back to the conversation. "Yes, Santores threw me a similar question during my testimony," he said. "In my case, he wanted to know what I knew about navigational systems on Cobra Worlds ships."

"What did you tell him?" Jody asked from across the table.

Jin focused on her daughter. The question had been an innocent one, delivered in a mostly innocent way.

But there had been something in Jody's tone. And now, studying her face, Jin could see that there was something going on behind the young woman's eyes, as well.

"Everything I know, which isn't much," Paul said. "Typically, our nav displays show current location, previous location, and the route taken. I know the ship's computer also stores the locations of all of the Cobra

Worlds, plus the main Tlossie, Chriie, and Hoibie trading points. There's also supposed to be a limited history of recent trips, but I told them I'd never seen one."

"Did they *ask* about that last part, or did you just volunteer it?" Jin asked, most of her attention still on Jody. "Seems an odd question."

"Yes, it was; and yes, they did," Paul confirmed. "History files were specifically mentioned. My first thought was that they were trying to find where our trading partners' demesnes were located. But that's ridiculous. Half the merchants on Aventine know where to find them."

Corwin cleared his throat. "Actually—and this is all very confidential, so please keep it quiet—"

"If it's confidential, maybe you should start the quietness by keeping it to yourself," Paul interrupted quickly. "No offense, but Nissa Gendreves is still pushing hard for that treason trial. There's no point giving her extra ammunition by passing out state secrets."

"This isn't exactly a secret," Corwin told him. "And under the circumstances, I think you deserve to know. The Dominion isn't looking for the Tlossies. They're looking for Qasama."

"For *Qasama*?" Jin asked. "What in the Worlds for?"

"I don't know for certain," Corwin said. "But Qasama *is* a lost Dominion colony, and I know that Santores is already talking about bringing the Cobra Worlds' legal structure back in line with that of the Dominion. You're welcome to connect the dots however you choose."

"I don't think the Qasamans would like the way the Dominion does things," Jody murmured.

"Oh, I'm quite sure they wouldn't," Paul agreed grimly.

"Why don't they just ask Chintawa for Dome's records?" Lorne asked. "We've made, what, three different trips there?"

"Four, counting your grandfather's mission to rescue your mother," Corwin said. "The problem is—and this is where the confidential part comes in—all those records have been expunged."

Jin felt her mouth drop open. "*Expunged?*" she echoed, staring in disbelief at her uncle. "I never heard anything about that. Why didn't you tell me?"

"The Council and then-Governor-General Chandler ordered that the plan be kept quiet," Corwin said. "That veil of secrecy applied even to you." A muscle in his cheek twitched. "Maybe even especially to you."

"When did this happen?" Paul asked.

"About three weeks after she returned," Corwin said. "The Council was terrified that someone would go to Qasama for any of a number of reasons, get himself captured, and that the Qasamans would use his ship and the navigation history files to come charging across space and take their revenge."

"Which they'd essentially promised to do," Jin murmured.

"And which the Council of course knew all about," Corwin agreed. "So when the suggestion was made that Dome ban travel to Qasama and eliminate all records of its location, they jumped at the chance."

"Well, *that* was brilliantly forethoughtful," Lorne growled. "Whose clever idea was *that*?"

Corwin raised his eyebrows slightly. "Mine."

For a moment the room was silent. "And your reasoning?" Paul asked calmly.

"They were terrified of the Qasamans," Corwin said.

"And rightfully so, at least if you looked at what had happened from the Qasamans' point of view. But that kind of terror doesn't last forever. Sooner or later, whether it was this Council or the next, I knew that someone would eventually find themselves unable to resist the temptation to again go mess with the place."

He looked at Jin. "I knew how much Daulo Sammon and his family meant to you, Jin. How much the people there meant to you. So I used the Council's fear to make sure we would never bother them again."

There was another silence, a longer one this time. "The search of my quarters last night," Lorne said at last. "They weren't looking for incriminating evidence. They were hoping I had some data on Qasama."

"Probably," Corwin agreed. "I assume you *don't* have anything?"

"No, nothing," Lorne assured him. "I just wish I'd known they were coming. I could have put together a package with enough random numbers to keep them searching for the *next* hundred years."

"Just as well you didn't," Jin said. "It's dangerous to play with a screech tiger. Especially one that's already this mad at us."

"They can be as mad as they want," Lorne said flatly. "I don't really care." He snorted a sudden laugh. "You know the really fun part? The only way Santores is going to get to Qasama now will be to ask the Tlossies for directions."

"That irony hadn't escaped me," Corwin said. "Though I doubt the commodore is in the mood to appreciate it."

"I just hope the Tlossies don't give in to any such requests," Thena said, a shiver running through her.

"After what the Qasamans have been through, they don't deserve to be invaded again. Even if it's from their own people."

"Especially if it's from their own people," Corwin said. "And with that, this line of conversation is officially at an end. New house rule: when the discussion starts making Thena uncomfortable, it gets changed."

"I like that rule," Jin said, giving Jody a final surreptitious look. Sure enough, with the promise that the topic was about to change, some of the tension had left her daughter's face.

But only some of it. What was she hiding, Jin wondered, that she didn't want the others to know?

"Sounds good to me," Lorne seconded. "Dad, I notice you're hogging all the extra glaze sauce at that end of the table. How about sending the bowl back this way?"

Jody had made her decision right after dinner, as she and Lorne were gathering the dishes and taking them to the kitchen.

But she knew better than to say anything about it then. Nor did she say anything as they all dug into the cake Thena had prepared for dessert. Not until they were all gathered by the front door, saying their goodbyes, did she drop the bombshell.

"If you don't mind, Dad," she said, "could you and Mom just take Lorne back? I'd like to stay and talk to Uncle Corwin for a few minutes. I can get a cab home."

She braced herself, waiting for the inevitable flood of questions and concerns. But to her surprise, her parents just looked at each other and then back at her. "Sure," Paul said.

"And no cab needed—we'll take her home," Corwin added.

"Great," Paul said before Jody could protest. "We'll see you tomorrow, Jody?"

"Sure," Jody said, a pang of guilt digging at her. She hadn't meant to scramble everyone's schedules this way. Briefly, she thought about backing out and trying to reset this private conversation for another time. But it was too late for that now. "I wouldn't miss the annual Broom houseplant-repotting festival for anything."

"Great," Jin said. "See you then."

They left, the murmur of conversation following them down the twinkle-lit walkway toward the gate and the brighter street beyond it.

Jody gazed at their backs as they walked away from her, three shadowy silhouettes in the night. Her mother, who'd had a deadly brain tumor removed by Qasaman surgeons. Her father, who'd had a burned and useless leg regrown by those same doctors. Her brother, whose life had been inextricably intertwined with those of the Qasaman warriors he'd fought alongside in battle after battle.

Her family owed the Qasamans. *She* owed the Qasamans.

"Shall we go back inside?"

Jody shook away her thoughts. Corwin was standing beside her, but Thena had disappeared, probably to the kitchen to deal with the cleanup. "Sure," she said, taking a step back and letting her great-uncle close the door in front of her. "I'm just—I thought they'd put up more of a fight."

Corwin chuckled as he took her arm and steered

her back into the living room. "If you think we're *that* easy to fool, you're sadly mistaken. We all saw the look that settled across your face during the Qasaman part of the conversation. We were just waiting for you to make up your mind about what you were going to do next."

"Sorry," Jody apologized. "But I have to talk to someone. And—"

"There's no need to apologize," he chided her gently as he settled her onto the couch and sat down beside her. "We're family. That means we're here for each other. So. What's the problem?"

Jody took a deep breath. Unfortunately, there was no way to ease into this. "I know where Qasama is."

Corwin's face went rigid. "How?"

"The Troft transport that Mom and the Qasamans took to Caelian," she said. "It was wrecked in the crash, but Rashida Vil and I had to go back there to—well, it's a long story. The point is that Kemp and Smitty realized there was too much food for the spine leopards they were supposed to be transporting here to Aventine, so I downloaded the course history to try to figure out later where the transport was supposed to go."

"And since the transport had just come from Qasama," Corwin murmured, "its coordinates were in there, too."

"Exactly," Jody said. "So what should I do? Erase the whole thing and keep it quiet? I could. Only—" She broke off, wondering suddenly if she should keep this particular strange thought to herself.

But Corwin was already ahead of her. "Only wherever the transport was supposed to take those spine leopards," he said quietly, "might also be the place where they took Merrick."

"Yes," Jody said, feeling thoroughly miserable now. "But if I keep it, and Santores finds it—" She shook her head. "We owe the Qasamans our lives, Uncle Corwin."

"I know," he said. "Can you get into the file and edit out the Qasaman part?"

"Not anymore," Jody said. "I multi-laced everything to protect it better, and I can't edit without transferring it all onto a computer. But if I do that now, with the Dominion here—"

"They might be able to pull it out of the system," Corwin said, nodding. "And they've surely tapped into the network by now."

"That's what I was afraid of," Jody said. "I wish I'd done it before they came. But I never expected—" She lifted her hands helplessly. "What do I do?"

"You get out of here," Thena's voice came from the kitchen door.

Jody turned, her chest suddenly tight. The older woman was standing there, a dish and polishing cloth still clutched in her hands. "What?" Jody asked.

"You get out of here," Thena repeated. "I don't mean *here*, this house. I mean you get off Aventine, as quickly as possible."

"She's right," Corwin said. "So far Santores seems to be focusing his attention here. If we can get you off Aventine, you may be able to bury yourself away for awhile."

"At the very least, you can bury your recorder," Thena added. "When the Dominion goes away, we can dig it back up."

"If they ever do," Jody said, her brain racing. Somehow, the thought of leaving Aventine had never occurred to her.

And, really, why would it? Her family was here, and they were in serious trouble. The last thing she would ever do was run off and desert them.

Unless there was a critical reason to do so. "You're right," she said reluctantly. "Okay. How do I do this?"

"As quietly as possible," Corwin said, pulling out his comm and punching keys. "The *Southern Cross* is currently at Creeksedge," he said. "Due to leave for Esquiline . . . tomorrow afternoon at three. Perfect— you can go visit your Aunt Fay. They're not showing any berths free, but maybe Chintawa can pull some strings and get you aboard."

"And maybe keep your name out of it," Thena added. "We don't want Santores bumping into your name on a ship passenger list."

"Chintawa will know how to do that," Corwin said.

"*If* we can trust him," Jody warned.

"I think we can," Corwin said. "As long as we don't tell him *why* you're leaving, I don't think he'll be a problem." He started to punch in a number on his comm, muttered something, and put the device away. "And of course we don't want this on the comm system any more than we want it on a computer," he continued, standing up. "Let's wander over to the Dome, shall we, and see if he's still there?"

"Okay, but I should probably go alone," Jody said, standing up, too. "You're in enough trouble just being related to me."

"Technically, we're in trouble being related to your father," Corwin said with a wry smile. "He's the one most prominently in Nissa Gendreves's sights these days. On a more practical level, you need us along because I doubt Chintawa owes you nearly as many favors as he owes me."

"So it's settled," Thena said, setting down the dish and cloth. "I'll bring the car around."

"Maybe you'd better stay here," Corwin said, looking across at her. "If there's fallout from this later, it would be safer if you weren't on any of the Dome's security records."

"I used to work there, too, you know," Thena reminded him. "We're just a happy, innocent couple doing their grandniece a favor while taking the opportunity to catch up with old friends."

Without waiting for a response, she turned and disappeared into the hallway leading to the garage. "I guess she's going to bring the car around," Corwin said dryly. "Let's get your coat."

Traffic was surprisingly thin tonight, Jody noticed as they headed through the glow of the overhead streetlights. It had been equally sparse earlier when her parents had driven them to the Island for dinner. Maybe everyone had simply gotten used to staying indoors, as they'd been forced to do during the Troft occupation.

Or maybe they didn't like the Dominion presence any more than they had the Trofts'.

No one talked as Thena drove through her usual maze of back streets. As a child, Jody had fantasized that her great-aunt was a secret operative, believing that she drove the city's back streets as a way to evade capture by shadowy enemies. Only later did she realize that Thena took the slower route simply because she didn't care for the crowds and higher speeds on the main thoroughfares.

Now, long after the fact, reality and her daydream were finally merging. Thena was, in fact, driving the back streets in an attempt to escape notice.

Only now it was their own government, not enemy operatives, whom she was trying to avoid.

They were out of the maze of back streets and had just settled onto Appletree, one of the local roads paralleling the wide swath of Cavendish Boulevard, when a pair of headlights behind them suddenly surged forward. Before Jody could do more than glance over her shoulder, the car roared past. Thena reflexively tapped the brakes, and Jody grabbed for her armrests as she rode out the car's slight bucking. "Well," Jody murmured. "*He* sure was in a big—"

She broke off as Thena hit the brakes again, this time hard enough to throw all three of them against their restraints. There was a stomach-churning second of fishtailing, and then the car came to a jolting halt behind the vehicle that had stopped abruptly right in front of them. "What in the *Worlds*?" Jody managed through suddenly chattering teeth.

"Stay put," Corwin said, his voice tight. "Keep the door locked."

Before Jody could find anything to say, a pair of figures suddenly appeared beside the car. There was the brief screech of a lockpop and one of the figures wrenched her door open. "Are you Jody Broom?" he demanded.

Jody shrank back against the seat, her mouth frozen, her heart thudding. In the glow of the overhead lights she could see now that the man was wearing the uniform of a Dominion Marine. "Are you Jody Broom?" he repeated.

"I'm Corwin Moreau," Corwin said calmly from the front seat. "Stop yelling—you're frightening her. What's this about?"

"Something that doesn't concern you," the Marine growled, his eyes still on Jody. "We want your brother, Broom. Where is he?"

For that first frozen instant Jody thought he was asking about Merrick, that they knew about her recorder, and that it was all over. But a heartbeat later she realized that he had to be asking about Lorne. "You mean Lorne?" she managed. "I don't—"

"Damn it, *talk* to me," the Marine snarled, leaning halfway into the car.

"She doesn't know," Corwin said, putting some steel into his tone. "Why don't you just call him and ask where he is?"

The Marine muttered something under his breath. "Fine," he said.

And to Jody's horror he reached in and grabbed her arm. "Come on—unbelt. You're coming with us."

"She'll do no such thing," Thena snapped.

"Absolutely not," Corwin seconded, opening his door. "Who do you think—?"

He broke off as the second Marine slammed the door closed again right in his face. "I said she's coming with us," the first Marine said. The fury that had been in his voice was gone, leaving a quiet coldness behind. "You want to appeal it, you're welcome to come to the Dome and talk to Colonel Reivaro. But until her brother comes out of hiding, she's ours."

"Okay, okay," Jody said, her brain finally coming

unstuck. She had no idea what might have happened to Lorne, but she had no particular problem with them taking her to the Dome for a few hours. That's where she'd been headed anyway, and the *Southern Cross* wasn't leaving Aventine until tomorrow.

But at all costs she had to make sure they didn't get hold of her recorder. "Fine. Let go a second, will you?"

Silently, he released his grip on her arm. She turned halfway around in her seat, putting her back to him, and reached one hand down to the restraint release. As she did so, she slipped her other hand into her jacket, pulled out her recorder, and pushed it beneath the armrest. The restraints popped free, and she turned again and climbed out of the car. "But I really *don't* know where he is," she added, starting to close the door.

But it was too late. Before the door could shut the Marine reached past her, caught the edge, and pulled it open again. "In that case, you've got nothing to worry about," he said. Taking her arm again, he pulled her away from the car.

And then reached in and retrieved the recorder from under the armrest. "Unless this is something you aren't supposed to have," he continued, holding it up to the streetlight and peering at it. "What is it?"

"It's mine," Corwin said, again trying to open his door. "And unless you have a search and seizure order—"

Once again, the other Marine simply shoved the door closed. "Come on," the first said, dropping the reader into his pocket and pulling Jody toward their car. "The colonel will sort it out."

A minute later, they were back on the road, the two Marines in the front seat, Jody in the back.

Her pulse thudded in her neck.

There had to be a way out of this. She couldn't let the Dominion get into her recorder and find the Qasama data.

Blinking back tears of anger and frustration, she gazed out at the cityscape rolling past. They were fifteen minutes from the Dome, she estimated, maybe twenty if the Marines weren't familiar with the tangle of streets and the ramps that fed into Cavendish Boulevard.

She had that long to figure out what she was going to do.

CHAPTER THREE

They had just taken the ramp onto Cavendish Boulevard and were heading for central Capitalia when Lorne first realized they'd picked up a tail. "Dad?" he said into his parents' quiet front-seat conversation. "Don't look now, but we're being followed."

"I know," his father said calmly. "The blue Savron two cars back with the overheating left headlight."

Lorne keyed his infrareds and eased a look over his shoulder. Sure enough, the Savron back there was showing extra heat around its left headlight.

"Probably a couple of Gendreves's people making sure I don't leave town," Paul added. "Just ignore them."

"I'd love to," Lorne said. "Problem is, that's not the car I was talking about."

Paul half turned, his forehead wrinkled in a frown. "It isn't?"

"Nope," Lorne said. "Mine's three cars back from it, a green Max-7."

"You're sure they're following us, too?" Jin asked.

"Positive," Lorne told her. "He was parked around the corner when we first got to the Island. He, or they," he amended. "I never saw who was in it."

"Perhaps we should try to get another look," Paul said, his voice going a little darker. "How's your sling-frog technique these days?"

"Haven't done one in years," Lorne said, frowning as he looked around them. Out here in the open in the middle of a wide street, a slingfrog would be next to useless.

An instant later he grabbed at his restraints as his father abruptly veered off the boulevard onto an exit ramp. "Where are we going?" he managed.

"Aunt Thena's old neighborhood," Jin said. "She's been driving through the area every time she goes to the Dome for the past twenty years. I'm guessing I know it a lot better than either of our friends back there."

"Both of whom got off Cavendish along with us," Paul reported, studying the image in the mirror. "They're keeping their distance, but we've still got a parade going. Where do you want to do this?"

"Three blocks straight, then take a right," Jin said, pointing ahead. "The hairdressers' at that corner has a deep setback doorway—Lorne can duck in there after he jumps out."

"Okay." Paul looked over his shoulder at Lorne. "You game for this?"

"Sure," Lorne said, trying to sound more confident than he felt. The slingfrog was one of the military tactics they'd practiced a few times back at the academy. While many of those techniques had been adaptable to the Cobras' predator hunts, the slingfrog wasn't one of them.

Still, the maneuver was pre-programmed into the nanocomputer nestled beneath his brain. As long as he keyed into it properly and let the computer and servos do their job, he should be all right.

"Almost there," Jin called over the seat.

Unfastening his restraints, Lorne got a grip on the door release with his right hand and the edge of his mother's seat with his left. Rolling onto his right hip, he bent his knees and braced both feet against the center storage console. "Ready."

The soft click of the turn signal went on. Lorne took a deep breath. The car made a hard right around the corner—

And as the corner shop momentarily blocked the lines of sight from the pursuing vehicles, Lorne wrenched open the door, straightened his knees convulsively, and leaped out into the night.

The move would have been impossible for a normal human, fighting upstream against momentum and inertia as the car finished its turn. But the servos implanted in Lorne's arms and legs had the strength, and the ceramic laminae made his bones strong enough to take the sudden stress. He shot out of the car in a shallow arc, the door edge nearly smashing into his shin as it slammed shut behind him. The angle of his jump had put him into a sideways position relative to the ground, but his nanocomputer was already on it, having added just the right amount of spin to his body as he pushed off the center console. Even as he reached the top of his arc and started down he found himself swiveling around, and by the time he landed on the walkway his feet were positioned to take the impact and turn him upright again.

The deep doorway his mother had described was ten meters straight ahead. Using the residual momentum of his jump, he sprinted into the shadowy alcove and skidded to a halt, turning to face the opening and dropping into a crouch. As the sound of his parents' car faded away, he heard the growing rumble of the first pursuing car. Keying his optical enhancers for light amplification, he pressed against the side of the alcove and held his breath.

A second later, with a squeal of tires, the Savron with the bad headlight roared into view. There were two men in the front seat, he saw, with the passenger holding a set of night binoculars to his eyes. The engine roar changed pitch as the driver suddenly increased speed, and as the car disappeared past the other side of the alcove Lorne saw the passenger lower the binoculars.

And then they were gone. Lorne listened as their engine noise faded away, an eerie feeling creeping up his back.

Those weren't just a couple of Nissa Gendreves's warrant enforcers. They were Dominion Marines.

Had Nissa somehow persuaded Commodore Santores to take the treason investigation away from Chintawa? That could be good, or it could be very, very bad.

But there was no time to weigh the possibilities now. He'd had his look, and now he had to figure out what to do next.

Should he go into hiding somewhere? Or should he head back to the Dome on foot and play innocent if someone called him on the stunt he'd just pulled?

And someone *would* call him on it. The Marine with the binoculars had almost certainly spotted Lorne's sudden disappearance. Their assumption might be that he'd merely ducked down in the seat, either to get something or just to mess with them. But that engine surge right at the end implied they were going to check it out anyway. Somewhere along the line they would pull his parents over, at which point they would discover that Lorne had indeed vanished.

If the Marines were following Paul and Jin, whether on orders from Nissa or Santores, that would probably be the end of it. They would most likely be annoyed by Lorne's trick, as well as the fact that their surreptitious pursuit had been exposed. But there certainly weren't any official charges they could bring.

But if they were following Lorne, someone was going to be very unhappy indeed.

He caught his breath, a sudden belated thought flooding in on him.

There had been two cars following them. Only one had continued the chase around the corner.

Where the hell was car number two?

Cursing his inattention, he keyed in his audio enhancements. The distant sounds of his parents' and the Marines' cars jumped in volume, along with the city's other background noises. But there were no other engine sounds nearby. Had the car turned off somewhere else?

And then, he heard footsteps. Two sets, moving stealthily along the walkway.

Coming closer.

His right hand curled into stunner mode. Whoever was out there was about to take an unexpected nap. The footsteps were nearly to his doorway now...

"Lorne?"

Lorne felt the tension drain out of him, a combination of relief and annoyance taking its place as he straightened up. No Dominion Marines or legal annoyances this time—just Badger Werle, one of his teammates out in DeVegas province. He should have guessed that only another Cobra could have anticipated Lorne's slingfrog maneuver. "Here, Badj," he called back, and walked around the doorway wall.

It had only been a few weeks since Lorne had last seen Werle. But with all that had happened it felt more like a lifetime. It was therefore something of an odd shock to see that the man looked pretty much exactly the way Lorne remembered him.

That wasn't the case with the second man. To Lorne's shocked surprise, Dillon de Portola now had a long, ragged laser-burn scar across his right cheek and up along the side of his head. "Hey, Dill," he said. Even to himself his voice sounded strained and forced.

But if de Portola noticed the sudden stress, he ignored it. "Hey, Lorne," he replied calmly. He tapped the backs of his fingers against Werle's shoulder. "I told you he'd pulled a slingfrog."

"Yes, you did," Werle agreed, rolling his eyes. It was a game the two of them had been playing for years: de Portola pointing out a bit of his own brilliance, and Werle pretending that it irritated him. "What's going on?"

"I could ask you the same thing," Lorne said. "How come you two were following us?"

"Mainly because they were," Werle said, nodding down the street. "Dill and I came to your great-uncle's place looking for you and spotted them skulking around. We talked it over and decided we were intrigued, so we hunkered down out of their sight and waited to see what they were up to. When they took off after you—" He shrugged. "We decided to tag along."

"So what does the Dominion want with you?" de Portola asked. "Ishikuma said you finished your testimony this afternoon."

"Maybe Ishikuma was wrong," Lorne said.

"Cobra commandants are never wrong," de Portola said. "You know that."

"He reminds us about it all the time," Werle added. "He's especially never wrong when his information comes from Chintawa himself. That's actually why we're here—Ishikuma sent us to haul your butt back to Archway so you can, quote, do some actual Cobra work for a change, unquote."

"Ah," Lorne said, nodding. "Yes, I'm afraid I've been loafing lately."

"And don't think we haven't noticed," Werle said severely. "Out playing with Trofts when there are spine leopards that need killing."

"Luckily, Ishikuma sent us by aircar, so you won't have to worry about how to fill the long hours of a land drive." De Portola raised his eyebrows. "Unless there's some reason you want to stay here a few more days. We can always say we couldn't find you."

Lorne looked around. He'd grown up in Capitalia, and there were plenty of things he liked about the place. Ever since his assignment to the small towns and rural areas of DeVegas Province, he'd looked on his occasional big-city trips with a kind of nostalgic anticipation.

But not anymore. From now on, the tall buildings and masses of steel and concrete would forever be associated in his mind with the Qasaman city of Azras, and the death and destruction he'd seen there.

Cities no longer felt like refuges. Cities felt like death traps. "No, I'm ready," he assured de Portola. "The aircar's at the field?"

"Ready and waiting," de Portola confirmed. "Soon as we drop off this rental, we'll be on our—"

"Hold it," Lorne said as his comm signaled. He pulled it out, frowned briefly at the ID display, and keyed it on. "Hey, Uncle Corwin," he said. "What's up?"

"We've got trouble," Corwin said grimly. "Jody's been taken from our car by a pair of Dominion Marines."

Lorne felt his mouth drop open. "What in the Worlds for?"

"I don't know," Corwin said. "But it has something to do with you—they wanted to know where you were. Are you all right?"

"I'm fine," Lorne said between clenched teeth, a red rage boiling up inside of him. So their response to his little escape prank had been to take it out on his sister? "Don't worry—I'll get straight over to the Dome and raise whatever hell is necessary to get her out."

"You can't wait that long," Corwin said. "One of the Marines has her recorder. It's absolutely vital you get it back before they get there."

Lorne frowned. Her *recorder*? "Understood," he said, wishing he actually did. "Any idea which way they're going?"

"Last we saw, they were heading north on Apple-tree in a tan Celera, starting at the intersection with Mitchell," Corwin told him. "But they may be heading back to Cavendish."

"Got it," Lorne said, visualizing the map of the

city. That intersection was about six blocks behind them and two streets over. Even if the Marines were planning to get on Cavendish, he should be able to intercept them before they reached the ramp. "Got to run—I'll call you."

He keyed off the comm. "Sorry—"

"Yeah, we heard," de Portola said tightly, pointing the direction opposite from Appletree. "There's a patroller station about two blocks that way."

"I don't have time for—"

"Shut up and listen," de Portola cut him off. "Get to the station and get in their faces about your sister being snatched. Badj and I will go get Jody."

"And there's no time to argue, so don't," Werle added. "Make noise for ten or twelve minutes, then head over to Hollenvar Car Parts—we'll meet you out back. *Go.*"

Without waiting for a response, he and de Portola took off, sprinting down the street toward Appletree with servo-enhanced speed.

For a second Lorne stared after them, his brain still trying to process everything that had been dumped on it in the past thirty seconds. Then, spinning on his heel, he headed toward the patroller station. There would be time later to sort it all out.

He hoped.

They had reached the intersection of Appletree and South, and Jody was working on her fifth ridiculously heroic and utterly impractical scheme to get her recorder back when there was the muffled thud of a blowout and the car suddenly swerved violently to the side. For a handful of seconds she hung onto her restraints until the driver wrestled the car to a halt.

The Marine in the passenger seat swore under his breath. "Damn backwater junk," he growled, shoving open his door. "Stay here," he ordered, and climbed out...

...slowly, Jody drifted back to consciousness, vaguely aware that she was cold and uncomfortable and that she shouldn't, in fact, be waking up from anything.

A murmur in the back of her brain coalesced into voices. Two of them, male, somewhere nearby. The darkness around her grew lighter, and she realized she was lying on her back on a cold surface, her neck and head on something softer and not as cold. She opened her eyes.

And found herself looking up at two strangers. One was crouched over her, looking off to his left, the other standing on her other side and looking in the other direction.

Apparently, she'd been kidnapped.

With an effort she forced her eyes away from the men and focused on her surroundings. She was in a service alley somewhere, she decided, with three- and four-story buildings to either side of her and the only illumination coming from a streetlight half a block away in both directions. Above her, the sky was a faint haze that blocked out all but the brightest stars.

Which meant she was still in the city. A quiet, semi-deserted part of the city, probably, but still Capitalia.

And being in the city meant she was surrounded by patrollers and ordinary citizens and maybe even a few Cobras.

Carefully, she filled her lungs. She had no idea if anyone was even within earshot, but she had to

try. And she would only have one shot at this. She
opened her mouth—

Like a striking snake, the crouching man's hand
snapped up from his side and clamped solidly over
her mouth. "Hey, none of that," he admonished.

Jody grabbed at his arm, trying to wrench his hand
away. She might as well have tried to lift her parents'
car. She tried to open her mouth far enough to bite
him, but his palm was pressed too tightly against her
lips. "Easy, there—easy," the man said as she tried to
twist her head away. "We're not going to hurt you."

"I'm Cobra Badger Werle," the standing man added.
"This is Cobra Dillon de Portola. We're friends of
your brother Lorne."

Jody paused, peering more closely at the face leaning over her. Sure enough, she recognized them now
from that single trip she'd made out to Archway to
visit Lorne two years ago.

She nodded. Or rather, she tried to nod—de Portola's grip was still holding her head immobile. But
enough of the movement got through. He pulled his
hand away, letting the nighttime air flow over her face
again. "Sorry," he apologized. "But we didn't want you
screaming. Someone might have heard."

"And then we'd all be in trouble," a new voice said.

And to Jody's relief Lorne trotted up to the group.
"Lorne!" she said, getting a hand under her and starting to get up.

"No—just stay there another minute," Lorne said,
squatting down beside de Portola and gently but firmly
pushing Jody's shoulders back onto the cold pavement.
"You caught a sonic blast, and your balance is probably still shaky. You okay otherwise?"

"Yes, I think so," Jody said. "I was—"

And suddenly, it all flooded back to her. "Lorne—my recorder!" she gasped. "The Marines have it."

"No, it's okay," Werle said quickly. He dug the recorder out of his pocket and pressed it into her hand. "We got it back."

"Thank you," Jody breathed, closing her fingers tightly around the recorder, feeling the sudden spike in her heart rate start to slow down again.

"You can thank us by telling us what the hell is going on," Lorne said a little gruffly. "What's Uncle Corwin afraid of? That the Dominion will find out about your embarrassing taste in music?"

Jody flashed a look at each of the other two Cobras. "I don't—"

"And if you're thinking about going all dark and mysterious, don't," Lorne said firmly. "Badj and Dill just attacked a pair of Dominion Marines. Their necks are stuck out all the way into the next province on this one. They deserve to know what fire they just pulled your butt out of."

Jody grimaced. But he was right. "You remember Uncle Corwin telling us at dinner that the Dominion is looking for Qasama?"

Lorne nodded. "Of course."

"They're looking for Qasama?" Werle cut in, frowning. "What in the Worlds for?"

"Nothing good, I'll bet," de Portola said. "From everything I've read of Dominion history—"

Lorne silenced him with a gesture. "What does this have to do with you?" he asked Jody.

She braced herself. "Qasama's coordinates are on my recorder."

The three men looked at each other. "So erase them," de Portola said.

"Or if you want them *really* erased, let me do it," Werle suggested, holding out his hand. "A couple of arcthrower shots, and they won't even be able to tell that it was a recorder anymore."

"It's not that easy," Jody said, clutching the recorder to her chest. "There's other data there that I have to keep, and it's all multi-laced. I can't explain any further."

"Okay," Lorne said, clearly puzzled but also clearly willing to let her run with this. "So what's the plan? I assume from the fact you were with Uncle Corwin that there *was* a plan?"

"I was trying to get to Esquiline," Jody told him. "The *Southern Cross* is right across town, but it's full. He was hoping he could twist Chintawa's arm and get me aboard."

"No chance of that now," Lorne said, scratching his cheek. "Dill; Badj? Any ideas?"

"She could come to Archway with us," de Portola suggested doubtfully. "Lots of places there where we could stash her for awhile."

"No, I have to get off-planet," Jody insisted. "I need to be able to...go. Other places."

"Like Qasama?" de Portola asked pointedly.

"Just other places," Jody said. "Look, if you can't help—"

"What about the Troft ship?" Werle asked suddenly.

"What Troft ship?" Lorne asked.

"There's a Hoibie merchant on Aventine," Werle said. "He was in Capitalia this morning, but I think he's in Pindar right now."

"Yes, he is," de Portola confirmed. "I heard a couple

of people in town talking about Hoibie shipments being due in this afternoon, and about damn time, too."

"If we hurry, we should be able to get her there before he leaves." Werle looked at Jody. "If you don't mind traveling with Trofts, that is."

"Riding a Hoibie ship will be a lot safer than sticking around here right now," Jody said, suppressing a fresh flicker of uneasiness. A Tlossie ship she would have jumped at without hesitation, especially after all the time they'd spent with the Tlossie demesne-lord's third-heir. But she didn't know the Hoibies nearly so well.

But it was her best chance. Possibly her only chance. "The question will be whether or not I can get them to take me aboard," she added.

"We'll manage," Lorne said, eyeing her closely. "*My* question is, where are they headed after they leave Aventine?"

"Anywhere will do," Jody assured him, a sudden thought flicking across her mind. Esquiline was out, she realized now. With the Dominion fully aware that her entire family was involved, Aunt Fay's house would be the first off-planet location that would pop up on their list. Depending on how badly they wanted her, they could find her there without much trouble.

On the other hand, if she could persuade the Hoibies to tweak their delivery schedule, maybe she could get them to take her somewhere a little less obvious.

Specifically, Caelian.

She didn't have any family there, but she had friends. Lots of friends. Also lots of places she could hide from any Dominion force foolish enough to come after her. "And we're wasting time," she said,

once again getting her hands beneath her. This time
Lorne didn't push her back down, but simply caught
her arm and helped her to her feet. She wavered a
moment, clenching her teeth as a wave of dizziness
washed over her. "Okay, I'm ready."

"Right," Werle said. Scooping up the folded jacket
that Jody's head had been resting on, he shook it out
and put it on. "I'll go get the car. With luck, we'll be
in the air before the Marines even wake up."

Barrington just managed to get his last tunic fastener
closed before the conference room door slid open
in front of him. "All right, I'm here," he growled.
"What's all the—?"

He broke off, silently cursing himself for his care-
lessness. Colonel Reivaro, the man who'd sent Barrington the urgent wake-up call, was standing behind
the long table, his expression just short of explosive.

But he wasn't alone. Seated at the head of the
table was Commodore Santores.

And even a Dominion captain didn't barge into
the presence of a superior officer without the utmost
decorum. "My apologies, Commodore," Barrington
said hastily, coming to quick and belated attention.
At least he'd managed to have his uniform in proper
order before the door opened.

"Sit down, Captain," Santores said, his voice giving
no indication that he'd even noticed Barrington's lack
of proper manners. "We have a situation."

"Yes, sir," Barrington said, sitting down in his usual
place at Santores's left.

Santores made a small gesture. "Colonel?"

"Earlier this afternoon, as ordered, I placed Cobra

Lorne Broom under observation," Reivaro said, his voice stiff and formal. "The Marines were instructed to make sure he returned to his quarters after dinner." His throat tightened. "Somewhere on the drive back to the Dome he managed to give them the slip."

Barrington looked at Santores, but the commodore's face was giving nothing away. "How?" he asked Reivaro.

"We still don't know," the colonel admitted. "His disappearance was quickly noted, though, and immediately reported. Also reported was the fact that Cobra Broom's sister Jody had left the Moreau home shortly after Cobra Broom's departure in a car with her great-uncle and aunt. As we now had indications of coordinated action, I ordered a second Marine dyad to intercept the Moreaus and bring Jody Broom here."

"As bait to lure in her brother?" Barrington asked.

"Or as leverage," Reivaro said. "But the point is moot. The car bringing her in was ambushed, the dyad rendered unconscious, and Ms. Broom has also now disappeared."

Barrington winced. Dominion Marines didn't take well to being bested, especially not as quickly and easily as Reivaro made it sound. "Her escape was engineered by Cobra Broom, I assume?"

"Oh, there's no doubt about *that*," Reivaro said icily. "But he didn't do it directly. We have security footage of him at a patroller station at the time of the attack. Obtained after the fact, unfortunately. Obviously an attempt to buy himself an alibi while a group of his fellow Cobras carried out the actual extraction."

"Do we know how many Cobras there were?"

"No," Reivaro growled. "The Marines didn't see their attackers, and we haven't found any visual record of the incident itself. I'm told the city's security monitor system was deactivated by the Trofts during the occupation, and Chintawa hasn't yet seen fit to reactivate it."

"I see," Barrington murmured, his own comment earlier that afternoon flashing back to mind. The Cobras might be utilizing hundred-year-old technology, but that tech was apparently good enough to take out two Dominion Marines.

Of course, the Marines had been taken by surprise, with their movements severely limited by the car they were in. Under those conditions, a mob armed with nothing more than wooden clubs could probably have taken them out. "Do we have any idea where either the brother or sister are now?"

"Not yet," Reivaro said, clearly clamping down hard on his temper. "But we've questioned the parents and the Moreaus, and stress-matrix analysis indicates that Jody was trying to get off-world. Possibly Lorne, too—the family wasn't sure about him."

Barrington felt his eyebrows rise a millimeter or two. A surprisingly brazen move, trying to sneak off-world, especially considering that there were three Dominion of Man warships orbiting overhead. "The spaceport's been locked down, I presume?"

"Yes, sir." Reivaro snorted. "For all the good that'll do."

"Because," Santores said heavily, "we believe they're already off Aventine."

Barrington frowned. *How could they have—?*

And then he got it. "The Troft merchant ship."

"So we believe," Santores confirmed. "By the time Colonel Reivaro had sorted through the information and interrogation data, the Troft had already left

Aventine. It lifted from the city of Pindar...where an aircar from Capitalia arrived approximately an hour before his departure."

"Which I again don't believe was a coincidence," Reivaro said. "As far as I'm concerned, we have growing evidence of a massive conspiracy."

Barrington gave a little shrug; agreement or acknowledgment, however Reivaro wanted to take it. "Do we have a plan yet on how to proceed?" he asked, turning to Santores.

"We do," Santores said. "While Colonel Reivaro continues the investigation here, you'll take the *Dorian* to the Hoibe'ryi'sarai home world and bring the fugitives back."

Barrington felt his eyes widen. "Excuse me, sir?" he asked carefully.

"Relax, Captain," Santores said, smiling slightly. "We're not talking about a one-ship invasion of a Troft demesne. You'll merely be carrying a message from Governor-General Chintawa requesting the Brooms' extradition. He's already assured me that their demesne-lord will honor it."

"I see," Barrington said, trying to read past his commander's controlled expression. "In that case, why not send one of my couriers? I can have the *Hermes* detached and ready to fly in five hours."

"I'd prefer that our initial show of presence be a bit more dramatic," Santores said. "And with a ranking officer in command."

"Yes, sir," Barrington said, forcing back a frown. Something felt off-kilter here, but he couldn't figure out what. "In that case, Commodore, I need to return to the *Dorian* and make preparations for our departure."

"Indeed you do, Captain," Santores agreed. "Check in with me before you leave orbit for any final data or instructions. Dismissed."

It wouldn't do, Barrington knew, to question a superior's orders or information in that superior's presence. He therefore waited until he was two corridors away from the conference room before keying his comm for Meekan.

Barrington had been called out of bed for his emergency meeting with Santores and Reivaro. By all rights his aide should have answered the call in a similar bleary-eyed state. But to Barrington's complete lack of surprise, his cornea projector came on to show Meekan awake and properly dressed in full day uniform. Once again, the unofficial ship's grapevine had done an efficient job of alerting subordinates to sudden changes in their superiors' schedules. "Yes, Captain?" Meekan said briskly.

"I want you to do a search through Aventine's official computer system," Barrington said. "I'm told that Cobra Lorne Broom and his sister Jody have disappeared and are possibly off-world. I want some evidence one way or the other."

"Yes, sir," Meekan said, taking the order in his usual calm stride. "Anything else?"

"That should do for now," Barrington said. "Connect me to CoNCH, then get busy."

"Yes, sir."

The projected image winked out and was replaced a few seconds later by a view of Commander Garrett in the CoNCH command chair. "Captain," Garrett greeted him as briskly as Meekan had. "You're up early."

"You have no idea," Barrington told him. "New

orders, Commander. We're taking the *Dorian* to the home world of the Hoibe'ryi'sarai Troft demesne. We have the coordinates?"

Garrett's eyes widened, just noticeably. But, like Meekan, he'd been in the Fleet long enough to have learned how to take even the most bizarre orders without question. "Yes, sir, we do," he confirmed. "Do we have an ETD?"

"Nothing official," Barrington said. "But I doubt the commodore will be pleased if we dawdle."

"Understood, sir," Garrett said. "I'll start prep immediately. When will you be back?"

"I have a few things to finish up down here first, but I should be leaving within the hour."

"Yes, sir," Garrett said. "I'll alert your launch crew to begin pre-flight."

"Very good, Commander," Barrington said. "Captain out."

He keyed off the comm and resumed his walk toward his quarters. He hadn't brought very much down from the ship, but those few items needed to be packed. Someone else could do that, and probably should, but at this point it would be quicker for Barrington to do it himself than to roust a yeoman out of bed.

His comm toned with Meekan's ident, and Barrington again twitched on his projector. "Is there a problem, Lieutenant?"

"No problem, sir," Meekan said. "I have a preliminary report. So far I haven't found anything current for Jody Broom. But Lorne Broom has been added to today's Cobra duty roster in DeVegas province."

"Really," Barrington said, frowning. Still, it could be nothing more than a leftover scheduling fragment from when Broom was supposed to be heading back there this morning. "When was the update?"

Meekan twitched his eyelid. "Thirty-seven minutes ago."

"I see," Barrington said, forcing his voice to remain calm. "See if there's anything more on Lorne, and continue looking for Jody."

"Yes, sir," Meekan said.

Barrington keyed off, and for a moment he stared blackly at the Dome corridor in front of him. Then, spinning around in a parade-perfect one-eighty, he stalked back toward the conference room.

Meekan knew. And if a lowly captain's aide could figure this out from a simple remote search of Aventine's computer system, anyone could. Including Colonel Reivaro.

Including Commodore Santores.

Someone had lied to him. And Barrington Jame Moreau did not take kindly to being lied to.

Santores and Reivaro were still at the table, talking together in low tones. Both looked up as Barrington strode into the room. "We need to talk, Commodore," Barrington said without preamble.

For a moment Santores eyed him in silence. Then, he inclined his head fractionally. "If you'll excuse us, Colonel?"

"Of course, sir," Reivaro said, his usual annoying bluster momentarily subdued beneath his instinct for self-preservation. Avoiding Barrington's glare, he made a hasty exit.

"You have a question, Captain?" Santores asked.

"Lorne Broom hasn't left Aventine," Barrington said. "There are indications he's in DeVegas province."

"I know," Santores acknowledged calmly. "He arrived at the Cobra station in Archway early this morning and reported for duty."

"I see," Barrington said stiffly. Other flag officers he'd worked with would have either dragged out the lie as long as they could or else tried to shift the blame elsewhere. At least Santores had opted for honesty. Eventually. "Do I assume you're canceling my orders to take the *Dorian* to Hoibe'ryi'sarai?"

"Not at all," Santores said. "You yourself pointed out that Broom's sister is still unaccounted for."

"We don't need her," Barrington said.

"Don't we?" Santores countered. "Consider, Captain. Jody Broom heads for the Dome, allegedly hoping the governor-general can get her aboard a ship bound for Esquiline. When she's intercepted, she tries to hide a device we've since identified as a recorder. After the Marines are ambushed, not only is Ms. Broom gone, but so is the recorder." He cocked his head. "I, for one, am interested in knowing what's on that recorder. Aren't you?"

"I'm mildly curious, yes," Barrington conceded. "But I was under the impression that our first priority was finding Qasama. Lorne Broom is still here. If you think the MindsEye can pull Qasama's location out of him, why not just bring him back and put him under?"

"For how long?" Santores asked. "The six hours Captain Lij Tulu wanted?"

"I'd prefer the full week that'll allow him to live through the procedure," Barrington said stiffly. "Fortunately, as of now, that should be possible. With his sister's disappearance, you should be able to tag him as a material witness and announce you'll be holding him aboard the *Algonquin* until Jody Broom surrenders herself."

"I see your patron's instructed you in the art of the convenient half-truth," Santores said. "Unfortunately, it's not that easy. As Colonel Reivaro said, there's growing evidence of a conspiracy between the Aventinian government, the Cobras, and the Trofts. Lorne Broom's open reappearance in DeVegas *might* be his attempt to draw our attention and make us forget about his sister. But it might equally well be his version of a challenge for us to come and get him."

"So do it," Barrington said, frowning. "What's the problem?"

"The same problem we had earlier today," Santores said, impatience creeping into his voice. "We still need Chintawa's cooperation, and he's made it clear that he won't release any of the Broom family into our custody until the treason charges have been worked through. It could very well be that Lorne's attempting to push us into trying to take over the Cobra Worlds before we have sufficient cause. If we react to his reappearance too hastily and without careful consideration, we could find ourselves having to choose between a planetary revolt or a public and embarrassing positional retreat." He raised his eyebrows. "I have no interest in doing either."

"Understood, sir," Barrington said, trying without success to read what was going on behind Santores's eyes. "I presume, then, that you've found another option?"

For a moment Santores's eyes held Barrington's. Then, to Barrington's surprise, the commodore's gaze drifted away. "You know, it's really quite interesting," he said meditatively. "I've been reading up on Cobra Worlds history, and it's remarkable how often the

Moreau family has ended up at or near the flashpoint of some critical moment."

"It's been the same with my branch of the family," Barrington murmured, a shiver running up his back. "Am I to understand that they're about to be the flashpoint again?"

"We're three ships against an entire planet, Captain," Santores reminded him. "Several planets, actually. We can't bring Lorne Broom in for a week of interrogation against the wishes of a hostile government. We need for the government in question to voluntarily cede us that authority, or to make a flex-wrapped case to that government as to why we need to invoke martial law. And to bring that about—" His lips compressed. "Things may get a bit unpleasant."

Barrington took a careful breath. "That's the *real* reason I'm going to Hoibe'ryi'sarai, isn't it? You don't really care about Jody Broom and her recorder. You just want me out of the way so that I can't object to what's about to happen."

"It's for your own good, Captain," Santores said. "Both for your career, and for your standing with your patron."

"And if I refuse to be shunted to the side so that Lij Tulu has free rein to play with his MindsEye toy?"

"Walk carefully, Captain Moreau," Santores warned, his voice and words suddenly gone formal. "The consequences of disobeying a direct order are something even your patron would be unable to remedy."

"I don't disobey, sir," Barrington said, matching his tone. "I merely appeal the order in the strongest terms possible."

"And that appeal is denied," Santores said. "Never

forget, Captain, that you're not the only one with a patron. Mine also demands certain results. And he *will* have them."

And whoever Santores's patron was, he was probably higher on the political food chain than Barrington's was. "Then I'll content myself with pointing out that martial law is a twin-ended torch," he said. "If we end up at war with these people, we might as well have stayed home."

"I'm aware of that, Captain," Santores said. "But whatever happens, at least you'll be clear of any repercussions. That should keep you out of trouble with your patron."

"My patron is not so easily beguiled," Barrington warned. "And as long as we're talking about trouble, remember that sending me into Troft space just to get me out of your way will reduce your fighting force here by a full third. That's not a good position for any commander to be in."

"If our ships' weaponry is needed, we'll have already lost," Santores said heavily. "The decision has been made, Captain. My order stands."

"Yes, sir." Barrington straightened to full attention. "With your permission, Commodore, I'll return to the *Dorian* and prepare for our departure."

"Very good, Captain," Santores said, just as formally. "And content yourself with the fact that things seldom turn out as badly as one anticipates."

A minute later, Barrington was again striding down the corridor, his heart aching with anger and frustration and dread. Santores was right, of course. Things were seldom as bad as expected. Sometimes, they were better.

Sometimes, they were much, much worse.

CHAPTER FOUR

Merrick Broom had been through a war. He'd seen destruction and violence on a scale he'd never imagined. He'd seen men and women killed and maimed, soldiers and civilians alike. He'd been injured himself, badly, and in some ways was still not fully recovered. Even if a full healing somehow managed to happen, he knew there were physical and emotional scars that would be with him for the rest of his life.

Given all that, life aboard a Troft slave ship turned out to be almost like a vacation.

Not a perfect vacation, of course. Not the kind he'd gone on with his family when he was a boy, relaxing and comfortable and carefree. For one thing, it was hot and cramped down here at the lowest part of the ship. There was also the engines' low and pervasive rumbling, which had just enough random variation in it that his brain could never quite learn to ignore it. The food, sleeping, and sanitary facilities were wildly inadequate for the sixty men and women who eventually ended up being crowded into the narrow spaces.

And as for his fellow travelers—

"Hey!" a deep voice growled from behind him. "You—Merk. You're in my spot."

Reflexively, Merrick curled his hands into fingertip laser firing position. Consciously, he uncurled them again. It was Dyre, of course. It was always Dyre.

"Merk!"

Not turning around, Merrick lifted a hand in silent acknowledgment.

"Yeah, put your wobble hand down and get your squatter out of there," Dyre growled. "You're in my spot."

Merrick lifted his eyes from his shallow bowl to the slender woman seated across the narrow table from him. Anya Winghunter was gazing back, her pale eyes locked on his, her bright blond hair almost glowing in its contrast with her slightly darkened skin. Her lips parted a couple of millimeters, but she didn't speak.

But then, she didn't have to. She and Merrick had already been over this territory a hundred times, and they both knew what he had to do.

Which wasn't to say that either of them liked it.

"I said *move*."

A dozen sarcastic retorts flashed into Merrick's mind. Once again, he forced it all back. The men and women of Anya's world spoke an odd dialect, and while he was mostly able to understand it, he had a long way to go before he could speak it without drawing unwelcome attention. Anya had suggested early on that their safest course would be to pretend he was mute, and he'd reluctantly gone along with her reasoning.

"Merk—"

"Give him a moment," Anya interrupted, her voice

and expression stern as she stared up over Merrick's shoulder. "His hearing is not so good."

"He's in my spot," Dyre repeated.

Merrick clamped down on his teeth as he stood up and started working one leg out from under the table, trying not to jostle either of the two men sitting beside him on the long bench. There were no assigned seats, of course. Not that Dyre would have cared if there were. Merrick and Anya had tried several different spots over the course of the past few meals, and Dyre had claimed every single one of Merrick's choices as his.

"Come on. Come *on*."

Neither of the men beside Merrick was giving him so much as a millimeter of extra space, either, which made it twice as awkward. Either they were afraid of Dyre, or else they agreed with his assessment that Merrick was the person to pick on during this trip. Maneuvering carefully, trying to avoid kicking anyone, Merrick got one leg over the bench and was finally able to turn around.

And since there wasn't much room between the bench and the wall, he found himself looking up into Dyre Woodsplitter's glowering face.

Dyre was a big man, a good fifteen centimeters taller than Merrick, with a broad-shouldered fighter's physique that filled out even the extra-large version of the slaves' standardized gray jumpsuit. His hair wasn't quite as blond as Anya's, but it wasn't far behind. As far as Merrick had been able to tell from their brief interactions, the man's emotions had just two settings: silent brooding and loud anger.

So far that anger hadn't actually overflowed into physical violence. But it never seemed far from the

edge. The big man had joined the transport ship a
week after the slaves from the Qasama invasion force
had been put aboard, and for whatever reason he'd
taken an instant dislike to Merrick.

"I'm sure he apologizes," Anya continued. "We will
find another place."

"Just him," Dyre said, not taking his eyes off Merrick. "You can stay where you are."

"I choose to go with him."

"And *I* choose that you don't." Dyre jabbed a finger
toward the far end of the table. "Go. Now."

There was nothing to do but obey. Merrick turned
and picked up his bowl, sending a questioning look at
Anya as he did so. Her face was puckered, but she
gave a small confirming nod in the direction Dyre
had indicated. Merrick nodded back, and with bowl in
hand, he headed down the line of other diners. He'd
never liked bullies, and it galled him like a festering
sore to have to back down in front of this one.

But he had no choice. Standing up to Dyre would
probably precipitate a fight, and exposing even a hint
of his Cobra strength and reflexes could prove fatal,
not only to Merrick but also to Anya and the other
slaves. For now, he had to swallow his pride, keep
a low profile, and wait until this voyage ended and
they reached Anya's village.

Where he would do something. He still didn't know
exactly what.

He found an empty place near the end of the table,
across from a couple and their five-year-old daughter.
He worked his way between the men on either side of
the narrow gap—again, without any cooperation from
them—and sat down. Trying to ignore the sudden

conversational silence that had settled around him, he returned to his meal.

It wasn't supposed to have been like this. When Commander Ukuthi, the Troft in charge of the Balin'ekha'spmi contingent on Qasama, had come to Merrick with this plan, it had looked a lot more promising. Ukuthi had told him about Anya's people, apparently the survivors of another lost human colony, whom the Drim'hco'plai demesne had found and enslaved. Many of those slaves were tasked with fighting each other for the amusement of their owners, Anya and Ukuthi had told him, while others worked as house or outwork slaves.

But when the Drims had suddenly announced that all the slaves they'd sold to other Troft demesnes were to be immediately returned, Ukuthi had suspected their demesne-lord was up to something sinister. Given the sometimes intense rivalry between the demesnes—and probably given the Balin demesne-lord's reluctance to stick his own neck out on this one—Ukuthi had come to Merrick and asked him to join with the returning slaves and find out what the Drims were planning. Merrick had tentatively agreed, provided Ukuthi got him some disguised combat and survival gear and added a few combat-suited Qasamans to the infiltration team.

Only it hadn't worked out that way. The battle that the Drim commander had expected to be the final blow against Qasaman resistance had been turned suddenly and violently against him, and in a fit of frustrated rage he'd ordered that Ukuthi's two slaves—Merrick and Anya—be handed over to him immediately instead of waiting to join the rest of the group being collected from the other Balin slave owners. Ukuthi had tried to argue the point, but he'd had no choice but to give in.

Which had left Merrick and Anya unceremoniously dumped aboard this transport with no preparation, no planning, and no equipment.

And no allies.

The oddest thing about the whole situation, to Merrick's way of thinking, was that none of those setbacks seemed to matter to Anya. She had accepted Merrick's unexpected lone-wolf status without comment or qualm, simply and calmly starting him on an intensive private training course on her culture, ethos, and the parameters of slavehood.

At times he wondered whether she truly understood the magnitude of the task Ukuthi had dropped in his lap. To figure out what the Drims were up to, they were first going to have to escape her village, then infiltrate whatever garrison the Drims had monitoring that batch of humans, and *then* probably find a way off-planet to wherever the main work on the project was being done.

Merrick had seen what the Qasamans could do. With half a dozen of them at his side, he was pretty sure they could have made a respectable showing of themselves.

But by himself?

"Daddy?" a soft voice murmured into his brooding.

He looked up. The girl was staring across the table at him, her face a mixture of fascination and fear. Merrick gave her an encouraging smile—

"Leave him be, Gina," the girl's mother admonished her, making no attempt to keep her voice low. "Just leave him be."

"But his *hair*—"

"It's a different tribe," the girl's father put in, his tone warning her to drop the subject.

"And he doesn't talk," her mother added.

The girl subsided. But her eyes remained on Merrick's hair for another few seconds before she returned her attention to her bowl.

Suppressing a sigh, Merrick returned to his own meal. There was enough variant in the slaves' hair color that his own light brown didn't stand out too noticeably. But even in the two weeks he'd been aboard, he'd noticed a definite cultural bias among the slaves toward the pure blonds like Anya and Dyre.

How that figured into the culture he didn't yet know. But it was definitely something he needed to nail down before he and Anya reached her village.

"Mommy? I'm still hungry."

Merrick looked up again. The girl's bowl had been scraped clean, but the look of hunger was still in her eyes. He shifted his attention to her father in time to see his lips compress as he replaced her empty bowl with his nearly empty one.

Merrick looked down at his own meager meal. Between the run-in with Dyre and his forced move down the table, he hadn't made much headway. Ignoring his growling stomach and trying the encouraging smile again, he slid his bowl toward the girl.

She looked up, her eyes brightening. But before she could say anything her father reached across the table and firmly pushed the bowl back toward Merrick. "Thank you," he said, his voice stiff. "But she is ours to feed. Not yours."

But she's just a child, and she's hungry. Ruthlessly,

Merrick forced back the words. He was a mute, and he had to stay a mute.

There was the sound of footsteps far above. Merrick looked up, blinking against a trickle of falling dust, to see a pair of Trofts walking along the catwalk grid three meters above his head. From the heavy tool belts and the grime on their leotards, it was a fair bet they'd just come from some repair work in the engine room and were on their way back to the living areas for their own evening meal.

Unlike the slaves, they would probably get plenty to eat.

He looked back at Gina. She was working on her father's bowl, carefully scraping every bit of food from it as she had her own. There were two other human children aboard the ship, the products of marriages through the years of their parents' captivity.

Adult slaves were bad enough. Child slaves made Merrick's skin crawl.

He looked up again as the two Trofts reached the end of the catwalk, keying his optical enhancers for telescopic as one of the aliens punched in the five-digit code that opened the heavy door at the end. A minute later they were through, closing the door behind them.

Merrick nodded to himself. That was the fifth time over three days that he'd watched Trofts open that door. All of them had used the same code, with no system of personalization or daily rotation.

And to be fair, the simple approach should have been all that was needed. The slaves were way down here, with locked doors in one direction and height and a metal grid in the other. There was no reason for the Trofts to expect any trouble.

Glowering at his bowl, Merrick returned to his meal. For whatever reason of pride or culture, Gina's parents wouldn't accept food, even for their daughter, from a dark-haired stranger.

Like hell they wouldn't.

The slave quarters consisted of a pair of long, relatively narrow spaces set on either side of the engine core, tall open areas which Merrick guessed normally did double duty as access corridors and convection heat-flow regulators. During the day, the two spaces were connected around the core's aft end, with the slaves free to travel back and forth. At night, after the table and benches had been stowed, the slaves were separated, with the men bedding down in one side and the women and children in the other.

Merrick had never figured out the purpose of that separation, since the crowded conditions and complete lack of privacy would dampen all but the most serious ardor anyway. His best guess was that it was meant as a punishment, like the just-barely-insufficient food being ladled out at each meal. The Drims had been kicked off Qasama, and possibly the Cobra Worlds as well, and someone aboard was looking for a group of humans to take his frustrations out on. The slaves, being the only humans within his reach, had been elected.

Still, the forced separation did make for limited lights-out conversation and a quicker settling down to sleep. Tonight, that was going to work to Merrick's advantage.

He waited half an hour after his auditory enhancers confirmed the last of the men had settled into the slow breathing pattern of deep sleep. Then, being careful not to disturb those on either side of him, he got up, rolled his sleeping pallet, and tucked it under his right arm. He set a target-lock on the catwalk to give his nanocomputer the range, bent his knees, and jumped. As the top of his leap brought him beneath the catwalk he slipped the fingers of his left hand through the grating, curling and locking the joints in place.

The grate, he'd seen earlier, was made up of meter-square sections secured with bolts at each corner. He lifted his legs and braced his feet against the wall, then unrolled the pallet and laid it across his chest and legs to absorb the droplets of molten metal he was about to create. With four quick shots from his fingertip laser, he cut through the four bolts on one of the sections. Easing the gridwork out of its frame, he lifted it up and over and set it down on the next section, then pushed his pallet though the opening and followed. He replaced the loose section, spot-welded it back in place with four shorter bursts from his lasers, and headed down the catwalk, his pallet again rolled and tucked under his arm.

Thirty seconds later, he was through the door and inside the Troft section of the ship.

For a moment he stood still, listening with full audios to the hum of the engines, fighting against the sudden urge to do something more meaningful than simply steal a little food. If he could slip through the darkness to the heart of the ship and take control—

Then all of them would be dead, because he hadn't the foggiest idea of how to fly a Troft spaceship. Or even a human one, for that matter. For better or worse, he had no choice but to see this through the way Ukuthi had laid it out for him. He would find some extra food, and he would get back to the slave quarters, and that would be it for tonight.

He took another deep breath, focusing this time on the smell. The kitchen would be the best place to look, but he had no idea where it was, and he could detect no likely aromas that might lead him there.

But there were other possibilities. Taking a final sniff, wondering briefly if anyone had ever proposed adding olfactory enhancements to the Cobras' repertoire, he started down the darkened corridor.

One turn later, he found what he was looking for: an open door with soft light spilling out. Notching up his hearing, he glided toward it.

It was, as he'd surmised, some kind of engineering monitor station. A lone Troft was sitting in front of a bank of monitors, his back to the door, his posture that of someone in a state of either complete relaxation or utter boredom.

Throwing a quick glance both ways down the corridor, Merrick stepped inside the room. He'd been in Tlossie merchant ships a couple of times, and had noticed that monitor stations usually included a small selection of snacks and drinks for the crewers on duty. If Drim protocol worked the same way...

It did. Just as he'd hoped, there was a small flat case fastened to the wall.

Only instead of being beside the door near Merrick, which was where it was on Tlossie ships, this one was fastened to the left-hand wall, well within the duty crewer's peripheral vision.

Merrick scowled. This was going to be risky. But the option was to go back empty-handed and spend the rest of the trip watching Gina and the other children stay hungry. Bracing himself, moving as quietly as he could, he eased forward.

He closed to within a meter of the Troft. Then, lifting his right arm, he pointed his little finger at the back of the alien's head and triggered his stunner. The low-power current arced across the empty space, and with gratifying swiftness the Troft slumped in his seat.

Merrick moved to the alien's side, feeling his stomach tighten as he activated his opticals' infrared. But the stunner had worked exactly as it was supposed to: the heat pattern in the Troft's face showed that he was indeed unconscious. Leaning the chair back, Merrick adjusted the alien into a more comfortable position, the kind a tired and bored crewer might have settled into just before nodding off. With luck, that would be the conclusion the Troft would come to upon awakening, and would decide the better part of valor would be to keep his guilty conscience to himself.

With even more luck, he'd do all that waking and thinking before someone else wandered in and found him. Merrick had no idea how hard it was to wake a Troft from a stunner blast, and he wasn't anxious to find out.

The snack case was half full of meal bars and bottled drinks. Merrick wasn't familiar with this particular type of bar, but he knew from years of Cobra Worlds experience that human and Troft metabolisms were close enough that each group could eat any but the most exotic of the others' food. He selected three of the bars and slipped them inside his jumpsuit, closed the case, and started to leave.

And paused. The Trofts mostly ignored the slaves

except when it was time to feed them. But the overhead catwalks saw plenty of traffic. If one of the aliens spotted the children with the bars, there would be serious trouble.

Unless he could turn potential inquiries in the wrong direction.

It took a minute to find a small scratch pad and stylus tucked away in a drawer of the center monitor array. Quickly, he scribbled out a note in the best cattertalk script that he could manage.

The extra food, it is for the children. Hunger, it is not proper for the young to feel it. Secrecy, I beg you to keep it.

He folded the note and stuffed it into his jumpsuit beside the meal bars. It wasn't a particularly brilliant diversion, he knew. But with all the slaves theoretically locked away it would give any investigation someplace else to start.

Assuming that at least some of the slaves in there could read cattertalk. If not, Anya would have to translate for them. Hopefully before someone started excitedly waving the bars around and drawing unwelcome attention.

He'd had some concerns that the doors into the slave areas would have a different access code than the one at the end of the catwalk, which would have forced him to get back into his sleeping room the same way he'd left it. But just as the Trofts had seen no need to rotate their codes, they also apparently didn't want their engineering staff having to remember different numbers for the various doors in their sector. The code he'd used upstairs unlocked the door, and a moment later he was inside the women's sleeping area.

As Merrick had instructed, Anya had taken the position nearest the door tonight. She was sound asleep as he tiptoed over to her, and stayed that way as he tucked the meal bars and the note under the edge of her pallet. He slipped out again, closing the door behind him, and walked around the bulk of the engine core to the men's side.

A moment later, less than five minutes after he'd left, he was back inside.

It took another minute of careful maneuvering to make his way between the closely-spaced pallets. But finally he reached his spot and unrolled his own pallet. Lying down, relieved that it was all over, he closed his eyes, keyed off his opticals, and settled down to sleep. Almost as an afterthought, he boosted his hearing for a moment, listening to the soft sounds of breathing around him.

And froze. Amid the murmured sea of slow breathing was a single, distinctly faster rhythm.

Someone else in here was also awake.

He held his breath, trying to pinpoint the other's location. But between the background engine hum and the rest of the breathing around him, he couldn't even pick out a general direction.

But if he sat up and used his infrareds, he should be able to identify the other by his stronger facial blood flow.

Except that if he did that, the other might spot him, too.

Or had he already seen Merrick's stealthy return? If he had, and if he'd already identified him, Merrick would have nothing to lose.

But there was no way to know if that was the case.

In fact, the odds were probably stacked in the opposite direction. Chances were high that the insomniac had simply come briefly awake during the natural rhythm of his sleep cycle and was already starting to go back under again. He might not even have opened his eyes.

And even if he had, he surely couldn't have seen Merrick very clearly in the dim light. He might also have lost track of Merrick's movements as he crossed the room, adding to the likelihood that he didn't have a clear idea who the midnight traveler had been. Even if he'd seen everything perfectly, his logical assumption would be that Merrick was simply returning from a trip to the lavatory.

Which meant that Merrick's best course of action was to stay low and not draw extra attention to himself by sitting up and looking around.

In other words, to do nothing.

Reluctantly, he rolled onto his side, tucking one arm beneath his head. The logic was sound enough. But if worse came to worst—if all those long odds had indeed stacked up against him—it was an even surer bet that the watcher out there would be telling the Trofts about it as soon as they showed up with the slaves' breakfast. In that case, this might be the last full night's sleep Merrick got.

It would probably be best not to waste it.

CHAPTER FIVE

The Dome's hallways were deserted, the windows and skylights showing nothing but an empty, street-lit city. Jin's footsteps echoed unnaturally loudly in her ears as she and the two Dominion Marines walked along, the sounds forming an eerie counterpoint to the thudding of her heart.

The Marines were just as silent as the hallways, having not spoken since opening the door of her holding cell and ordering her to come with them. The other pair of Marines standing guard at the conference room door were even less talkative, merely nodding acknowledgment to her escort and opening the door at their approach.

Taking a deep breath, Jin stepped through the doorway.

Commodore Santores was seated alone at the head of the table, staring down at the tabletop, his eyelids occasionally twitching. Reading something, apparently, from their fancy data system. The Marines ushered Jin to a seat a few chairs down from him and motioned for her to sit. She did so, noting that Santores hadn't yet looked up or given any other sign that he was aware of her arrival.

She smiled cynically. If the early-morning wake-up call followed by the seemingly oblivious and uncaring interrogator act was supposed to impress her, they were going to be disappointed. She'd been through a war and back, and the intimidation value of stern, authoritative disapproval didn't even begin to register. Settling back in her chair, wishing her generation of Cobra infrareds was sophisticated enough to allow her to track Santores's emotional state, she waited for him to make his move.

"You're smiling, Cobra Broom," Santores said, his eyes still on the table. "You find something about this amusing?"

"Just admiring the theatrics, Commodore," Jin said. It was risky, she knew—for some people, even a suggestion that they were being laughed at could turn pompous arrogance into cold fury. But a senior military officer should have better self-control than that.

To her mild surprise, Santores actually chuckled. "Touché," he said, finally looking up at her. "Do you still use that term? Touché?"

"We do," Jin said, relaxing slightly.

And immediately chided herself for it. If intimidation didn't work, she knew, false friendship was the next most promising tactic.

"Sorry to drag you out of bed so early," Santores continued, giving his eyelid one final twitch. "I trust your quarters weren't too uncomfortable?"

"They couldn't have been nicer," she assured him. "Paul and I had no idea how pleasant the Dome's holding cells were. We're already talking about changing next year's vacation plans."

"I understand your frustration," Santores said. "Actually, the *Megalith*'s brig is more comfortable, and I suspect the food is considerably better. But Governor-General Chintawa insisted you remain on the ground."

"I'll be sure to take that up with him later," Jin promised. "Was putting Paul and me together his idea, too? Or were you the one who hoped we'd spill some deep, dark secrets in a bugged cell?"

Santores shrugged. "You'd be surprised how many people equate solitude with privacy," he said without embarrassment. "Not on a conscious level, of course—people aren't *that* gullible. But on an emotional level, many still can't resist the chance to compare notes or seek solace."

"Well, you obviously didn't bring me here for solace," Jin said. "Does that mean you want to compare notes?"

"I have no interest in your notes, Cobra Broom," he assured her. "But as a courtesy, and in recognition of your service during the recent Troft incursion, I thought I'd offer you a brief look at mine."

Jin felt her eyes narrow. "I'm listening," she said cautiously.

"Here's what's about to happen," Santores said. "Later today, your son Lorne is going to do something foolish. He'll either attack a member of my crew, allow a member of my crew to be harmed, or defy a direct order by that same crewman. When that happens—"

"My son would never disobey a legal order."

"When that happens," Santores continued emotionlessly, "he'll have broken Dominion law, and we'll be able to bring him up on Dominion charges. Chintawa will resist, but he'll have no choice but to release him into our custody."

"And what do you expect that to gain you?"

Santores pursed his lips. "There's a device aboard the *Algonquin* called the MindsEye," he said. "For various legal and political reasons it's under the control of Captain Lij Tulu." A grim smile touched his lips. "And the captain is *very* eager to use it."

Jin forced herself to relax. Even the name of the device was sending chills up her back. "You going to tell me what it does? Or do I have to guess?"

"No guessing required," Santores assured her. "The MindsEye sifts through the neural patterns and connections within the subject's brain in an effort to reconstruct his or her visual and auditory memories."

Jin stared at him, her stomach tightening. "What sort of memories?"

"All of them," Santores said calmly. "Personal memories. Private memories. Embarrassing memories. Sometimes even legally actionable memories."

"And you can do this to *anyone*?"

"Anyone whom the law permits us to examine. There are legal safeguards, of course."

"I'm sure there are," Jin said, fighting to keep the sudden fear and anger out of her voice. And Lij Tulu wanted to use this hellish machine on her *son*? "What kind of state is the victim in after you're finished with him?"

"The subject, not the victim," Santores corrected. "If it's done properly and there are no complications, he walks out of the chamber in perfect health and with all his memories intact." He shrugged. "Though, depending on what the survey reveals, he may face other legal problems."

"And if it *isn't* done properly?"

"It will be," Santores promised. "Once he's under official charges, we can take him to the *Algonquin* and take the time necessary to do the job right."

"Instead of rushing through it like a wrecking hammer?"

"You're joking, but that's basically what Captain Lij Tulu originally proposed," Santores said. "He wanted your son brought back here this evening on the pretext that we needed another day's worth of testimony from him. Unfortunately, that would have given us only a few hours to run the procedure before someone noticed his absence and started asking questions." He shrugged. "As you may have noticed, Governor-General Chintawa is very protective of you."

"That's because we're up on treason charges and he doesn't want to anger the Syndics who are on Nissa Gendreves's side of this," Jin said mechanically, her attention still back on the MindsEye. "Rushing the procedure is bad, I assume?"

"We would get what we wanted," Santores said obliquely. "The point is that, hopefully, we won't have to go that route."

"And what exactly is it you want?"

"Nothing terrible," Santores said, eyeing her closely. "I certainly wouldn't use anything illegal we discovered to bring charges against your son. All we want is his image of the navigational display of the Troft ship that took you to Qasama."

Jin curled her hands into fists. So Uncle Corwin had been right. The Dominion wanted Qasama, and they were willing to turn her son's brain inside out to get it. "I doubt he even looked at the display," she said as calmly as she could. "I know *I* didn't. There were more pressing matters on all of our minds."

"He doesn't have to have looked directly at it," Santores said. "A peripheral image might be enough. The only way to know is to try."

"I'll take your word for it," Jin said. "I hope you're not too disappointed when it doesn't happen."

Santores shrugged. "As I said, we can but try."

"I meant when Lorne doesn't fall into your trap," Jin said, getting to her feet. "If you'll excuse me, the Cobra guards at our holding cell are probably wondering where I went, and we wouldn't want them getting concerned. As you said, the governor-general is rather protective."

"Sit down, Cobra Broom," Santores said, his voice suddenly dark and ominous. "I'm not finished with you yet."

"Yes, you are," Jin said. "I'm under Cobra Worlds authority, remember?"

"And if I order my men to detain you?"

Jin looked measuringly at the two Marines standing behind her, their faces expressionless. Unlike the ceremonially-garbed group that had played escort to Santores and the other Dominion officers at the hearings, these men were dressed in high-collared burgundy-black outfits made of a heavy-looking material that shimmered strangely in the room's indirect light. The men had small sidearms belted at their waists, but Jin guessed those were mostly for show, and that the suspiciously thick epaulets on their shoulders were where they carried their main firepower. "I doubt Captain Moreau would be pleased with such an action," she warned.

"I'm sure he wouldn't," Santores agreed. "Unfortunately for you, Captain Moreau isn't here. He and the *Dorian* left Aventinian space thirty minutes ago."

Jin stared at him. "He's *gone*? Where?"

"To the Hoibe'ryi'sarai home world to collect your wayward daughter," Santores said. "A six-day round trip, according to Chintawa, plus whatever time he requires to serve Chintawa's extradition request. Plenty of time for us to arrest your son in Archway and start the MindsEye procedure."

"Jody's never been to Qasama," Jin protested. "Leave her alone—she's of no use to you."

"Most likely not," Santores agreed. "On the other hand, she has a recorder she and your son worked very hard to keep out of our hands. I'm rather curious to see what she has on it."

"If it's of any use to you, she'll already have erased it."

Santores raised his eyebrows. "But she *will* have looked at it."

Jin felt her blood go cold. "Are you suggesting—?"

"Why not?" Santores gave an odd sort of finger twitch. "You see, Cobra Broom, there's no way for you to win. Even if you're right about your son avoiding Colonel Reivaro's provocations, it won't matter. In a few days we'll have your daughter."

Jin took a deep breath. "You will not do this," she said quietly, enunciating each word like it was a hand-crafted threat. "Not to my family."

"We're the Dominion of Man," Santores said, his tone matching hers precisely. "We do whatever we want. Now sit down. Or my men will make you."

"You have no authority to give such an order," Jin said, trying to force back her fury. He was goading her, she knew, using the same tactic he'd already said he was going to use on Lorne. Trying to force her into making a move that would let him snatch her out from under Chintawa's protection and put her under Dominion law.

But knowing the facts didn't matter. Her whole body was shaking with the overwhelming desire to wipe that superior look off the man's face.

No, she told herself firmly. *Not now. Not yet.* "And your men don't dare attack without provocation or legal authority," she managed. "But they're welcome to walk me back to my cell."

"Perhaps they'll walk you to the gates of hell," Santores said.

A whisper of air brushed the back of Jin's neck as one of the Marines behind her took a step forward. A quick ceiling flip, she knew, would land her behind Santores and put him between her and his men's weapons...

With a final, supreme effort, she forced herself to stand perfectly still. "Are you threatening me, Commodore?" she asked instead.

For a moment no one moved or spoke. Then, with a small, ironic smile, Santores gestured to the Marines. Jin turned her head far enough to see them each take a step backward. "You're a cool one, Cobra Broom," Santores said, a hint of grudging admiration in his voice. "I would have bet heavily that just hinting at danger to your children would drive you into an attack."

"You should be damn glad it didn't," Jin told him darkly. "I'm already charged with treason. The murder

of a Dominion commodore could hardly have made
things worse."

Santores shook his head. "You'd never even have
reached me."

"You think not?" Jin looked at the Marines again.

"I know not," Santores said scornfully. "These are
Dominion Marines, with the best personal weaponry
ever created. Your hundred-year-old Cobra technology
wouldn't have had a chance."

"Really?" Jin countered. "When did the human
body become immune to lasers, sonics, and high-
voltage current?"

"Since we created uniforms that deflect or disperse
lasers, ear implants that block sonics, and conductive
micromesh that drains away current," Santores said
calmly. "And with shoulder-mounted lasers that fire
wherever the soldier is looking, even your target-lock
system is obsolete."

"I see," Jin said in a subdued voice. So the Dominion had scrapped the whole Cobra concept in favor
of a version of the Qasaman combat suits. Interesting.
"Can I go back to my cell now?"

Santores exhaled a slightly frustrated-sounding sigh.
"For the moment. Marines, return her to confinement."

A minute later Jin was again walking down the corridor through the darkened dome and the darkened city.

So Santores liked to play cliff-edge games, did he?
There'd been plenty of politicians like that during
Uncle Corwin's days in the Dome, she remembered.
In the end, every one of them had either been taken
down by someone who played the game better, or else
had outsmarted themselves right off the cliff.

Santores would go the way of all the others. That

much she was sure of. She just hoped he didn't take down her family or her world before that happened.

In the meantime, she'd survived his first move. She could only hope Lorne would do the same.

The Hoibie merchant ship captain hadn't been happy with Jody's request to hitch a ride. He'd been even less happy when he learned she was hoping for that ride to take her to Caelian, nearly two days and exactly 180 degrees off his plan of heading straight for home.

None of that exactly surprised Lorne. What *did* surprise him was the fact that it took less than ten minutes for Jody to persuade him to accept her request anyway.

On Aventine, the Broom name might be linked to treason, he mused as he and the other two Cobras continued their trip toward DeVegas province and the provincial capital of Archway. But for the Hoibies, the Broom name was linked to victory.

What that victory consisted of for them, he had no way of knowing. Maybe it had manifested in a major restructuring of the local demesnes' precedence order. Maybe it had created a situation where resources or cash traded hands. Maybe it had simply been a welcome humiliation of a rival demesne and its allies.

But whatever the Hoibies had gained, it had apparently bought enough goodwill to get Jody safely off Aventine. For now, and for Lorne, that was all that mattered.

Getting Jody away from Santores's people had been Lorne's primary goal. Now, with that accomplished, he was ready to tackle his next task: drawing the Dominion's attention toward himself and hopefully deflecting it away from inquiries about his sister's whereabouts until the Hoibies were ready to lift. Keeping himself out of Santores's target-lock as long as possible would be an added bonus.

Fortunately, there was a way for him to accomplish both.

Ten minutes after Werle set the aircar down at the Archway field, Lorne had signed himself into the Cobra duty roster for the day. Five minutes after that, as Werle headed for his apartment and some long-overdue sleep, Lorne and de Portola headed the opposite direction: through one of the gates in the city's perimeter fence on nighttime patrol.

If the Dominion people had any brains, their first try at a computer check would spot the roster and mark him as being back in DeVegas. But with night patrols by definition following semi-random paths through the province's fields and grazing lands, anyone Santores sent out to bring him back to Capitalia would have the devil's own job finding him. They would first have to track everyone who was out and about, then figure out which of them were Cobra teams and which were ordinary citizens getting a jump on the day's chores, and *then* get close enough for a positive identification. By the time they did all that, Jody should be well on her way to Caelian.

They'd been on patrol for three hours, with dawn less than an hour away, and were circling through the western part of Dushan Matavuli's grazing land when a sleek aircar of unfamiliar design suddenly appeared directly above them, the red glow from its grav lifts blazing as the vehicle dropped like a stone. It braked at the last possible second and settled with only a small bounce across the dirt road twenty meters ahead of them.

"Nice," de Portola commented as he let their car roll to a stop. "Makes you want to hop right out and applaud, doesn't it?"

"I always like to wait until the orchestra stops playing and the performers take a bow," Lorne said, eyeing the two big men who had now emerged from the aircar and were striding toward them. Unlike the fancy dress uniforms the Dominion men had worn at the Capitalia hearings, these outfits were unadorned burgundy-black suits that shimmered strangely in the car's headlights. A quick check with his opticals' infrareds indicated the men's stony expressions were hiding some serious annoyance.

More interesting was that the infrareds also showed a noticeable heat signature in the thick rank epaulets on both men's shoulders. "Dill, take a look at those epaulets," he said.

"Yeah, I see it," de Portola said thoughtfully. "Any ideas?"

"Back in my great-grandfather's day, Dominion Marines had weapons called parrot guns on their shoulders," Lorne told him. "Automatic target tracking, with a choice between pulse lasers or short-range antipersonnel missiles. The pictures I've seen showed the things as being pretty bulky, which I gather was part of the point."

"Like snipe dots," de Portola said, nodding. "You're obviously being targeted, so you behave yourself."

"Right," Lorne said. "Looks like the Dominion's dropped blatant in favor of subtle this time around."

"Could be," De Portola agreed. "I wonder how you target-lock the things."

"Maybe we'll find out," Lorne said, unfastening his

restraints as the two Marines split formation, one heading down each side of the car. "Okay; nice and innocent."

The Marines reached the two car doors simultaneously. There was a screech of a lockpop, and the man on Lorne's side pulled the door open. "Lorne Broom?" he demanded.

"Morning, soldier," Lorne greeted him genially. He nodded at the door. "It *was* unlocked."

"Are you Lorne Broom?" the other repeated.

"Yes," Lorne said. "And you?"

The Marine glanced over the top of the car at his companion, then looked down at Lorne again. "It's Marine, not soldier," he corrected stiffly. "Marine Sergeant Singal Khahar."

"This is Cobra Dillon de Portola," Lorne said, nodding at his companion. "You here to try your hand at killing some spine leopards?"

The Marine on de Portola's side of the car snorted. "Hardly. We came to drag your—"

"Squelch it, Chimm," Khahar cut him off. "Sure, why not? Where do you keep them?"

"Everywhere you want, and most places you don't," Lorne said, gesturing Khahar back. The sergeant's eyes narrowed, but he obediently stepped back to make room for Lorne to get out of the car. "Down along Sutter's Creek is usually a good place to start," Lorne continued, pointing toward the wooded slope fifty meters away.

"We're always clearing nests and way stations out of the groves bordering the creek," de Portola added as he also got out of the car. "You two should probably hang back a little—they can come at you from unexpected directions. We'll show you how it's done."

"You just worry about yourselves," Khahar said. "We'll be fine."

"I'll take point," de Portola offered, and headed toward the cluster of trees and high grass. Keying in his infrareds and light-amps, Lorne followed.

They'd reached the tall grass on the edges of the grove, ten meters from the bank, when he caught the first hint of something warm in the middle branches of one of the trees. It was too diffuse to get a positive identification, but the positioning suggested that it was an adult, probably a male.

De Portola had spotted it, too. He snapped his fingers softly and pointed to the tree. Lorne snapped twice in acknowledgement, and as de Portola angled to the right of the tree, Lorne shifted toward the left. A straightforward flanking maneuver would draw out the spine leopard and force it to choose between the two targets.

Lorne was still focused on the tree when, to his stunned disbelief, the two Marines strode between him and de Portola and headed at a brisk walk straight for the tree. "Wait!" Lorne whispered. "Don't go that—"

Too late. With a crackle of displaced branches, the spine leopard leaped out of concealment. It hit the ground running, headed straight toward the Marines.

Lorne swore under his breath. The timing of that bonehead move had left him off-balance, his weight on his left leg, unable to bring the antiarmor laser running along that calf to bear on the attacker.

Fortunately, de Portola had been on his right leg when the spine leopard made its move. Even as the predator put on a burst of speed, he twisted to his right and swung up his left leg. The blue beam flashed from his heel to cut across the spine leopard's head and flank. Its legs collapsed beneath it, and it plowed into the ground with a mournful screech.

As its final howl faded into the night, a dozen spine leopards boiled up into view from beneath the bank and charged.

Lorne dived to his right, flicking target locks on the three nearest predators as he sailed through the air. He landed hard on his side, his vision jolting with the impact as he triggered his antiarmor laser. His body swiveled around as his nanocomputer took control of his servos, pivoting him around his shoulder and swinging his left leg up to fire a triple blast into the spine leopards he'd targeted. He blinked to clear his vision, only to spot the rippling wakes in the tall grass that meant two more of them were headed toward him.

There was no time for even his nanocomputer to get his leg into position for these two. Rolling over onto his back, he pointed his right-hand little finger at the first of the predators and triggered his arcthrower. The high-voltage current snapped through the grass, riding the ionized path that his fingertip laser had burned through the air a microsecond earlier, and the spine leopard jerked and collapsed. There was a multiple flash of blue laser fire from somewhere to his left, and the second predator skidded to a halt in the brush.

And with that, the world was suddenly quiet.

Lorne frowned, running a quick mental count. That couldn't possibly be it—he and de Portola couldn't have accounted for more than half the predators he'd seen charging them. And with a group this big there was usually a second wave, as well.

"You chirpies always make such a big a deal about these things?" Khahar asked into the silence.

Frowning, Lorne sat up. The two Marines were just standing there, more or less where they'd been when the attack began, their faces wreathed in self-satisfied smirks.

Scattered on the ground around them were eight dead spine leopards.

"They're getting themselves all dirty, too," Chimm added. "Not very professional, are they?"

"Hey, we can't *all* be Dominion Marines," Khahar chided his partner. "Give them some slack."

"Sure thing," Chimm said. "But they promised to show us some action." He raised his eyebrows blandly at Lorne. "That wasn't it, was it?"

For a couple of heartbeats Lorne was seriously tempted to flatten both men with a blast from his sonic. But common sense kicked in, reminding him that it wouldn't gain him anything except a brief moment of childish satisfaction.

On the other hand, if he kept his temper he might be able to learn something. Getting slowly to his feet, he adjusted his opticals' infrared settings and gave the two Marines a good, hard look.

Mostly of what he saw was the standard human infrared pattern, topped off with the condescending cheerfulness he'd already noted. But there were two interesting anomalies. The first was the thick rank epaulets, which had an strong layer of heat everywhere except along the inside edges close to the Marines' necks. Parrot guns, almost certainly. The second anomaly was a close-knit grid of slightly higher warmth throughout their uniforms, especially along the front of their torsos and down their thighs to their knees.

"Nicely done," de Portola said with a grunt as he

hopped back up and brushed at his back and butt where he'd been rolling around on the ground. "I never even saw you draw."

Lorne looked down at the Marines' belted sidearms. Neither of the guns had so much as a hint of infrared to them.

The sidearms hadn't been fired. They'd probably not even been drawn. Pure camouflage, put there to distract a potential enemy form their real weaponry.

"You weren't supposed to see us," Chimm said loftily. "Like the sergeant said, not everyone can be Dominion Marines."

"I'm sure we backwater amateurs have a lot to learn," de Portola said with far less sarcasm than Lorne would have felt justified in using. "Spine leopards aren't easy to kill, either. Those things must pack a real punch."

"And have some nice targeting capabilities on top of it," Lorne agreed, notching up his opticals' magnification a little and studying the nearest of the dead spine leopards. Instead of the massive laser burn he'd expected to see, there was a figure-eight pattern of perhaps twenty smaller burns across the predator's head, neck, and chest. Three or four of the shots had hit kill points, but the others had done little but burn more or less uselessly through hide and muscle.

"Regardless, I think we can safely scratch off that way station for the moment," de Portola said, throwing a lingering look at one of the other spine leopards before turning back to the Marines. "Next likely spot should be about half a kilometer up the road. You coming?"

"No, and neither are you," Khahar said briskly. "We need to get back to Archway. Colonel Reivaro wants to see you."

"We're not done with our shift," Lorne pointed out, impressed in spite of himself. So Reivaro had come all the way out here in person? Clearly, Lorne's plan of drawing attention away from Jody had worked. Possibly too well. "We can't put the citizens here at risk."

"Point accepted," Khahar said calmly. "Fine. Your buddy de Portola can stay here on patrol. The rest of us can head back in our flitter."

Lorne felt his throat tighten. The last thing he wanted to do was get into an aircar alone with these jokers, especially with Reivaro waiting at the other end of the flight. Out of the corner of his eye he saw de Portola lift a finger. "I suppose I could do that," Lorne said, rubbing his forehead. Under cover of the movement he flicked a look at de Portola.

One more, the other mouthed silently. *One more.*

"Or we could compromise," Lorne continued, dropping his hand back to his side. "Let's check the grove de Portola mentioned, and then all four of us can head back together."

Khahar's eyes narrowed. "The colonel doesn't like being kept waiting."

"And we really shouldn't press their luck," de Portola offered helpfully. "Just because they survived one attack doesn't mean they could get through another one. You go ahead, Lorne—I can handle the rest myself."

"I seriously doubt that," Khahar ground out. "Just show us where they are."

The second encounter was pretty much a repeat of the first. Lorne tried hard to stay on his feet this time, hoping to see firsthand how the Marines' combat gear worked. But the attack had barely started when his nanocomputer once again threw him out of the way of a charging predator, and he spent the rest of the fight leaping and dodging and rolling on the ground.

De Portola didn't have it any better. In fact, he had it worse—at one point Lorne spotted him flat on his back, holding off a spine leopard that had somehow gotten past his lasers and was going for his throat. He was still flailing around, and Lorne was trying to get a clear shot at the animal, when Khahar killed it.

Naturally, the sergeant's back was to Lorne at the time, which meant he got nothing but a silhouetted view of the man's head and torso against a quick stutter of blue laser fire.

Sometimes, he thought sourly, he could practically hear the universe snickering at him.

He made one more effort to persuade the Marines to tackle another way station, but Khahar would have none of it. He announced in no uncertain terms that he and Chimm were heading back, and that Lorne was riding with them.

Which gave Lorne the small satisfaction of watching the sergeant's face heat up when both Cobras politely but firmly told him that they would be riding together in their own car.

Given the still-early hour, the parking area at the Cobra command center should have been nearly deserted. It was therefore a disquieting surprise when de Portola rounded the corner and Lorne saw that there were already four cars in the lot. They hadn't been sitting there for long—a check of the engines' infrared signatures showed they'd barely begun to cool down. "Is that Eion Yates' car?" he asked as de Portola angled them into a parking space.

"The fancy one on the end, yeah," de Portola confirmed. "I don't recognize the others, but I'll bet a week's pay it's connected with this Colonel Reivaro character."

"No bet," Lorne said, opening his door and climbing out. "Let's go see what's going on."

There was another Dominion Marine waiting just inside the main door. He looked the two Cobras up and down and then wordlessly pointed them along the darkened corridor toward the assembly room.

Inside the assembly room, as expected, they found Colonel Reivaro.

"Ah—Cobra Broom," Reivaro called from the table at the front as Lorne and de Portola entered. "We wondered where you'd sneaked off to."

"I didn't sneak anywhere," Lorne said mildly, looking around the room. Werle was there, looking somewhat bleary after only a couple of hours of sleep. Cobras Randall Sumara and Jarvic Whitherway were with him, looking only marginally better rested. None of the cars out in the lot were theirs: either they'd walked to the command center or else Reivaro had rented or commandeered some vehicles and sent Marines to roust them out of bed.

There were certainly enough of the latter for the job, he noted uneasily. Eight of them, to be precise, standing stiffly at various points around the room, all wearing the same shimmery burgundy-black outfits as Khahar and Chimm.

Standing even more stiffly beside Reivaro, looking like a storm cloud a minute away from opening up, was Eion Yates.

The DeVegas Cobras in general, and Commandant Ishikuma in particular, had had a somewhat rocky relationship with Yates over the years. As the province's premier industrialist and third largest employer, Yates had a lot of money to throw at parks, roads, and general humanitarian causes. And for the most part he threw that money with generosity, grace, and occasionally even enthusiasm.

But he was also used to getting what he wanted when he wanted it, and Ishikuma's eagerness to comply with his requests wasn't always up to the man's standards. Still, all in all, on most days Yates was less trouble than he was worth.

Judging from the look on his face, today wasn't going to be one of those days.

"Apparently your definition of *sneak* is at variance with mine," Reivaro said. "You never signed out or even said goodbye."

"Commodore Santores said you were finished with me, and I had work to do," Lorne said. "And we don't have to sign in or out everywhere we go."

"Ah, yes—your so-called *work*," Reivaro said, his tone managing to make the word into something mocking. "Slaughtering animals."

"Killing predators," Lorne corrected, knowing full well that Reivaro was trying to bait him. Santores and his people had had the Cobra Worlds' complete records for a full week now, and Reivaro would have to be a complete idiot not to understand the threat spine leopards posed to people and livestock. "Comes under the heading of citizen protection."

"Of course," Reivaro said in that same condescending tone. "But don't flatter yourself—we didn't come all this way just to see why you ran out on us." He gestured to Yates. "You know Mr. Yates, I presume?"

"Of course," Lorne said, nodding to Yates in greeting. "He's one of our most prominent citizens."

"More importantly, he also owns a large-scale manufacturing facility," Reivaro said. "We're going to be borrowing it for a bit."

"Colonel Reivaro uses *borrow* the same way a thief does," Yates growled, the words clipped and precise. "He wants to take over the plant and completely retool and re-staff." He gestured to Lorne. "I believe your great-uncle Corwin still has the Governor-General's ear. Would you kindly get on the comm and ask him to tell Santores and his crew of highway robbers to go stick their heads in a spiny burrow?"

"I'm sure Commandant Ishikuma will be able to clear this up," Lorne said as soothingly as he could. "I presume he's on his way?"

"Whether he is or isn't is irrelevant," Reivaro said offhandedly. "Commandant Ishikuma has been relieved of his command."

Lorne looked at Werle and Sumara. Both men's expressions had turned to carefully neutral stone. "I don't understand."

"Was I not clear enough?" Reivaro asked, shifting his eyes to de Portola. "Cobra de Portola, isn't it?"

"Yes," de Portola confirmed stiffly.

"I understand you and Cobra Werle were in Capitalia last night with Cobra Broom."

"We were ordered to give him transport back to Archway after he'd finished his testimony," de Portola said. "Why was Commandant Ishikuma relieved?"

"Forget Ishikuma," Yates cut in impatiently. "So he gets some extra vacation while the Dome sorts it out—so what? What's important is this military idiot's got his thugs in my plant right now sending my people home."

"For a little extra vacation," Reivaro murmured.

Yates spun to face him, his face reddening dangerously. "*Look*, you sorry excuse for a—"

"It might help if we knew what you wanted with his factory," Werle cut him off.

"As Mr. Yates said, I'm going to retool and re-staff it," Reivaro said. If Yates's anger was bothering him in the slightest, he hid it well. "Tell me, Cobra Broom: how many starships do the Cobra Worlds possess?"

"Four," Lorne said. Reivaro should know that one, too.

"Are they armed or armored?"

"Of course not," Lorne said. "They're freighters. They carry passengers and cargo."

"Get to the point," de Portola growled.

"The point is simple," Reivaro said. "We're going to use Mr. Yates's facility to turn your freighters into warships."

Again, Lorne looked at Werle and Sumara. Apparently, they hadn't heard this part yet, either. "You must be joking."

"I don't joke about defending Dominion people and property," Reivaro said icily. "Surely you haven't already forgotten the recent Troft invasion? Your world is in danger, and we won't always be here to protect you."

"You weren't exactly here to protect us before," Yates countered. "What makes you think we need you now?"

"He's right," Lorne said. "I don't know how things work at your end of the Troft Assemblage, but at this end, military victories bring friends and allies out into the sunshine. We have plenty of both, thank you."

"Only for the moment," Reivaro warned. "Alliances based on mutual advantage are never stable. Those Trofts you're counting on could turn into enemies in a single heartbeat."

"Not a chance," de Portola said firmly. "We've been trading with some of those demesnes for nearly a century. As Cobra Broom said, they're not just our allies. They're also our friends."

"Friends?" Reivaro snorted. "Don't make me laugh. We have no friends out here. *You* have no friends. No friends, no allies, no one who cares whether you live or die. We're all we have, Cobra de Portola. We're all we'll ever have. We stand together, or an uncaring universe will erase us from an uncaring history."

For a moment no one spoke. Then, Yates lifted his hands and clapped them together three times. "Beautiful," he said acidly. "Patriotic and poetic both. I'm impressed."

"You seem to think this is some kind of joke," Reivaro said, his eyes flashing. "As it happens, your so-called allies have already begun their campaign against you. Earlier this morning, one of their ship captains kidnapped a young human woman." He looked at Lorne. "To be specific, Cobra Broom's sister Jody."

Lorne felt his mouth go dry. So that was what this was all about. Santores hadn't been able to keep Jody here, so he was going to use her disappearance as his excuse for taking over Aventine and the rest of the Cobra Worlds.

And the only chance he had of stopping that was for him to come clean about the real reason why Jody had left the planet. "Actually—"

"What makes you think she was kidnapped?" Werle cut in. "Maybe she just wanted to get away for awhile."

"*Did* she?" Reivaro asked.

Werle shrugged. "I hardly know the woman. How should I know what she wants or doesn't want?"

"Yet you raise the question of her mental state without even being asked about it," Reivaro said, giving Werle a hard look. "Interesting. But also irrelevant." He looked back at Yates. "Because Jody Broom did not, in fact, simply leave of her own volition. She was attacked while in the company of two Dominion Marines, her escort was neutralized, and she was subsequently taken to Pindar and put aboard a ship of the Hoibe'ryi'sarai demesne."

He turned to Lorne. "But don't worry. The *Dorian*, under the command of Captain Moreau, is on its way there even as we speak, with orders to bring her back. Using whatever means necessary."

With an effort, Lorne forced himself to hold the other's gaze, his pulse thudding in his throat. This was insane. Completely and utterly insane. Was Santores actually going to risk war with the Hoibies just to find Qasama? No—that couldn't be. Reivaro had to be bluffing.

But what if he wasn't?

Lorne clenched his teeth. He had to stop it. He had to tell Reivaro the truth about what had happened.

Only if he did that, he would also have to finger Werle and de Portola as the men who'd attacked those two Marines.

Behind Reivaro, Lorne saw the two Cobras exchange looks. They saw Reivaro's trap, all right.

But Lorne could see his same uncertainty reflected

in their eyes. If Santores had really sent one of his ships to the Hoibies...

"In the meantime," Reivaro continued, "we need to plan for war. You in DeVegas province—and you in particular, Mr. Yates—have been assigned to start building armor plating in your factory."

"If I refuse?" Yates demanded.

"Then your factory will no longer be yours," Reivaro said flatly. "Cobra Broom, you will escort Mr. Yates to his facility. You will have him unlock the computers so that our people can go in and reprogram the manufacturing lines."

"The hell I will," Yates said, just as flatly. "And the hell *he* will."

"Cobra Broom?" Reivaro said, ignoring Yates's outburst. "You've been given an order. You will carry it out. Now."

Lorne took a deep breath—

Behind him, the assembly room door slammed violently open. "Broom?" Ishikuma's voice echoed angrily off the walls and ceiling. "What the *hell* do you think you're doing here?"

CHAPTER SIX

Lorne spun around. Ishikuma was standing just inside the open doorway, his hair wild and tangled, his face unwashed, apparently freshly hauled out of bed. His expression was thunderous, his eyes flashing with more simmering danger even than Reivaro's. "Commandant—" Lorne began.

"Shut up," Ishikuma snarled. "Just shut the hell *up*."

The order had been directed at Lorne, but it was one that apparently no one else in the room felt the need to challenge. Even Reivaro kept his peace as Ishikuma stalked his way to the front of the room, his footsteps unnaturally loud in the taut silence. He reached the front and for a long moment just stared into Lorne's eyes. "You," he said, his earlier fire turned now to subzero ice, "have a hell of a lot of nerve coming to my town."

Lorne swallowed hard, trying to figure out why his universe was suddenly skewing in all different directions. What in the *Worlds* was going on? "I was told you wanted to see me," he said carefully.

107

"Who the hell told you that?" Ishikuma demanded. He twisted his head toward Werle and de Portola. "Did *you* tell him that?"

"No, sir," Werle said, his voice as cautious as Lorne's. "We said you wanted him back here."

"Here to DeVegas," Ishikuma retorted. "Not here to Archway." He turned his glare back onto Lorne. "We wanted that Isis machinery, Broom," he said bitterly. "We *needed* it. But you never even once thought about that, did you? You never thought of *us*, did you? No. All you thought about—all you *cared* about—was your precious Qasama."

I was thinking about trying to win the war! With an effort, Lorne forced the words back. For whatever bizarre reason, Ishikuma was clearly on hair trigger, and anything Lorne said might send his rage into actual violence.

And with Dominion Marines all around him, the first result of that violence would be Ishikuma's own instant death.

"So they get new Cobras, and we don't," Ishikuma continued. "I guess that means we're all going to have to work a little harder, doesn't it? Cobra de Portola?"

Out of the corner of his eye Lorne saw de Portola straighten to full attention. "Commandant?"

"Bitter Creek's been without a resident Cobra for over a month," Ishikuma said, his eyes still on Lorne. "Cobra Broom's just volunteered to take up that slack. You'll check out an aircar and fly him out there."

"Just a moment," Reivaro said, finally breaking free of the paralysis that had settled over the room. "You have no authority to give orders to these men."

Ishikuma looked at him as if seeing him for the first time. "Who the hell are you?"

"Colonel Milorad Reivaro," Reivaro said stiffly. "You've been relieved of command, Commandant. The Dominion of Man is in charge here."

"You need to take another look at the statutes, Colonel," Ishikuma said. "I'm not relieved until Commandant Dreysler says I'm relieved. He hasn't. So I'm not. I gave you an order, Cobra de Portola."

"Yes, sir." De Portola unglued himself from the floor and headed for Lorne. "Cobra Broom?"

"Marines, seal that door," Reivaro snapped. "No one leaves here without my permission."

The two Marines closest to the door took three long steps each, stopping in front of the door and turning back in perfect unison to face the rest of the group.

Once again, the room filled with a rigid silence. "Colonel Reivaro," Ishikuma said, almost too quietly for Lorne to hear without his enhancements, "you have thirty seconds to order your men away from the door and permit Cobra de Portola to carry out his orders."

"And if I don't?" Reivaro asked just as quietly.

"There will be bloodshed," Ishikuma said, his voice dropping into liquid nitrogen range. "And because you have no legal reason to impede the movements of my men—and you *don't* have one, or you'd already have stated it—the blame and the blood will be squarely on your hands. I doubt very much that Commodore Santores will have any option but to throw you to the wolves. Possibly literally."

For a long moment the two men stared unblinkingly at each other. Keeping his head motionless,

Lorne put targeting locks on the four Marines within his field of vision.

The thought that the standoff might escalate to actual combat both horrified and sickened him. But if it did, he was damned if he would stand here and not do whatever he could to protect his fellow Cobras. The seconds counted down...

And as his clock circuit reached Ishikuma's thirty-second ultimatum, Reivaro finally stirred. "Stand down," he growled. "They can go about their business."

"Thank you," Ishikuma said, his voice about as far from actual gratitude as Lorne had ever heard. "Cobra de Portola?"

"Yes, sir." De Portola stepped to Lorne's side and gestured toward the door. Throwing a last look at Ishikuma's profile, Lorne followed de Portola between the two glowering Marines and out of the room.

As the door closed behind them, de Portola picked up speed. Lorne matched his pace to keep up, canceling the target locks he'd set up. A few seconds later they passed the Marine door warden—who was also glowering—and emerged once again into the chilly morning breeze.

Lorne took a deep breath, marveling at how clean the air smelled after what had nearly gone down in there. "What the *hell* was that?" he murmured.

"That was Ishikuma saving your hide," de Portola said grimly, angling toward the car they'd arrived in. "Come on, we'll take the car. It'll be faster than walking."

"Saving my *hide*?" Lorne frowned, playing back his memory of the showdown. No—that couldn't have been an act. Could it?

"Believe it, buddy," de Portola said, wrenching open the car door and sliding behind the wheel. "You really think Ishikuma's too stupid to realize that giving Isis to the Qasamans was the move that won the whole damn war? Come on—get in before Reivaro's blood pressure drops back to normal and he figures out his next move."

"But this is crazy," Lorne protested, getting in beside him. "I can see why they want Jody, what with—you know. But I've already told them I don't know where Qasama is."

"Maybe they don't believe you," de Portola said, backing out of the parking space and gunning the car out onto the deserted street. "Maybe they just think you'll be good leverage when they finally track her down. But they *do* want you. Why else would Reivaro have tried so hard to force you into confessing you'd been involved in last night's incident?"

"Or trying to get me to refuse his order to make Yates give up his factory," Lorne said as the pieces finally fell into place. "He wants to get me on some Dominion charge so that he and Santores can pry me away from Chintawa."

"Bingo," de Portola said. "And as a side note, I'll point out that by laying into you in front of all those witnesses Ishikuma made it clear that none of us are going to lift a finger to help you out in any way." He hunched his shoulders. "Hopefully, this will all blow over and that won't be necessary. But if it doesn't . . ."

For a minute they drove in silence. Lorne gazed out the window, again feeling the disorientation of watching his universe shift around him. He'd just been through the hell of one war. Was Commodore

Santores really this determined to push them to the edge of another?

He stole a sideways look at the scar on de Portola's cheek. The Cobras in Capitalia might have obeyed Chintawa's order to sit out the Troft invasion. But it was clear that the Cobras out here in the expansion regions hadn't.

And if Santores ordered those Cobras into a war against the Hoibies...

"How did you knock out those Marines?" he asked suddenly.

De Portola shot him a suspicious look. "Why? You thinking about trying it?"

"I'm thinking it would be a nice thing to have in my skill set," Lorne said. "You and Werle seemed to do just fine."

"Only because we were lucky," de Portola said. "We caught them by surprise. And we caught them in their dress uniforms instead of these night-fighter things they all seem to be wearing now. Or weren't you paying attention during our joint spine leopard hunt this morning?"

"Yeah, I saw the lasers in the epaulets and the electrical grid pattern in the torso sections," Lorne confirmed. "Any idea what that grid thing was all about?"

"I'm guessing it had something to do with rigidity," de Portola said. "You notice the pattern was only over the core body sections and didn't extend over the major limbs or joints. I'm guessing it was a sort of instant armor, with the positioning a compromise between protection and mobility."

"Not that they seem to do a lot of moving when they fight," Lorne pointed out. De Portola's analysis made sense—the Qasaman combat suits had similar stiffeners running through the material, also triggered by small currents.

Except that the Qasaman suits had used that rigidity in conjunction with strength-enhancing servos, allowing their Djinn warriors to mimic Cobra combat abilities. If de Portola was right, the Dominion Marines were mainly interested in the protection aspects of the system.

"Yeah, well, it's not like they *have* to do much moving," de Portola said sourly. "Did you happen to catch the fire pattern from their epaulets?"

"They were punching out figure-eights," Lorne said, nodding. "Scatter-gun approach—they weren't sure where the spine leopard kill points were, so they fired everywhere and hoped for the best."

"Basically," de Portola said. "Except for one small detail. They weren't doing that targeting manually. I mean, I'm sure they were *firing* manually, but the figure-eights were pre-programmed."

Lorne raised his eyebrows. "Really? I thought parrot guns just fired wherever the gunner was looking."

"Maybe that's how they worked a hundred years ago," de Portola said. "But they've gotten more sophisticated since then. Another thing: I got a good look at their tactics on that second encounter, and neither of them so much as looked over their shoulders during the attack. Either they're more arrogant or stupid than they have any right to be, or else they've got some kind of sensor array watching their backs."

"Tied into the parrot guns, no doubt," Lorne agreed. "I wonder how they keep from shooting each other if one of them happens to come into range."

De Portola shrugged. "Must have some kind of Identify Friend/Foe setup. They'd be stupid to run that kind of weaponry without one."

"True," Lorne said. "On the other hand, the Trofts on Qasama had IFF systems, too, and we found a way to turn them to our advantage. I'll bet we can do it here, too."

"Maybe," de Portola said. "One more thing. As near as I could tell, their right forefingers twitched each time they fired, so that must be the firing mechanism. And you were right, the targeting is optical—they looked at each spine leopard before they fired. *But* it seemed to be a single, real-time system, without the multiple sequential targeting locks we have."

"Maybe those extras come with a helmet or visor or something," Lorne said, looking curiously at the other. "You got all this while you were wrestling with a spine leopard?"

"What wrestling?" de Portola asked with a shrug. "The thing was already dead. I just wanted an excuse to flail around in one place while I watched them work."

Lorne shook his head. "You always were a little nuts."

"Yeah, I got a lot of that from people during the war," he said ruefully. "So. You have anything to add to our little library?"

"Only that all that fancy figure-eight programming is probably tucked away inside the inner edges of the epaulets," Lorne told him. "Those were the only places that weren't warm after all the firing."

"Really," de Portola said thoughtfully. "Nice—I missed that one. I wonder what happens if you fry those spots."

"I doubt it totally disables the lasers," Lorne said.

"That would be a pretty stupid design. I'd guess it probably kills any programming presets, though. So how *did* you take them out back in town?"

"Like I said, we were lucky," de Portola said. "Badj blew out a tire as they passed, and when they opened their doors we dropped in from above and behind and zapped them with a combination of sonics and our stunners." He gestured. "But don't count on getting away with that one now. Any material as shiny as those combat suits has to have some serious conductivity going. I wouldn't even trust a full-power arcthrower to get through, let alone a stun blast. And if they're smart, they'll already have a defense ready against sonics."

"Though you *could* go for a head shot with your stunner," Lorne pointed out.

"Bad idea," de Portola warned. "Current designed to overload voluntary-muscle nerves might have nasty side effects when blasted straight to the brain. It might even kill him."

"Which is the last thing we want right now," Lorne agreed, wincing. Still, if it ever came down to one of them or one of his fellow Cobras . . .

Firmly, he pushed the thought away. His job—*all* the Cobras' jobs—was to make sure it *didn't* come to that. "What happened to Tristan?" he asked.

De Portola's lips compressed briefly. "He was killed in a raid on one of the Troft ships," he said. He threw Lorne a tight smile. "Did you know they had to bring a second warship to Archway? We made *that* much of a nuisance of ourselves that they actually needed reinforcements."

"Good for you," Lorne said, inclining his head. "I wish I'd been here to help."

"Yeah." De Portola's smile faded. "You know . . . I'd like to think it all meant something. All the work. Especially all the lives."

"It did," Lorne assured him. "Believe me. The victory at Qasama might have been what brought the Tlossies and other demesnes into the war, but it was you and the Caelians and everyone else who convinced the invaders not to argue the point when the Tlossie ships showed up. Not to mention that every ship and Troft you pinned down here was one the Qasamans didn't have to deal with. No, you guys did your part. And everyone knows it."

"Yeah," de Portola said. "Maybe."

A minute later they pulled onto the field. Ten minutes after that, they were in an aircar headed for the tiny farming and logging community of Bitter Creek.

Where Lorne would try to step into the shoes of a favorite son. A man who'd been killed in a war that Lorne had fought, not alongside the rest of them, but on a foreign world forty-five light years away.

He sighed. It was looking to be a long, long day.

For the first six hours after Jin's confrontation with Commodore Santores, she'd been unable to rest, her heart and brain working feverishly and uselessly, wondering if Lorne was indeed going to fall into Santores's trap.

Occasionally she was able to sit on the edge of her bed for a few minutes at a time. But she was too tense to stay there for long. Mostly she paced back and forth across the tiny holding cell, her enhanced hearing on nervous edge as she waited for the sound of arrogant Dominion footsteps in the corridor outside.

Paul, for his part, had listened to her hurriedly whispered summary of the meeting, and then had stayed out of her way, letting her work it through the only way she could. For a couple of hours, to her guilty annoyance, he actually managed to get some sleep.

But for those first hours the corridor outside had held only the occasional non-arrogant footsteps and murmurings of the two Cobra guards on duty. Once, a meal was delivered by a silent jailer. No one came to gloat, or threaten, or even remind them that the Dominion still cared they were in here.

Eventually, Jin had managed to persuade herself that that was in itself good news. Had Lorne been caught in the Dominion's scheme, surely *something* would have happened by now. Santores wasn't the type to pass up the opportunity to personally bring the news that Lorne was in his hands.

And so, for the past two hours the tension had been slowly draining away, allowing her to lie down, even doze a little.

It was eight hours and seventeen minutes after the Marines had returned her to her cell when they finally had a real visitor. But this time it wasn't Dominion Marines or even a gloating Santores.

"Cobras," Governor-General Chintawa greeted them gravely as he stepped into the cell. He gestured, and some unseen person outside closed the door behind him. "How are you holding up?"

"We're fine," Paul said, "considering we're being held without charges." He raised his eyebrows. "Or is that by deliberate design?"

"Of course it's by design," Chintawa confirmed sourly. "The minute I file specific charges, Gendreves and

Santores will have something tangible they can deal with. As long as you're nothing but vague persons-of-interest, there's nothing either of them can get a grip on."

"So they've teamed up?" Jin asked.

"To be honest, I'm not sure what their relationship is," Chintawa admitted. "If there's any relationship at all. Frankly, I'd be afraid to ask, lest it give one or both of them any ideas. So far I've been able to mostly outmaneuver them individually. I'm not so sure I could do so if they joined forces."

Jin braced herself. "What's happening with Lorne?"

"What do you mean?" Chintawa asked, frowning. "The last I heard, he was back on duty in DeVegas."

Jin and Paul exchanged glances. "Are you sure?" Paul asked.

"I *was*," Chintawa said, pulling out his comm and punching in a number. "Status check, please: Cobra Lorne Broom . . . yes . . . thank you."

He keyed off. "Commandant Dreysler's office confirms he's in DeVegas," he said, putting the comm away. "Were you expecting him to be elsewhere?"

"We were concerned," Paul said. "Commodore Santores seems to have developed an unhealthy fascination with our family."

"I see." Chintawa shifted his eyes to Jin. "And the reason for this fascination?"

Jin hesitated. Should they tell Chintawa about the MindsEye? Would that help, or would it just make things worse? "You'd have to ask Santores that," she said evasively.

"I may do that," Chintawa said, eyeing her another moment before turning back to Paul. "Let me rephrase: is this fascination going to make it dangerous for me to let you out, or will you be safer in here?" He sniffed. "Or should I ask Santores *that* one, too?"

"Thanks for your concern, but I think we've had enough of the Dome's hospitality for one day," Paul said, standing up. "We'll take our chances with Santores."

"Fine." Chintawa gave each of them a hard look. "But let me give you a warning. I'm not happy about the Dominion being here, and I'm even less happy about some of the changes Santores has been talking about. The last thing I need is someone rocking the boat. *Especially* someone from the Moreau or Broom families. Do I make myself clear?"

"Very clear," Paul said. "Just remember that we're not the only ones doing the rocking."

"I know," Chintawa said with a scowl. "And I'll do my best to keep Gendreves on a legal leash. All I ask is that you don't give her any additional ammunition."

"We'll try," Jin said dryly. "Believe me."

"Do more than just try." Chintawa nodded toward the door. "Come on. Let's go to the desk and I'll walk you through the sign-out procedure."

Between their own release forms and the slightly more complicated de-impoundment procedure, it was nearly an hour before they were finally back in their car, staring at the gateway leading from the car park back into the city.

"We should call Uncle Corwin and Aunt Thena and let them know we're all right," Jin said into the silence.

"Yes, we should," Paul agreed. "And then?"

Jin stole a look at his profile. His expression was calm enough, but she could see the determination lurking beneath the surface. "What are *you* thinking?" she countered.

He was silent another moment. "I was just wondering," he said slowly, "whether I should just march into Santores's office and offer to go under this damn MindsEye contraption myself."

"Absolutely not," Jin said firmly. "I don't care how they spin it—the thing doesn't sound even remotely safe."

"Santores wouldn't dare hurt me," Paul assured her. "If he even looked like snatching away one of Nissa Gendreves's prize fish she'd be on him like a rabid spine leopard. I was mostly thinking that if I let him look into my brain, he'll find out I didn't see the nav display on Warrior's ship clearly enough to do him any good."

"Fine; but what if you *did* see it?" Jin countered. "What if you can point him at Qasama? We can't take that risk."

"I'm almost positive I didn't," Paul said. "I know it's a gamble. But if I can persuade him we're no use to him, maybe he'll leave us alone."

"I doubt it," Jin warned. "He strikes me as the vindictive type who'd go ahead and pull all the actionable stuff out of your brain, just for spite."

"I thought he promised he wouldn't do that."

"He said *he* wouldn't use anything they discovered to bring charges against Lorne," Jin corrected. "That doesn't mean he wouldn't turn everything over to Gendreves. No, this thing could blow up in your face in any number of ways."

"Then so be it," Paul said firmly. "Better me than Lorne."

And there it was at last. Jin gazed at him, his image going blurry as her eyes filled with tears. "It wasn't your fault, Paul," she said quietly, reaching over and taking his hand.

For a moment his hand resisted, staying rigid within the circle of her fingers. Then, almost unwillingly, the skin and muscle relaxed and softened, and his fingers wrapped around hers. "Of course it was my fault," he said, the words dark with fear and anger and hopelessness. "I should have stopped him. I should have—" His hand squeezed hers tightly. "I should have done *something*."

"There was nothing you could do," Jin said, reaching over to enfold his hand now in both of hers. "You were trying to protect Merrick. Merrick was trying to protect you. You couldn't both have what you wanted."

"I know." Paul took a deep breath, let it out in a slow, controlled sigh. "But that just makes it all the more important for me to protect the son I have left."

Jin looked out through the gate at the bustling city beyond. Barely a week since the Dominion ships had arrived, and already Santores had insinuated his people into the highest levels of Cobra Worlds politics and was talking about changes. How much longer, she wondered, before he went ahead and took over everything?

"He wouldn't stop with you," she said, the words coming out with an edge that startled even herself. "Santores was highly disappointed that I didn't give him an excuse to send me to his ship. He's probably equally disappointed that whatever he was trying to do with Lorne has also failed."

"He needs to get used to disappointment," Paul murmured.

"He's used to getting his own way. He's going to keep going until he gets it here, too."

"So what do you propose we do?"

Jin looked at their hands, still entwined. *In unity there is strength*, the old adage whispered through her mind.

Merrick was gone. Jody was out of Santores's reach, at least temporarily. Corwin and Thena and the rest of her extended family were of no use to the Dominion. That left only her, Paul, and Lorne.

"He wants the three of us," she said. "Fine. Let's make it easy for him."

She felt Paul's eyes on her. "You mean we should put all his eggs in one basket?"

"I was thinking more of giving him a mouthful he'll choke on," Jin said grimly. "He needs to learn what it means to deal with Cobras." She lifted her eyes to Paul's. "And he *definitely* needs to learn what it means to take on the Broom family."

"Okay." Reaching down, Paul started the car. "You want to head out now, or shall we get a good night's sleep first?"

"I drove through the night on Qasama," she reminded him. "I can do it here, too."

"Good enough," Paul said, pulling out of the parking space. "We'll grab some food on the way and just hit the road."

He snorted. "And under the circumstances, I think we should wait to call Corwin and Thena until we reach Archway."

CHAPTER SEVEN

Merrick had worried about repercussions over the meal bars he'd stolen for the three slave children. To his relief, there weren't any. In fact, as far as he could tell, it was possible the Trofts hadn't even missed them.

More importantly, they also apparently hadn't made any connection between the slaves and the monitor crewer's unplanned on-duty nap. That had been the much more worrisome possibility, and ever since that night Merrick had made a habit of checking every Troft who passed by for signs of suspicion, anger, or even uneasiness.

It all added an extra layer of tension and sleeplessness on top of the rest of the stress Merrick was already putting up with. But it was worth it every time he caught a glimpse of one of the children furtively taking a bite from his or her precious private food supply after the inadequacy of their meager Troft-supplied meals. The expressions of gratitude and furtive curiosity on their parents' faces added that much more to his private satisfaction.

Of course, the Trofts' failure to react might not have been due to negligence. It might simply have been because they decided they didn't have time for a proper investigation. Barely two days after Merrick's midnight raid, considerably earlier than he'd expected, the ship put down on Anya's planet.

"Welcome to Muninn," she said quietly as the two of them stood off to one side, away from the rest of the thirty disembarking slaves, watching as the Trofts tossed out the bags containing the humans' small collections of personal items. "Once a joyous and peaceful place, if the legends are to be believed." She gestured across the landing field toward the dense-looking forest encircling the landing field about half a kilometer away. "Our village of Gangari is that direction, about forty kilometers distant."

Merrick keyed in his telescopics. There was a road leading off the field in the direction she was pointing, paved with some sort of black stone or ceramic similar to the rocktop the Qasamans used on their own roads. It looked wide enough for two Aventinian-style passenger cars or about one-and-a-half cargo trucks. On either side of the road was a wide shoulder that looked like plowed ground. The forest vegetation ran right up to the shoulders' edges, but without any visible penetration into that zone, which suggested that some kind of sterilization or poison was at work. In the distance, a line of rugged mountains rose above the trees. "Are they sending cars for us?" he asked.

She gave him a puzzled look. "Cars?"

"You said it was forty kilometers," he reminded her. "We're not going to walk the whole way, are we?"

"Of course," she said, still looking puzzled. "Is that a problem?"

Merrick looked at the rest of the slaves, now busily sorting through the pile of bags the Trofts had thrown out. Standing behind the adults, fidgeting with impatience or nervousness, were two of the three children who'd been aboard the transport. "I was thinking of the children," he said. "Forty kilometers is a long way for someone that young to walk."

"It's not so bad," Anya assured him. "Only one of them will be coming with us. The others will be going there." She pointed the opposite direction from the blackstone road, toward a considerably wider opening in the surrounding forest and a much smoother-looking roadway. "The town of Runatyr is only five kilometers distant. That's where most of them will be going. It's the largest settlement in this part of the world."

Merrick felt his lip twist. A major town, maybe even a city. Whatever the Drims were up to, a locale with a high concentration of slaves was the logical place for them to set up shop.

Only he and Anya weren't going there. They were going to some little backwater village multiple kilometers away.

He shook his head in frustration. With every minute, Commander Ukuthi's simple little espionage mission got better and better.

"Ours will be only an eight-hour journey," Anya said. She paused. "With a child, perhaps ten," she conceded.

Merrick looked at the sky. The sun was already past

the midpoint, and Anya had told him earlier that there were twenty-six hours in Muninn's day. No chance of making Gangari before nightfall. "Are there places nearby where we can camp?" he asked. "I assume we'll wait for tomorrow to head out."

"No, we'll start as soon as we're ready," she said. "A journey of this length is better split into two parts."

"What about nighttime predators? Or are there safe houses along the way?"

"There are no shelters. But none of the darktime animals will be of danger to us."

"Mm." Merrick wrinkled his nose doubtfully. Still, this was Anya's world. She presumably knew what she was talking about. "Any idea how many are traveling with us?"

"Not many," she said. "A moment, and it will become clear."

A moment later, it was. As the grav lifts flared and the ship lifted back into the sky, the majority of the slaves shouldered their bags and headed toward the road to Runatyr, a murmur of quiet but relieved-sounding conversation moving along with them. The remaining five turned and headed toward Anya and Merrick.

That group, Merrick noted, was strangely silent.

No wonder, really. Gina was one of the group, the little girl who'd been fascinated by Merrick's unusual hair color, as were her parents, who'd been even less friendly to the stranger who'd offered their daughter some of his dinner. Two other men strode along at their sides, big men with hard faces and muscles to match. One was a slightly darker-haired man whom Merrick had seen aboard ship but never talked to.

The other was Dyre Woodsplitter.

Merrick sighed. Terrific.

The feeling was clearly mutual. "What's *he* doing here?" Dyre demanded as the group approached, his eyes on Merrick.

"He travels with us," Anya said. She gestured to Gina and her parents. "Merrick Hopekeeper—"

"I don't want him," Dyre interrupted. "Let him go to Runatyr with the others."

"No," Anya said calmly. "Merrick Hopekeeper, I present Leif and Katla Streamjumper and their daughter Gina."

Merrick bowed his head in the low nod of first-formal that Anya had coached him in. Leif and Katla returned the gesture, though neither seemed any happier about his presence than Dyre did. "This is Ville Dreamsinger," Anya continued, gesturing to the other man.

"Merrick," Ville repeated, giving the greeting nod. Unlike Dyre and the Streamjumpers, he seemed more intrigued than annoyed.

"And this is Dyre Woodsplitter," Anya concluded. She hesitated just a fraction of a second. "My betrothed."

Merrick felt his jaw drop. Her—?

"Her betrothed," Dyre repeated, making the word both a warning and a challenge. "If we're going, let's go. Where are your possessions?"

"We have none," Anya said. "You will take lead?"

"What do you mean, you have none?" Dyre demanded. "You have my pledge."

"Your pledge was lost," Anya said. "We waste sunlight—"

"*Lost?*" Dyre's eyes shifted to Merrick and narrowed into a glare. "How did this happen?"

"I was a slave," Anya said, her voice chilling noticeably. "Slaves are not always permitted to do as they wish. We waste sunlight with this conversation."

"She speaks truth, Dyre," Ville said. "I'll take lead. You take follow."

Dyre muttered something vicious-sounding. "This isn't ended," he warned, resetting his bag violently over his shoulder. "Go."

"Follow closely," Ville said as he strode briskly off toward the blackstone road. "The fafirs will be especially active this time of year."

Leif touched his wife's shoulder and put a hand on his daughter's back, silently nudging the two of them into line behind Ville. Anya gestured Merrick to follow them, then moved into a spot just behind Merrick and to his left. Glancing over his shoulder, Merrick saw a brooding Dyre fall into step a meter behind her.

He turned back again, his stomach churning with guilt.

Because Anya *had* had possessions. A whole bag of them, in fact, probably twice the size of the one Dyre had bouncing against his back. Commander Ukuthi had sent one of his soldiers to get it for her after the Drim captain had ordered her and Merrick to his own slaves' quarters for the journey home.

But Anya had refused to accept the bag, asking the Troft instead to return it to Ukuthi for safekeeping. When Merrick had asked why, she'd pointed out that he had no such trinkets or treasures, and being the only unburdened slave might draw unwelcome attention. Two impoverished slaves would be less noticeable, especially when they were the two who'd supposedly been under the ownership of a Balin ship commander.

Merrick had accepted her logic, admiring her dedication to the mission all the while. Never had it occurred to him that something in the bag might hold a particular significance for her.

Never had it occurred to him to even ask.

And now the man whose gifts had been deliberately tossed away was walking directly behind him. Apparently convinced that Merrick was the one responsible for their loss.

In a way, he was right.

The road material turned out to be pretty much as Merrick had guessed: bits of black rock of various sizes embedded in a glassy-looking black substrate. The forest pressing in around them was filled with a variety of subtle sounds and aromas, similar yet markedly different from those of the forests of Aventine and Qasama.

Most of the scents were pleasant or at least exotically neutral. One, though, was distinctly different: acidic and nose-curlingly unpleasant when the breeze came just right. Apparently, Merrick had been right about the road's shoulders being laced with some kind of powerful herbicide. Maybe it was just as well, he mused, that the Cobras' designers hadn't included olfactory enhancements.

The group traveled mostly in silence. Gina was the one exception, asking questions end to end, mostly about the various plants and small animals she spotted and the twittering bird calls she could hear. Her parents were far less inclined toward conversation, and their answers were short and perfunctory.

For an hour the girl kept at it, undeterred by the curtness of her parents' answers or the silence of the others. But after that her excitement at her new surroundings began to wane. By the start of the third hour she either ran out of questions or the energy to ask them, and fell silent as she concentrated on her walking.

They'd been at it for a full three hours, and Merrick was idly trying to match the various songbird calls with the names Leif had given Gina, when the songs and other noises on the left-hand side of the road suddenly faded away.

He looked behind him. Anya's face was turned toward the ominous silence, her eyes darting around. Behind her, Dyre was doing the same.

Merrick scowled. Terrific. Keying in his infrareds, he scanned the trees.

Most of his Cobra service had been in Capitalia, where the most vicious animal he was likely to run into was some obnoxious person's obnoxious pet. But his training had included a unit on wildlife, and if he remembered those lessons correctly most predators were either ground attackers or liked to jump from trees.

This group had apparently skipped that part of the manual. There were eight large-animal infrared images lurking out of sight along the side of the road, and they were evenly distributed between the ground and the lower branches of the nearest trees.

Two entirely separate types of animals, perhaps? That was certainly possible. They could either be working together, like the mojos and razorarms on Qasama, or be rivals jockeying for first grab at the tasty-looking human travelers.

"Ville?" Dyre called softly.

"I hear them," Ville said, glancing around. "There," he said, pointing to the right and turning off onto the shoulder.

"Yes," Dyre confirmed, heading that same direction. "Leif, get your family to cover."

"Get one for me," Anya called, giving Merrick a light but insistent shove toward a bush that seemed to be made entirely of fuzzy green bamboo-like spikes clustered together. The Streamjumper family was already moving in that direction, Leif pressing his palms against his wife's and daughter's backs as he hurried them along, his eyes on the quiet forest behind him. "Go with them," Anya added quietly to Merrick. "Protect them, especially the child."

Merrick started to object, remembered in time that he was supposed to be mute, and instead pointed toward the hidden predators.

"Yes; fafirs," Anya said, giving him another push, a more forceful one this time. "They're not too dangerous—we can easily drive them away. But you must protect those who cannot fight."

"What, *him*?" Dyre growled. There was a sudden *crack* of breaking wood, and Merrick saw him pull a thick section of branch as long as his arm from beneath the flowing foliage of one of the trees. At one end the branch was studded with thorns the size of razorarm fangs.

"Dyre speaks truth," Ville agreed. Two quick wood-breaking *cracks*, and he strode back onto the road, swinging a thorn stick in each hand. "If you want them safe, you'll need to protect them yourself."

"Merrick can do it," Anya insisted. She gestured to Ville, and he tossed her one of the sticks, giving it a midair half-turn so that she could catch the non-thorny end. Glaring at Merrick, she jabbed the stick toward Leif and his family. "Go!" she ordered.

Glowering, Merrick headed toward the Streamjumpers, throwing another look at the woods on the left side of the road. More infrared images had appeared, with the total now up to nearly twenty. They were spread out over a good ten meters, too. If they all attacked together, Anya, Dyre, and Ville would be quickly outflanked.

And unless the predators were a lot tamer than anything that size had any business being, one or more of the human defenders was going to get hurt or killed.

He looked back at Leif and his family, huddled together in front of the bamboo bush. On the other hand, Leif didn't look like much of a fighter at all. If some of the predators got past Anya and made it over here, he and his family were even more likely to die. At least Anya and the others had weapons.

Which, come to think of it, would probably be a good idea all around. Stepping over to tree where Ville and Dyre had gotten their sticks, he eased his hands into the curtain of soft leaves and found another of the thorn branches. Getting a grip at its base, he gave it a pull.

Nothing happened.

He frowned. The same sort of branch had come off in Dyre's hand like it was a dry piece of kindling. Ville had managed to get two of them without even working up a sweat. Locking his fingers around the branch, he tried again, this time putting servo strength into the effort.

For a moment the branch continued to resist. Then, with a protesting *crunch*, it broke free.

Merrick backed away from the tree, staring at the stick in uneasy wonderment. It had taken a fair level of his enhanced strength to break something that Ville and Dyre had done with unassisted muscle power.

Anya had told him that many of the human slaves were used in combat together for the amusement of their owners. Apparently, some of those owners had experimented with strength-breeding among their stock. Maybe they would do all right against the fafirs, after all.

He started back toward Leif and his family, again keying his infrareds as gave the situation a quick assessment. Anya and the two men were standing in a line down the center of the road, spaced about three meters apart where they would be far enough to have freedom of movement but close enough that they could quickly go back-to-back if they started becoming overwhelmed. The predators were still holding position, but as Merrick notched his auditory enhancers up he could hear restless-sounding movements in some of the closer trees. Someone up there was impatient to get started. From somewhere behind Merrick came the soft crunch of something moving through the underbrush—

There was a sudden squeal, startlingly loud in his enhanced hearing. "Look out!" Gina's voice boomed.

Merrick spun around, his left hand curling automatically into fingertip laser firing position. There was an animal there, all right, barely three meters away, its body pressed close to the ground as it gazed at him.

But it wasn't a fafir, whatever the hell a fafir was. It was something more familiar, and far more dangerous.

It was a razorarm.

And it was definitely the Qasaman version, not a spine leopard that had been taken from the expansion regions of Aventine. Merrick could see the scarred and toughened skin on its shoulders, evidence that it had once carried a mojo raptor bird there.

For that first instant Merrick gaped at the predator in sheer frozen surprise. A heartbeat later, his brain caught up with him. Back on Qasama, he and Commander Ukuthi had both noted the curious fact that Troft ships were still capturing razorarms from the local forests despite the fact that the attackers had apparently already moved on Aventine, where they should have a ready supply of the predators. Part of the impetus for this mission, in fact, had been Ukuthi's curiosity as to what the Drim demesne was doing with all of those animals.

Apparently, Merrick had found one of the answers to that question. And with that answer had come a sudden huge problem.

Because he couldn't simply target one of the predator's kill points and fire a laser at it. It was absolutely vital that he keep his true identity a deep, dark secret. That was why Anya had spent all those hours trying to teach him how to fit in with her people. That was why he was still pretending to be mute, so that even after that coaching his foreign accent wouldn't raise eyebrows and questions. His mission—hell, his *life*—depended on it. So did Anya's.

But his mission also depended on him surviving the next thirty seconds. The razorarm's forearm quills were already fanning outward, the first indication that it was preparing to attack. Without his lasers or arcthrower, he didn't have a chance in hell.

From somewhere behind him, dimly heard through the thudding of his heart and his single-minded focus on the razorarm, came the violent rustling of vegetation and a chorus of whooping barks. Apparently, the fafir attack had begun.

And suddenly, he remembered the stick gripped in his hand.

It was an insane plan, really. But unless he wanted to simply give up and proclaim to the world that he was a Cobra, it was the only plan he had. Turning to put his torso square-on to the razorarm, hoping the noise of the battle behind him would cover up any stray sound, he fired a burst from his sonic.

The razorarm staggered slightly, its balance temporarily thrown off. Before it could recover, Merrick leaped forward and slammed the thorny end of the stick squarely across its face.

The predator howled in rage and pain, its quills snapping all the way out. Merrick continued his lunge forward, shifting the angle of his stick and slapping it across the predator's right foreleg. The impact flattened a section of the quills back against the leg. Before they could bounce out again he threw himself chest-first against the leg, his body pushing the quills the rest of the way down. At the same time he snaked his right arm up under the predator's head and around the back of its neck, squeezing his upper arm against its throat.

And as the angry howling abruptly turned into a labored snarl, he pressed the little finger of his left hand deep into the fur over one of the animal's kill points and fired his laser.

The razorarm went limp. Still holding its neck, he

shifted his left hand to another kill point and fired again, just to be sure. Then, careful of the still-protruding quills, he released his grip and pushed himself away.

Only then did he notice that the sounds from behind him had stopped.

He spun around, fearing the worst. To his relief, Anya and the two men were still standing, still apparently in good shape, though Ville had a shredded jumpsuit sleeve and a long cut beneath it. Scattered around them were the fafirs: lean, hairy animals that seemed to be some strange combination of wolf and ape. A couple of them were sprawled unmoving on the road, but most of the handful still in sight were limping or loping rapidly away.

Apparently, the defenders' focus had been more on driving the attackers away than actually killing them. Merrick took a quick look at the downed fafirs, wondering if any of them might still be a danger, then raised his eyes to Anya.

She was staring back at him, her face suddenly carved from stone.

Ville was staring, too. So was Dyre. So were all three of the Streamjumper family.

Merrick hissed out a sigh. So much for his attempt to keep a low profile.

It was Gina who finally broke the silence. "Wow!" she said, leaning against her father's grip, straining to get a better view of the carnage. "What's *that*?"

Merrick felt a sudden surge of hope. So it wasn't his killing of the razorarm that had them all so awe-struck. Or at least not *just* the killing. It was the razorarm itself.

Which, now that he thought about it, made perfect sense. Razorarms hadn't existed on Muninn until the Drims started hauling them here a few weeks ago. There was no reason why any of the others would ever have seen one before.

Anya apparently reached that conclusion the same time he did. "They're called razorarms," she told the others. "Merrick was trained to kill them in my master's version of the Games."

"Was he, now," Ville said, striding toward Merrick and the dead predator, his now-battered thorn stick swinging idly in his hand. "Impressive."

"I don't believe it," Dyre said flatly. "It's some kind of trick. Look at that thing—look at the muscles around its throat. He couldn't possibly have choked it to death."

"Maybe he beat it to death," Ville suggested, pointing at Merrick's stick and wiggling his fingers in silent request. Frowning, Merrick handed it over.

"Not a chance," Dyre said insisted. "*Look* at him. He hasn't got the strength for it."

"Your truth is lacking," Ville said. "He has strength aplenty." He lifted up the stick. "See for yourself—he didn't twist this off. He tore it off the trunk. Just tore it straight off."

Merrick winced. So that was how the others had done it. No superhuman strength, just a trick that probably everyone on this part of the planet knew.

Only he hadn't known it. And now, he'd exposed his genuine superhuman strength.

Or maybe not. Where there was one trick, why couldn't there be a second?

He looked back at Anya. Her face had gone rigid

again. Forcing an awkward smile, Merrick gave a little shrug.

Once again, she caught on instantly. "Please—he's not *that* strong," she said scornfully. "It's simply a different technique."

"I don't know," Ville said, running his fingers across the torn end. "It looks pretty solid to me."

"Trust me," Anya said. "And as we speak of solid, the solid dark of night is soon approaching. We need to gain further distance before we settle for the night."

"She speaks truth," Leif spoke up. "The scavengers will soon be coming for their feasting. I don't wish to be here when they do."

"As do none of us," Ville agreed. Tossing aside both his stick and Merrick's, he headed back to the road. "I'll again take lead."

Merrick frowned at the discarded sticks, then looked at Anya and raised his eyebrows. She shook her head and beckoned to him. "Another hour, I think, and we'll find a spot for our overnight rest," she said. "We don't wish to weary the young one overmuch."

"If she tires, I'm certain our overstrong Merrick can carry her," Dyre muttered as he took his place at the end of the line.

"Enough talking," Ville called back from the front. "The fafirs are become active. We must now listen closely for their presence." He threw a small smile back at Merrick. "Perhaps Merrick will later show us his technique for obtaining thorn maces."

Merrick made a face as he fell into step beside Anya. Inventing a magic trick for them, right on the spot. He could hardly wait.

❖   ❖   ❖

Fortunately, it didn't come to that. They saw a few stray fafirs along the way, but there were no more large packs and no further attacks.

They walked the hour that Anya had recommended, plus half an hour more, before Ville called the evening's halt at a small clearing that had been carved from the edge of the forest by a pair of fallen trees. Leaving Merrick and the Streamjumpers to gather dead wood, Anya, Ville, and Dyre went off to hunt for dinner.

Even listening with his audio enhancers as much as he could, Merrick never heard any sounds other than normal movement through the grass, bushes, and flat-leafed ferns. Nevertheless, by the time Leif had a fire going and he and Katla were collecting fuzzy bamboo spikes to build into a shelter, the others returned with a pair of rabbit-sized animals.

Briefly, he considered taking Anya aside and asking how they'd caught and killed their prey so quietly. But as he watched Ville and Dyre set about skinning the animals with fist-sized chunks of some kind of rock, he decided he probably didn't want to know.

And as the dinner cooked over the open fire, and he helped Leif and Katla weave the bamboo spikes into an elegant and deceptively strong set of walls for their shelter, another thought slowly occurred to him. A thought that, like the details of the hunt, he wasn't sure he wanted an answer to.

But in this case, he needed that answer. And he needed it tonight.

His first concern was how to sneak out past whatever sentry the group ended up posting. That problem disappeared when it was decided that no guard would, in fact, be posted. All of them apparently agreed with

Anya that none of the nocturnal predators was a threat to them, especially once they were inside the woven-spike A-frame structure they'd constructed.

That didn't take the razorarms and their unpredictable hunting schedules into account, of course. But the A-frame was reasonably sturdy, and as long as they stayed inside they should be all right.

Especially if what Merrick suspected turned out to be true.

He waited until the rest of the group was asleep. Then, moving silently, he left the shelter and headed out into the night.

An hour later, he returned to find Anya sitting beside a tree a dozen meters from the shelter, waiting quietly for him.

"I saw you were gone," she murmured as he sat down beside her. "I wondered if you'd decided to go to Runatyr instead."

Merrick winced. That thought *had* occurred to him. Several times, in fact, during the day's journey. "Why would I do that?" he asked.

"You didn't come here to settle down in a distant and unlively village," she reminded him. "Runatyr is more likely to be the center of the Drim'hco'plai plot among us."

"You'd think so, wouldn't you?" Merrick agreed. "But in this case, Commander Ukuthi was right on target."

Anya's eyes were steady on him. "The razorarms?"

"Yes," Merrick said, nodding. "Ukuthi wondered why the Drims were still taking them off Qasama. A better question might have been why they were taking them from the populated areas, where the villagers could take pot shots at them, instead of harvesting them from more distant parts of the planet."

"And you've solved this puzzle?"

"I think so," Merrick said. "Tell me, are there other villages near Gangari? And do your people and theirs typically go back and forth a lot?"

"Yes, to both questions," Anya said, nodding. "We trade frequently with five other villages, and have occasional contact with seven or eight more." She hesitated, just noticeably. "There are also small family groups in the forests and at some of the river cross-ings who we deal with. Are the Drim'hco'plai trying to stop that trade by planting razorarms around us?"

"That may be part of it," Merrick said. "I'm think-ing they're trying for a strange sort of balance here: they want to isolate the villages, but at the same time don't want a mass slaughter of the people. That would explain why they picked razorarms from the inhabited areas, where they had some experience with humans. They figured those would be good at discouraging people from traveling the roads, but would be leery enough of actually attacking anyone."

"Even without the mojo birds to make that deci-sion for them?"

"Apparently so," Merrick said. "Actually, that makes a certain amount of sense. However the neural or tele-pathic link worked, the razorarms clearly got enough from the mojos to influence their actions."

"Yet the razorarm today *did* attack," Anya pointed out. "So did the ones in the Games back on Qasama."

"The ones in the Games definitely did," Merrick agreed. "But remember that those weren't Drim razorarms, but ones that Commander Ukuthi brought in specially for the purpose. I'm guessing he had his people grab them from areas a long ways from the Great Arc, where humans are few and far between."

He felt his stomach tighten. "And as for the one today, I may have jumped the gun. It didn't attack—in fact, I'm not convinced it was even *thinking* about attacking. It was looking us over, certainly, and it might have been nervous or agitated by the fafirs gathered across the road. But it didn't made a move until I hit it with that thorn stick—"

"Mace," Anya corrected. "It's called a thorn mace."

"Right," Merrick said, feeling his face warming. A stupid mistake. "The bottom line is that it didn't attack until I attacked first." He hissed out a sigh. "Which meant I killed it for nothing."

Anya was silent a moment. "You had no way of knowing," she reminded him. "But you know now?"

Merrick nodded. "I ran across two more razorarms while I was out just now. Both saw me. Neither attacked."

"I see," Anya said slowly. "So. They want us alive, but kept apart. Why?"

"That's the big question, isn't it?" Merrick agreed. "Hopefully, we'll find out when we reach Gangari." He reached out to touch her arm, then changed his mind and pointed to the shelter instead. "We'd better get back before someone misses us."

He started to get up, but stopped as she put a hand on his arm. "One more thing," she said.

Merrick braced himself. If this was going to be about Dyre, he really didn't want to hear it. "Yes?"

"It's still twenty-five or more kilometers to Gangari," she said. "If the masters wish to isolate our group of villages, why are there razorarms *here*? Shouldn't they be closer to us?"

Merrick frowned. That was a damn good question. Even knowing how razorarms could sense open territory, they still shouldn't have made it this far from Gangari in the short time since the Drims started collecting and dumping them.

Unless he'd been wrong about Gangari being the center of the Trofts' attention. Maybe it was something closer to their current position. "Are there any other villages or towns in this area?" he asked.

"None that I know of," Anya said. "But it's been twelve years since I was taken from my home. Something could have been built in that time."

A shiver ran up Merrick's back. Anya couldn't be more than twenty-three or twenty-four years old. To have spent half of her life as a slave...."We need to find out for sure," he said, forcing away the image of a twelve-year-old child being forcibly taken from her home. "Do people from Gangari get out this way at all?"

"A few of them do," Anya said. "Mostly hunters and trappers. Some of the smaller family groups may also know this area." She considered. "Though with new predators in the area, they may be staying closer to their homes. I'll ask when we reach the village."

"Okay," Merrick said. "Was there anything else?"

Her forehead wrinkled. "No. Should there be?"

"No, no," he assured her. So there would be no discussion of her relationship with Dyre, at least not tonight. Briefly, he wondered whether he was relieved or sorry. "I was just wondering. Come on, let's get back inside."

CHAPTER EIGHT

The strangest thing about being back on Caelian, Jody thought as she left the Hoibie merchant ship, was that it felt like coming home.

Which, on the face of it, was faintly ridiculous. She'd spent less than two months here, hardly even twice the length of the semester breaks she'd taken back in college. In fact, her family had once had a vacation longer than that, back when she was in seventh grade and Great-Uncle Corwin had taken them on a tour of the fledgling Cobra Worlds of Viminal and Esquiline.

But then, strict passage of time wasn't necessarily the best measure of a life. In her two months here Jody had squeezed in a good fraction of a lifetime, first pressed on all sides by deadly plants and animals, then hammered and crushed together with the Caelians in the swirling tidepool of war. She'd seen death and destruction, heroism and chaos, and had come within a splintered hair of losing everything she held dear. She'd aged tremendously, far more than a simple count of sunrises would indicate.

Still, the homecoming feeling was still just plain weird.

The capital city—or, more properly, the small, compact town—of Stronghold was pretty much the way it had been when she left, with a few significant changes. Part of the sterile zone outside the city had been reestablished, though it didn't stretch as far from the wall as it had before the invasion. The section of the wall itself where the Troft ship had fallen on it was still gone, but there was now a somewhat slapdash-looking barrier of wood and cloth that had been erected in the gap. Above the barrier, she could just see the tops of the two wrecked Troft ships, one lying on top of the other where they'd both been knocked over on their sides.

Just before she'd left to head back to Aventine, Governor Romulo Uy had been talking to the Tlossies about getting the ships upright again and seeing if either could still fly. Obviously, those plans hadn't gotten very far.

The Hoibie car that had taken her from the landing area had dropped her off just inside the main gate, then turned and headed immediately back toward the ship. She'd made it maybe another hundred meters in when she turned a corner and nearly ran into one of the people she'd met during that brief eternity she'd spent here.

And suddenly she realized why it felt like coming home.

"Jody!" Kemp exclaimed, covering the ten meters between them in three long servo-powered steps and wrapping her in a bear hug that would have crushed her to death if he'd put his full Cobra strength behind it. As it was, it just felt very, very comfortable.

"This is a surprise," he murmured into the side of her head. "When did you get back in town?"

"About fifteen minutes ago," Jody said into the side of his, frowning as she replayed the image of him bounding toward her. His face had been badly burned during their climactic battle with the Troft invaders, and when she'd left three weeks ago that raw flesh had been well on its way to becoming a an impressive collection of scar tissue.

But while his face didn't exactly look baby-smooth, it was a long way from the leathery mask she'd been fearing. In fact, aside from a few small indention lines, it hardly looked marked at all. "You're looking good," she added.

"Aren't I?" Kemp agreed, pulling back from the hug and giving her a closer look. "Qasaman medicine is about as close to miraculous as we're ever likely to see. Harli's looking good, too. Of course, with Harli that's a much trickier bar to reach. You said you just got here?"

Jody nodded. "On the Hoibie merchant ship that just came in."

"You mean the Hoibie merchant ship that's just leaving?"

She turned to look. He was right—the ship was already in the air, its grav lifts glowing. "Huh," she said as she watched it rotate a few degrees and pull for the sky. "I kind of assumed they'd at least check around and see if they could do some business here before they took off."

"They didn't have any business already set up?" Kemp asked, frowning. "So, what, the only reason they came here was to give you a ride?"

"Well...yes, mostly," Jody admitted.

"Uh-*huh*," Kemp said, his voice gone suddenly wary. "You in trouble at home or something?"

Jody hesitated. But the last thing she would ever do was lie to any of the people here. "A little," she admitted.

"Uh-huh," he said again, eyeing her closely. "You got time to talk about it?"

"I've got all the time in the world," Jody said. "Is there somewhere quiet we can go?"

"Sure," Kemp said, glancing down at her tunic and slacks, the outfit she'd been wearing when she made her hasty departure from Aventine. "I'd start with a clothing shop, though—you're already starting to turn green."

Jody peered down at her sleeves. Sure enough, they were already showing signs of green as the microscopic spores began to gather on the carbon-based cloth. "Oops," she said, brushing reflexively and uselessly at the material. "I'd forgotten how fast these things collect."

"Right," Kemp said dryly. "You were gone, what, a whole two weeks?"

"Closer to three," Jody said. Unfortunately, the only cloth that could fend off the airborne vegetation was the stiff silicon-based stuff that Kemp and everyone else on Caelian wore.

Unless one of the Qasaman combat suits Siraj Akim and the other Djinn had left were still lying around unused. Those also had the purely accidental ability to keep off the spores, and they were a lot more comfortable that the silliweave stuff. "Are Geoff and Freylan still here?" she asked.

"Here on Caelian, yes," Kemp said. "Here in Stronghold, no. They're out in Aerie running some tests."

"Ah," Jody said with a quiet sigh. So much for the combat suits. Geoff Boulton and Freylan Sonderby, her two erstwhile partners, were nothing if not thorough. If they were out running tests, they undoubtedly had both suits with them. "Okay, then, but someplace cheap. I didn't bring a lot of money with me."

"So you left in a rush," Kemp said thoughtfully, eyeing her again. "Interesting. Are you hungry?"

Right on cue, Jody's stomach growled. Her body was still on Capitalia schedule, and for her it was way past dinner time. "I could eat," she conceded.

"Great," Kemp said, stepping forward and taking her arm. "In that case, let's see about getting you a cheap outfit *and* a late lunch."

"You know a place that does both?" Jody asked dryly.

"As a matter of fact, I do," he assured her. "The most exclusive place in town."

The most exclusive place in town turned out to be the top floor of the Government Building and Governor Uy's residence.

"It's so good to see you again, Jody," Elssa Uy said cheerfully as she hurried around the kitchen putting together a meal. "How long are you here for?"

"I'm not really sure," Jody said, hunching her shoulders beneath the silliweave tunic Elssa had insisted on loaning her. "I'm sort of . . ." She looked at Kemp.

"Marooned," he supplied, looking distinctly uncomfortable as he fidgeted in the chair beside her at the informal breakfast bar. His intent, he'd protested at least twice, was merely to drop off Jody and then wait downstairs until she'd eaten and was ready to talk. Instead, Elssa had insisted that he sit down and join them, pointing out that it was as easy to prepare a meal for two as it was for one and that she and Jody would enjoy the company. "The Hoibie ship she was on has already taken off."

"Really," Elssa said, pausing long enough to throw Jody a curious look. "Is there some trouble at home?"

Jody hesitated. She'd been willing to share her concerns about the Dominion's hunt for Qasama with Kemp, privately and off any official record. But relating those same concerns to the governor's wife would take things to an entirely different level.

She was still working on her decision when Kemp made it for her. "That's exactly what *I* asked her," he said. "She wanted a quieter place to talk about it. I figured this was as quiet a place as any." He raised his eyebrows at Jody. "My guess is that it has to do with the Dominion."

"Does it, Jody?" Elssa prompted.

"Sort of," Jody hedged. "But I'm not sure this is the right time and place to talk about it."

"Absolutely not," Elssa agreed calmly. "We need to wait until Rom gets here."

Jody threw Kemp a startled look. "I didn't mean—"

"Too late," Kemp said wryly. "Once the Queen of Caelian has made up her mind, there's no changing it."

"Kemp, I've told you a hundred times not to call me the Queen of Caelian," Elssa said, mock-severely. "It's either *Ms. Power Behind the Throne* or just plain *Swimbo*."

"Sorry," Kemp apologized. "I always forget."

Jody frowned. "Swimbo?"

"It's an acronym," Kemp explained. "Short for *She Who Must Be Obeyed*."

"Ah," Jody said. "Sounds like my mother."

"Which is probably why we all get along so well together," a new voice came from the doorway.

And as Jody turned, Governor Uy stepped into the room.

Actually *stepped* into the room, on his own, with no assist and no cane. "Governor," she greeted him, standing up and giving him a quick once-over. No limping, no pressure cast visible through his clothing, not even any obvious favoring of the side where he'd caught that Troft laser blast. Like Kemp, the man had made a remarkable recovery. "I'm impressed. The last time I saw you, you were barely even able to stand."

"Caelian toughness and stamina," Uy said, waving a nonchalant hand as he continued on into the room. He was moving carefully, Jody saw now, but he *was* still moving. "And, of course, a little help from our new friends." He half-turned and gestured to someone out of view behind him. "Please—come. I don't believe you and Jody Moreau Broom have yet been introduced."

"Indeed we haven't," an unfamiliar voice said. An old man walked into view, his walk nearly as careful as Uy's, a thoughtful smile on his face. "She looks very much like her mother did at that age," he went on, his speech slow and deliberate, his words as carefully chosen as his steps.

Jody frowned, studying his face. She would have sworn she'd met all of her mother's old friends and acquaintances over the years. But she couldn't remember ever seeing this man before. "Yes, people have mentioned that," she said. "Were you a friend of hers?"

The old man's smile went a bit brittle. "Not then, no," he admitted. "I would hope that's now changed."

"Jody Moreau Broom," Uy said quietly, "may I present His Excellency Moffren Omnathi of the Qasaman Shahni. Your Excellency, may I present Jody Moreau Broom."

Jody felt her whole body go rigid. *That* was Moffren Omnathi? The man who'd once been one of the Cobra Worlds' most ingenious opponents before turning his talents against the invading Trofts?

And he was *here*?

"I'm honored to meet you, sir," she managed, trying furiously to remember the Qasaman sign of respect her mother had once shown her. Her fingertips went... here? "I'm told you're one of the chief reasons my family is still alive," she added, making her best try at the sign.

Omnathi's smiled eased, the brittleness replaced with what seemed to be affectionate amusement. Apparently, Jody hadn't quite gotten it right. "You honor me, Jody Moreau," he said, inclining his head. "I point out in turn that your family is one of the chief reasons Qasama is free today."

"*And* Caelian," Uy murmured.

"And Caelian," Omnathi agreed. "Did I hear correctly that you're in some sort of trouble?"

"Yes, and we were just about to browbeat her into telling us all about it," Kemp spoke up. If he was overawed by the presence of a senior Qasaman statesman, Jody reflected, he was certainly hiding it well.

But then, she'd seen plenty of instances where Kemp had treated his own governor with the same outwardly casual respect. "No browbeating needed," she said. "In fact, I'm glad you're here, Your Excellency, because it concerns Qasama as well."

"Really," Uy said. "In that case, and with your permission, Your Excellency, I'd like to invite Harli in for the conversation. You may wish want to call Ifrit Akim, as well."

"Siraj Akim is here?" Jody asked, surprised. From what her parents had said, she'd assumed they'd left Siraj and all the rest of the elite Djinn warriors back on Qasama.

"Yes, he and a few others accompanied me," Omnathi said. "I agree, Governor Uy. I'll call him at once."

"And we should also should have Rashida Vil," Kemp suggested.

Omnathi seemed a bit taken aback, and Jody saw Uy wince a bit. Small wonder, given the rigid and subordinate position women held in Qasaman culture. "Your reasoning?" Omnathi asked, his voice giving nothing away.

"She's the only Qasaman who was here when the Dominion ship came for their brief visit five days ago," Kemp said. "Her insights might be useful."

Omnathi's lips puckered, just noticeably. But, cultural biases or not, the man clearly knew logic when he saw it. "A valid point," he agreed. "Yes, have Cobra Uy bring her, as well."

"Well, if we're going to have a crowd, we're going to need more room," Uy said, gesturing them toward the archway leading into the dining room. "And possibly more food. Elssa?"

"I'll make it stretch," Elssa assured him. "And Jody, don't you dare start on your story until I get in there. Or else speak up loudly. I want to hear everything."

There really wasn't much to tell. But with the questions that came after Jody had finished, many of which she wasn't able to answer, the whole thing took nearly an hour.

And at the end, it still didn't make any sense.

The governor's son Harli was the first to voice that thought. "I don't get it," he said into the latest moment of silence. "You have no military bases, at least nothing the Dominion could use. You have no maintenance or drydock facilities, no one trained in such things even if you had them, your population has been hammered, and your basic infrastructure has been shot to hell. What in the Worlds can they possibly want with you?"

"A fair question," Omnathi agreed. "Rashida Vil, what was your opinion of the Dominion personnel you met?"

"Wait a minute," Jody said, frowning across the table at the young woman. Like Siraj Akim, Rashida was wearing a combat suit, though hers had the scars and discoloration it had picked up during the final battle she and Jody had ended up being involved in. Apparently, Geoff and Freylan hadn't taken both suits to Aerie with them after all. "You met them? I mean, actually *met* them?"

"It's all right," Harli assured her. "She was part of a group, and we had her put a silliweave outfit over her combat suit. They never knew who she was. Besides, Smitty was with her, and you know perfectly well that no one ever looks at Smitty twice if they can avoid it. He made sure she stayed anonymous and that they didn't ask her any questions." He nodded toward his father. "We thought she should get a chance to see them up close and personal."

"What do you mean by questions?" Jody asked. "You mean as in hearings?"

"Nothing so formal," Uy said. "They mostly wanted an overview of what had happened here. I gathered they already had sources back on Aventine they would be questioning about the details."

Jody nodded. Her parents and brother for the first big battle; Nissa Gendreves for everything after that. "I see. My apologies for the interruption, Your Excellency."

"No apology needed," Omnathi assured her. "It was a useful question." He gestured at Rashida. "Rashida Vil?"

Rashida's lips puckered slightly. Clearly, she was uncomfortable at having been brought into a meeting with such high-level people, especially when that group included a Qasaman Shahni.

But it was equally clear that she was determined not to let her nervousness get in her way. "They were polite enough," she said. "Though at the beginning they seemed more polite to Governor Uy and the city leaders than to the average citizens." She looked at Harli. "And they seemed quite contemptuous toward the Cobras."

"Really?" Uy said, frowning. "I didn't notice that."

"It changed over the hours they were here," Rashida said. "They seemed to become more respectful after their tour of the ship wreckage."

"And saw what we'd done to the invaders," Harli said, nodding.

"I believe so, yes," Rashida said. "But while they

now respected your accomplishment, it still felt that they didn't respect you personally." Her lips puckered again. "I don't know if that makes sense."

"I think it does," Uy said. "I can respect the work Nissa Gendreves did on the barrier cloth Geoff and Freylan came up with, but I don't think much of her as a person."

"It seems strange, though, that anyone could dis-respect Cobras," Siraj murmured. "We've seen you fight. Haven't they?"

"Not really," Uy said. "Not for about a hundred years, anyway."

"It's worse than that, actually," Jody pointed out. "They got to Aventine first, before they came here, and on Aventine the Cobras were ordered to basically sit on their hands after the invasion."

"They didn't fight at *all*?" Harli demanded, staring at Jody in disbelief.

"That's what Uncle Corwin said," she told him. "Well, no, that's not quite right. The ones in Capitalia and the other major cities didn't. But a lot of the Cobras in the expansion regions ignored the order and made a first-class nuisance of themselves."

"Good for them," Elssa murmured.

"But I don't know if the Dominion people got out there before they sent out whoever it was who came to look you over," Jody continued.

"Which means they already had a low opinion of us," Harli said.

"I believe that was part of it," Rashida said. "Yet even when they were being polite, and even when they'd seen the destruction you'd caused, there was a sense of arrogance and pride that never quite went away."

Out of the corner of her eye, Jody saw Uy stir and pull out his comm. "Was it mostly the officers who had that attitude?" she asked Rashida.

"The officers were certainly that way," she agreed. "But all the troops had some of that same sense about them." She hesitated. "In some ways, it reminded me of the way city dwellers on Qasama treat those from the villages."

"Not all that surprising, I guess," Harli said. His eyes, Jody noted, were on his father. "As far as the Dominion of Man is concerned, we have to be the most out-of-touch backwoods group of worlds they've ever seen."

"Interesting," Omnathi said thoughtfully. "I would have assumed that with your more open attitudes—" he inclined his head toward Jody "—they would be more accepting of your differences."

"I didn't see any such acceptance," Rashida said. "But I'm not a trained or experienced observer."

"True," Omnathi said. "In some ways, it's a shame we arrived too late to see them ourselves."

"That's one of the things about life, Your Excellency," Uy said, his voice suddenly grim as he put away his comm. "Sometimes missed opportunities sneak back up behind you." He gestured toward the sky. "They're back."

"The *Dominion*?" Harli demanded. "But that's—" He broke off, his eyes shifting to Jody. "Oh, hell."

"We have to hide her," Siraj said, standing up. "Where would be a safe place for her to go?"

"Let's not be too hasty, Ifrit Akim," Omnathi said calmly as he gestured the Djinni back to his seat. "It might be instructive to see their reaction to her presence."

"Before they take her away?" Siraj countered, still standing.

"No one's taking anyone off my world," Uy said, sounding equally thoughtful. "But His Excellency has a point."

"Indeed," Omnathi said. "Especially if her presence before them is combined with mine."

"What?" Harli demanded, standing up beside Siraj. "Not a chance. I mean, not a chance, Your Excellency."

"Your concern is appreciated, Cobra Uy," Omnathi said dryly. "But I have nothing to fear from them. I have no idea where my world is located, and never entered the control areas of the Tlos'khin'fahi ship that graciously brought us here. I have nothing to fear, for I have nothing to offer them."

"Except possibly yourself as a hostage," Harli said ominously.

"A *hostage*?" Elssa said, staring at him. "You can't be serious."

"You didn't see as much of them as I did, Mom," Harli said. "The way they talked to the people out there . . . Look, I may be overreacting. But I've read the Dominion's history, and after their last visit I wouldn't put anything past them. Better safe than sorry."

"I have to agree, Your Excellency," Siraj said. "Your safety is our first priority."

"Incorrect, Ifrit Akim," Omnathi said mildly. "Our first priority is to gather knowledge of this possible new threat. That will be my task." He gestured to Rashida. "*Your* task will be to protect Rashida Vil. She, who has actually guided a ship between these two worlds, is far more of a danger to our people than I am. You will therefore find a place to conceal her where she'll be safe from discovery."

"Understood," Harli said. "Kemp?"

"I have just the place," Kemp said, nodding. "Come on, Rashida. We'll grab Smitty and a couple of others along the way and have you buttoned up before they land."

"And take this," Jody said, suddenly remembering her recorder. "Keep it safe."

"I will," Rashida promised, tucking the recorder into a pocket of her combat suit.

"Where are you taking her?" Elssa asked. "No, wait—don't answer that. We shouldn't know, should we?"

"No, because you can't tell what you don't know," Uy confirmed. "We'll set up in the main conference room downstairs, Harli, make sure any staff down there is cleared out of the way. I'm guessing our visitors may arrive in some force, and I don't want anyone overreacting. And you, Kemp, get back as soon as you have Rashida hidden."

"I will," Kemp promised as he, Rashida, and Harli headed for the door.

"And don't let them say anything interesting until we get back," Harli added.

The rest of the group followed directly after them, heading downstairs to the conference room. Jody elected to stay behind for a few more minutes, both to help Elssa clear away the remains of their impromptu meal, and also for the better view the third-floor windows afforded of the landing area a couple of kilometers to the south.

Jody had seen plenty of holos of the Dominion warships orbiting Aventine, and she'd seen several of the landing shuttles Santores and his people had used getting back and forth between their ships and the Dome.

But the ship now settling to the ground was entirely different from either of those two types. It was much bigger than the landing shuttles, maybe half again as big as the Hoibie freighter she'd arrived in, with a sleekness that probably allowed it to be as maneuverable inside an atmosphere as it was in the vacuum of space. It had a pair of blister-like bulges on both sides about halfway back from the bow, but whether they contained weapons or sensors Jody couldn't tell. The ship's underside was curiously shaped: slightly curved, in a way that reminded her of a slice cut from a melon.

It was only as the ship sprouted landing gear and settled onto the grassy plain that she suddenly realized where she'd seen the underside's distinctive gridwork pattern before. This vehicle was designed to fit into a cutout slot in one of the warships, its underside actually functioning as a section of the warship's curved hull.

Offhand, she couldn't see how that design could possibly make sense, given that once the ship had been launched it would leave a gaping and presumably highly vulnerable opening in the warship's outer skin. But it obviously made sense to *someone* in the Dominion's ship-design department.

Briefly, she wondered if the passengers would head across the open ground on foot, which on Caelian was an engraved invitation to get yourself killed. But the advance group that had checked the place out five days ago had apparently filed the proper warnings. Even as the glow of the grav lifts began to fade, a small hatch on the top of the ship opened and a long aircar appeared. It floated upward about fifty meters, gave a casual three-sixty as if doing a quick survey of the area, then straightened out and headed toward the city.

For a moment, Jody considered just staying where she was. It was only an assumption, after all, that the Dominion was here for her. If they didn't actually know she was on Caelian, but were just here for another survey, they might not even ask about her. And if they *were* looking for her, there was something to be said for not making their job any easier than she had to.

But on the other hand, it sounded like Omnathi was planning to announce himself to them. There was no way she was going to miss that.

She was in the conference room, seated between Harli and Siraj and trying not to fidget, when Kemp opened the door and announced the arrival of their guests.

Considering there were only five of them, it was quite an entrance. They strode past Kemp into the room like they owned the entire planet, or else were preparing to take it in a quick and bloody battle. There was one senior-looking officer, his blazing blue-and-gold dress uniform visibly brightening the room, and four Marines dressed in muted outfits of burgundy and black that made his uniform look even brighter by comparison.

And all four Marines had handguns holstered at their sides.

Jody felt a shiver run up her back. The Marines

she'd seen parading around Capitalia had been in fancier dress uniforms and hadn't been armed, at least not so obviously. Someone was expecting trouble.

"Good afternoon, citizens of Caelian and the Dominion of Man," the officer said briskly as he stopped a meter from the end of the table. He was tall and handsome, his face an exotic combination of dark skin, short-cropped black hair, and piercing blue eyes that would have looked perfect on a recruitment poster. "I'm Lieutenant Commander Tristan Tamu, fourth officer of the Dominion Cruiser *Algonquin* and currently in command of the *Algonquin*'s courier ship *Squire*. Which of you is Governor Romulo Uy?"

"I'm Governor Uy," Uy spoke up. "Welcome to Caelian, Commander Tamu."

"Actually, sir, I doubt I'm all that welcome," Tamu said, his voice flat.

"And why would you think that?" Uy asked.

Jody had thought Tamu was as stiff and straight as humanly possible. She was wrong. "We're here, Governor Romulo Uy, to place you under arrest," he said, his voice suddenly clipped and formal. "I've been ordered to escort you back to Aventine for trial."

His eyes flicked once around the table, then returned to Uy. "The charge," he added, "is treason."

CHAPTER NINE

In other places, Jody thought distantly, and with other people, a statement like that would have been followed by gasps or shouts of outrage and disbelief.

Not in this place. Not with these people. All that Tamu got for his verbal bombshell was a dead, dark, ominous nothing.

Uy broke the silence first. "I presume you have a warrant?" he asked calmly.

Tamu gestured, and one of the Marines walked around behind Jody and the others to the head of the table. He pulled an envelope from his sleeve and handed it to Uy, then took a step backward.

Uy opened the envelope, and another silence settled onto the room. Jody looked furtively around the table, noting with uneasiness the hard look on Harli's face.

Even more ominous, while the Marine had been delivering the warrant, two more Cobras had stepped silently into the room and were now standing in a loose line beside Kemp, the three of them blocking the door.

"And while we head back to Aventine to deal with that," Tamu continued, "my men will be organizing and directing the construction of new defenses for you. We have the plans and equipment aboard the *Squire*."

"What do we need defenses for?" Harli growled. "The war's over."

"A particular war may end," Tamu said. "The institution of war never does. If the Trofts tried to conquer you once, they'll try it again."

"And if we don't want to waste our time playing fort-building games?" Harli countered.

"I would hope you wouldn't take that attitude," Tamu said coolly. "Since in that case Commodore Santores would have no choice but to place Caelian under martial law."

"What?" Harli turned to his father. "Dad?"

"Yes, that's in here, too," Uy said mildly, gesturing to the papers in his hand. "We're to give Commander Tamu our fullest cooperation, or else he'll have it by other means." He raised his eyebrows at Tamu. "The Dominion seems to think we're vulnerable to threats here on Caelian."

"Then the Dominion needs to take a closer look at the Troft warships we took out," Harli said.

"I don't make these decisions, Cobra Uy," Tamu said. "I just carry out my orders, and expect you to do the same." A faint smile flicked across his face. "Oh, yes, I know who you are, Cobra Harli Marco Uy. I know who all of you are."

He looked over his shoulder at Kemp and the other two Cobras, and Jody noticed his left eyelid give a small twitch. "Cobras Popescu, Tammling, and Kemp. I'd stay back if I were you, gentlemen. I wouldn't want you to get hurt."

He turned back to the table, his eyelid twitching again. "Elssa Onella Uy, the governor's wife." He paused as his gaze shifted to Omnathi, his eyelid twitching twice this time. He frowned slightly and moved on to Siraj. "You are..." He stopped, his eyelid again twitching. His eyes flicked to Siraj's scaled gray combat suit, then turned to Jody. "You—"

He stiffened. "Jody *Broom*?" he said. "But you're—" His eyes flashed briefly to Uy, then back to her. "I was informed you were taken to the Hoibe'ryi'sarai demesne."

"Obviously not," Jody said. "Why? Is that a problem?"

"No, not at all," Tamu said. The brief surprise was past, and he was back on balance again. "In fact, it's extremely convenient that you're here. Commodore Santores is most anxious to speak with you. As I'm already tasked with bringing Governor Uy to Aventine, you can travel with us."

"I don't think so," Harli said. "You're not going to be taking anyone anywhere."

"And why is that?" Tamu asked.

Pushing back his chair, Harli rose dramatically to his feet. "Because there's something you don't know."

Abruptly, there was a multiple flash of light from somewhere behind Jody, followed by a muffled curse.

She twisted her head around. Tammling was staggering back, clutching at his arms and chest where a dozen black spots had suddenly appeared in his silliweave tunic. Two of the three Marines had half turned to face him and the other Cobras, one of them with his forefinger pointing warningly at Kemp. The third Marine, along with the one still standing behind Uy, still had their full attention on the group at the table.

"You mean that one of your Cobras was attempting to sneak up behind me?" Tamu asked, his voice heavy with contempt. "If that was his idea, Cobra Uy, it was extremely foolish. If it was your idea, it was criminally foolish. Consider yourselves lucky that our backstab systems were set on riot control. His fresh collection of burns are painful, but not life-threatening."

He looked back at Tammling, standing in stoic silence now beside Popescu, his eyes boring into one of the Marines as Popescu helped him ease out of his tunic. "Also be aware that riot control is stage two. There are six more stages above that. The next time one of your men tries a stunt like that, it may not end so well."

"I'll keep that in mind," Harli said, his voice under rigid control. "I suggest you do likewise."

Tamu turned back, his eyebrows raised. "Is that a threat against the Dominion of Man, Cobra Uy?"

"Take it any way you want," Harli said. "Just take it as truth that you're not taking my father or Ms. Broom away."

Tamu snorted gently. "Words of emptiness," he said scornfully. "I've already proved you can't harm us physically. Do you really think anyone on Caelian will deliberately open themselves to their own charges of treason by interfering with our lawful duties?"

"Your words carry an emptiness of their own,"

Omnathi spoke up calmly. "Not everyone on Caelian is subject to the laws and pretentions of your Dominion."

"Really?" Tamu asked, his eyelid doing another twitch. Accessing some kind of personnel databank? "And how precisely do you compute that?"

"Truth does not need to be computed," Omnathi said with a sudden diplomatic weight and strength that sent a shiver up Jody's back. "I am Moffren Omnathi, Shahni of the sovereign world of Qasama."

It seemed to Jody that Tamu actually paled. "You are—?" His eyes darted to Uy, to the still-standing Harli, then back to Omnathi. "I'm honored to meet you, Mr. Omnathi—"

"*Your Excellency*," Siraj cut in, his own eyes unblinkingly on Tamu and as unfriendly as Jody had ever seen them. "The proper address is *Your Excellency*."

"My apologies, Your Excellency," Tamu said, looking pained at his gaffe. "May I ask what you're doing on Caelian?"

"I'm engaged in diplomatic discussions with Governor Uy," Omnathi said.

"What sort of discussions?"

"*Private* discussions," Omnathi said, leaning on the first word.

"I see," Tamu said, his voice stating to show some strain. "May I suggest that as a representative of the Dominion of Man, Commodore Santores would be a more appropriate person to negotiate with?"

Omnathi's eyebrows rose microscopically. "Define *appropriate*."

Tamu's throat worked. Clearly, the conversation was already way outside his mission parameters. "I simply meant that Commodore Santores has the authority to

speak on behalf of the Dominion of Man. Governor
Uy doesn't." He looked back at Uy. "Especially under
the present circumstances."

"And if I ask that the charges against him be
dropped?"

Tamu's eyes flicked to the Marine standing behind
Uy. "I may have some flexibility in my orders," he
said. "If you'd care to accompany me back to my
ship, perhaps we could discuss it in more comfortable surroundings."

"The surroundings here are adequate to my needs,"
Omnathi said. "Whatever you wish to discuss, we may
do it here."

Tamu's lips compressed. "Very well," he said reluctantly "As I've already suggested, Commodore Santores
is most anxious to speak with a representative of your
world. If you were willing to travel to Aventine to meet
with him, I would be honored to provide transport for
you. The flight would take less than a day."

"And Governor Uy?"

"He would be permitted to remain on Caelian until
we return," Tamu said. "But I have no doubt that
you and the commodore could work out a mutually
acceptable resolution to his situation."

"As I said, I prefer my current surroundings,"
Omnathi said. "If you wish to return to Aventine—
alone—to consult with your superiors and bring back
a full reversal of the charges against him, I'll consider
holding further discussions."

"You'll *consider* it?" Tamu retorted, his face darkening. "Have a care, Your Excellency. One word from
me and you'll be on your way to Aventine whether
you wish it or not."

"You could give that word," Omnathi agreed, his voice gone cold. "But it would be your last. Or do you truly believe I came here alone?"

Tamu's eyes flicked to Siraj and the Djinni's combat suit, and Jody had the sense of a rapid reassessment. "No, of course not," he said. "But I've intruded on your time too much already. With your permission, I'll take my leave. Governor Uy, we'll speak more on this matter later."

He gestured, and the Marine standing behind Uy retraced his steps around the table. Then, in perfect unison, all five of them turned and strode past the three Cobras through the doorway. The Cobras followed, closing the door behind them. Straining her ears, Jody heard the faint thud as the building's outside door closed.

"An interesting dilemma," Uy said.

"Not exactly the word I would have chosen," Harli said sourly.

"I didn't mean ours," his father told him. "I meant Commander Tamu's."

"Indeed," Omnathi agreed thoughtfully. "As I see it, he has three possible paths. First, he can attempt to take us by force. But that path is pitted with danger. Not only do you have many Cobras who would resist, but there may be an unknown number of Djinn as well. A well-schooled military commander would never go against such uncertainties unless he had no other options. Second, he can send his ship back to Aventine to alert his superiors and bring back new instructions and more warriors. But that would leave him stranded without his ship's tactical support. Third, he and his entire force could leave and return for instructions.

But he then risks the chance that we would be gone when he returned." He looked at Uy. "Do you find any flaws in my reasoning?"

"No, your reasoning is solid," Uy said heavily. "I only wish it wasn't built on a castle of cards."

"What do you mean?" Jody asked.

Uy looked at Omnathi. "I'm not sure..."

"He means that my threat was hollow," Omnathi said calmly. "There are only four Djinn currently on Caelian, and Ifrit Akim is the only one in Stronghold."

"The other three are in Aerie assisting the Cobras who are testing the combat suits we brought," Siraj added.

"Fortunately, Tamu doesn't know that," Uy said. "The trick is to maintain the illusion. *And* to not back him into a corner where he feels he has to call our bluff."

"I see," Jody said, a shiver running through her. Tamu had called the *Squire* a courier ship, but given that it was a Dominion craft, she didn't doubt that it was also heavily armed. Not that it would take much weaponry to flatten what was left of Stronghold.

"There's also Damocles," Harli said.

"What's Damocles?" Jody asked.

"Something the less said about, the better," Uy told her.

"Okay," Jody said, a shiver running through her. She'd seen the Caelians come up with all sorts of crazy combat schemes. If Uy didn't even want to talk about this one, it must be even crazier than usual. "New tack. Your Excellency, is there any way to get you out of here if Tamu goes with option three?"

Omnathi shook his head. "That, too, is a castle of

cards. The Tlos'khin'fahi ship that is to take us home is not scheduled to return for three more weeks."

"Wait a minute," Harli said, frowning off into the distance. "What about the Troft warship we left in the Octagon Caves? Do you think we might be able to get that one back in the air?"

"I doubt it," Jody said. "We left it pretty firmly wedged in."

"Yeah, I know," Harli said. "But if we could get it unstuck—use shaped charges to blast away the stone above it or something—we know that you, Smitty, Kemp, and Rashida can fly the thing. Even if we couldn't get Shahni Omnathi all the way back to Qasama, we might at least get him out of the system where Tamu couldn't find him."

"And perhaps move Governor Uy away, as well," Siraj suggested.

"Oh, wouldn't *that* just fry him?" Harli said dryly. "What do you think, Dad? Should I send a couple of miners to the caves and see what they can do?"

Across the room, the door abruptly swung open. "Sorry," Kemp said. "Governor, we've got trouble. Tamu's got a whole bunch of his Marines out in the streets trying to get people into his ship."

"You mean *kidnapping* them?" Uy demanded, straightening in his chair.

"No, no—so far they're just talking," Kemp said. "But they're talking real big—promising food and money and help. The whole niners."

"Is anyone listening to them?" Harli asked.

"*Everyone's* listening to them," Kemp said grimly. "They've got twenty corralled already and they've only gone three blocks."

Jody felt her stomach tighten. On her walk into the city she'd noticed that several of the large gardens that supplemented Stronghold's food supply were still out of commission, their crops torn up and trampled during the battles with the invading Trofts. With the additional deaths of so many Cobras and civilians, it was likely that the normal hunting schedule had also been disrupted.

The Caelians were hungry. Tamu had obviously noticed that, too. "Looks like he's found a fourth option," she murmured. "But aside from good will, I don't see what this gains him."

"Maybe it gains him hostages," Harli said tartly, moving toward the door. "How many Cobras have we got out there?"

"Just a minute, Harli," Uy called, gesturing him back. "Let's think this through. Kemp, are they picking specific people, or just gathering them at random?"

"I couldn't tell," Kemp said. "Some of the people were working. Others were just standing there chatting with each other or minding their own business."

"I cannot imagine a warrior allowing random civilians past his barriers," Omnathi said. "He must be doing some form of screening."

"I'm sure he is," Uy agreed. "We know that the first Dominion survey team pulled the city records. We've also seen that Tamu has either a prodigious memory or access to some computerized face-recognition system. If he wanted specific people, he could probably find them."

"If they're looking for hostages, they should be going after Council members or other community leaders," Elssa said. "Is that who they're approaching?"

"No, none of them are in the group," Kemp said, frowning. "Wait a minute—I take that back. Pivovarci was one of them."

"*Pivovarci?*" Harli snorted. "Terrific."

"Who's Pivovarci?" Jody asked.

"One of our chief malcontents," Harli growled. "He didn't like the way Stronghold got torn up while we were fighting the Trofts, he didn't like the Isis deal with the Qasamans, and he *really* doesn't like the food rationing we've had to impose."

"So he's not buying hostages," Kemp said grimly. "He's buying allies. Using food as his lure."

"All the while whispering words of betrayal in their ears," Omnathi said, nodding agreement. "A slower tactic than force of arms, but just as likely to yield results in the long run."

"Too bad we can't hear what those words consist of," Harli said. "Kemp, was there anyone in the group we can pull aside later and ask what they talked about?"

"No one I'd trust to tell me the truth," Kemp said sourly. "But they're still collecting. Maybe Tamu will slip up and pick someone who'll be a little more on our side."

"Lord knows we don't need any more enemies right now," Elssa murmured.

Jody braced herself. "Then maybe we should see about bringing in a few more allies."

"Meaning?" Uy asked.

"You said there were three more Djinn out in Aerie and a bunch of new combat suits," Jody said, thinking quickly. She was going to need some fancy verbal footwork if she was going to sell this. "How many suits are there?"

"There are fifty," Uy said, gazing hard at her. "All of them out in Aerie."

"Are you suggesting we dress up a few citizens and pretend they're full-fledged Djinn?" Kemp asked.

"Because if you are, it won't work," Harli added. "They have the population records, remember? One flick of his eyelid and Tamu will know they're not Qasamans."

"Unless all he got were Stronghold's records," Jody pointed out. "Do we know for sure that they got Aerie's, too?"

"It's a good bet they did," Uy said.

"I still think it's worth trying," Jody said stubbornly. "All I need is an aircar."

"You also need *not* to get picked up by Tamu," Elssa warned. "I doubt he left here without putting a Marine on guard at our doors."

"Actually, he left two," Kemp confirmed. "But I can get her past them."

"Besides, what Tamu doesn't know is that I'm not worth nearly as much as he thinks I am," Jody said. "As long as he doesn't get my recorder, there's nothing I can give them that they want."

"Doesn't mean they won't lock you away until they figure that out," Harli pointed out.

"I'm willing to risk it," Jody said. "Besides, Aerie deserves to know what's going on."

For a moment the room was silent. Uy and Omnathi looked questioningly at each other, and Jody saw Omnathi give a small nod. "All right," Uy said reluctantly. "Baxtern's the Cobra in charge out there. Just tell him what's going on, and have him coordinate with Ifrit Ghushtre on a cautious—a *cautious*—response."

He made as if to say something else, then seemed to change his mind. "Kemp, are you going to need a field radio for this?"

"No, we can do it pick-up," Kemp said. "Come on, Jody—we need to get to the roof."

"The roof?" Jody echoed, frowning, as she stood up and headed across the room.

"The roof," he confirmed. "Trust me—you're going to love this."

"Good luck," Uy called after them.

"And be careful," Elssa added.

Two minutes and three flights of stairs later they emerged onto the roof. "We actually have your mother to thank for this one," Kemp commented as he led the way across the tiles at a fast jog. "It was her last maneuver before the Trofts surrendered that inspired us to come up with it. Well, hers and the Qasamans'."

He trotted to a halt right at the roof's edge and peered down at the streets and people below. Jody stopped a more cautious meter away, a sudden sense of foreboding tingling up her spine. The way *she* remembered it, her mother's last maneuver in that battle had nearly gotten her killed.

Abruptly, Kemp gave a short whistle and snapped his fingers. He paused, snapped his fingers again, and gave a sort of pancake-flipping motion with his hand. He nodded, gave whoever was down there a thumbs-up and gestured to Jody. "Okay, we're ready," he told her as she came up. He took hold of her wrist—

And to her stunned bewilderment pulled her toward him, leaned over, and scooped her up into his arms. "What—?"

"Happy landings," he said.

And before she could more than gasp in surprise and terror he straightened his arms and hurled her high into the air off the edge of the roof. The city flashed dizzily around her as she spun around twice like a high diver who'd lost her way and orientation. On the second spin she thought she saw a figure flying up to meet her—

A second later her spin came to a sudden halt as a pair of strong arms closed around her shoulders and knees. She jolted slightly with the impact, and there was more disorientation as she belatedly realized she was still falling. The arm cradling her shoulders shifted, the hand reaching up to support the back of her head.

And then, with another jolt and a sudden but controlled deceleration, they were down.

Down, spinning around, and bouncing rhythmically across the ground. Blinking against the wind blowing across her face, Jody looked down.

She'd been wrong. They weren't running along the ground, but along the top of a two-story building. Peering past the shoulder pressed against her cheek, she saw the Government Building receding behind her.

"Hope that wasn't too frightening," a soft voice murmured in her ear.

"No, I'm okay," Jody said, bending the truth only a little as she looked up.

To find the last face on Caelian she'd expected smiling tightly down at her. "*Tammling?*" she breathed. "But I thought—" She broke off, dropping her eyes to the burn marks the Marine's lasers had cut through his tunic. "You just got *shot*."

"What, *that*?" He made a rude-sounding burble with his lips. "I got hit way worse during the war. We just wanted to see how close you could get before the Dommies' auto-target stuff kicked in."

"You mean the backstab thing Tamu mentioned?" Jody asked, turning her head to look the other direction. They were coming up fast on the edge of the roof. "Uh—"

"Right—backstab," Tammling said. "Nice appropriate name for it, huh? Anyway—"

"Tammling—the *edge*—"

"Hang on," Tammling said.

A second later Jody found herself once more arcing through the air as Tammling leaped over a narrow alleyway to the next building over.

A much smaller building than the one they'd just left, with another wide street beyond it. "How much more of this is there?" Jody asked, hoping the bouncing covered up the quavering in her voice.

"Almost there," Tammling soothed her. "Hopefully, Williams is in position."

Jody felt her eyes bulge. "*Hopefully*?"

"Relax," Tammling said with a chuckle. "Here goes nothing. Good luck."

Jody clenched her teeth and folded her arms tightly across her chest. A second later, she was once again flying solo through the air with the city spinning beneath her.

The flight this time seemed shorter than the first one, though that might just have been because she was marginally more used to it. However it happened, a frozen moment later she landed with another disorienting thud in someone's arms, followed by the same short drop and controlled deceleration as Cobra knee servos took the impact. "Jody Broom?" an unfamiliar voice asked.

Jody's first impulse was to ask who else he was expecting to be flying over the streets this afternoon. But she resisted the urge. "Yes," she said. "Who are you?"

"Jameson Williams," he said as he bent over and set her feet back onto solid ground again. "We've never met, but I wanted to tell you how much I admire your family. It was mainly because of your mother and father that I decided to became a Cobra."

"Oh," Jody said. She'd been hit with similar comments in the past, and she had yet to figure out a good answer. "Thanks. I'm sure they appreciate it." She glanced around at the people moving along the streets, all of them studiously ignoring the couple who'd just dropped out of the sky. "Where are we?"

"Oakleaf and Sun," he said. "Where are you trying to go?"

"Aerie," Jody said, frowning. "You telling me you don't even know *that*?"

"All I got was the whistle to get ready for a sky-hook and a handflap with your name," Williams said, taking her arm and starting down the street. "Come on—we're parking the aircars indoors these days."

Jody kept an eye on the streets and the people as Williams hurried her along, watching especially for burgundy-black Dominion uniforms. But apparently the Marines hadn't made it to this part of town yet.

They ended up two blocks later in a small warehouse with a large gash through its glazed-stone facing. "Used to be a food processing area," Williams grunted as he forced open the door from its visibly distorted frame. "One of the Troft missiles blew it open to the air, and that was pretty much that."

"Doesn't look like there's much food to be processed right now, anyway," Jody said as they went inside. There were three aircars parked inside the building, none of them in terrific shape, but none of them looking like it would disintegrate out from under her, either. "How do we get it out?"

"Loading door in the back," Williams said, heading toward the darkness at the rear of the building. "Pick one and get it started—keys should be on the seat."

"Right." Jody stepped to the closest vehicle, a bright red six-seater that seemed to have fewer dents and scrapes than the other two. She pulled open the door, spotted the keys on the seat—

"Hold!" a voice ordered tersely from behind her.

She spun around. Three Dominion Marines were standing just inside the building, two to the right of the doorway, the other to the left. "Who are you?" she demanded, trying to put some outrage into her voice. "What do you want?"

"Marine Sergeant Tapper," the man on the left said. "And you, Jody Broom, are under arrest."

Jody stifled a curse. "On what charge?"

"Attempting to flee possible felony charges will do for starters," Tapper said, motioning the other two men forward. "You were ordered not to leave the Government Building, and yet here you are."

"I was given no such order," Jody insisted.

"I was told you had," Tapper said. If he was disturbed by the discrepancy, it didn't show in his voice. "That'll be for you and Commander Tamu to work out. As for you, Cobra, whatever you're planning back there, I strongly suggest you reconsider."

Jody looked over her shoulder. She couldn't see

Williams anywhere, but she had no doubt he was lurking somewhere.

And after what had happened to Tammling...

"It's all right," she called, moving toward the Marines. "It's all right. Don't do anything—please. I'll go with them. It's all right."

There was no response. Nothing but a brooding silence from the rest of the building. Tapper took Jody's arm as she reached him, pulling her gently but firmly in front of him. He motioned his men to leave, then backed through the doorway after them.

Jody had half expected to find a Cobra ambush waiting out on the street. But there were only the ordinary citizens moving about their business. Unlike earlier, though, Jody could see many of them furtively eyeing the strangers as Tapper marched them briskly in the direction of the gate.

"How did you know I'd left the Government Building?" Jody asked as they walked. "Did you just happen to spot me, or what?"

"Trolling for information?" Tapper gave a derisive snort. "Go ahead—it doesn't matter. I could give you the whole schematic stack for inversion-layer reflectives and it still wouldn't help. How back-wash people with century-old technology think they can just sneak around without us knowing all about it is beyond the senses."

"Must be something about frontier life," Jody said, fighting back her reflexive anger. "Speaking of which, if you're thinking about walking across the field to your ship, I strongly suggest you reconsider."

"No fears," he said, pointing at the sleek aircar just visible around the next corner. "The ordinaries can walk. Important snags like you get to ride."

A minute later, they were in the aircar and soaring over the city, heading toward the Dominion ship.

Jody gazed down as they flew, noting the small but growing crowd behind Tamu and his Marines. The commander would probably be highly pleased when he learned that she'd been picked up and spirited away from the protection of Uy and his Cobras.

Hopefully, he would be pleased enough that it would never occur to him that this was exactly what she'd been going for in the first place.

Uy had wanted ears on Tamu's pitch to Stronghold's people. In just a few minutes, he would have them.

Of course, she would then have to find a way to slip into the main group and listen. After that would come the task of getting the information out of the ship and back to Uy and Omnathi. After *that* it would be handy if she could find a way to get out of the ship herself.

But she would figure it out. She was a Broom, and a Moreau. Somehow, she would figure it out.

CHAPTER TEN

Lorne's first day at Bitter Creek wasn't as bad as he'd feared. Mayor Mary McDougal welcomed him politely enough, the people he met were civil, and the spine leopards hadn't encroached as much on the edges of town as he'd feared they would during the couple of weeks the town had been without full-time Cobra protection.

Best of all, there was no mention of Tristan's death during the invasion, or how Lorne hadn't been there during their local war against the Trofts, or how Lorne would never measure up to a fine local boy like Tristan.

At least, none of that got said within Lorne's hearing.

The biggest challenge, in fact, looked like it was going to be adjusting his biological clock to a sleep schedule consisting up of two- to three-hour, round-the-clock naps.

It was just after dawn on his first full day in town, and he was very much looking forward to one of those naps, as he parked the grav-lift cycle they'd given him and headed inside the grocery-goods store that doubled as the city building. Mayor McDougal was already at her desk behind the counter, working at her comboard. "Morning," she said, a distracted smile on her round face as she nodded to him in greeting. "Any trouble?"

"Not really," Lorne said, hungrily eyeing the other chair behind the counter next to McDougal. But he was still officially on duty, and tradition and professional pride dictated that he remain standing in the presence of his supervisor. "I chased away a couple of families snooping around a livestock shelter to the southwest, and I cleaned out a way station along one of the big creeks further north."

"One of the ones that goes through the forest?" McDougal asked, frowning. "Which one?"

"I'm not sure," Lorne said, wincing. He'd studied some of the area maps yesterday, but the local geography was still something of a jumble in his mind. "It went through a culvert under the perimeter road. But I guess they all do that, don't they?"

"Were its banks mostly just mud and reeds, or were there a lot of stones and big rocks at the waterline?"

"There were a fair amount of stones," Lorne said, thinking back. "At least at the spot where I found the way station."

"Stony Creek." McDougal smiled lopsidedly. "Yes, I know—we're not very creative with our names around here." Her smile faded. "Stony Creek. Damn."

"Trouble?"

"There's a crew supposed to be taking down a stand of blueleaf trees this morning along that creek about half a kilometer from the road into the forest," McDougal said. "Tristan always said that if you saw one way station, there were two more you didn't see."

"That's about right," Lorne said heavily. And he'd been so looking forward to a couple of hours of sleep. "Do you want me to head back and see if I can find them?"

For a moment McDougal seemed tempted. Then, reluctantly, she shook her head. "No, you need to get some sleep," she said. "Besides, Tristan also said it was easier to find the way stations at night when the beasts were on the move." She scrolled down her comboard. "Let's see if we can get clever. Okay. If they reschedule to that oak stand out north this morning, then shift to the blueleaves after you've had a nap..."

A faint noise in the distance caught Lorne's attention: the sound of an approaching aircar. "You expecting company?" he asked.

"Not me," McDougal said, frowning toward the window. "Doesn't sound like one of ours, either. Maybe your new friends from Archway are back to see how you're doing."

Lorne scowled. Now that she mentioned it, the grav lifts *did* sound like the ones on the aircar Khahar and Chimm had swooped in on yesterday morning. "Could be," Lorne told her, heading for the door. "Better stay inside. I'll go see what they want."

It was indeed a Dominion aircar that settled to the ground outside the store a minute later. The two men who got out were equally familiar. "Good morning, Sergeant," Lorne said as politely as he could as Khahar and Chimm strode toward him. "Bored with life in Archway already?"

"That's funny," Khahar said with a grunt as he stopped a couple of meters away. "Get in the car."

Lorne frowned. They walked all they way over here

from the car just to tell him they were all getting right back in and leaving? "Why?" he asked.

"Because there's trouble, and we need you back there," Khahar said. "We'll explain on the way." He stepped forward and to his left, clearly heading to get behind Lorne.

"Whoa," Lorne protested, taking a quick step to his own left to keep both Marines in sight. "I can't just run off, not even to Archway. I've been assigned here, and I'm on duty."

"And Colonel Reivaro is reassigning you," Chimm said.

"Reivaro's not in my chain of command," Lorne countered. "I can't leave without a good reason."

"How about a general riot?" Khahar growled. "That a good enough reason?"

Lorne felt his eyes widen. "A *riot*? What the hell have you been *doing* down there?"

"Hey, it's *your* people who've gone off the deep end, not ours," Chimm shot back.

"Like I said, we'll explain on the way," Khahar said, taking another step forward. "Come on, come on—the colonel needs every man he can get, and that includes you Cobras."

Another quiet alarm went off in the back of Lorne's mind. Reivaro was *still* in Archway? That didn't make any sense at all.

Unless, of course, this whole alleged riot was nothing more than Reivaro taking another run at getting Lorne into a dark room and trying to squeeze Qasama's location out of him. "I understand," he said, taking another step back and pulling out his comm. "But like *I* said, I'm on duty. Any changes have to be cleared with the commandant first."

"Are you tired, Broom, or just naturally stupid?" Khahar demanded impatiently. "Commandant Ishikuma has been relieved. You know that. Colonel Reivaro's in command now."

"I wasn't talking about Commandant Ishikuma," Lorne said, punching in a number. "I was talking about Commandant Dreysler, supreme Cobra commander on Aventine. He has final say on everything we do."

Khahar and Chimm looked at each other. "Fine," Khahar growled. "Make it fast."

The comm clicked and a woman answered. "This is Cobra Lorne Broom," Lorne identified himself. "It's urgent that I speak with Commandant Dreysler right away."

The night's drive had been long and tedious, the monotony punctuated mainly by soreness in Jin's hips, soreness in her lower back, and an occasional fatigue cramp in one of her legs. There had been several times through the long hours when she'd nearly given up and asked Paul to stop at a motel where they could get a few hours of real sleep.

But most of those times had been when Paul was driving, and Jin had usually been drifting off to sleep anyway, and on further consideration it had seemed like too much trouble to get out of the car, even if there was a real horizontal bed at the other end of the walk.

Now, with the sun rising in the east and Archway only a few kilometers ahead, she was glad she'd kept her silence. A few more minutes, and she and Paul would be reunited with Lorne, and they could start figuring out a strategy for dealing with the Dominion and their obsession with Qasama.

From her pocket came the muted signal from her comm. She glanced at Paul, dozing in the passenger seat, and glanced at the comm's display.

And felt her lips curve into a relieved smile. The caller was none other than Lorne himself. What an unexpectedly pleasant way for her and Paul to end their long, wearying trip. Tapping it on, she held it to her ear. "Good morning, Lo—"

"This is Cobra Lorne Broom," Lorne said, his voice stiff with proper protocol and tension. "It's urgent that I speak with Commandant Dreysler right away."

Jin's muscles went rigid, her smile vanishing, her sleep-starved brain scrabbling frantically for an innocuous explanation for such a bizarre beginning to this conversation.

But there wasn't one. Lorne knew her number, and he knew her voice, and Dreysler's office answered with a much more formal identification. There was no way any of this could be a simple mistake on her son's part.

Which meant it was deliberate.

Which meant he was in trouble.

"One moment," she said, dropping her voice into the same official cadence. Keying the comm to mute, she let go of the wheel with her other hand long enough to give Paul a quick slap on the shoulder.

He came awake in an instant. "We there?" he asked, blinking against the sunlight.

"It's Lorne," Jin told him, holding up the comm. "Only he's pretending he's calling Commandant Dreysler."

Paul sat up straighter, his slightly befogged manner gone. "Where is he?"

"I don't know," Jin said. "He just said it was urgent that he talk to Dreysler."

"Some kind of trouble, then." Paul gestured to the comm. "Put it on speaker."

Jin nodded and switched the comm to her other hand, holding it between them, and keyed on the speaker. "This is Dreysler," Paul said in a surprisingly good imitation of the commandant's voice. "This better be good, Broom."

"Yes, sir, and I'm sorry about the hour," Lorne said. "I have two Dominion Marines with me here in Bitter Creek. They're telling me I need to abandon my assigned post and accompany them immediately back to Archway."

Jin flashed a startled look at Paul. *Bitter Creek?* she mouthed.

He gave a small shrug in return. "Is there some trouble in Archway?" he asked.

"They said there was trouble simmering," Lorne said, "but they haven't given me any details. I was hoping you could clarify the chain of command for me, or maybe contact Governor-General Chintawa and see if there's been some arrangement in place that I'm not yet familiar with."

Jin felt her stomach tighten. So that was why Lorne had called them. He'd naturally assumed they were still in Capitalia, within easy contact of the Dome, and was hoping they could get Chintawa to intervene in whatever was going on in DeVegas province.

Only she and Paul were a long way from any official contact, even if there'd been anyone in Chintawa's office who would actually listen to them anymore. If that was indeed Lorne's plan, then they needed to clue him in right away that it wasn't going to work, and then try to figure out a new strategy.

Unfortunately, there was no way to give Lorne the situation without coming right out and saying it. If the Marines were listening in, the whole thing was about to come crashing down on them.

But it was a risk they had to take. "Can the Marines hear our side of the conversation?" she asked quietly.

"I don't think so," Lorne said, his voice subtly changing pitch as he moved the comm a few centimeters away from his mouth. "You two have any papers or documentation on this supposed change in my orders?"

There was a muffled and indistinct voice. "No, they've got nothing like that," Lorne said, speaking directly into the comm again. "They claim the new order's coming from Colonel Reivaro, if that means anything."

"Okay, here's the situation," Paul said softly. "We're actually on our way to Archway now—don't ask, it's a long story. We'll try to find out what's going on and get back to you."

"Do you think you can stall them long enough for us to do that?" Jin added.

There was an odd sort of snort from the comm. "Yes, I think I can do that," Lorne said, a hint of grim amusement in his voice. "Let me know what you find out."

He keyed off. "This is not good," Jin said tightly, keying off from her end. "You think we should call Commandant Ishikuma and see if he can tell us what's going on?"

"If the Dominion has any sense, they've got Ishikuma's comm flagged," Paul said, taking the comm from her and punching in a number. "Let's try a little lower on the chain of command. We'll start with Badger Werle, and if he's not answering we'll try Dillon de Portola."

"Their comms may be flagged, too," Jin warned.

"So could the whole comm system," he countered. "In which case, any subterfuge is so much wasted effort anyway."

"You're right," Jin said, grimacing. "Sorry. You going with the dumb approach?"

"I think that's our best bet," he said. "A couple of clueless parents here to visit their son."

And if the Dominion was flagging all calls, she and Paul would probably be picked up before they even reached Archway.

On the other hand, if the Dominion had taken over the whole system, they probably already knew that Lorne had called his mother and not Commandant Dreysler.

"Cobra Werle?" Paul said into his comm. "This is Paul Broom. Can you tell me what's going on?"

Ahead, a sign marked the spur into Archway. Giving the area a quick visual sweep, Jin settled into the final leg of the drive.

And wondered what the hell was happening to her world.

It started with a low rumble of a badly-tuned grav-lift cycle, humming distractingly in Lorne's other ear as he tried to carry out his charade conversation with his parents. Slowly but steadily the rumble grew louder, and as it did it was joined by a second hum, and then a third, and then by the deeper rumble of an unmuffled car engine or two or three.

By the time his father began describing their proximity to Archway, the first of the grav-lift cycles appeared, a burly man in a heavy jacket with a rifle slung over his shoulder astride the saddle. By the time his mother asked about stalling the Marines, the second, third, and fourth vehicles had coasted to a halt a dozen meters from the three men standing their face-off.

By the time he keyed off the comm and put it away, over a dozen of Bitter Creek's citizens had taken up positions in a rough semicircle around the front of McDougal's store. All of them looking wary, angry, or determined.

All of them armed.

If the Marines were worried about the sudden influx of weapons, it didn't show in their faces. "I see we rate the A-Squad welcoming committee," Khahar said calmly. "This your doing, shopkeeper?"

"It is," McDougal said from where she now stood, just outside her store, with a shotgun gripped in her hands. "And for the record, you can address me as Mayor McDougal."

Chimm turned to frown at her. "*You're* the mayor?"

"We're more egalitarian here than you are back in the Dominion," Lorne told him. "On the Cobra Worlds, our leaders are the ones who have the talent for actual leadership."

"Or we go with whoever's willing to take the damn job," McDougal said. "Either way, I trust we've made our point?"

"What point is that?" Khahar asked. "That even a woman can command a military unit if the unit's standards are low enough?"

"That you don't just stroll into our town and snatch

away our people," McDougal said, ignoring the taunt. "Now get back in your aircar and let's see you make some dust."

Khahar shook his head, mock-sadly. "They're so earnestly pathetic, aren't they, Chimm?"

"Yes, sir, they are," Chimm said. "Almost a shame, isn't it?"

"Almost," Khahar agreed.

And without a single hint of warning the entire area exploded into an eye-searing firestorm of blue laser fire.

Reflexively, Lorne slammed his eyes shut as his nanocomputer took over his servo network and threw him in a low dive to the side. He hit the ground and rolled back to his feet, his hands snapped up in front of him as he flicked target-locks onto the two Marines.

But it was already over. The men in the cordon circle were staggering back in shock, dismay, and pain, their half-melted guns smoldering on the grass in front of them.

"I trust we've made *our* point," Khahar said, raising his voice. "It could just as easily be your bodies lying smoking on the ground as your weapons. Consider it your one and only warning."

Lorne took a deep breath, fighting hard against the almost overwhelming urge to drop both Marines where they stood. Out here, in spine leopard territory, a working firearm could mean the difference between life and death. "What the hell was *that*?" he demanded in a low voice.

"As I said: a warning," Khahar said coolly. "Certainly more warning than an actual enemy would have received."

"You fired on your own people."

"Who had drawn weapons on uniformed enforcement personnel," Khahar snapped. "For a world that professes to be a loyal and upstanding member of the Dominion of Man, Cobra Broom, your citizens are remarkably hostile. Not to mention slow to learn." He gestured impatiently. "Enough of this. For the last time, *get in the vehicle.*"

Lorne looked around. A grim and watchful silence filled their little circle of drama, the newly disarmed men watching him closely.

Waiting to see what their new Cobra would do.

Once again, Lorne longed to drop the Marines. Even a non-lethal sonic burst would give at least some momentary satisfaction to the insult and injury that had been arrogantly handed out.

Once again, he forced back the temptation. The last thing any of them wanted was for this whole incident to escalate further.

Or was it?

Lorne focused on Khahar again, this time keying his infrareds. The sergeant's face was brimming with anticipation, as if he was actually hoping Lorne would make some move against them.

Which he was, of course, Lorne realized. Both Marines were hoping that. After all, their mission was to get Lorne back to Capitalia and the main Dominion force. What better way to accomplish that than to goad him into attacking them?

Of course, it would be a pretty hollow victory for Khahar and Chimm personally if they both died in the process.

Earlier, Lorne and de Portola had speculated that

the Marines' combat garb had some kind of defenses built into them. The fact that Lorne could see no fear in either man's face implied they had a lot of confidence in those defenses. Still, could any outfit really be strong enough to block a full Cobra attack?

There was one way to find out. But not here. Not now. Their mission might be to bring Lorne in; Lorne's was to stall them off long enough for his parents to find out what the hell was happening in Archway.

Fortunately, he had an idea how to do that.

"In a minute," he said, glancing around. Six meters behind him was an arrowcrest, tall and serene, with the spindly yet strong branches jutting out from the trunk that made it a favorite climbing tree for the province's children. "See that tree?" he asked Khahar, pointing as he walked toward it. "Let me show you something."

"Broom—"

"It'll only take a second," Lorne promised. "It's something you may not know about us."

He walked to the base of the tree, his shoulders tensed the whole way with the foreboding sense that he was about to catch a laser blast in the back. But the attack didn't come. Either Khahar was intrigued enough to hold his fire, or else he figured that he could handle whatever Lorne had up his sleeve.

"This is called an arrowcrest," Lorne identified it, stopping and turning back to face them. The townspeople, he noted, seemed as baffled by his gambit as the Marines were. "You want to know its biggest claim to fame?" he asked, glancing up at a clump of branches eight meters above his head.

"Wood?" Khahar suggested sarcastically.

Lorne shook his head. "This," he said, crouching down and pointing to the base of the tree as if indicating the roots.

And with a surge of servo-enhanced strength he leaped straight up.

The move caught the Marines completely off-guard. Before they could even goggle, let alone fire, Lorne was balanced astride two of the branches, his hand on the trunk behind him for stability. "It's one of the best climbing trees on the planet," he called down.

"How wonderful for it," Khahar growled. "What the hell was that supposed to accomplish? You don't think we can fire above our heads?"

"No, I'm sure you can," Lorne said. "I'm also sure you won't. Because I'm pretty sure Commodore Santores's orders were for you to bring me back alive."

"Don't be ridiculous," Khahar said scornfully. "I've seen the vids. You can jump up and down like that all day without hurting yourself."

"*Jump*, yes," Lorne agreed. "*Fall*, no." He tapped the side of his head. "Just because my brain is encased in ceramic doesn't mean it won't slosh around badly if I hit the ground from this height."

Keying in his telescopics, he focused on Khahar's face and took his hand away from the tree trunk behind him. "But if you want to experiment, I'm game to give it a try." Deliberately, he let his body wobble a little, as if he was losing his balance.

Just as he'd expected, Khahar's lips gave an involuntary twitch. Whatever his orders were, they didn't include Lorne plummeting to his death. "You're bluffing," he bit out.

"I'm not planning suicide, if that's what you mean,"

Lorne agreed. "But it hardly qualifies as suicide if a couple of gung-blaze Dominion Marines shoot me down, does it?"

Khahar looked sideways at Chimm. "You've got chutz, Broom—I'll give you that. But you can't stay up there forever."

"I wasn't planning to," Lorne said. "I just want to wait until I get some word about what's going on in Archway."

"We already told you," Chimm said. "The people are planning a riot."

"Then you'd better get back in case you're needed, hadn't you?" Lorne suggested.

Khahar's eyes were all but spitting laser fire of their own. But he and Chimm were clearly expected back at Archway, and standing here looking like idiots while they had a face-off with a Cobra in a tree was apparently below Khahar's personal dignity level. "Fine," he said darkly. "But this isn't over. Not by a long shot." Gesturing to Chimm, he spun around and stalked toward the aircar.

Lorne switched his attention to the ring of silent townspeople. There seemed to be some mild disappointment on a few of the faces, those men in particular who'd probably been hoping to see Bitter Creek's new Cobra deal out some mayhem. But most of them seemed satisfied to see the intruders slapped down without the use of force. Especially since any such violence would undoubtedly have repercussions for the whole town somewhere down the line.

And speaking of the use of force...

"You're right, it's not," Lorne called after Khahar. "Mayor McDougal is going to prepare a receipt for the guns you just destroyed. Both of you will sign and print it, and the Dominion will have three days to reimburse the owners."

Khahar spun back around, a look of disbelief on his face. "Like hell we will," he said. "It was self-defense."

"Hardly," Lorne said. "None of the guns were pointed at you."

"They had them out and ready."

"Everyone traveling outside a town fence has a weapon out and ready," Lorne countered. "That's how life is in the expansion regions." He cocked his head. "But I understand how paperwork is. If the receipt thing is too much trouble, I'll bet there are some nice weapons in your aircar you could hand out instead."

Khahar's eyes narrowed. "Don't even think it," he warned. "The first move anyone makes toward our car, the next volley will be to kill."

"Only if you're ready for all of us to die together," Lorne said. "I've already got you target-locked. And don't forget, your superiors need me alive. I doubt they'd even miss you."

"Don't count on it," Chimm snarled. "You try assaulting us, and they'll be sifting your brain aboard the *Algonquin* by nightfall."

"They could certainly try," Lorne said, feeling his forehead crease. They'd be sifting his *brain*? What in the Worlds did *that* mean? "But you're right—today *would* be a rotten day to die, what with you being missing from the Archway riots and all. So I guess we'd better go with the receipt thing instead. Mayor?"

"Got it," McDougal said, making a last flourish on her comboard and stepping up behind the two Marines. "If you'll both sign and thumbprint, please?"

For another couple of seconds Lorne thought Khahar might be rethinking the whole blaze-of-glory approach. But he merely snorted and yanked the comboard from McDougal's hand. He signed and thumbprinted the document and watched, glowering, as Chimm did likewise. Then, with a final glare at Lorne, the two of them stalked back to their aircar. A minute later they were above the treetops, gaining altitude and heading toward Archway.

Lorne waited until the sound of their grav lifts had faded completely from his enhanced hearing. Only then did he drop back to the ground, making sure to let his knee and hip servos take the impact. "Thanks," he said, looking around the circle. "That could have been awkward."

"It *was* awkward," McDougal said sourly. "But thanks at least for trying to get our guns back."

"You'll get them," Lorne promised. "I'll make sure of that."

"Yeah," McDougal said. "We'll see." She gestured to the others. "Looks like that's it for now. I'll let you know if and when I need you again."

The men glanced at each other, and still without speaking a word they got back in their cars or onto their cycles and headed out. A minute later, Lorne and McDougal were again alone. "You know you're not going to get any real news out of Archway, don't you?" she said. "They've got the whole province comm system locked up tighter than a switchback."

"That's okay," Lorne said. "My parents are there. They'll find a way to get word to us."

"Yeah," McDougal said, not sounding like she believed that any more than she believed the Dominion would come through with money for the lost weapons. "You heading for bed?"

Lorne snorted. "Like I'm going to be able to sleep *now*. No, I think I'll head back to Stony Creek and see if I can sniff out those other way stations."

"Sounds good to me," McDougal said, and this time Lorne thought he could detect a hint of respect in her voice. "You got a field radio?"

"Right here," Lorne said, tapping his inside pocket. "I'll let you know when it's safe to send in the loggers, and I'll stay with them until they're done."

"We'll see," McDougal said. "You're way behind on sleep, and you won't be any use to anyone if you fall asleep across a brambler bush."

"I'll be all right," Lorne assured her, walking over to his grav-lift cycle and climbing back into the saddle. The adrenaline rush had faded, and fatigue was pulling at his eyelids like five-kilogram weights.

But there was no way he was going to back out now. Questions of pride and professionalism aside, he had no intention of being asleep and snoring when Khahar came back for another try.

And he *would* be back. That was as guaranteed as tomorrow's sunrise.

"I'll call you later." Turning on the engine, he raised the vehicle to operating height and headed back toward the woods.

And hoped that, whatever was happening in Archway, his parents would be able to deal with it.

CHAPTER ELEVEN

In Jin's opinion, the crowd that had gathered outside Yates Fabrications hardly qualified as a mob, which was how Badger Werle had described it during their hurried comm conversation. True, there were about a hundred people clustered together twenty meters back from the building's main entrance, and there was a low rumble of tense and ominous conversation rippling through them. But no one was shouting or brandishing weapons, and no one was loudly demanding freedom or death. For all she could tell, they might have been attending an open-air meeting sponsored by some political hopeful.

But then, Jin and Paul were seeing the crowd from the rear. Werle and the other twenty Cobras standing a sentry line between the townspeople and the plant's entrance were seeing the group's other side. From that vantage point, it was entirely possible that the crowd looked more like a mob.

And whatever it was, it was growing bigger by the minute as more vehicles pulled up at the edges or people strode in on foot. If it wasn't a mob yet, she realized soberly, it could easily turn into one.

"Not good," Paul murmured as they headed across a parking lot already packed with cars toward the milling crowd. "Maybe Lorne's Marines weren't exaggerating as much as he thought."

"I don't understand," Jin murmured back. "What in the Worlds is going on?"

"They're trying to repurpose the plant," a voice said.

Jin turned. The man coming up beside them from somewhere in the mass of parked cars was middle-aged, maybe a year or two younger than she was, with the wrinkled skin of someone who'd spent much of his life outdoors. "Excuse me?" she asked.

"The Dominion's trying to repurpose the plant," he repeated. "You're Lorne Moreau's folks, aren't you?"

"Yes," Paul confirmed. "Paul and Jasmine Broom."

"Good—glad I caught you," the man said. "I'm Lester Kalhandra. Badj Werle asked me to try and intercept before you got close enough for the Marines to spot you."

"You've got Marines here?" Paul asked, frowning as he looked around. "Where?"

"They're mostly inside," Kalhandra said. "But I don't doubt Reivaro's got a few out here keeping an eye on things. That man's a class-A weasel."

"What did you mean, they're repurposing the plant?" Jin asked.

"They want to make armor plate for the *Dewdrop* and our other ships instead of farm machinery like it's supposed to," Kalhandra said. "Though what the hell use they think four armored freighters are going to be I haven't a clue. But some brain-wizard seems to think it's a clever idea, and they're hell-bent on carrying it out. They're in there right now reprogramming all the design modules."

"Can they even *make* armor plate with the machinery they've got in there?" Jin asked, frowning. "I'd think you'd need specialized equipment."

"And you'd be right," Kalhandra said grimly. "Odds are they'll wreck every fabricator in the place within a week. And once they do—" He gestured at the ever-growing mass of people in front of them. "Every last one of these people will be out of work."

"Including you?" Paul suggested.

"Including me," Kalhandra confirmed. "Plus my son and daughter-in-law."

"Hasn't Yates warned them that this will destroy the plant?" Jin asked.

"Often and loudly," Kalhandra said. "Maybe they don't realize how much these machines cost to repair or replace. Maybe they just don't care. Who the hell knows?"

Jin craned her neck, eyeing the line of Cobras standing between the people and the plant. "So why are the Cobras there?"

Kalhandra snorted. "Why do you think? Reivaro ordered them to come in and keep order."

"I thought you said he had his own Marines," Paul said.

"He does," Kalhandra said. "But according to him, their weapons are lethal, whereas Cobras have stunners and sonics and other more humane methods of crowd control. Badj said he made it sound like he was doing Archway a favor by making the Cobras face everyone down instead of putting his own men there."

"Trying to drive a wedge between the Cobras and the rest of the people," Paul said.

"You think?" Kalhandra said sourly. "What *I* don't get is why Ishikuma didn't refuse. He should at least have appealed to the Dome or something. I can't see Dreysler putting up with this."

"I wouldn't throw it all on Dreysler's shoulders," Paul said. "He's undoubtedly getting pressure from Chintawa, and Chintawa's walking a thin line of his own with Commodore Santores."

"And don't forget the anti-Cobra faction in the Council," Jin added. "They're probably salivating at the idea of moving Dominion forces into the positions Cobras have always held before." She gestured toward the crowd. "The more people they can turn against us, the happier they'll be."

"Fomenting a battle between Cobras and the people they're supposed to be protecting would be a good start," Paul said soberly. "And the Cobras, for their part, know that if they don't hold back the mob, the Marines will do it for them. At probably a lot higher cost."

"You've got that right," Kalhandra agreed darkly. "I've heard that Santores has already gone on record that this plant is vital to the Dominion's war effort. If Reivaro can persuade Santores that an angry mob is about to wreck the place, he'll probably be able to do whatever he wants and skate on the consequences."

"Maybe we can pull together enough firepower of our own to force Reivaro to back down," Jin suggested. "How many Cobras are in DeVegas?"

"You're looking at them," Kalhandra said. "That line has every Cobra in the province except for Lorne. And they've probably got him on the way."

"Who all is inside the building?" Paul asked.

"Yates, Reivaro, and a bunch of Dominion people," Kalhandra said. "At least twenty of them, techs and Marines combined. Reivaro wasn't even going to let Yates in, but the techs said it would take days to crack the encoding on the computer systems without him."

"Or else Reivaro realized he'd be a fool to let Yates out of his sight," Paul said thoughtfully. "After all, the man who runs the plant is also the man who knows best how to wreck it."

Jin frowned at him. "You suggesting we *wreck* the place? Isn't that a bit counterproductive?"

"No, it's a *lot* counterproductive," Paul said. "But Aventine needs to draw a line in the sand and let Santores know he can't treat us like his personal slaves. Any idea what Reivaro's timetable looks like?"

Kalhandra shrugged. "From the little I know about the programming process, I'd guess he can probably get everything set up in another three or four hours. Once that's done, he can start building his damn armor alloys."

"How will we know when that happens?"

"Trust me—when the compressors and meldors start up, everyone within half a kilometer will know it." Kalhandra gestured to the crowd. "I'm guessing that's when we're likely to get a fast shift from watchful-waiting to what-the-hell-have-we-got-to-lose."

Jin felt her stomach tighten, her mind flicking to her lost son Merrick. "There's always more to lose," she murmured.

"Maybe," Kalhandra said. "But there's a school of thought that says if you're going to go down in flames anyway, you might as well be the one lighting the matches."

"So what we need to do is wreck it just enough to slow him down," Paul concluded. "Try to give the Dome enough time to come up with a response."

"Sounds like a plan," Kalhandra said. "Problem is, how do we do that? I don't have a clue how even a Cobra would wreck those fabricators. The damn things are like mechanical mountains."

"Then we ask someone who *does* know," Jin said.

"You mean Yates?" Kalhandra asked, frowning. "But he's already inside. I said that."

"Then we need to get inside with him," Paul said. "Are there any other doors?"

"Just emergency exits you can't open from the outside," Kalhandra said, his voice suddenly thoughtful. "But there *are* some big ceiling exhaust vents you can probably get through. Especially since nothing is running at the moment that needs venting."

Jin focused on the building behind the crowd. "Those walls are a little too tall to get to the top in a single jump," she said, keying in her telescopics. "They look awfully smooth, too. I don't think we can climb it."

"Oh, I'm sure you can't," Kalhandra seconded. "Knowing Yates, he probably deliberately designed it so that Cobras *couldn't* get up there. But I'm thinking that if I cup my hands and you jump while I throw you, the extra oomph might do the trick."

Jin frowned at the man's slender frame. "You aren't serious."

"Trust me—there's more than you can see on the surface," he assured her. "More than Reivaro and his goons can see, either. That's why Badj sent me to intercept you."

Jin felt her stomach tighten. "You're a—?"

"A failed Cobra," Kalhandra said. "Go ahead—you can say it. Medical discharge, if it matters. You game to try, or not?"

"I'm game," Jin said. A lot of failed Cobras nurtured deep resentments toward the whole Cobra system, especially those who had already received their enhancements and were bounced at the last minute for psychological reasons. But not everyone found their earlier love turned to hatred. Besides, if Kalhandra wanted to trap them in a compromising position, there were lots of easier ways for him to do that. "You have a spot in mind?"

"Just a second," Paul put in, taking her arm. "Before we go any further, let's make sure we fully understand the possible consequences. Santores is already looking for an excuse to lock us up. If one of us goes in there and gets caught, we're finished."

"And if I don't, the plant's ruined and people are out of jobs," Jin said. "I think it's worth the risk, especially since I've been doing some hard thinking and I'm ninety-nine percent sure I don't have anything Santores can use."

"Likewise," Paul said. "Which is why we draw straws to see who does this."

Jin shook her head. "*I* do this because your leg's still healing."

"You're still recovering from brain surgery."

"Which means they'll be more careful with me if I'm the one who gets caught," Jin said. "So that's settled." She turned back to Kalhandra. "How do we do this?"

"You're sure you don't want to talk about it some more?" Kalhandra asked snidely. "Fine. It'll be faster if we drive—my car's over here."

A minute later, Kalhandra was maneuvering them between the lines of vehicles toward a narrow circular drive that ran around the building, its edges lined with decorative clumps of trees. "This is mostly a service drive," he said as they reached the end of the parking lot and turned onto it. "Mostly used by the groundskeepers and some of the delivery people. And of course, the Dominion people don't know who those are. What's your husband up to?"

Frowning, Jin looked out the window. Paul was striding purposefully through the lines of parked cars toward the mob. "I don't know," she said. "Hopefully, not something stupid."

"Yeah, well, from what I've heard, doing stupid things runs in your family," Kalhandra said with a grunt. "But it usually works out."

"Usually," Jin murmured. "Whatever he's up to, there's nothing we can do about it now. Let's concentrate on our part, and let him do his." She grimaced. "Whatever that is."

The crowd wasn't very densely packed, and Paul was able to work his way through with a minimum of jostling and only an occasional request to let him pass.

Some of the men and women glanced at him as he went by. Out of the corner of his eye, he saw some of those glances turn into double-takes.

He was halfway through the crowd when he noticed a sudden change in the texture of the murmured conversation around him. Frowning, he keyed in his audios.

And felt a frown crease his forehead. The tone, the texture, the content—all three were totally unexpected, and on one level completely bizarre. In fact, he had to eavesdrop on four separate whispered exchanges as he made his way forward before he finally and reluctantly concluded that the reason for the sudden excitement was genuinely what he was hearing.

Paul Broom was here.

It made no sense, not even when he overheard one of the men explaining in whispers to some friends who exactly the famous visitor was. Especially since the man's assessment was just flat-out wrong. While Paul had played a role in both the Caelian and Qasaman victories, he'd hardly been a key figure in either battle.

But this wasn't the time to argue fine points of history. He'd started toward the front of the crowd, hoping to persuade them to stay calm long enough to give Jin enough time for her part of the plan. Whatever prestige the people were ready to give him toward that effort was more than welcome.

By the time he reached the front the crowd had gone completely silent. Giving the line of Cobras a quick look, noting with some uneasiness how the range of their expressions ran from tense to hostile, he turned back to face the assembly.

From this side, they did indeed look like a mob.

"Good morning," he called out. "My name is Paul Broom. Some of you may have heard of my modest contributions to the successful campaigns against the Trofts on Caelian and Qasama." He gestured toward the building behind him. "We've got another invasion of sorts going on here today. An invasion, not by enemies, but by allies."

"Since when are they our *allies*?" someone in the crowd challenged.

"Since we're all part of humankind, and since we've recently learned the hard way that it's a hostile universe out there," Paul said calmly. "The Troft invasion showed that the only way we're going to survive is for all of us to stick together." He lifted a hand. "That being said, there are smart allies and there are idiot allies. At this point, I'd have to say that Colonel Reivaro and his men fall into the latter category."

A small chuckle ran through the crowd, and Paul felt some of the tension ease. "Let me tell you some of the things I learned fighting the Trofts," he continued. "Some of those lessons might not be applicable here. But some of them might."

Once again, he gestured behind him. "Let's start with the Cobras."

The run, catch, and toss/jump maneuver had gone as smoothly and successfully as if Jin and Kalhandra did it every day. The vent he'd directed her to was as passable as he'd promised, and not nearly as filthy as she'd expected.

Beneath the opening was a meter-wide, square-sided conduit. Her experience traversing a similar pathway in the Sollas hospital just after the Troft invasion stood her in good stead, and she worked her way down the shaft with a maximum of speed and a minimum of noise.

The latter part being especially important, she discovered as she worked her way through the hoppers and cranes high above the factory's main work floor. Aside from the hum of the ventilation system, the low rumble of a few machines on standby, and a few scattered pockets of muttered conversation, the place was as silent as a graveyard at midnight. She had no idea if the Dominion troops had audio enhancements built into their combat suits, but prudence dictated that she assume they did.

Fortunately, the lack of other noise made the main group easy to locate. She found them gathered around a computer console set in the middle of one of the rooms and surrounded by a ring of large machines. There were seven in the party: Yates, Reivaro, two Marines, and three other uniformed men. Two of the latter were seated at the console, with the third man and Reivaro watching over their shoulders. Yates was a couple of meters away, with the two Marines standing close watch on either side of him.

Nobody looked very happy. Reivaro, especially, seemed particularly irritated.

"I tell you, that *is* the proper passcode," Yates was saying with some serious annoyance of his own as Jin eased herself to a shadowed viewing position between a girder and one of the crane rails. "Like I told you before, some of the foremen add in their own codes for convenience. The only way you're going to get through is for me to look up the list of everyone who oversees this division, get them all in here—"

"We're through, Colonel," one of the men at the console announced.

"You were saying?" Reivaro said.

Yates swore feelingly, his eyes darting around the room with the restlessness of a trapped animal. He looked up, his eyes touching each machine and piece of equipment in turn, almost as if he was taking inventory of a treasured family business he might never see whole again.

And as he did so, his gaze locked onto Jin.

She winced, trying to get a finger up and to her lips before he could blurt out anything. But eyes had already moved on, continuing around the room as if he hadn't even noticed there was someone perched up there above their heads. He eyed the two Marines, glared at the back of Reivaro's head.

And abruptly stepped to the console and picked up a notepad and stylus. Sending another glare at Reivaro, he started scribbling on the pad.

"I trust you're writing out the passcode for the next station?" Reivaro asked.

"Hardly," Yates growled. "It occurred to me that I might as well put this time to some constructive use."

"Poetry?" Reivaro hazarded. "Your memoirs?"

"Your indictment," Yates retorted. "You're going to be on trial someday for this, Reivaro. Count on it. It would be good to have a contemporaneous document to add to the case against you."

"Very courageous of you," Reivaro said calmly. "But a waste of effort. History is written by the winners, Mr. Yates, and whatever happens over the next few weeks or months, the Dominion of Man *will* be the winners." He gave Yates a casual flick of his fingers. "But feel free to write whatever you want. I'm told that purging your anger with words is a good way to cleanse the soul."

"*You're* the one whose soul needs cleansing," Yates said, his stylus digging into the pad as if he was trying to poke the tip straight through the paper. "I'm going to take great pleasure in reading this personally at your trial—"

"Quiet," Reivaro said suddenly.

Jin froze. Had someone spotted her? She keyed her audios, hoping she might catch a clue—

"*Broom?*" Reivaro demanded softly, taking a few quick steps away from the console. "Where in hell did *he* come from?"

There was a moment of silence, and Jin felt her muscles relax a bit. Clearly, Reivaro's sudden reaction had been to a call from one of his people.

Who apparently was outside in view of Jin's husband. She notched up her audios a little more, wondering uneasily what Paul was up to out there.

Whatever it was, Reivaro wasn't happy about it. "No," he bit out. "*Damn* him. Are they listening?... Damn it, Jerrant, I want *rioters*, not peaceful happyface protesters."

Jin smiled tightly. Apparently, Paul had taken it upon himself to try to spread some of his own natural calm over the frustration and anger of the workers outside. And if Reivaro's reaction was any indication, he was succeeding.

"No, no, that's a *terrific* idea," Reivaro said sarcastically. "Can you make it look like the shot look came from Broom or one of the other Cobras? No? Then don't bother. Matter of fact, don't bother with anything. Just stand down and watch. I'll handle it."

He spun back around. "You finished with that yet?" he demanded.

"I've got a start," Yates said. He tore off the top sheet of paper, pressed it up against the screen of his comboard, and punched the copy key. "This will do for the moment. Now we just..." He broke off, frowning at the comboard.

"Did you really think I was stupid enough to allow

comm functions in here?" Reivaro asked. Stepping forward, he plucked both the paper and the comboard out of Yates's hands. "Very eloquent," he commented as he looked at the comboard. "But you should have stuck with poetry." Pressing the erase key, he handed the comboard to one of the Marines. "Keep it away from him," he ordered as he crumpled the paper and stuffed it into his pocket. "We don't want him hurting his fingers against all those buttons. You finished here, Synchs?"

"Yes, sir, just about," one of the men said.

"As soon as you are, get to the next node," Reivaro ordered. "I need to deal with something out front. And make *damn* sure he doesn't get near anything breakable."

He strode off across the room and out the doorway into the next room. The others remained at the console another few seconds, then at a murmured comment from Synchs the whole group trooped off in the opposite direction. A moment later, Jin was once again all alone.

Staring at the pad of paper still lying on the console.

Yates had seen her—she was sure of that. The big written indictment of Reivaro had to be his response to that. Some kind of message that he'd hoped to slip to her.

But Reivaro had stood right there and read it. If it had been a message for Jin, surely he would have realized that.

The key had to be the paper, and why Yates hadn't just written it directly on the comboard instead of going through that extra step. Somehow, the message on paper had lost its hidden meaning once it was on the comboard.

Jin was never going to see the note, she knew. Reivaro would hold onto it until he destroyed it. But she didn't have to see that particular sheet of paper. The way Yates had been pressing down on his stylus, there should be a clear impression of the message on the next sheet down.

Keeping her audios at full power, she made her way down to the factory floor. She picked up the pad, realized just in time that the whole pad disappearing might be a dangerous tipoff if someone came back here, and instead pulled off the top two sheets. Retreating into a narrow gap behind one of the machines, she studied her prize.

She'd been right about one thing, anyway: the message pressed into the paper was as clear as the stylus's ink would have made it.

The actual meaning, though, was anything but.

> *To Cobra Worlds legal authorities of the first circuit court: Dominion efforts to utterly break citizen rights in the west and southwest sections of DeVegas and to corner the workers, citizens, and industrialists by using the power of their office will quickly, permanently, and utterly wreck our infrastructure. This will destroy all aspects of our economy, primary plus secondaries, and leave a dismal future for first and last citizens alike.*

She read the note three times, becoming more confused with each pass. The phrasing was certainly eloquent, even poetic, but it told her nothing.

Was there something in the way the words were written, some flourish or additional markings that the comboard would have eliminated or ignored when it scanned and reformatted the note? But she couldn't see anything in the script that looked like it might be a code or clue. Could it be something involving the order of the words themselves, or maybe the placement? That also would have been changed by the comboard's reformatting.

And then, suddenly, she saw it. The second word of each line, read down the paper instead of across:

> *Cobra circuit break southwest corner by*
> *office wreck all secondaries first*

Mentally, she threw Yates a salute. It was, in retrospect, the simplest and most elegant way to bring a modern factory to a sudden halt. No need to damage the machines themselves if you could cut off the power running to them.

Especially since these circuit breakers probably weren't the kind you could pick up at a home-supply store.

The main breaker panel was easy to find: a large roll-up panel door with the words MAIN BREAKER PANEL printed on it in bright white letters. Behind the door were ten fuse-type circuit breakers twice the size of Jin's upper arm, fastened vertically to the panel's back wall and linked at both ends to shielded cable conduits as big around as her wrist. The secondaries mentioned in Yates's note weren't nearly so obvious, and it took her a couple of tense minutes to locate them in one of the drawers of a large storage cabinet a few meters away.

Her next move was even more problematic. She turned one of the spares over in her hands a few times, trying to figure out the best way to disable it. Unlike her home's breakers, which could be reset after they were popped, these were single-use devices: through the heavy plastic window in the center she could see a wide strip of metal that was apparently designed to melt if it got too hot, or if the current through it ran too high.

Fortunately, heat and current were two items Cobras had literally at their fingertips. A little experimentation showed that a couple of seconds' worth of fingertip laser fire into one of the breaker's connections conducted enough heat into the strip to snap it across its center. Jin gave the connector a couple more seconds of fire, watching as the half still connected to that end melted into a small reservoir cup at the breaker's bottom.

Three minutes later, all the rest of the backup breakers had similarly been turned into scrap and were back in their drawer.

The breakers in the panel weren't going to be quite so straightforward. The cables they were wired to were big and heavy, with thick grounding sheaths that would wick away most of the heat from her laser. Either she was going to have to remove the breakers, one by one, from their positions, or leave them where they were and use her arcthrower instead.

She eyed the conduits, an unpleasant chill running up her back. Normally, the arcthrower was easy enough to use, and as safe as any weapon that involved thousands of volts of current could possibly be. Unfortunately, in this case there was a hidden but potentially lethal threat lurking beneath the surface. The arcthrower worked in conjunction with a low-power precursor blast from her fingertip laser that partially ionized the air and created a path for the current.

She'd never tried the weapon on a line that already had high-voltage current running through it. If the voltage was high enough to run backwards along the ionized path, her first shot might end up electrocuting her.

Still, chances were good that with the whole plant on standby, the voltages running through the breakers were pretty low. She could also hedge somewhat against the danger by being off the ground when she fired. But whatever the risks, she had to try it. Putting targeting locks on the first two breakers in line, she jumped straight up and fired her arcthrower.

She'd expected a repeat of the quiet demise of the spare breakers. No such luck. Alloys that would melt with a relatively gradual increase in heat weren't in any way prepared to suddenly have thousands of extra volts slammed into them. The strips vaporized instantly, the force of the explosions shattering their plastic enclosures and cracking the rest of the ceramic casing.

And suddenly, Jin was on borrowed time. Every Dominion tech and Marine within a hundred meters would have heard that double crack. She had to wreck the rest of the breakers before someone decided to come see what all the noise was about. Hitting the floor, she targeted the next four, jumped, and again fired the arcthrower.

Only to find that her capacitors only had enough juice for three shots fired that closely together. Cursing under her breath, she again landed, targeted the next three in line, leaped and fired, then landed and target-locked the final two. She gave herself a three-second pause to make sure she had enough current, then leaped one final time.

Only this one wasn't one of the short hops, but a full-servo jump that should get her all the way back up to the line of hoppers and girders above her head. She fired her arcthrower on the way up, and had the satisfaction of hearing two final pops. As she reached the top of her leap, she caught the edge of one of the wider girders and pulled herself up and over on top of it.

The nearest cover was another four meters away, but some instinct warned her that she didn't have time to get there. Dropping flat onto her stomach on the girder, she pulled her arms tightly into her sides and lay still.

Just in time. She'd barely settled herself against the cold metal when there was the clatter of multiple footsteps from below and at least four people rushed into the room.

"What the—?" someone snarled, his voice so twisted with fury and disbelief that she was barely able to recognize it as Yates's. "What in the name of hell did you do *this* time?"

"That wasn't us," Synchs protested, sounding even more horrified by the sight of the ruined breaker board than Yates did. Small wonder—he and his fellow workers would probably bear the brunt of Reivaro's anger when he found out about this. "We haven't even fired up any of the—"

"Can it, butterboy," a new voice cut him off, this one hard and suspicious. "Don't you know sabotage when you see it? You've got five seconds to tell us where he is."

"Where *who* is?" Yates countered angrily, fresh footsteps and a shift in his voice's location showing that he was hurrying the rest of the way to the breaker box. "*You're* the ones who supposedly cleared the whole place out this morning."

"You told the colonel we had everyone," the voice said. "Hey—get away from there."

"Sure—like there's anything more I could do," Yates bit out sarcastically. There was the creak of metal hinges— "At least the main wiring's still okay. We should be able to replace the breakers and get it back online. Might need to hammer out the connectors and casings a little."

"The alarm's out, Lieutenant," another new voice said. "Perimeter's ninety percent contained. If he's still in here, we'll get him."

"I tell you, none of my people did this," Yates insisted, the last word nearly lost in the metallic thud as he slammed the access door closed again. "You probably misprogrammed something when you were retasking one of the meldors—"

"Shut up," the lieutenant said. His voice was quiet, but there was something in his tone that made Yates abruptly stop talking. "Call in the outer ring and organize a search of the building. While you do that, Mr. Yates and I are going to have a chat with the colonel."

"What about us?" Synchs asked nervously.

"You get back to work," the lieutenant told him. "Yates is right—we'll have this mess fixed soon. When it is, you won't want to be the ones holding up the colonel's parade. Get moving."

Once again, the room echoed with the sounds of footsteps heading swiftly across the room. But even as they faded away, Jin had the impression that not all of the men had left. She waited another moment, then keyed in her audios.

Sure enough, there was the sound of breathing coming from directly below her, and a set of quieter footsteps as someone moved toward the ruined breaker box. "Record damage profile," the lieutenant's voice came softly. "Key for analysis." There were a few more seconds of breathing, followed by a loud creak, which startled Jin until she realized it was the sound of the service door Yates had opened earlier. Another pause as the Marine apparently looked inside, then another creak and thunk as he closed it again. "Search leader, acknowledged," he murmured, and now his footsteps were crossing the room in the direction the rest of the group had taken. "Cross-confirm all emergency exits are still set to alarm when opened. If he was able to slip outside after his attack, we'll need an immediate mag of the search area."

Jin grimaced. It sounded like they already had the outside of the plant buttoned up, with another team on its way inside to hunt her down. It was lucky for her that she had a backup plan.

Or rather, that *Yates* had had a backup plan.

Because there was no reason she could think of why he'd made such a point of checking the wiring behind the breaker panel. Even the lieutenant had apparently found it odd enough to go look in there himself. The best explanation was that Yates had known she was still here and had wanted her to know about that specific access panel.

She waited until the lieutenant's footsteps faded completely away, raised her head for a quick look, then rolled off the girder and dropped as silently as possible to the floor. Crossing to the access door, she eased it open.

Yates had a plan, all right. Not only did the door give access to the heavy wiring behind the box, but it also led upward into a narrow ventilation conduit. Jin had no idea where the conduit led, but right now it didn't matter. What she needed was a place to ride out the initial search, and this was probably the best she was going to get.

Getting a grip on the cables, she pulled herself up and in, closing the door behind her. Now if Paul and the mob gathered outside could slip away while Reivaro was distracted by the job of finding her and fixing the damage, they might actually pull this one off.

Of course, Yates himself was probably going to be in hot water for awhile. Hopefully, he had enough pull with the Dome to keep Reivaro off his back.

Three meters up from the breaker box, she found a place where she could wedge herself in place without risk of falling. Getting as comfortable as she could, she closed her eyes, concentrated on her hearing, and settled in to wait.

The crowd was slowly settling down, and Paul was starting to hope that the worst of the riot threat had passed, when a sudden wave of fresh uneasiness ran through the assembly.

"What we have to do is make sure we don't over-react," he continued his current point, watching the group closely. Their eyes were on the building entrance, he saw, a focus that was steadily changing. Someone, apparently, had left the plant and was coming up behind him. "We have to think things through, and to explore all options—"

"Such as sabotage?" Reivaro's voice came from behind him.

Paul turned. Reivaro and three Marines stood between him and the line of Cobras, the colonel's expression unreadable, the Marines' faces hard-edged. Back by the door of the plant, he could see Yates glowering in the grip of two more Marines. "I'm sure your men have been listening closely," Paul said. "I never once suggested sabotage or violence of any sort."

"No, you didn't," Reivaro agreed. "But what you said or didn't say hardly matters now. The plant has been sabotaged. And with that action, you people have left me no choice."

He lifted a hand. "In the name of the Dominion of Man," he called, his voice suddenly booming across the open space, "I declare the city of Archway and the region of DeVegas province to be under full martial law."

And as the last echo of his voice faded from the air, three large air vehicles rose from concealment from behind rows of trees a kilometer away and shot across the landscape to a sudden and simultaneous halt at the edges of the crowd. There they sat, hovering on their grav lifts like monstrous metal birds of prey.

"Impressive," Paul said, striving for calm. The aircraft bristled with weapons, all of them trained on the crowd now frozen like terrified rabbits beneath them. "The synchronization was especially nice. Good for impressing the simple natives."

"If the evidence of force is sufficient, sometimes force itself doesn't have to be used," Reivaro said calmly. "Let's hope you Cobras learn that lesson as fast as the other simple natives."

"Meaning?"

"Meaning this." Reivaro turned to face the line of Cobras, their expressions ranging from confused to wary to fuming to calculating. "As part of that martial law," he called, again raising his voice loudly enough for the entire assembly to hear, "all Cobras are to be immediately brought into the Dominion military, under my command locally and through the hierarchy to the ultimate authority of Commodore Rubo Santores."

"Like hell we are," one of the Cobras spat. "We're under the authority of—"

"As token of your new rank and position," Reivaro continued, gesturing to two of the Marines, "you'll be fitted with red insignia neckbands."

The Marines stepped to opposite ends of the line and pulled bright red neckbands from hip pouches. They reached up to fasten the bands around the two nearest Cobras—

And staggered as both were thrown a meter backward by simultaneous stiff-arm shoves. "We don't take orders from anyone but Commandant Ishikuma," one of the Cobras said.

"And we aren't wearing your damn collars," the other added scornfully. "Collars are for dogs."

"And Dominion Marines," the first Cobra added.

"Like I said," the second replied.

"Commandant Ishikuma has been relieved of duty," Reivaro said. "As to chain of command, you'll be receiving confirmation from the Dome within the hour as to the declaration of martial law and your new status."

"That's fine," Paul spoke up, trying to ease some

of the tension. The anger out there was getting dangerously close to the flash point. "When we do, we'll resume this conversation."

"I think not," Reivaro said, an odd edge of anticipation on his face. "By then, you'll have scattered across the province where you'll be difficult to track down. No, we'll do this now."

"Over our dead bodies," the first Cobra.

"If necessary, yes," Reivaro said coldly. "And I urge you not to take that as hyperbole. Dominion martial law permits summary judgment *and* summary execution."

A fresh ripple of uneasiness ran through the crowd at Paul's back. "You can't be serious," he said.

"We're at war, Cobra Broom," Reivaro said. "Treason during wartime is punishable by death." He gestured to the Marine still facing the first Cobra, the neckband gripped his hand. "Proceed."

"I'm warning you," the Cobra said softly, and Paul winced as he caught the small twitch of the other's eye that indicated he'd put a target lock on the Marine. "Don't."

Reivaro gestured again. "Proceed."

The Marine stepped forward. He reached up to the Cobra's neck, and again fell back as the Cobra gave him a second servo-powered shove. The Marine regained his balance and started forward again. The Cobra lifted a hand, fingers curled into laser-firing position—

And all but burst into blue flame as a blazing flurry of laser blasts raked across his body from the Marine's epaulets. The Cobra gave a gurgling scream and collapsed.

And as his charred body hit the ground, all hell broke loose.

The neat line of Cobras disintegrated as their nanocomputers reacted to the sudden attack and sent them leaping or dodging or rolling away in all directions. A dozen laser shots flashed out, the nearest salvo part of the same programmed reaction, the rest deliberate counterattacks driven by disbelief and fury at the attack against one of their own. The Marine staggered again as the shots blew sections of his burgundy-black uniform into clouds of smoke and ash, his parrot guns and those of the other Marines once again returning fire. The battle raged on, the fury of laser shots punctuated now by shouts and screams. The first Marine fell to the ground; the Cobras' main attack shifted to one of the others—

"Cease fire!" a bellow rose from somewhere in the crowd. "Cobras—cease fire! Damn it all, *cease your damn fire!*"

Reluctantly, it seemed, the firestorm trailed off. Paul turned to the frozen, horrified crowd as Ishikuma strode into view, his face red with fury and anguish and helplessness. "Reivaro, you rotten son of a—"

"They were warned," Reivaro cut him off harshly. "Maybe now they'll realize how serious the Dominion of Man is taking this." He gestured. "And they'll see that kicking against the spurs does nothing but waste men and resources vital to our common cause."

Paul turned, his stomach knotting. All around him, the Cobras were slowly getting to their feet, their expressions disbelieving or pained or shaken. Some of them were clutching hands or legs where Marine counterfire had turned healthy skin into reddened or blistered hideousness.

Three of their number, including the one who'd

died in that first volley of fire, didn't get up with them. From the looks of their charred and smoking bodies, they never would.

And then, as if a final macabre joke to the Cobras and the people of Archway, the first Marine, the one who'd taken the brunt of the first Cobra attack, stirred and carefully worked his way to his feet. He was in pain, certainly, with multiple burns and slash marks across his body. But he was alive.

And with that, the full scope of Reivaro's demonstration sank into Paul's heart and soul. Twenty-one Cobras had gone against three Dominion Marines in a head-to-head fight . . . and the result had been three dead Cobras and one wounded Marine.

He turned to Reivaro to find the colonel gazing back at him. "Lesson learned?" Reivaro asked quietly.

Paul took a careful breath. "Lesson learned."

"Good," Reivaro said, all brisk business now. "The Marines will now affix the new neckbands. I presume there will be no further trouble?"

"No," Ishikuma said heavily.

"Good," Reivaro said again. "The neckbands aren't simple strips of cloth, by the way. They contain locators, so that we'll always know where our forces are."

"Do your Marines have similar locators?" Ishikuma asked.

"My Marines have already proved their loyalty," Reivaro said pointedly. "Your Cobras have yet to earn any such trust. To that end, the neckbands are also designed so that they cannot be removed." He considered. "At least, not safely."

"Meaning?" Ishikuma asked.

"Meaning attempts to remove them will trigger the

small explosive charges hidden within," Reivaro said calmly. "I know that Cobra bones are reinforced to protect against such dangers. Sadly, Cobra throats, veins, and arteries are not."

Paul looked at Ishikuma, bracing himself for a fresh blast of fury. But the commandant had apparently exhausted his supply. "I see," he said, almost calmly. "So much for the lie that you want us as partners or allies. All you really want is slaves."

"You can think of it that way if it aids your sense of dignity," Reivaro said. "But in reality, we're really all little more than slaves of the greater good that is the Dominion of Man. Those of us who grew up among its worlds have long since accepted our proper place in that structure. Now it's your turn." He nodded toward one of the dead Cobras. "I hope there'll be no need for further lessons of this sort."

"No," Ishikuma said quietly. "There won't."

"Good," Reivaro said. "And now, Cobra Broom, as the apparent ringleader of this mob and a likely co-conspirator in the sabotage of Yates Fabrications, I hereby place you under arrest. You'll be transported immediately to Capitalia for questioning."

Paul hissed out a sigh. And no doubt the majority of that questioning would take place with him under the influence of the MindsEye device.

But it would be all right. He was positive there was nothing in his memory that would give Santores any help in finding Qasama.

And it would be far better for them to try their machine on him instead of on Jin.

He flicked a glance at the factory, feeling a twinge of guilt. With all that had happened he'd completely

forgotten about the trouble Jin herself was in. He had
no idea whether she'd been able to get out after her
sabotage, or even if she'd been able to go to ground
before Reivaro's people moved in. If she could stay
clear of the Dominion forces for a while longer, she
might find a way out of Archway and get someplace
where she could wait out this madness.

If not, he'd probably be seeing her again all too soon.

Something touched his throat. He started, then
subsided as he realized it was just one of the Marines
putting on his new slave collar. Beside him, Ishikuma
was standing in grim silence as another Marine fastened
one around the commandant's own neck.

They'd learned their lesson, all right. Never again,
if Paul had any say in it, would Cobras make a frontal
assault against Dominion men and weapons. Next time,
they would fight smarter, with cunning and subtlety
and strategy.

And next time, they would win.

"Cobra Broom?" the Marine said. "It's time."

Paul looked over to see one of the three hovering
transports settle to the ground. Back on Qasama, he'd
tried to protect his son Merrick by setting himself up
for capture by the Trofts. Maybe this time he could
protect his wife and other son.

And if the MindsEye ended up killing him, that
was a price he was willing to pay.

"I'm ready," said. "Let's do this."

CHAPTER TWELVE

"Coming up on the Hoibe'ryi'sarai home world," the *Dorian*'s navigation officer called, his voice clear and calm on the CoNCH speakers. "Ten minutes to break-out."

"Acknowledged," Barrington called back from his command chair. "All CoNCH stations, run final diagnostics."

On the wall across from him, the lower left-hand corner of each status display began to blink amber as the command crew ran their system diagnostics. Slowly, as the seconds passed, the amber lights turned green with confirmation that everything aboard the *Dorian* was running smoothly.

Barrington stroked his lower lip as he watched the procedure, feeling a small but persistent knot deep in his gut. Normally, this was simply a standard part of the break-out checklist, one of the hundreds of routine procedures that took place every day on a Dominion warship.

But today was different. Today the *Dorian* was entering the heart of a Troft demesne. And no matter what the Cobra Worlds' relationship might be with this particular group of aliens, Dominion doctrine was that all Trofts were potential enemies and to be treated as such. Today, nothing was routine.

Because something out there was wrong. Something was very wrong.

"Sensors all show green," Commander Garrett murmured from Barrington's side. "Seems to me we should have collected some pings by now."

So the *Dorian*'s first officer had spotted the anomaly, too. "One would think so," Barrington agreed. "Your analysis?"

"I see two possibilities, sir," Garrett said slowly. "The lack of pings could mean the Trofts are simply asleep at their stations. You'd never find that on the other side of the Assemblage, but it's conceivable this side isn't worried about intrusion enough to watch for incoming ships."

"Possible," Barrington said. "Your second thought?"

Garrett's lip twitched. "That they've come up with a new tag system we can't detect."

Barrington nodded. Those were the same two scenarios he'd also come up with. And the first one was laughingly unlikely. "So why haven't they tried to stop us?"

"A good question," Garrett admitted. "It's possible their system recognizes us as a human ship, and we know they're accustomed to human ships coming in and out. But I can't see how any decent tag system could possibly mistake the *Dorian* for one of the Cobra Worlds freighters. Our size alone ought to trigger a major alarm. Every web and flicker-mine this side of the system should have been activated long ago."

"Yet still we travel."

"Still we travel," Garrett confirmed grimly. "Either they don't care, or they're trying to lure us into a trap."

Barrington nodded heavily. The *Dorian* was a powerful ship of war, one of the finest in the Dominion's fleet. But he had no illusions about their chances of taking on an entire Troft home world by themselves.

His eyes drifted to the nav display. It wasn't too late to abort, he knew. He had simply to order a few degrees' worth of course change, veer clear of the star's gravity well, and head back for Aventine. Given that Santores had all but admitted the whole mission was little more than a way to get Barrington clear while Lij Tulu did what he wanted with the Broom family, there was no reason for him to risk the *Dorian* and her crew this way.

"Break-out in one minute," the nav officer called.

Barrington squared his shoulders. Unfortunately, the reasons for his orders were irrelevant. All that mattered was that the orders themselves had been explicitly and lawfully given. "Stand by for break-out," he repeated into his all-ship mike. Briefly, he considered raising the battle preparedness level from three to two, decided that such a declaration less than a minute from space-normal would be more confusing than helpful. "All stations, hold at BatPrep Three."

Across from his station, the large forward displays came on, ready to show whatever was out there the moment the ship left hyperspace. The nav counter ran to zero, and with a distant thud from the relays, the *Dorian* reentered space-normal. Across CoNCH, the displays lit up, showing the edge of a distant yellow-orange star on one side and the half-lit curve of a planetary mass on the other. Barrington looked at the status display, noting with approval that the *Dorian* had emerged a bit over a hundred thousand kilometers from the planet, exactly as he'd ordered—

"We're being pinged, Captain," the sensor chief called. "Multiple pings—multiple sources—" He broke off, his mike picking up a soft but sharp intake of air.

"I see them, Lieutenant," Barrington said, forcing calm into his voice. He'd never visited a Troft home world personally, but he'd seen the reports from scouts who'd successfully slipped into the core systems of some of the demesnes bordering the Dominion. None of those systems had ever had more than four capital warships on duty to support their orbital defense systems.

But not the Hoibe'ryi'sarai Trofts. Here, on the outer fringes of the Assemblage—with the Dominion a hundred and fifty light-years away and no other threats to speak of anywhere around—here, the Hoibe'ryi'sarai Trofts had sixteen of the damn things in place.

Sixteen.

They weren't simple patrol ships, either. They were full-bore ships of the line, all of them frigate class at least, three of them fully half the *Dorian's* size. They were arranged in a layered deployment, twelve spaced out more or less evenly along a common high equatorial orbit, the other four huddled more closely to the planet in a lower, atmosphere-skimming zone.

It was just as well, the thought flashed through Barrington's mind, that they weren't here to make trouble.

He keyed the radio. "This is Captain Barrington Moreau, commanding the Dominion of Man War

Cruiser *Dorian*," he called. "We're on a peaceful mission from Cobra Worlds Governor-General Chintawa to the Hoibe'ryi'sarai demesne-lord. I respectfully request that a representative of the demesne-lord respond, that we may discuss our errand."

The radio remained silent. Barrington looked back at his board, wondering if he'd forgotten to tie in the translator. But no, the message had gone out in both Anglic and cattertalk.

"Movement," the tactical officer called tensely. "Multiple marks."

Barrington looked over at the tactical display. All twelve ships in the outer orbital ring were on the move, the white circles marking their positions beginning to sprout multicolored vector arrows as they began to shift out of their orbits. Three of the ships were dropping inward, moving closer to the four already in low orbit, while the other nine were heading outward. From the angles of the vectors, it was clear their target was the *Dorian*.

And as the arrows lengthened and changed direction, the circles marking their positions began to turn yellow, then orange, and then bright red.

The Troft ships were powering up their weapons.

"Respectfully suggest that we go to BatPrep One, sir," Garrett murmured.

"Easy, Commander," Barrington murmured back, tapping the key that would send a repeat of his previous broadcast. "We're on a peaceful mission. Let's continue to look peaceful."

There was a sudden burst of cattertalk from the CoNCH speakers. "Captain Barrington Moreau, this is Deputy Kopdji, speaker for the Hoibe'ryi'sarai demesne-lord," the translation came. "Your presence is not desired in the Hoibe'ryi'sarai demesne. You are requested to depart immediately."

Barrington frowned. Chintawa had assured him that the demesne-lord would welcome him with at least a modicum of hospitality. "Perhaps you misunderstood the reason for our visit," he said. "My errand is one of peace. Moreover, I bring greetings and a personal request from Governor-General Chintawa, whom I'm told is well-known in the Hoibe'ryi'sarai court. All I ask is that you permit me to approach and present his request to you."

There was more cattertalk— "My demesne-lord knows no human by that name," Kopdji insisted. "Now be gone."

One of the lights on the radio board went off as the Trofts broke transmission. "That's a flat-faced lie," Garrett said darkly, his eye twitching as he did a quick search through the ship's data stream. "We've got records of at least three occasions where the demesne-lord personally traveled to Aventine and met with Chintawa."

"Yes, I remember that report," Barrington said, frowning at the ships still rising from their orbits. Why in space would Kopdji make a statement that could so quickly and easily be proven false? The demesne-lord had no need to make excuses or explanations to an intruding human ship. Especially not when he had as much firepower as he had backing him up.

Unless that firepower wasn't his.

"Analysis of the Troft ship hull markings," Barrington called across CoNCH, his stomach knot back to full strength. "Confirm they're all Hoibe'ryi'sarai. If they aren't, I want to know who they are."

"Acknowledged," the sensor chief acknowledged.

"Interesting," Garrett said thoughtfully. "I thought everyone out here was more or less at peace with everyone else."

"Chintawa may have oversimplified the situation," Barrington said. "And being under siege would certainly explain Deputy Kopdji's surliness."

"And that lie about Chintawa was the demesnelord's attempt to tip us off that there was trouble?"

"Possibly," Barrington agreed. "Let's gather a little more data before we start speculating on motives."

"Enemy weapons at full power," the sensor officer called.

"At current rates of acceleration, estimate eight minutes thirty to effective laser range," the tac officer added. "Ten minutes twenty to missile range."

Assuming, of course, that the *Dorian's* data on Troft weapons, defenses, and countermeasures that had been gleaned from the other end of the Assemblage also applied here. Unfortunately, there was no way to know for sure until someone actually opened fire.

Either way, it was time to stop looking peaceful. "Go to BatPrep One," Barrington ordered. "Repeat, BatPrep One."

There were a flurry of terse acknowledgments from across CoNCH. On the wall of displays, the nav and engineering system monitors flicked over to their alternate weapons and hull-integrity modes. "I need some answers on those hull markings," Barrington called.

"They're difficult to read at this distance," the sensor officer called back as a graphic of three different lines of cattertalk script appeared on Barrington's command display. "But those on the twelve outer ships appear to be the same, or at least very similar. No idea which demesne—they're not markings we're familiar with. Of the four inner ships, three carry Hoibe'ryi'sarai markings, while the fourth is again unknown, and of a different pattern than the outer group."

"Interesting," Barrington said. "So it's not, in fact, one against sixteen. It's four, possibly five, against twelve."

"So you were right about the Hoibe'ryi'sarais being under siege," Garrett commented. "I wonder what the story is on that sixteenth ship. Friend or ally?"

"Possibly," Barrington said. "He could also be a hostage."

"Seven minutes to laser range," the tac officer called. "All weapons and defenses at full readiness."

"Acknowledged," Barrington said, keying his radio again. "Deputy Kopdji, this is Captain Moreau. There are nine ships from an unidentified demesne moving toward us with possibly hostile intent. Are they allies of yours, that we should leave them undamaged?"

The radio remained silent. "Sounds to me like he wouldn't object to having them blown to dust," Garrett suggested.

"Or at least chased away," Barrington said. "Only he can't say that on an open channel where they can hear him. Maybe showing we're capable allies will loosen his tongue a little."

"Yes, sir," Garrett said reluctantly. "That of course assumes we *want* to be their allies."

Barrington suppressed a grimace. That was the question, all right. And it was hardly a trivial issue. The Cobra Worlds might have a friendly trading relationship with these particular Trofts, but that didn't mean they were the best choice of allies for the Dominion.

For that matter, there was no guarantee that the Dominion would be able to get *any* Troft allies, even if they wanted them.

But those were matters for the policy-makers of the Dome to work through at some future date. Barrington had neither the authority nor the training to make any long-term agreements or commitments.

Fortunately, he didn't have to. The Hoibe'ryi'sarai demesne wasn't sending aggressors at his ship. The unidentified demesne was. From where he sat this was a purely military matter, and Dominion standing orders were very clear on how he was to deal with it. "We'll leave that to the politicians," he told Garrett. "Assessment?"

"Looks like they're going for a straightforward flanking maneuver," Garrett said, pointing at the diverging vector angles on the tactical. "Three per side low, three down the middle high. They might diverge into singlets somewhere along the line, but I'm guessing they'll stick to triads for maximum fire support."

"Weaponry?"

"No way of knowing what their missiles are capable of until they fire off a few," Garrett said. "But from their engine-power profile I don't expect their lasers to be any stronger than those of other comparably-sized Troft warships." He gestured to the aft display, currently showing nothing but the distant starscape. "The aft horizon still shows clear, which implies that our appearance here was a surprise."

"Our appearance, or anyone else's," Barrington agreed thoughtfully. The lack of a backup force might imply that intruders had been expecting this to be a quick in-and-out snatch, not a prolonged siege. As

Garrett had suggested, maybe Sixteen was a friend under Hoibe'ryi'sarai protection.

Or else they were simply holding him there while they bargained up the price for handing him over.

"Six minutes to laser range."

"Stand by ECM," Barrington ordered. "And lock a Pluto cone into all incoming ships." There was only a slim chance, he knew, that electronic countermeasures designed to work against missiles and targeting algorithms at the other end of the Assemblage would work on this group of warships. Pluto cones, on the other hand, worked directly and physically to block incoming missiles. Between them and the point-defense systems, the *Dorian* should have a good chance of making it through the Trofts' first salvo.

"ECM, Pluto cones, aye," the weapons officer confirmed. "Targeting orders?"

Barrington studied the tactical. One of the smaller ships coming in directly in front of them, he saw, was lagging slightly behind the two others in its group. "Scrambler cone on Four," he ordered. Scramblers, like ECM, were tuned to specific types of electronic firing mechanisms, and there was a good chance that it would be ineffective here. But if it worked, it might befuddle Four's systems enough to get it firing at random, and some of those wild shots could hit its companions. "Laser locks on One, Six, and Eight; missile triads on One, Two, Five, and Nine. Hold for my order."

There was another flurry of acknowledgments, and the weapons and tactical displays adjusted as the crews gave the targeting computers their orders. "Shall we prepare decoys, sir?" Garrett suggested.

"Not yet," Barrington said. Decoys were the ultimate

in missile defense, but they were expensive, and the *Dorian* had a limited number of them. "Let's give the ECM and Plutos a chance first."

And with that, it was down to the waiting. With nine opponents on the way, a preemptive strike would be the most prudent course of action, especially since the *Dorian*'s reactor size probably meant its lasers had a greater range than those of her attackers, especially the smaller ships of the flotilla.

But the *Dorian* wasn't here to make war. Not here and now, anyway. Barrington needed the attackers to make the first move, and to trust that his defenses would get it through that attack. Only then could he legitimately open up with the full power and fury of his massive arsenal.

"Movement!" the sensor officer snapped. "Sixteen is dropping orbit—moving in toward the planet."

Barrington frowned as one of the displays shifted to a closer view of the four ships hugging the planet's atmosphere. Sixteen had indeed dropped inward, where the physics of orbital mechanics gave it a boost in its speed and sent it shooting ahead of its three Hoibe'ryi'sarai watchdogs. The latter ships, for their part, seemed to be maintaining their original orbits, as if taken by surprise by the maneuver.

Not so the three siege ships above them. Sixteen was only a few seconds into his bid for freedom when they reacted, dropping inward and accelerating toward the fleeing ship. "Well, *that* was foolish," Garrett murmured. "As long as Sixteen stayed with the Hoibe'ryi'sarai ships the others couldn't make a move against him. Now, there's nothing to stop them."

"Yet they're still not firing," Barrington pointed out.

"They must want him alive," Garrett said. "He must have thought that with nine of the siege ships moving out he had a chance to make a run for it."

The words were barely out of his mouth when the fleeing ship abruptly rolled up onto its stern and blasted full-power away from the planet, heading straight toward the three siege ships dropping down the gravity well toward it.

This time, the pursuers were caught flat-footed. Before they could do more than fire their engines, Sixteen had shot straight through their formation and was headed for deep space. The tactical's vector arrows swiveled madly as the three ships tried to get back on target, but their momentum and inertia were working against them. By the time they would be in position to resume their chase, Barrington saw, the fleeing ship would be well beyond their reach.

"More movement," Garrett called, pointing to the main tactical. "Four, Five, and Six are breaking off."

Barrington looked back at the main tactical. Garrett was right: the three ships that had been heading for the *Dorian*'s bow were scrambling to decelerate and change direction. Falling back, abandoning their part of the attack and turning instead to try to intercept the fleeing ship.

And Sixteen was playing right into their hands. Instead of turning hard away from them, which he should have done as soon as he was clear of his original pursuers, he was cutting away at only a shallow angle. Worse, he wasn't pulling anywhere near the acceleration necessary he needed to get clear of them.

"What the hell is he doing?" Garrett muttered, sounding bewildered. "He'll never get away like that."

Barrington leaned forward in his chair, as if moving a few centimeters closer to the displays would force them to make sense. What in hell *was* Sixteen's commander playing at?

And then, suddenly, he got it. "Get me a reading on Sixteen's engines," he called. "I want to know if that's the best speed he can make."

"Aye, sir."

"Are you suggesting he's deliberately drawing them away from us?" Garrett asked.

"The only other explanation I can see is that he's utterly incompetent," Barrington said. "Given the slickness of his previous move, that one doesn't seem likely."

Garrett huffed out a breath. "They must *really* want him," he said.

"And, as you said, want him alive," Barrington said. "And he knows it. So instead of simply running, he's decided to draw some of his enemies off our back."

"Captain, I estimate Sixteen's engines are running at about two-thirds capacity," the sensor officer called. "Four, Five, and Six are still decelerating toward intercept courses on Sixteen. The other six ships are holding their previous vectors toward us."

"He's taking a lot on faith," Garrett commented thoughtfully. "Not just that we're people he wants to make friends with, but also that we'll even survive this whole thing."

"Agreed," Barrington said. "Clearly, he understands the concept of the calculated risk."

"Two minutes to laser range, Captain," the tac officer called.

"Acknowledged," Barrington replied. "Cancel scrambler cone on Four; shift scrambler to Two. Cancel

Pluto cones on Four and Six, laser on Six, and missile triad on Five. Stand by to fire on my order."

"Yes, sir." the officer said. "What about the Pluto cone on Five? Shall I cancel and shift?"

"Hold that lock for now." Barrington looked at Garrett. "Sixteen is trying to run us a little interference," he explained. "We may want to return the favor somewhere down the line."

"Or he'll just take off as soon as the shooting starts," Garrett pointed out. "Nothing we can do to make sure that doesn't happen, I suppose."

"Not unless you want to try to talk the Hoibe'ryi'sarais into moving on him," Barrington said. "Still, I'm guessing he'll at least stick around long enough to thank us. We'll just have to see where it goes from there."

"Enemy ECM coming up," the tac officer announced. "Primary projection cones from Two and Eight."

"Profile?" Barrington asked. Figuring out what exactly the enemy countermeasures were designed to do would be crucial to neutralizing their effects and getting the *Dorian*'s missiles through those particular barriers.

"High-level," the officer said. "Looks like navigational scrambler type."

Designed, in other words, to affect missiles' steering and tracking capabilities. Bad, but not as bad as the type that attempted to trigger premature detonations. "Tuning?"

"Very high, sir. About eighty percent."

"Interesting," Garrett murmured. "Looks like they've tangled with Dominion missiles before."

"Or they know someone who has," Barrington said, an odd thought striking him. Santores's task force had been in space for eight months, but it was a considerably shorter trip from one end of the Troft Assemblage to the other. "We were given several sets of potential ECM upgrades before we left the Dominion," he reminded the tac officer. "Run those against the Troft ECM and see if that raises the tuning."

"Yes, sir." A handful of seconds ticked by— "The overlays give a revised tuning of seventy-seven to eighty-nine percent."

"Acknowledged," Barrington called. "Activate ECM, stand by missiles, and prepare to fire Pluto cones." He looked at Garrett. "So that's it," he said lowering his voice. "Our friends out there apparently have data on current Dominion missiles and ECM profiles. Data *we* don't even have."

"Yes, sir," Garrett agreed grimly. "Question is, how big is this particular clubhouse?"

A cold chill ran through Barrington's body. A hundred years ago, though no one had known it at the time, the war the Dominion had thought it was waging against the entire Troft Assemblage had actually only been against the handful of border demesnes who'd felt threatened by human encroachment. The Dome and Asgard had been hoping fervently that it was the same situation this time around.

Only now, here at the extreme far end of Troft space, at least one of the local demesnes possessed current data on Dominion weaponry. If that meant the entire Assemblage was united in this latest war against humanity—

He squared his shoulders. "Apparently not big enough for everyone," he reminded Garrett firmly. "Whoever Sixteen represents, he clearly has issues."

The words were barely out of his mouth when the Trofts attacked.

The first assault, as expected, came as a coordinated burst of laser fire from all six of the closing ships. The blasts raked over the *Dorian's* hull, bow to stern tracking from two of the enemy triads, stern to bow for the third. "Damage?" Barrington called.

"Minimal to portside sensor arrays," the damage control officer called. "Main hull shielding is holding."

"Looks like we're right on the edge of their effective range," Garrett said, his eyes narrowed as he studied the analysis section's rolling data stream. "Probably hoping they can knock out some of our sensors and ECM before the serious combat begins."

Barrington nodded. That was a standard Troft technique, though it worked better against Troft ship design than against human.

The lasers winked off, their capacitors probably needing to recharge. "Minimal additional damage," Garrett continued. "Sensors down three percent; lasers and launchers undamaged. Do we reply, sir?"

Barrington looked at the tactical. The *Dorian* was within laser firing range now, but not close enough to do serious damage to hull metal. More importantly, they were also out of optimal missile range, particularly given that the enemy had up-to-date ECM to use against them.

He pursed his lips thoughtfully. Unless their ECM was *too* up-to-date. If the Trofts thought they were facing one class of missile, but would actually be on the receiving end of another, their ECM screens would be less effective than they expected.

He rechecked the range. If this was going to work, he needed to make sure the Trofts didn't have enough time to recognize their mistake and correct it. That meant closing another few seconds' worth of distance without the Trofts veering off their current vectors or deciding to start their own barrage.

Which meant giving them something to focus their attention and targeting systems on something besides throwing missiles...

"Launch Pluto cones at One, Four, and Eight," he ordered. Pluto cones, dense clusters of shrapnel traveling at high speed, were technically an anti-missile weapon, but they were also useful for drawing out, distracting, and draining a target's point-defense systems. "Stand by ECM," he continued. "I want a sixty-percent drop in transmission levels on my mark."

"A sixty-percent *drop*?" Garrett echoed, frowning.

"A sixty-percent drop," Barrington confirmed. The displays lit up as the Trofts, their laser capacitors recharged, fired off a second volley. Once again the energy beams swept across the *Dorian*'s hull—

"Mark!" Barrington snapped.

The lines on the ECM status display dropped precipitously. "ECM sixty percent down," Garrett confirmed, his professional tone colored with confusion. "Sir, if they launch their missiles now—"

"They won't," Barrington assured him. "Not yet." He pointed at the display. "See where they're concentrating their fire?"

Garrett's forehead creased in puzzlement as he flicked back through the data stream. Then, suddenly, the frown smoothed out. "That's the spot where their lasers were targeted when the ECM went down."

"Exactly," Barrington said.

Which the Trofts now clearly assumed was part

of the ECM system. Only it wasn't. What they were wasting energy on was in fact nothing more crucial than one of the docking system's sensor clusters. Something the *Dorian* could easily do without for the foreseeable future.

And with the Trofts' attention focused on opening the way for their own missiles, the *Dorian* had now slipped into range to use its own. "ECM to full power," he ordered. "Fire lasers at locked targets."

From the bow and stern of the ship came the dull rumble of sequentially cascading capacitors as the lasers were pulsed. "Laser damage to enemy ships appears minimal," Garrett reported.

Barrington nodded acknowledgment. They were still well beyond laser kill range, as he and Garrett both knew.

But as the Trofts themselves obviously knew and were counting on, even undamaged sensors could sometimes be temporarily dazzled.

The attackers' main error was that they hadn't followed up their laser sweep with missiles. The *Dorian* wasn't going to make that mistake. "Fire missile triads," he ordered. "Follow up with a Pluto cone at all attacking ships."

The *Dorian* shuddered with the multiple vibrations as the rail-launched missiles were thrown from their tubes. "Missiles away," Garrett reported.

"Enemy ECM?" Barrington called.

"Marginal," the tac officer called, his voice grimly satisfied. "Missiles targeting true. Enemy ECM retuning— point defense engaging—"

And then, the main display lit up in a stuttering flicker of light as the missiles began detonating.

"Damage?" Barrington asked, scanning across the displays and resisting the temptation to dip a quick look at the *Dorian*'s data stream. That was Garrett's job; Barrington's was to maintain a general overview of the entire battle sphere without getting bogged down in any particular set of details.

"Direct hits on Two and Five," Garrett reported. "Looks like they took some major damage—we'll know more when the debris clears. Near misses and probable minor damage to One, Two, and Nine."

"Missiles incoming," the tac officer called. "Two each from One, Two, and Seven; four from Nine. Pluto cones on the intercept."

"Second salvo," Barrington ordered. "Triads on One, Two, and Nine."

"Missiles away."

"Incoming missiles engaged," Garrett said. "ECM is slowing them...Pluto cones engaging...incoming missiles destroyed."

"Salvos detonating," the tac officer called. "All missiles wide. Enemy ECM appears to have retuned."

So as often happened, this was going to end up as a laser duel. "Stand by lasers," Barrington ordered. "Target damaged ships—"

"Enemy disengaging!" Garrett snapped.

Barrington blinked in surprise. Already?

Already. The Troft vectors were once again changing, shifting from intercept to a multiple-angled dispersal pattern. "Watch them," Garrett warned. "They could be going for a encirclement spread."

"I don't think so," Barrington said. "At this range, dispersal won't gain them much."

"Picking up break-in sequence," the sensor officer

called. "All attackers . . . make that all unidentified ships, Captain. They're running."

"What do you know?" Garrett murmured. "Six to one odds, and they *still* run. No stomach for a fight, I guess."

"Or no orders for one," Barrington said. He watched the fleeing attackers another moment, then shifted his eyes to the long-range display.

He'd told Garrett earlier that Sixteen would probably hang around until after the battle. Still, it was nevertheless to his mild surprise that the Troft had actually done so.

It was, though, considerably farther ahead of its pursuers than it had been when Barrington last saw it. Apparently, its captain had decided the *Dorian* was handling things well enough that he didn't have to serve as a lure anymore.

Especially now that its three pursuers were also breaking off and preparing for hyperspace. Even as Barrington watched, they flickered and were gone.

"We could still take out a couple of them, sir," Garrett said into his thoughts. "Three and Eight are moving a lost slower than the others."

"So I see," Barrington said. And yet, the other ships of the attack force hadn't simply abandoned their damaged comrades. They were still nearby, ready to break in but still holding station. Presumably still prepared to fight if the *Dorian* insisted.

"Sir?" Garrett prompted.

"Let them go," Barrington told him. "Stand ready, but if there are no additional attacks, just let them go."

A minute later, Three and Eight flickered into hyperspace. A couple of heartbeats later, the others were also gone.

"I hope that was the right move, sir," Garrett said, a little doubtfully.

"We may need to deal with some of these demesnes someday, Commander," Barrington reminded him. "Until we know which, we'd do well to limit the amount of blood on our hands." He gestured. "Speaking of dealing, let's give Deputy Kopdji another call. The Hoibe'ryi'sarai demesne-lord may be more willing to talk to us now."

He wasn't.

"What the *hell*?" Garrett demanded when Deputy Kopdji had once again curtly broken off communication right in their faces. "Sir, this is ridiculous."

"Easy, Commander," Barrington soothed, his eyes on the long-range display. Sixteen had sprouted another vector arrow, this one leading away from the planet and toward the *Dorian*. "I doubt we're the kind of diplomatic entanglement the demesne-lord was expecting today. He's probably busy weighing us against whoever it was we just chased away, and until he figures out the best course it makes sense for him not to talk to anyone."

"Even someone carrying Governor-General Chintawa's blessing?"

"Maybe *especially* someone with Chintawa's blessing," Barrington said dryly. He nodded toward the display. "Sixteen, on the other hand, looks like he might be interested in a conversation. Let's find out, shall we?" He keyed his radio. "Unidentified Troft ship, this is Captain Barrington Moreau, commanding the Dominion of Man War Cruiser *Dorian*. I appreciate your assistance in drawing off some of our attackers."

There was a short stream of cattertalk from the CoNCH speakers. "As I also appreciate your aid, Captain Moreau," the translation came. "As you no doubt surmised, the Drim'hco'plai warships you bested had arrived here in hopes of removing me from my ship and taking me to their demesne-lord for interrogation."

"*Had* we surmised that?" Garrett murmured.

"We knew they wanted him alive," Barrington murmured back, tapping the mute key and double-twitching his left eyelid. If he was remembering correctly...

He was. The Drim'hco'plai demesne had been one of the coalition who had attacked and occupied the Cobra Worlds. "We just didn't know why," he added, unmuting the radio. "Was there anything in particular their demesne-lord wanted to know?" he asked the Troft.

"Several things," the Troft said. "And given this fortunate meeting, I would very much like to discuss those same matters with you, Captain Moreau. Is there a way for us to meet in private?"

Barrington lifted an eyebrow at Garrett. "Is there something you feel a need to hide from my officers?" he asked.

"Not from your officers, but from the universe at large," the Troft said. "There is little I can say on an open channel, but I can say this: it concerns your kinsman, Merrick Moreau Broom."

Barrington felt his breath catch in his throat. Merrick Broom, son of Paul and Jasmine Moreau Broom, who'd mysteriously vanished in the last days of the Troft invasion on Qasama. "What about him?" he asked carefully.

"I know where he is," the Troft said. "I also know

that he's in great danger. Is there a way for us to meet in private?"

Barrington chewed at his lip. Bringing a Troft aboard his ship could be dangerous. It was also expressly forbidden except in the most extraordinary of situations.

But there were ways to minimize the risk. "I can meet you in one of my hangar bays," he said. "If you're willing to come across, we can talk there."

"Have I your word that you'll allow me to go free and unharmed after our discussion?"

"Yes," Barrington said without hesitation. The Dominion had no policy for the taking of hostages or noncombatant prisoners. "I have your word in turn that you'll make no attempt at espionage or sabotage?"

"Yes," the Troft said. "How close may I bring my ship before boarding a shuttle to complete my journey?"

"You can close to one tenth of our present separation," Barrington told him. The Cobra Worlds had introduced the metric system to the Hoibe'ryi'sarai and their other trading partners, but he had no idea whether or not his new contact's demesne was familiar with it. "I'd ask that you also leave your weapons uncharged."

"Of course," the Troft agreed. On the tactical his ship's vector arrow shifted to an intercept course. "I shall be there within the hour."

"I'll look forward to our meeting," Barrington said, suddenly realizing that he'd somehow forgotten to ask the two most obvious questions. "May I have your name?"

"I am Commander Ukuthi, fourth demesne heir to the Balin'ekha'spmi demesne," the Troft said.

Beside him Garrett muttered something under his

breath. Barrington nodded: the Balin'ekha'spmi demesne had also been part of that Troft invasion coalition. A recent enemy of the Cobra Worlds; and one of their demesne heirs wanted to come aboard his ship? "And how exactly do you know of Cobra Broom's danger?" Barrington asked, forcing his voice to remain calm.

There was an almost-sigh from the speakers. "Because, Captain Moreau," Ukuthi said, "I'm the one who sent him. Please prepare your conference room; I am most anxious to speak with you."

CHAPTER THIRTEEN

Merrick's nanocomputer clock circuit indicated he'd slept less than five hours by the time the sunlight and the activity around him dragged him awake.

Somehow, in all their talks together, Merrick and Anya had never covered her people's morning rituals. Certainly he'd never noticed anything like that aboard ship, nor had Anya performed any such rituals during the time they'd spent together as Ukuthi's prisoners.

But now, as he left the shelter, wincing with aching muscles, Anya took his arm and led him to where the others were gathered in a line facing the rising sun. They joined the end of the line; and as they did, the ritual began.

Leif started it off, speaking solemnly in a language Merrick didn't recognize or understand. A few sentences later, his wife joined in, followed a few sentences after that by Gina. For a minute all three spoke in unison, and then both adults fell silent while the child intoned the final three sentences alone.

And with that, it was apparently over. "Let's get moving," Ville said briskly as he picked up his bag from beside a dead log. "Same marching order as yesterday."

"That was our village's sunrise greeting," Anya explained to Merrick as the group set off down the road toward the red-tinged sky. "It's performed whenever there are families present and the sun can be seen or its position inferred." She gave him a sideways look. "I'm sure your morning ritual is much different."

Merrick nodded, agreement and understanding both. So that was why she hadn't mentioned it before. As someone who was supposed to be from elsewhere on Muninn, he wouldn't be expected to know how Gangari's customs worked.

He just hoped no one would be courteous enough to ask about his own town's customs. Maybe he ought to work up a few, just in case.

The rest of the trip was mostly uneventful. Around noon they ran into another pack of fafirs, but Anya, Ville, and Dyre again easily drove them off. There were no spine mace trees in the area this time, so the defenders instead used whips made from tapering vines they tore off a cluster of nearby trees.

As with the last fafir attack, Merrick was ordered to stay with the Streamjumper family. This time, he obeyed.

It was late afternoon and Anya was estimating only a couple of kilometers left to go when Merrick began seeing razorarms again.

They were, for the most part, a mixture of aggression and caution. Six of the seven that Merrick spotted stayed behind the first line of trees, paralleling the humans for a few minutes before turning back into the forest. The seventh came all the way out onto the shoulder, its foreleg spines quivering as it scowled at the intruders. But even that one never set foot on the road itself. It was as if the predators had decided the road was the humans' section of territory and were treating it just as they would that of another razorarm family.

Which might be exactly what they were doing. The mojos, which had been the razorarms' symbionts on Qasama, had known how deadly humans were and had been careful to steer the predators away from potentially lethal confrontations. Somehow, the birds' caution had been impressed on the razorarms' more limited minds.

From Anya's description of her hometown as a village, Merrick had pictured it being similar to the Qasaman version: small and rustic, with high walls surrounding it as protection against dangerous animals.

Gangari was certainly small enough. The whole thing looked to be no more than a kilometer across, with a good two-thirds of the cleared area taken up by cropland stretching between the forest and the village proper. The rest of the landscape was also more or less as he'd envisioned it: around the cleared area was more forest, while behind it the ground rose sharply into the line of rocky, tree-covered mountains he'd seen in the distance from the landing area. To the north, a narrow white-water stream rolled down from the mountains and disappeared among the trees.

But the rest was nothing like Merrick's mental image. The homes and community buildings were made of smooth-planed wooden planks, laid out in an elaborate cross-hatch design. The roofs were peaked, with carvings at the upper and lower corners that reminded him of upside-down ocean waves. Unlike the buildings in Qasaman villages, the ones here were well-spaced, with small gardens filling many of the spaces between them. The people he saw were dressed in a variety of clothing styles, ranging from bright colors to quieter and more muted tones. Here and there, in the distance toward the center of the town, there were occasional glimpses of people wearing copper-trimmed black.

Another surprise was that the road didn't go all the way into the village. Instead, it split at the edge of the cropland, disappearing into the masses of trees to the north and south. "Is there a path?" Ville asked, coming to a halt at the edge of the blackstone.

"Yes," Anya said, her voice tight. "But it has most certainly been changed in the twelve years since I last walked it."

Dyre snorted. "Perhaps we should let your out-village friend find it," he suggested maliciously. "He hasn't proved useful anywhere else. He could at least offer us some amusement as he twitched like a chicken."

Merrick tapped Anya's shoulder and gestured questioningly. "Crossing a bersark field is dangerous," she said. "Crushing the plants underfoot releases the poison."

Merrick stared at her. They surrounded their village with poisonous plants? He gestured again, more urgently this time.

"He really *is* ignorant, isn't he?" Dyre said with another snort. "Don't cower, courageous one—it'll be properly refined before they allow you to take it."

Merrick frowned at him. Before they allowed him to *take* it?

"Is there any other way through?" Ville asked. "Surely the bersark doesn't surround on all sides."

"Not on all sides," Anya said. "But the stream is

swift and its banks treacherous, and the marsh on the southern edge is likewise impassable. We shall have to wait for someone to notice us."

"But will they notice us before nightfall?" Ville asked, looking behind them at the sun. "And even if they see us, will they invite us in?"

"You both grew up here," Katla pointed out, looking back and forth between Anya and Dyre. "Surely there's a way for wayward travelers to find the path."

"There was no such clue set when I was taken," Dyre said.

"Nor when I left," Anya said, an odd tone to her voice. "Still, I've seen no flights of kilerands in the past minutes. We may be able to risk a shout."

"And lest the ignorant be further confused," Dyre added, looking pointedly at Merrick, "kilerands often ingest bersark when they feed. Loud noises draw them."

Merrick looked across at the village. There were several people out and about, but none of them seemed to have spotted the group standing out here on the village's doorstep.

They weren't really stuck out here, of course. The stream might be swift and treacherous, but it wasn't so wide that he couldn't easily jump it.

Unfortunately, that would reveal more about himself than he wanted at this point. Shouting across the field, and possibly drawing birds he might have to use his lasers to drive away, would be worse.

But there might be another way. Lowering his gaze to the plants stretched out in front of them, he activated his infrareds.

The fine-tuning that had been added to his generation's enhancers had been designed primarily for reading and distinguishing human emotions. But Merrick remembered reading that some plants also had different infrared characteristics. If the bersark and the path plants were dissimilar enough, maybe he could spot that difference.

To his mild surprise, the trick worked. Snaking its way in a smooth pair of S-curves from the edge of the road to the far edge of the field was a slightly brighter swath of vegetation about two meters wide. Focusing on one edge of the path, he keyed in his telescopics.

There were different species of plants on Aventine that looked virtually identical, yet had drastically different properties. Mushrooms, in particular, were extremely dangerous for amateurs to deal with. The bersark and path plants were evidently another of that same class. Even knowing where the edge was, he couldn't see a single clue in the normal visible spectrum that he could latch to distinguish one from the other.

Earlier, he'd wondered about the lack of a fence to guard against unwanted guests. Now, he saw that the villagers didn't need one. They had a barrier of poison to protect them.

"But waiting until nightfall to call to the village would be even worse," Dyre pointed out. "I say we let Anya's out-village friend turn aside to right or left and give a shout. If the kilerands descend, we can try to drive them off before they cause too much damage."

"Don't speak venal foolishness," Katla chided. "If we need to retreat and build another shelter for the night, then that's what we'll do. Surely cultivators will be out among the dawn mists."

"I've spent twelve long years away from my home,"

Dyre said darkly. "I will not turn my back on it now when it's so close."

"It's my home too," Katla said, a bit sharply. "I yearn for it as deeply as you do. But I have no wish to die within sight of its edges."

Keying off his telescopics, Merrick took a deep breath. For once, he was with Dyre. He touched Anya's arm again and pointed at the field.

And before she could say anything, he stepped off the edge of the road into the middle of the infrared-bright path.

Someone behind him gasped—Katla, probably, though it could have been Gina. He took another step, wondering if he'd just done something extremely foolish.

Wondering, too, if it was the kind of poison that would at least warn him that it was starting to kill him.

But nothing happened. No acrid or bitter aroma, no light-headedness, no confusion or paralysis or convulsions. Either the stuff was slow-acting, or he'd guessed right about the path. He took two more steps, then stopped and looked back.

The others were staring at him, their eyes wide, their mouths hanging a few centimeters open. Katla was standing behind Gina, gripping her daughter's shoulders, looking like she was preparing to spin the girl's eyes away from the awful spectacle that everyone was clearly expecting.

Everyone, that is, except Anya. Her mouth was closed, her eyes showing no signs of stunned fear or morbid anticipation. In fact, there was just the faintest hint of an approving smile on her face. Merrick gave her an equally faint smile in return, then turned again and continued on his way.

It took until the first S-curve for them to be convinced. Anya was first, stepping off the road's shoulder and following the line of Merrick's footsteps. Ville was next, gesturing the Streamjumper family to follow.

Not until Merrick had reached the second S-curve did Dyre grudgingly join the procession.

They were halfway across the field when a woman tending one of the gardens finally noticed them. Her eyes widened for a moment, and then she dropped her tools and ran off between two of the houses. By the time Merrick reached the last section of curve a crowd was beginning to form. There were no excited shouts of either greeting or challenge, which bothered Merrick until he remembered Dyre's warning about neighborhood birds that didn't react well to loud noises.

But there was no mistaking the gradual brightening of faces through the crowd as they realized that some of their lost children had finally come home. Some of those faces brightened even more when they mentally added in the years and realized which specific children they were.

By the time he and the others reached the end of the field and made their way into the crowd, the hugs and tears were waiting.

Dyre got the most attention, Merrick saw as he stepped discreetly to the side out of the way of the quiet jubilation. The Streamjumper family was a close second, especially with the surge of interest that was focused on the young daughter no one in Gangari had ever met before. Ville was clearly recognized and politely received, but Merrick could sense some distance lurking beneath the greetings. Merrick himself garnered a few civil nods and curious looks, but he had expected nothing more.

What *was* puzzling was that Anya was ignored almost as completely as Merrick. What was even more puzzling was that she didn't seem surprised by the treatment.

The mass greeting was still in progress when Merrick began to hear odd thudding sounds from somewhere in the distance. Taking a few casual steps away from the crowd, he keyed in his audios. The thuds grew louder and resolved into the impacts, grunts, and groans of hand-to-hand combat.

He frowned. Even without his enhancers he'd been able to hear the sounds. The villagers around him should be able to hear them, too. Yet they seemed completely oblivious. Turning his head back and forth, he placed the sounds as coming from somewhere in the center of the village. He gave the well-wishers a final look, decided they could easily do without him for the moment, and set off to hunt for the trouble.

He didn't have to go very far. About a hundred meters away he passed between two houses and found himself at the end of a rectangular patch of open ground about twenty by thirty meters. Around the edges were lines of four-meter-tall vertical poles, set a couple of meters apart, with attachments along the sides that suggested sections of fencing could be added between them. In the center of the field were a pair of young boys, ten or twelve years old, wearing hand and head protectors and attempting to beat the sand out of each other. One of the men Merrick had glimpsed earlier wearing copper-trimmed black was hovering at the edges of the fight. A trainer, probably, or else a referee.

And at the far end of the field, watching the proceedings from in front of a low-slung aircar, were two Trofts.

Merrick's first semi-panicked impulse was to put a targeting lock on both aliens' foreheads. A second later, though, he realized it wasn't as bad as he'd thought. The Trofts were dressed in civilian-style leotards, not the armored versions the aliens' soldiers wore, and they had no helmets or weapons.

Or rather, they had no lasers or blades. But both aliens carried half-meter-long sticks that had the distinctly sturdy look of weapons about them. A check with his telescopics showed that there was something at the end of each stick, either a gas-spitter nozzle or a capacitor electrode.

"Your first happenment with the Games?"

Merrick turned. Another of the black-and-copper men had come up behind him and was eyeing him with open curiosity. Merrick opened his mouth, remembered just in time that he was supposed to be mute, and quickly brought up his hand to point at his mouth as he shook his head.

"Merrick Hopekeeper is unable to speak, Henson Hillclimber," Anya said, coming up to Merrick's side. "And no, it's not his first happenment."

Merrick gestured toward the boys, holding out a horizontal palm to indicate their height. "But the one I witnessed alongside him was more elaborate and risksome than this," Anya continued. "And as he now points out, in that Game the fighter was fully grown."

"Witnessed," Henson repeated the word, a knowing look in his eye. "So he didn't grow up in a Games-bred village?"

"No, that he did not," Anya conceded.

"And yet you brought him *here*?" Henson pressed. "Deny it not, Anya Winghunter. I know the others still enmeshed in greeting. They either would not or could not have been so bold."

"Yet Ville Dreamsinger is also here," Anya pointed out. "I did not bring *him*."

"Ville is at least one of the Games-bred," Henson countered. "By your own admission Merrick is not. So again I ask: why did you bring him here?"

"I met him during my period of slavery. When we were ordered back to our homes, he had no place to go."

"Why not?"

"Do you truly have to ask?"

Henson's eyes flicked past Merrick's shoulder at the Trofts. "No," he said, some of the truculence finally leaving his voice.

"He wished to come with me, to my village," Anya continued. "I accepted his wish, and him."

Henson hissed between his teeth, muttering something under his breath at the same time as he eyed Merrick. "So you still have the death of this village at heart?"

"I never wished our death," Anya insisted, her voice firm but with an edge of pleading beneath it.

"Your actions belie your words." Henson gestured to Merrick. "For truly, an adult male without Games abilities could be disastrous to us all."

"He can fight," Anya said firmly. "Our village will not be shamed or isolated."

"We shall see," Henson said. "And as to whether Gangari will continue to be *your* village is a matter for further discussion."

There was a sudden, louder thud from the center of the field. Merrick turned to see that one of the boys was now on the ground, lying still but with his fingers still twitching. His opponent stood over him, a mixture of satisfaction and guilt on his face. Apparently, the fight was over.

Across the field, one of the Trofts took a step away from the aircar and called out something in that odd dialect that Merrick had yet to completely figure out. Henson lifted his hand in acknowledgment and called back something in the same dialect. Gesturing the other black-clad man to move back, he started toward the two boys.

And was jerked to a stop as Anya caught his arm. "You cannot," she said urgently. "They're too youthsome. It could be dangerous."

Henson shook off her hand. "Better a *could* than a *would*," he countered darkly. "It has been ordered. Stand aside, or face the wrath."

Anya glared at him. But she let go of his arm without further argument. Henson turned again and strode off across the field, digging into a small pouch hanging from his belt.

Merrick took a step closer to Anya. "What's going on?" he asked quietly.

"The masters demand the Game continue," she said, her tone angry and pained. "Henson must therefore give the downed boy a dose of bersarkis."

Merrick stared at her. "*Bersarkis*? That poison we just walked through?"

"No, no—that is *bersark*," Anya said. "*Bersarkis* is the refined form, a potion that aids in healing and recovery."

A memory clicked: the vial of light-brown liquid that Anya had always been trying to push on him during his imprisonment on Qasama. He'd never trusted her enough to take any of it. "So if it heals him, what's the problem? Just that he'll get up and they'll keep trying to kill each other?"

"You don't understand," she said tightly. "Henson won't give merely a healing dosage. He'll quatro the amount . . ." She trailed off.

Merrick focused on the boy who was still standing. He was trying hard to look calm, but a closer look with Merrick's infrareds told a different story. The boy was all but shaking with fear as he watched Henson approach and kneel down beside his unconscious opponent. "What does quatroing the amount do?" Merrick asked.

Anya gave a shuddering sigh. "It creates mindlessness."

Merrick was still trying to figure out how to respond to that when Henson pressed a small white patch of something onto the unconscious boy's upper arm and gave it a sharp slap. The boy jerked, lay still another moment, then jerked again and opened his eyes. For perhaps three seconds he stared up at the man leaning over him.

And then, abruptly, he reached a hand to Henson's chest and gave him a shove that sent the man toppling over backwards. Pushing off the ground with his other hand, the boy shot to his feet and hurled himself at his opponent.

The other boy did his best. But it was like stopping a summer storm. His attacker was all over him, flailing with hands and feet and occasionally even butting furiously with the front of his head. The blows weren't all that accurate, and the defending boy was able to block or avoid many of them. But the ones that got through were powerful enough to stagger him.

And through it all, the attacker filled the air with shrieks, snarls, and animalistic grunts.

Merrick looked over at the Trofts. They were watching the fight closely, with no indication that they were appalled by the carnage. In fact, judging by the quivering of their upper-arm radiator membranes, both of them found the bout highly exciting.

Maybe exciting enough that they wouldn't want it to simply end with the drugged boy beating the other into the ground?

Merrick swallowed hard. Because it would apparently be simplicity itself to keep the fight going. Another order to Henson, another white patch or two, and the loser would get his chance at some revenge.

One of the attacker's blows missed and the boy fell heavily to the ground, giving the defender just enough breathing space to scramble a few steps away. His face was pinched with fear and blotched with spots of oozing or trickling blood, and for a moment Merrick thought he might take advantage of the momentary lull to run away.

But despite the obvious reluctance in his movements, he nevertheless slowed to a stop and remained still, his breath coming in great heaving gasps as he waited stolidly for his opponent to get back up.

It was at that exact moment that it suddenly occurred to Merrick that he still had target locks on both Trofts.

It would be so easy. A quick pair of antiarmor laser shots—hell, even his fingertip lasers would probably do the job at this distance against unarmored aliens—and Anya and Henson could break up the fight and get both boys the medical attention they surely must need by now. He could load the aliens' bodies into the aircar, fly it out into the forest somewhere, and find a big tree to crash it into. By the time anyone found the wreckage, scavengers would probably have eaten enough to obscure any evidence of how they'd died.

Only it wouldn't work. The rest of their garrison or settlement would surely know that the pair had planned to come to Gangari today. They would send someone to investigate, and while Anya might be willing to cover for him, Henson almost certainly wouldn't.

Unless Merrick was also able to take out the investigators before they could report. But that would do nothing but postpone the inevitable, because even the stupidest Trofts wouldn't buy the idea that two teams disappearing in the same general vicinity was pure coincidence. The next Trofts would arrive in force, and in the end the entire village would suffer.

Time and again during the Troft invasion of Qasama, Merrick had seen the Shahni and other leaders make decisions about who would go into danger, and probably die, so that others might live. At the time, Merrick had been glad he wasn't the one who had to make such decisions.

Now, suddenly, he was.

And in this case, there was no doubt as to what he had to do. If the fight continued, one of the boys could indeed die. But if he interfered, the whole village would be devastated.

As Henson had said, better a *could* than a *would*.

The drugged attacker made it back to his feet and lurched again for his opponent. But something now seemed to be happening to the boy. He was moving slower, more hesitantly, and a quick check of his facial infrareds showed that the rage or fear that had been driving him was receding into a pain-wracked bewilderment.

He tried another couple of steps. His opponent kept his distance, watching warily. The drugged boy took a final step forward and stumbled, going down on one knee.

And to Merrick's surprise, the defender took a quick step forward and delivered a roundhouse punch to the side of his head that sent him once again sprawling flat on the ground.

Merrick caught his breath. What the hell kind of trick was *that*? The kid had been ready to fall over all by himself. He certainly hadn't needed someone's fist to help him along.

But at least the fight was over.

Maybe.

He looked over at Henson, wondering if he would step forward and slap the unconscious kid with another white patch. But apparently the Trofts had had enough of the Games for one day.

Possibly more than enough. The two aliens were chatting amiably with each other, like a pair of bored spectators waiting for the timer to run down so that they could go home.

For a moment Henson waited, probably making sure there would be no further orders. Then, turning to the other black-suited referee, he motioned him forward and gestured to the two boys.

"It's over," Anya murmured, sounding tiredly relieved.

"*That's* for sure," Merrick growled. "What the *hell* was that last punch—?"

"Keep your voice down," she cut him off. "You have no idea."

"Fine. Explain it to me."

Anya's lips compressed. "If the winner had simply let the loser collapse when the bersarkis had run its course, the Game would have been a draw," she said. "There's no gain in a draw."

"But there's gain in hitting someone when he's already down?"

Anya turned away. "I said you wouldn't understand," she said over her shoulder. "Stay here until the masters leave. Henson will find you a bed for the night."

"Anya Winghunter?"

Merrick turned. Henson was standing beside the Trofts, and all three were looking across the field at him and Anya. "Anya Winghunter, attend the masters." Henson's eyes shifted to Merrick. "And bring your companion."

Merrick looked at Anya. Her anger at his naiveté had vanished, a quiet dread now in its place. She flashed Merrick a look, then headed across the field. Making his face as blank as he could, Merrick followed. They passed the two boys as the loser was beginning to show signs of returning consciousness and came to a halt in front of Henson and the aliens. [The masters, what is their wish?] Anya asked in cattertalk.

One of the Trofts' membranes gave a brief fluff as he replied. Only this time, to Merrick's surprise, his dialect wasn't nearly as hard to understand as it usually was with members of the Drim'hco'plai demesne. In fact, aside from some strangely accented words, it was no worse than deciphering Anya's own slightly off-plumb Anglic usage. [Your language skills, your captivity has harmed them,] the Troft said.

[My apologies, I offer them,] Anya said, bowing

deeply. [My masters, this speech they used. My understanding of true speech, it has been affected.]

Which was, Merrick knew, a lie. Back on Qasama,
she'd had no trouble conversing with the Troft doc-
tor who used this same dialect. Why she would risk
the aliens' anger by forcing them to shift dialects
he couldn't imagine, unless it was for Merrick's own
benefit and ease of understanding.

[Slaves' minds, they are all too easily affected,]
the second Troft said scornfully. [Trof'te minds, they
are stronger.]

[The difficulty, I apologize for it,] Henson said,
flashing an angry look at Anya as he also bowed.

[The difficulty, there is none,] the first Troft said
loftily. [The dialect of our friends and allies, we have
no difficulty speaking it.] He pointed to Merrick. [This
slave, he does not appear familiar. His identity and
occupation, he will tell them to us.]

[The slave, his voice is damaged,] Anya spoke up
quickly. [His voice, an accident robbed him of it.
Merrick Hopekeeper, his name it is.]

[Merrick Hopekeeper, to the Games is he bred?]
the first Troft asked.

[The Games, he is not bred to them,] Henson
spoke up before Anya could answer. [His occupation,
a winghunter assistant it is.]

[A winghunter assistant, he is too old to be one,]
the first Troft said suspiciously. [A full winghunter, I
believe he is one.]

Anya's throat tightened as she looked at Merrick.
Once again, there was clearly something going on that
he wasn't getting. [A full winghunter, he is one,] she
confirmed reluctantly.

[Good news, that is some,] the second Troft said. [A hunt, the two winghunters will begin one at once. The delicacies, we will feast on them by moonlight.]

[And the hunt, we will observe its progress,] the first Troft said, his voice still suspicious as he eyed Merrick. [Their winghunting ability, we will evaluate it.]

[The hour, it is too late to scale the mountains,] Anya protested carefully. [The morning, we cannot leave until then.]

Merrick looked at the cliffs rising from the ground behind the aliens. The mountains were not only tall, but they were also steep and rugged, with quite a few places that were rocky enough to keep any trees or bushes from getting a foothold.

And winghunts started from somewhere up *there?*

[The hour, it is not too late,] the first Troft said firmly. [The dawn, we will not wait for it. The mountain, we will begin ascending it at once.]

[The mountain, you do not need to ascend with us,] Anya said quickly. [The way, it is very steep and difficult.]

[Fools, do you consider us them?] the first Troft demanded scornfully. [The mountain, we will not ascend it by foot. Your path, we will fly alongside it.]

[The decision, it has been made,] the second Troft said before Anya could say anything else. [The winghunter equipment, you will gather it.]

Anya looked at Henson, a quiet pleading in her eyes. But the other either didn't notice or didn't care. [The decision, it has been made,] he confirmed. [Their winghunting ability, with your own eyes you will see it.]

[That hope, you will nurture it,] the first Troft said ominously. He looked at Anya, his radiator membranes fluffing out from his arms. [The dark memory of years past, you still have it?]

Henson hissed between his teeth. [The dark memory, we still have it,] he confirmed. [The preparation, it will begin at once.]

He gestured to Anya. "The equipment's in the hunters' lodge," he said. "You remember where that is?"

"I can find it." Anya touched Merrick's arm. "Come."

She led the way from the combat field and onto a path leading toward the mountains. "I take it winghunting isn't something you learn in an afternoon?" Merrick asked quietly.

"No," she said grimly. "Especially not in an afternoon spent climbing a mountain after a long day of travel." She made as if to say something else, apparently changed her mind, and fell silent.

Merrick looked behind him at the sun. Still, it wasn't as bad as it could have been. It sounded like the rest of the day would be spent in climbing, with the actual hunt not beginning until tomorrow. That meant he theoretically had all night to examine the hunting equipment and learn whatever Anya could teach him. "We'll be all right," he said as encouragingly as he could. "Let's get geared up."

"And then what?" she countered with a sudden edge of bitterness. "Then what do we do?"

"We climb a mountain, of course," Merrick promised. "Come on, relax. Let's just take it one step at a time."

"You're right," she said. "I'd forgotten how special you are." She gave him an uncertain smile. "Perhaps you *can* learn winghunting in one night."

"Perhaps I can," Merrick said. "Let's find out."

CHAPTER FOURTEEN

Jody had assumed that she would be taken to wherever
Lieutenant Commander Tamu had gathered the rest
of the Stronghold citizens he'd persuaded to come
aboard his big fancy courier ship. It was clear that he
wasn't keeping them prisoner—on the aircar flight from
Stronghold to the landing area she saw a few of the
people already leaving, making their wary way across the
wide path that the Marines had cleared to keep Caelian's
plants and animals away. Tamu had also put four pairs
of Marines along the path, standing ready in case some
gigger or screech tiger decided to give it a try anyway.

All probably part of Tamu's plan, she decided as
the aircar put down beside the open hatch: a visible
demonstration that Dominion Marines could protect
the people of Caelian as well as the Cobras could. In
fact, they could probably do it even better, since the
Cobras had other work to do around the planet and
couldn't simply stand around looking brave the way
the Marines could.

Still, shows of force aside, the main thrust of Tamu's plan had to be taking place inside the ship where Uy's people couldn't watch. Her whole point in letting herself be captured had been to get inside, listen to the Dominion's propaganda or promises or bribes, and then get that information back to Uy.

Only it hadn't worked that way. Sergeant Tapper had escorted her up the ramp along with a new line of people heading in, but instead of continuing up the nearby stairway toward the murmur of voices coming from the next deck up, he'd taken her past the stairs and down the same-deck corridor.

It was a short corridor, considerably shorter than the ship itself, with an open door at the far end that gave a glimpse into the heavy machinery and blinking status lights of the ship's engineering section. Midway down the corridor, a crewer with a tool belt was kneeling in front of an open door. He stood up as Jody and Tapper approached, nodded, and gestured into the room. A minute later, Jody found herself locked inside.

And there she stayed.

For a day and a half.

It was six in the evening, local time, about the same time on the previous day that a taciturn Marine had brought her dinner, when Tamu himself finally showed up. "Good evening, Ms. Broom," he greeted her politely as he stepped through the doorway into her cell. "I trust my men have been treating you well."

"You mean your *jailers*?" Jody shot back, trying hard to hold onto her temper. She'd known this moment would eventually come, and she'd spent many of the long hours carefully rehearsing what she would say and how she would behave.

But now, with Tamu's smirking, condescending, superior face actually hanging there in front of her, all the simmering anger and frustration and helplessness had come roaring back. "You have no right to do this."

"On the contrary," Tamu said calmly. "You're a person of interest to the Dominion. I not only have a right to detain you, but a sworn duty."

"You have a duty to keep me locked up for over a day without even charging me with a crime?" Jody countered, trying to salvage something from the stack of brilliant legal and moral arguments she'd worked up. "Here in this—in this—"

"I already said you aren't being charged with any crimes," Tamu said, still with that maddening patience of his. "Though, depending on your behavior, that could change." He waved a hand around the tiny room. "And as to *this*, it happens to be my security officer's quarters. If you Cobra Worlds people had more experience with star travel you'd know that space is at a premium in a ship this size."

Jody took a deep breath, trying to come up with something else. But she could feel all her previous arguments melting away in the heat of one brutally simple fact.

Tamu had guns and a real spaceship and armed Marines. Caelian had a few Cobras and nothing else.

And despite the idealistic adages Jody had grown up with—the prattlings about democracy and the strength of public opinion—when it came to the final reckoning it was the people with the guns who called the tune that everyone else danced to.

"Personally, I thought you'd be more interested in why I was coming to see you now," Tamu continued.

"After all, as you already pointed out, it's been over a day since you joined us."

With an effort, Jody pushed back her frustration. She'd come here for information. It was time she focused her attention on getting some. "I *was* curious about that, yes," she said, pitching her tone more politely. "I'm also curious about why you haven't already headed back to Aventine."

"Because truth to tell—and don't take this personally— you're a very small fish," Tamu said. "I have my sights on bigger game."

"Governor Uy?"

"The governor was in fact my assigned target," Tamu confirmed. "But I'd be more than willing to pass him up in favor of bringing Shahni Omnathi back to Aventine."

"Ah," Jody said. Except that Omnathi didn't know Qasama's location any more than Uy did. She considered mentioning that, decided that Tamu probably wouldn't believe her. "Is that why you're working so hard to give ammunition to the governor's political opponents? You're hoping they can force Uy to give himself up?"

Tamu's lips puckered. "That was the goal, yes. I thought that giving food and aid to people like Assemblyman Pivovarci and his allies would raise their stature enough to challenge the governor's decisions."

Jody nodded as the light finally dawned. "Only it isn't working, is it? Pivovarci and the others are happy to take your food, but aren't interested in taking your orders."

"They're fools," Tamu growled. "All of them. Can't they see that you can't possibly win against us?"

"Just because you can't win doesn't mean you

shouldn't try," Jody said. "The Caelians are a proud people, with a long history of us-versus-them philosophy." She cocked her head. "For what it's worth, I'd guess the Trofts who invaded didn't think they could be beaten, either."

Tamu snorted. "The Trofts are fools, too. They sit in their little demesnes, fighting their petty squabbles, when they could instead be uniting under a single authority." Abruptly, he gestured. "Come with me. There's something I want to show you."

Jody had heard voices and periodic thuds and clangings outside her room during her isolation, and had spent some time puzzling over what it might be. Now, as she and Tamu headed down the corridor, she finally found out. One of the line of one-by-two-meter plates that ran down the center of the floor had been removed and propped up against the side wall, and two of the ship's crewers were pulling cream-colored boxes from a meter-deep storage bin beneath it. "More bribes?" she asked as Tamu led the way along the narrow strip of flooring that ran alongside the open bin.

"Humanitarian aid," he said stiffly. "The preliminary reports from Caelian said that their food supplies had been disrupted by the Troft invasion, so Commodore Santores had us bring extra food to pass out."

"Like I said. Bribes."

Tamu flashed her a glare and said nothing.

The murmur of conversation Jody had heard when she first came aboard the previous day was present again as the two of them climbed the stairway. An open door midway down the corridor seemed to be the source, and as they neared it Jody was able to start picking individual voices from the mix. Tamu reached the door, then stepped aside and gestured Jody to go in.

The room was larger than her prison downstairs, but still quite compact. It was apparently a mess room, with most of its floor space taken up by a long table and the fourteen chairs set around it. There were eight people at the table, all of them dressed in Caelian silliweave clothing, all of them eating earnestly from small bowls. At the far end of the room was a serving counter where a crewer stood ready with a stack of similar bowls and a steaming tureen. Standing at various spots around the room were Sergeant Tapper and four of his Marines, all of them looking intensely bored as they watched the others eat.

"The latest group of hungry citizens here to accept Dominion generosity," Tamu identified the diners. "I find it interesting that the numbers of people taking us up on our standing offer has been gradually diminishing since yesterday."

"They know now that all you've got is a propaganda meeting with refreshments," Jody said.

"Perhaps," Tamu said. "Yet they aren't boycotting us completely. I take that as a good sign." He pointed over her shoulder at the three men hunched over their bowls at one end of the group. "But I didn't bring you here to discuss crowd psychology. I simply thought you'd like to say hello to some old friends."

And without warning, the five Marines suddenly seemed to come to life. They strode across the room, converging on the three men Tamu had pointed out, and came to a halt surrounding them.

Jody frowned in surprise. What in the *Worlds*—?

And then, belatedly, she focused on the men's faces.

They weren't old friends at all. In fact, she'd never even met any of them. But their skin was deeply tanned, their hair dark, and their eyes were cool and calculating as they gazed up at the Marines.

Qasamans.

"Would you care to make the introductions, Ms. Broom?" Tamu asked.

The room had suddenly gone silent. The Caelians were still hunched over their bowls, some with spoons frozen halfway to their mouths, as they stared at the drama taking place at the end of their table. "Ms. Broom?" Tamu prompted.

The Qasaman in the middle stirred. "Leave her alone," he said. "Jody Moreau has no hand in this."

"I never thought she did," Tamu assured him. "Your name?"

"Ifrit Kaml Ghushtre," the man said, inclining his head slightly. "I command this squad of Djinn warriors."

"Not anymore you don't," Tamu said. "And your companions?"

"They are Djinn of Qasama," Ghushtre said. "Their names are unimportant."

"I'm sure they are," Tamu said coolly. "But Shahni Omnathi deserves to know the names of the men who may die because of him."

Jody spun toward Tamu, feeling her mouth drop open. *Die?* "What are you talking about?" she asked carefully.

"The Dominion needs Qasama," Tamu said, not even bothering to look at her. "For that we need Omnathi. We've tried ordering Uy to hand him over. We've tried persuading the people of Caelian to pressure Uy to give him up. Neither has worked. So we take it up a level."

"By kidnapping citizens of another world?"

"Don't you *dare* play that innocent act," Tamu snarled suddenly, his flash of anger sending Jody an involuntary step backward. "You came here as a spy. *They* came here as saboteurs. I'd be well within my legal rights to have all four of you executed on the spot."

"But you won't," Jody said. "Because we're the small fish, and we're more useful to you as bait. *Live* bait."

Slowly, the redness faded from Tamu's face as he regained control. "Yes," he said. "But in many cases the big fish is more cooperative if it knows how much longer the bait is likely to remain live." He turned back to Ghushtre. "Your companions' names?"

Ghushtre's lips compressed into a thin line. "Djinni Kaza," he said, nodding to his left. "Djinni Nisti," he said, nodding to his right.

"Good," Tamu said briskly. "Now, let me see these combat suits I've heard so much about. One at a time, of course. Stand up, if you will, Ifrit Ghushtre, and take off that silliweave tunic."

"We will not be hostages," Ghushtre said, making no move to stand up. "Nor will we be used to bargain against His Excellency's freedom."

"You'll do as I say or you'll die where you sit," Tamu countered bluntly.

"You've said already you can't kill us," Ghushtre reminded him.

"If you don't report, Omnathi will undoubtedly send in more of you," Tamu said. "I can use them as easily as I can use you. And don't hold onto any false hope about them slipping past our security—we have the faces of every genuine Caelian citizen on file. The next wave will be identified as quickly and easily as you were."

He gestured to the bowl in front of Ghushtre. "What you *should* concern yourself with right now is whether or not this is how you would choose to die. Do you really want your world's history to record that you met your end face-down in a bowl of soup?"

Jody braced herself. "Commander—"

"Shut it," he cut her off. "I've wasted over a day playing nice. I'm at the end of my patience. Now, *stand up and show me that suit.*"

For an agonizing second Jody thought Ghushtre was going to refuse anyway. Then, slowly, he rose from his seat, his glower burning the air between him and the nearest of the Marines. Unfastening his tunic, he slid it off his shoulders, revealing the gray, scaled combat suit hidden beneath it. Tucked away in his belt, just visible above the top of his silliweave trousers, were the suit's gloves with their fingertip lasers. "Nice," Tamu commented. "Now take it off."

Ghushtre sent a measuring look at each of the five Marines surrounding him. Then, with clear reluctance, he pulled off the rest of the silliweave and worked his way out of the combat suit. At Tamu's order, the other two Qasamans did the same.

"That wasn't so hard, was it?" Tamu said when the Qasamans finally stood dressed only in thin leotard undergarments. "Sergeant Tapper, you and your squad will escort our guests to their new quarters. After that, I want those combat suits taken to my cabin."

"Can't they at least put their other clothing back on?" Jody asked. Qasamans, she knew, were much more self-conscious about exposing their bodies than the people of the Cobra Worlds.

"There are fatigues waiting in their cabin," Tamu

said. "I don't trust Uy not to have slipped something nasty into their silliweaves." He gestured to the Qasamans. "But if you'd like to finish your soup first, please do so."

"We have had enough of your hospitality," Ghushtre said, his voice dark. "But know this, Commander. You may imprison us now. But the people of Qasama are no less stubborn than those of Caelian. We will not be your slaves. Not now, not ever."

"The Dominion does not make slaves, Ifrit Ghushtre," Tamu said. "But we're at war, and every human being must do his part." He raised his eyebrows. "*Will* do his part."

"You could just *ask* them for their help," Jody said acidly.

"We fully intend to," Tamu assured her. "But those matters are for Shahni Omnathi and Commodore Santores to discuss face to face." He gestured at the three Djinn. "There's no point in wasting time talking to men who have no actual authority."

Jody glared at him. But he was probably right. In many ways, the Qasamans' governmental structure was just as rigid and top-down as the Dominion military.

"And speaking of small fish," Tamu continued, turning back to Jody, "it's time to return you to your bowl."

Jody looked at the Qasamans again. Maybe if she could talk to them, they could all figure something out together. "Can't I at least eat first?" she asked.

"No," Tamu said flatly. "I want you back in your cabin where I don't have to watch you. Once all of you are behind locked doors I'll have someone bring your dinner."

"If I'm not eating, why am I here?" Jody asked.

"Just so I could see your cleverness in catching a couple of Qasamans?"

"Not at all," Tamu said, taking her arm and pulling her toward the door behind them. "It's hardly a secret that the Qasamans hold you and your family in high esteem. I thought they'd be less likely to start trouble if you might be caught in a crossfire."

Her last view of the room as they left was of the three Qasamans, standing straight and proud and silent. Waiting to be taken to their cells.

Later, through the silence of the long evening, she wondered over and over if they might have had a chance if she hadn't been there. If she'd refused to go with Tamu, or had tried to grab him at an opportune moment. If she'd just done *something*.

She wasn't a small fish, she realized bitterly. She was a tool. A tool the Dominion kept around purely because they thought it might be useful again someday.

She was trapped. She was all alone.

And she had never felt more helpless in her life.

As Jin had expected, the Dominion's search of the factory was quick, methodical, and thorough. During the first hour inside the somewhat claustrophobic press of the wiring conduit she heard the sound of voices five times, with the access door below her being opened for inspection each of those times.

Every time it happened she tensed up, bracing herself for the inevitable shouts of discovery or, worse, a no-warning burst of laser fire. But in each instance the access door was simply slammed shut again, and the voices eventually faded into the distance. Apparently, the way the cables clumped close together beneath

Jin's feet was fooling the searchers into thinking there was no room for anything or anyone else up there.

As to why sound or infrared detectors weren't picking her up, that one had been even more quickly answered. Through some combination of shape and position, the conduit seemed to act like a funnel for a host of other small sounds from nearby, everything from creaks and snaps and rumbles to the footsteps and muffled conversations of the searchers. Amid all that, any sounds of breathing or small movements on her part were apparently getting lost.

The conduit also functioned as an informal heat vent. Within her first five minutes of concealment, her clothing was damp with sweat.

Still, it was a small price to pay for staying undetectable. Whether Yates had been clever or just lucky in his choice of a hiding place, he'd done a good job of it.

And as the search came to an end, or moved elsewhere, her thoughts shifted away from concerns of her own imminent discovery to concerns of what might have happened to Paul.

The best-case scenario would be that in the presumed confused aftermath of her sabotage he'd managed to slip away and was in hiding somewhere. But Reivaro had already been on his way outside, and she doubted that he would have been so careless as to let Paul get away.

Still, no matter how furious Reivaro might be, even a Dominion colonel could only trump up charges so far. The crowd had been peaceful, and Paul would hardly have said anything to make them otherwise, and Cobra Worlds law entitled citizens to the right of peaceful assembly.

And there were a lot of Cobras in Archway and DeVegas province. Reivaro's Marines might be good, but they were seriously outnumbered, and they were on unfamiliar territory.

No, assuming the crowd had kept their heads, everything should be all right. Paul might end up spending a day or two in the Archway jail, but that wouldn't kill him. Sooner or later, Chintawa would get him out.

A sudden thud startled her out of her reverie. She froze, wondering if Reivaro had ordered yet another search.

But there wasn't the glimmer of reflected light from below that usually accompanied the access hatch being opened. There was another thud, and the faint sound of voices. Leaning forward, pressing her ear to the front of the conduit, she keyed in her audio enhancers.

"—telling you, it's not safe," an unfamiliar voice came. "There are serious issues with impedance matching, echo-transmissions, ohm compatibly—"

"You should have thought of that before you ordered your lady Cobra to wreck the panel and all the spares," a second voice interrupted, this one hard and cold.

"Hey, *we* didn't order anyone to do anything," the first man protested.

"You sure about that?" a third voice came. "Where exactly were you two when this whole thing came down?"

"We weren't anywhere near here," the first man said, and Jin could hear a fresh flood of nervousness in his voice.

"Relax, Rennie," a fourth voice said, a hint of suppressed anger in his tone. "We were with one of your guys, showing him the generator. You can ask him."

"Oh, we will," Third Voice said ominously. "In the meantime, you just focus on getting that panel out of there. It won't look good if the replacement arrives and you're not ready to install it."

"It'll look even less good if the whole plant burns down," Fourth Man countered. "Rennie's right, you know—there's a lot of high-volt, high-amp current that normally flows through these breakers. You can't just slap something else in there and expect it to run without a hitch."

"Especially stuff that doesn't even run Aventine specs," Rennie added.

"Don't be stupid," Second Man said scornfully. "Our equipment is a thousand times better than yours. If your breakers can handle the current, ours won't even notice it."

"It's not a matter of handling it," Fourth Man growled. "Weren't you listening? There are compatibility issues—"

"Let's try it this way," Second Man cut him off. "Did you see what our Marines did to your Cobras out there?"

There was a moment of taut silence. "We heard about it," Fourth Man said.

"You want to see it for yourself?" Second Man demanded. "Because we could call one of them in here for a demo. Of course, you and Rennie would have to draw straws to see who gets to watch and who gets to—well, you know."

"No," Rennie said hastily. "You don't need to—"

"Shut up, Rennie," Fourth Man bit out. "He's bluffing. He wouldn't dare have us shot down in cold blood."

"We don't bluff," Second Man said coldly. "And you'd be surprised what martial law lets us get away with."

"The Cobras found that out the hard way," Third Man said. "I hope you won't have to."

Jin felt a prickling across her skin. The Cobras had found out the hard way? What did *that* mean? What in the Worlds had happened outside?

Had Paul been part of it?

Whatever had happened, Fourth Man didn't seem all that intimidated by it. "Pretty big words from someone who hasn't the foggiest idea how any of this works," he scoffed. "You don't bluff? Fine—call in your Marines and have them kill us. In fact, have them kill everyone who works at the plant and actually knows what they're doing. Good luck then on getting a new breaker panel wired in."

"Don't be ridiculous," Second Man said scornfully. "You think you're the only ones who know how to do this job?"

"You think you can bully any of us into doing it?" Fourth Man countered. "In case you hadn't heard, we just came through a war where a lot of good men and women died. We're used to the idea of fighting for our freedom."

"No problem," Third Man said, his calm voice in stark contrast to the other two. "If we run out of high-voltage specialists in Archway, we'll just bring a few in from Capitalia. *They're* not so keen on dying big, noble deaths."

There was a brief silence. "Yeah, well, that's Capitalia," Fourth Man muttered. But it was clear that the mention of Capitalia had knocked a lot of the defiance out from under him.

It was clear to the Dominion men, too. "There's a lot to be said for being a live coward," Third Man said. "So let's pretend you want to go on living, too, and shut up the noise and get back to work."

And with that, the conversation was over. Jin continued to listen, but all she heard were the various clicks and quiet thuds as the men worked on the breaker panel, and the occasional request for a tool or helping hand.

Leaving Jin with a pounding heart and a roiling fear in her soul.

Something terrible had happened while she'd been in here sabotaging the plant. Something that had involved Cobras and Marines and death. Something bad enough to end in a declaration of martial law.

And suddenly the question was no longer whether Paul had gotten free or would have to spend a couple of quiet nights in jail. People had died out there this morning. If the Dominion men's taunts hadn't been lies, some of the dead had been Cobras.

Had one of them been Paul?

And the final horror was that there was no way for Jin to find out. She couldn't leave her hiding place, not with four men working just beneath her feet. She didn't know what the penalty for sabotage was under martial law, but she could guess that it involved a summary trial and a quick execution.

Even worse, if they took her alive—

Her breath caught in her throat as it abruptly became clear. Of course Reivaro hadn't had Paul shot down in the street. This whole thing was a setup, from taking over Yates's factory, to kicking out the workers, to forcing a deadly confrontation. All of it had been deliberately designed to give Santores an excuse to declare martial law and get the Brooms out of Chintawa's control and into his MindsEye machine.

And there was nothing Jin could do about it. Absolutely nothing.

Because if they had Paul, he was already on his way to Capitalia or one of the Dominion ships and long out of Jin's reach. If they *didn't* have him, they would probably go for Lorne next. If they somehow missed him, they would surely still be waiting for Jin to show herself.

One way or another, Santores was going to get one of them, and there was no way for her to keep that from happening. All she could do was wait, try to plan, and look for an opening.

And to hang on tightly to hope. Because for the moment, hope was all she had.

CHAPTER FIFTEEN

Commander Ukuthi wasn't at all what Barrington was expecting.

Except for being a Troft, of course. That part was completely as expected. Barrington had never seen a Troft this close before, but he was quite familiar with the vaguely insectoid torso and abdomen, the back-jointed legs, the flexible radiator membranes on the backs of the upper arms, the oversized head and chicken-like face, and the faintly disturbing contrast between the large main eyes and the small compound ones. Everyone in the Dominion military—everyone in the Dominion, for that matter—had seen enough holos and vids to know what humanity's deadliest enemies looked like.

But unlike the defiant posturing and threats that usually accompanied those vids, Ukuthi was calm and polite. Possibly it was the red sash he wore, the symbol of his place in line to someday assume the position of demesne-lord, that led to better manners than the typical Troft bothered with. Or maybe his completely unexpected mastery of the Anglic language had come with lessons on courtesy and how to deal with humans in a civilized manner.

Or maybe Ukuthi was simply an excellent con man using a better-than-average knowledge of humans to play his new acquaintances. That was a possibility Barrington was making sure to hold firmly in the back of his mind.

But if Ukuthi was a con man, he was a very good one.

And the story he had to tell was one blazing hell of a jaw-dropper.

"Interesting," Barrington commented, his voice echoing off the walls of the small hangar bay where he and Ukuthi had set up for their conversation. "And you're convinced these human slaves are from a lost colony and not simply the survivors of a captured ship or two?"

"The humans, they have a long history on their own world," Ukuthi said. "My demesne-lord has spoken with several of them at length, and has no doubt they have been in Trof'te space for at least three hundred years."

"I see." Barrington pursed his lips, surreptitiously double-twitching his left eyelid. Garrett, monitoring the meeting from CoNCH, would have started a records search as soon as Ukuthi raised the issue of a lost human colony. If Ukuthi was telling the truth, there should be some mention of that disappearance in the *Dorian's* records.

And there was. Maybe. He ran his eyes down the image, checking the dates . . .

"You have found it?"

Barrington focused on Ukuthi again. "Excuse me?"

"Your computer search," Ukuthi said. "The origin of the colony, you have found it?"

"Possibly," Barrington said, impressed in spite of himself. The corneal projector was subtle enough that even most Dominion citizens didn't notice when one was being used. Not only was Ukuthi a good storyteller, he was also an observant one. "We have records of at least fifteen colony ships over the past four hundred years that were headed in the general direction of the Troft Assemblage when they disappeared. Your lost colony could have come from any one of them, or it could be someone who was supposed to be heading in a different direction and got seriously lost. There's no way to pin it down more closely."

"Perhaps they have records or spoken history that will allow you to learn the truth," Ukuthi suggested. "We can seek those records once we have made full contact with them."

"Presumably," Barrington said. "Right now I'm more concerned with the present than the past. You said the Drim'hco'plai were shipping wild animals there from Qasama and possibly Caelian. What you *haven't* said is why."

"We do not know the Drim'hco'plai purpose," Ukuthi said. "But we fear it is part of a plot against those around them. Possibly against the Cobra Worlds; possibly against other demesnes such as our own." The radiator membranes on his upper arms fluttered. "Possibly against the Dominion of Man itself."

"And you said they were working for the—?" Barrington gave an exasperated snort. "Run all that by me again, would you? Your demesne names are hard for humans to keep track of."

"Certainly," Ukuthi said. "The Tua'lanek'zia demesne obtained a contract from another demesne, as yet unidentified but presumed to be one of those at war with your Dominion of Man. The Tua'lanek'zia then hired the Drim'hco'plai and Balin'ekha'spmi demesnes to assist in the invasions of Qasama and the Cobra Worlds."

"And your demesne-lord just went along with that?"

"My demesne-lord had little choice in the matter," Ukuthi said, his membranes fluttering again. "The Drim'hco'plai are very powerful, and he was fearful they would emerge from this action stronger than before and turn their wrath afterward upon us."

Barrington nodded. It was, unfortunately, an all-too-familiar scenario: antagonisms, grudges, alliances, and retaliations all tended to get tangled and amplified amid the haze of war. "So you joined in the attack. But then you changed your minds?"

"We never were truly committed to conquering the human worlds," Ukuthi said. "My orders were to cooperate as little as I could with the Drim'hco'plai and Tua'lanek'zia demesnes. My hidden mission was to observe both demesnes and determine their strengths and weaknesses and, where applicable, their hidden agendas."

"And these animal hunts told you that the Drim'hco'plai, at least, were running some game of their own on the side," Barrington said, nodding again. "Now, wasn't there one more demesne involved?"

"Yes, the Gla'lupt'flae," Ukuthi confirmed. "But they are a small demesne, and their role in the invasion was mostly one of supply and support." He cocked his head. "Is it clearer now?"

"Yes, thank you," Barrington said. In actual fact,

he'd gotten the whole thing the first time. He'd simply thought it might be instructive to see if Ukuthi could repeat his story again without mistakes or contradictions.

Which he had. Not that that proved anything, of course.

"We have made quiet enquiries, and are convinced that the animals were taken to the humans' world," Ukuthi continued. "We had hoped to trace the flights and learn its exact location, but have thus far been unable to do so."

"Yes," Barrington murmured, making a face. It wasn't bad enough that this lost colony was in the middle of hostile territory. Ukuthi and his fellow Balin'ekha'spmi didn't even know where exactly in the Drim'hco'plai demesne's five hundred cubic light-years the system was. "Which brings us to Merrick Moreau Broom. You said earlier that he was in danger. How do you know?"

Ukuthi's membranes fluttered again. "That much I've already told you," he said. "My intent, it was to send him with equipment and perhaps companions. But the circumstances forced him instead to go alone."

"But the Drim'hco'plai aren't on to your plan, are they?"

"The Drim'hco'plai have no reason to expect that a human spy has infiltrated their demesne," Ukuthi said.

Which wasn't exactly what Barrington had asked. "I'm sure they don't," he said. "On the other hand, a dozen ships from that same demesne had you pinned into a low orbit over the Hoibe'ryi'sarai home world less than two hours ago. I'll ask again: are the Drim'hco'plai on to you or your plan?"

"My reasons for being here were not related to Merrick Moreau's mission," Ukuthi assured him. "My demesne-lord asked me to bring the possibility of an alliance between our demesnes to counter the growing might of the Drim'hco'plai." His membranes twitched. "When I learned of your arrival at Aventine, I asked the Hoibe'ryi'sarai demesne-lord if he would provide an introduction. We were within that negotiation when the Drim'hco'plai ships appeared. It was fortunate for me that you arrived with such timeliness."

"Fortunate *and* convenient," Barrington said. "It got you out of a tight fix, and now you don't have to pay the Hoibe'ryi'sarai for an introduction. Two birds with one stone."

"Pardon?"

"An old Dominion saying," Barrington explained. "It means accomplishing two goals with a single action or set of actions."

"I see," Ukuthi said. "A useful phrase. There is nothing similar I know of among Trof'te adages."

"You should see about coining one," Barrington said, letting his eyes drift around the hangar bay. There wasn't much to see: just Ukuthi's shuttle, plus the table, chair, and couch that Barrington had had brought in.

But the sparse furnishings and tight quarters were fine with Barrington. Just as he'd never seen a Troft up close, so had he never seen an undamaged Troft ship. The vehicle's hull had an odd sheen to it, like some hybrid of metal and ceramic, and an even odder smell. More than once during the conversation Barrington had been tempted to surreptitiously signal Garrett and have him do a quiet scan. To make contact with a potentially friendly Troft demesne and also gain some information about their technology would make a nice two-bird combination.

But each time the temptation came he fought it back. Ukuthi had pledged not to spy on the *Dorian*. Barrington could hardly lower himself to a lesser standard.

Besides, there was one more bird poised at the end of the target range here. One which might yield better and quicker results than an analysis of Ukuthi's hull material. "It seems to me that the first thing we need to do is check out the situation on Qasama," he said, looking back at Ukuthi. "The Drim'hco'plai may have left behind records that could point us to the system where they took Cobra Broom. There might also be clues as to what exactly they're up to."

"Doubtful," Ukuthi said. "Commander Inxeba was a careful officer. He would have taken all such information with him, or else destroyed it."

"It's still worth a try," Barrington said. "I presume you can provide me with Qasama's location data?"

"Of course," Ukuthi said, his membranes fluttering uncertainly. "That data, you do not already have it?"

"We left Aventine before Governor-General Chintawa was able to locate the relevant records," Barrington said. "Given their history, the Cobra Worlds haven't exactly encouraged communication between their citizens and Qasama. The system's location was carefully hidden away, and it's proving difficult to retrieve."

"Indeed," Ukuthi said thoughtfully. "I had not heard of any such problems between the worlds. I shall have to inquire into the circumstances of this history you speak of." His membranes fluttered again, a decisive sort of movement this time. "But later will be soon enough. The fate of Merrick Moreau edges toward the precipice, and with it perhaps the fates of the Balin'ekha'spmi demesne and the Dominion of Man. Permit me to return to my ship, and I will transmit Qasama's location. To Qasama, you will then follow me?"

"I will," Barrington said, standing up. "When we get there, I may have more questions to ask you."

"The answers, I will endeavor to provide them," Ukuthi said, rising from his couch and stretching his legs. "Farewell, Captain Barrington Moreau."

"Farewell to you, Commander Ukuthi," Barrington said. "We'll meet again soon."

He waited until Ukuthi was back in his shuttle with the hatch sealed. Then, he signaled for the crewers waiting outside to collect the furniture, and together they left the hangar bay.

By the time he reached CoNCH, Ukuthi's shuttle was well on its way back to his ship.

Garrett rose from the command chair as Barrington approached. "Welcome back, sir," he greeted the captain.

"Thank you, Commander," Barrington said dryly as he took his seat. "It's been such a long and hazardous mission."

Garrett's lip twitched, and it wasn't hard to read his disapproval of such flippancy.

And to be honest, Barrington could hardly blame him. It may have been a lone Troft, and it may have been behind the *Dorian*'s hull and defenses. But it had still been a Troft, and not many Dominion officers had ever been that close to one of the enemy and returned alive.

But Garrett knew better than to bring that up, especially now that the meeting and the risks were over. "I did manage to get a little information about Jody Broom from Deputy Kopdji while you were talking with Uku-thi," the commander said. "He says the freighter that landed on Aventine three days ago hasn't returned yet."

Barrington frowned. Warships were typically faster than freighters, but the *Dorian* had taken the voyage at less than its top speed, taking extra care in crossing the unfamiliar stellography between Aventine and the Hoibe'ryi'sarai home world. Adding in the freighter's several hours of head start, it certainly should have been here by now. "You think he's lying?"

"Possibly," Garrett said. "But it could also be that the freighter decided to go somewhere else before it returned home."

"Is that common?" Barrington asked. "I'd think that keeping to a schedule would be as essential to their shipping infrastructure as it is to ours."

"Could be it's a tramp freighter," Garrett said. "Kopdji was rather vague on details."

Barrington snorted. "Probably hoping we'll go away so that he can claim he doesn't know us when the Drim'hco'plai come back in force."

"Probably," Garrett agreed. "Kopdji further says that they have exactly two hundred and ninety humans on the planet at the moment, all of them trade reps or import consultants, none of them Jody Broom. He sent me a list if you want to look at it."

"Did *you* look at it?"

Garrett nodded. "I also set up a cross-reference check. So far, it hasn't made any primary, secondary, or tertiary connections between any of the names and the Broom family. The computer's still looking, but I'm not hopeful."

"Keep it running anyway," Barrington said. "Did Kopdji offer any explanation as to why Ukuthi and the Drim'hco'plai were here?"

"He dodged the question every time I asked it," Garrett said. "You think Ukuthi was lying?"

"I think it's suspiciously convenient timing that he just happens to be here when the Drim'hco'plai show up," Barrington said. "I'm wondering if they might have been chasing him for some reason and he ran to the Hoibe'ryi'sarais hoping they'd give him refuge."

"Mm," Garrett said, rubbing his cheek thoughtfully. "I also notice that he never really answered your question about whether the Drim'hco'plai were on to him."

"No, he didn't," Barrington said. "It didn't seem worth pressing him on at the time, but it's something we'll want to remember for the future."

"Yes." Garrett shifted his gaze to the main display. "You really think he's just going to hand us Qasama's location?"

"I don't see why he wouldn't," Barrington said. "Qasama and the Cobra Worlds were clearly allies against him and the other invaders. The very least that allies typically share with each other is their location."

"Maybe," Garrett said. "But don't forget that these are Trofts, whose political and military viewpoint centers around living alone amid a cluster of potentially hostile neighbors. Just because he claims he didn't know about the bad blood between Qasama and Aventine doesn't mean he didn't."

"True enough," Barrington conceded. "On the other hand, he desperately wants our help. *That* much was clear."

"Or he's hoping to lead us into a trap."

"No," Barrington said firmly. "Possibly into a combat situation where we'll be over our heads, but not a trap per se."

Garrett grunted. "Not sure I see the difference, practically speaking."

"Captain?" the comm officer called. "We're getting a transmission from the Balin'ekha'spmi ship. It appears to be a set of navigational coordinates."

Barrington felt his pulse pick up. "Run them for distance and vector," he ordered.

"Yes, sir," the other said. "Distance is about forty-six light years, on a vector of twenty-seven by thirty-three."

"About ninety degrees from our current return vector to Aventine," Garrett murmured. "Could be a little tight."

Barrington keyed in a star chart, running the numbers in his head. Three days back to Aventine—maybe two now that they knew they could trust Aventine's stellography charts—then another five or more to Qasama. "Projected transit time?" he asked.

"Approximately—just a moment, sir," the officer interrupted himself. "Commander Ukuthi is sending a proposed course." On the nav display a squiggly white curve appeared, superimposed on the star map.

"Interesting," Barrington murmured, eyeing the course. Instead of a straight-line path from the Hoibe'ryi'sarai homeworld to Qasama, Ukuthi was suggesting the *Dorian* swing a few light-years back toward Aventine, then curve off and head more or less straight toward Qasama. "Any idea why this particular route?"

"He could be taking us back toward Aventine to avoid the edges of other demesnes," the tac officer offered. "But there's no way to prove that without knowing exactly where those edges are."

"Convenient, though," Garrett murmured. "It's almost as if he *wants* us to detour to Aventine."

"Not *wants* us to," Barrington corrected grimly. "*Dares* us to. See how the course meanders? That strongly implies he's already plugged in the stellography for us. If we divert to Aventine, we'll end up on a vector that's off just enough from his that we'll need to run at reduced speed. If, on the other hand, we divert to Aventine and then come back to his course, it'll cost us twice the diversion time."

"True, but that should only be a few hours," Garrett pointed out, his eyes darting back and forth as he ran the calculation through the data stream. "No more than fifteen or sixteen total."

Barrington gazed at the display, weighing his options. Time was critical—Ukuthi had made that abundantly clear during their conversation. But if the Troft was planning something underhanded and the *Dorian* went in alone, without support from the other two cruisers . . . .

"We can't risk it," he decided. "Especially since it's entirely possible that the coordinates he gave us aren't for Qasama at all, but for some other system."

"So you *do* think it could be a trap?" Garrett asked, frowning.

"Not necessarily," Barrington said. "If we show up on schedule at his coordinates, thereby proving that we keep our promises, he gives us Qasama's actual coordinates. If we show up late—especially if we show up late with the *Megalith* in tow—we find ourselves in the middle of nowhere with him long gone." He cocked an eyebrow. "In fact, the more I think about it, that's probably the way *I* would do it."

"But we can't just leave Commodore Santores out of the stream," Garrett protested.

"We won't," Barrington assured him. "As soon as we head off on Ukuthi's course we'll start prep on the *Hermes*. As soon as it's ready, we'll break out, drop it, then continue on our way. It shouldn't cost us more than ten minutes, and that short a time discrepancy will be easily explainable as mechanical problems if Ukuthi calls us on it."

"I suppose that'll work," Garrett said slowly, a frown still creasing his forehead. "If Commodore Santores reacts quickly, the *Megalith* shouldn't be more than a few hours behind us." He shook his head. "But if these *aren't* the final coordinates, they'll find themselves in the same middle of nowhere you just suggested."

"In which case, we'll drop a beacon behind with the proper coordinates before we leave," Barrington said. "Timered so that it won't start transmitting until we're long gone, just in case Ukuthi leaves someone behind to make sure we didn't leave a crumb trail."

"It still leaves us vulnerable," Garrett pointed out. "The fact he's pushing this so hard makes me suspicious. When someone insists on quick action, he's nearly always up to something."

"Could be," Barrington said. "But there is another possibility why he's in such a big hurry."

He looked back at the star display, and the tortured line that would be leading the *Dorian* into the unknown. "That Merrick Broom really *is* in immediate, serious danger."

❖   ❖   ❖

Merrick's introduction to the term *winghunter* had been during his imprisonment on Qasama, when Anya had first given him her name. She hadn't explained it or even referred to it after that, and Merrick had simply assumed that it was like a family name, harkening back to some kind of animal or bird that some founding member of her lineage had been particularly good at hunting. Later, aboard the Drim slave ship, he'd come to realize that the slaves' names weren't related to families that way, but were descriptive of the actual person who wore them.

Still, as he and Anya headed to the Gangari hunters' lodge, his mind continued to hold onto the mental image of the two of them moving up and down the mountain slopes in search of some elusive eagle or owl nest. The kind of hunt where his optical and audio enhancers might give him an extra edge to balance out his lack of experience.

It wasn't going to be like that. Because the *wing* in *winghunting* didn't refer to a bird. It referred to the delta-shaped wing of a hang-glider.

"It unfolds this way," Anya explained, opening the accordion-style folds as far as the cramped space in the lodge's storeroom would permit. "You strap yourself into this harness, lying in a face-down position beneath the wing, then use this control bar and the movements of your body to shift yourself left or right, up or down."

"Right," Merrick said, his mouth unpleasantly dry. He'd never had a particular fear of heights, certainly not in aircars or spaceships. But the thought of hanging hundreds of meters above the ground beneath a mere strip of cloth, his life at the mercy of air currents, storms, and his own ineptitude, was twisting his stomach into multiple knots. "I suppose there are techniques for keeping yourself from falling straight to the ground?"

"There are many such, yes," Anya said, giving him an odd look as she picked up a stack of thin, sheer white cloth. "While we fly, we'll each have one of these fastened to our ankles and spread out behind us." She unfolded the top layer and showed him the meter-wide opening. "We'll seek out swarms of jattorns and fly through them, capturing some in the net with each pass."

Merrick stared at her. "Is *that* what this is all about?"

"Of course," she said, looking puzzled. "Jattorns are a delicacy beloved by the masters."

So naturally they would set their slaves to capturing them, Merrick thought blackly. And just as naturally, they would order them to do it in the most dangerous way possible. "You can't just drop in on them with an aircar?" he growled. "Or shoot them from the ground?"

"They fly too high for arrows, and lasers and projectile weapons destroy too much of the meat," Anya said. "Aircars are also of no use, as the sound and emissions frighten and scatter the swarms."

She straightened up and gave him a surprisingly sharp glare. "And if there were no jattorn hunts for us to participate in, many more of us would be bred to the Games. Would you prefer *that*?"

Merrick sighed. It was so easy to forget—or to refuse to remember—that these people were slaves, under the absolute authority of their Troft masters. "No, of course not," he said. "Sorry. I don't . . ."

"Think like a slave?" Anya looked away. "I wish I didn't. I long for the day when I will no longer have to." She shook her head, a quick twitch as if shaking away unpleasant thoughts. "Have you ever used something like this?"

"Not even close," Merrick admitted. "I guess you're going to have to teach me on the fly. So to speak."

"I'll try," she said doubtfully as she refolded the wing and fastened its straps. "But there's no time now. The masters are waiting and will be suspicious if we linger. We'll speak later tonight, while they sleep. Come over here—there is clothing more suitable for mountain travel. We can take whatever we choose."

"Okay," Merrick said, following her as she moved down the narrow space between the shelves of equipment. Her proposed nighttime conversation assumed, of course, that the Trofts were comfortable enough in the presence of their slaves for both of them to sleep at the same time. If the positions were reversed, Merrick wouldn't be nearly so trusting.

On the other hand, if Merrick didn't think like a slave, he also didn't think like a slave master. Maybe the Trofts assumed their pet humans were so beaten down and servile that they had no fear of them.

If they did, great. If they didn't, Merrick would probably have to learn winghunting right on the job. From a few hundred meters in the air.

He could hardly wait.

The clothing Anya found for them was sturdy, warm, and considerably cleaner than the jumpsuits they'd worn since leaving Qasama. She selected two sets of shirts, trousers, boots, belts, and jackets, and they changed quickly into them. The fasteners were of unfamiliar design, but Merrick was able to figure them out without too much trouble.

Henson and the two Trofts were still waiting when they returned, but the two boys and the other referee were gone. Hopefully for medical attention, but of course Merrick couldn't ask about that. [The preparations, they are complete?] the second Troft asked, his membranes quivering with impatience.

[The preparations, they are complete,] Anya confirmed. [The mountain, we shall begin ascending it.]

[Your progress, we shall observe it,] the first Troft said, climbing into the aircar and motioning his companion to do the same. [The ascent, you will begin it now. Haste, you will make it.]

The aircar lifted from the ground and disappeared over the rooftops to the east. "You remember the path?" Henson asked stiffly.

"I remember it," Anya said. "Don't fear. We'll return safely."

"See that the Trofts return safely alongside you." Henson's eyes bored into hers. "If they don't, neither will you. Either of you."

He spun around, putting his back to them. Anya gazed at him a moment, a sequence of unreadable expressions flashing across her face. Then, silently, she also spun around and strode across the field toward the mountains. Merrick followed, wondering briefly if he should ask her what that had been about.

Staring at the rigidity of her back, he decided it would be smarter to keep his silence.

Earlier, as they'd approached Gangari, Merrick had had the impression that the mountain behind it rose directly from the edge of the village. Now, he found that sense had been correct. Barely five meters past the last house the ground turned rocky and angled upward. There were no trees right at the lower edge, probably having been removed long ago for fuel or building material, but there were plenty of bushes scattered along the edge. Between two of the bushes was a path that snaked upslope through the undergrowth before disappearing into the clusters of small trees that began about twenty meters past the village edge.

The Troft aircar was hovering over the path, its rear crash plate shining with the light of the sun now hanging low in the western sky. Without breaking stride Anya stepped onto the path and headed up. Trying to look as confident as she did, Merrick followed.

The lower parts of the mountain were easy enough. The slope increased only gradually, and the potentially foot-tangling undergrowth and half-exposed tree roots were easily visible where they intruded across the path's mostly open ground. The slope itself was nothing that Merrick and his servos couldn't handle, though he kept a close eye on Anya to make sure he didn't look like he was having it too much easier than she was.

More of a problem was the sunlight, which first hid potential obstacles in long shadows, and then, as the sun sank below the trees, concealed everything in a uniform gloom. They kept at it long after Merrick expected, certainly longer than he could have made it safely without his opticals' light-amplification enhancers. Why Anya was pushing so hard he didn't know, and was rather afraid to ask.

It was approaching full dark when her reason finally became clear. Rounding one final stand of scrubby trees, they stepped out into a thirty-meter-wide clearing with a small but sturdy-looking hut at one edge. "We'll spend the night there," she said, pointing to the hut. "It will be safer and more comfortable than sleeping beneath the sky."

"Assuming the Trofts don't commandeer it," Merrick murmured, looking at the aircar now settling to the ground at the opposite end of the clearing.

"They will stay with their vehicle," Anya predicted. "There's wood in the shed behind the hut—bring two or three pieces and some kindling, and I'll start a fire. Then I'll hunt our dinner."

By the time Merrick returned with the wood Anya had cleared the brush from a fire pit a few meters in front of the hut and added some kindling. "Put it here," she directed.

[The male human slave, he will come here.]

Merrick looked across the clearing. The two Trofts were standing in the gloom beside their aircar, gazing through a gap in the trees toward the forest stretching out beneath them, the tops of the distant trees catching the last hint of glow from the western sky. [The male human slave, he will come here,] the first Troft repeated more sharply. [A puzzle, the male human slave will explain it to us.]

Merrick flashed a look at Anya. [The male human slave, he cannot speak,] she reminded them, getting to her feet and gesturing Merrick to follow. [The puzzle, perhaps I can explain it.]

[The explanation, we will hear it,] the first Troft said.

A moment later, Merrick and Anya stopped beside the aliens. [The puzzle, may I hear it?] Anya asked.

[The puzzle, it is there,] the first Troft said, pointing out across the forest and handing Anya a small nightscope. [A gap in the trees, there is one. A naturally formed gap, it does not appear to be one.]

Anya took the scope and pressed it to her eye. Peering over her shoulder, Merrick activated his telescopics and keyed up his light-amps.

There was a gap in the woods, all right. It was long and narrow, more like a tear in some exotic fabric than any normal clearing. His opticals marked it as just over twenty-five kilometers away and about half a kilometer from the road he and the others had come in on.

[The gap, perhaps it was created by disease,] Anya suggested. [The gap, it doesn't look like it was created by fire.]

[Yet the gap, its edges show evidence of fire,] the second Troft pointed out. [A fire, what form of it burns only small areas?]

[The answer, I don't have one,] Anya admitted.

Merrick frowned, notching up his opticals a bit more. The Troft was right—the trees at the edge of the gap *did* appear to have been scorched.

Abruptly, he stiffened. It hadn't been a fire. It had been a crash. Some large aircraft or small spaceship had gone down at that spot, cutting a swath through the trees and scorching them as the ship itself burned or disintegrated.

Only it hadn't been just a random spaceship, he realized suddenly. It had been one of the transports bringing in razorarms from Qasama. *That* was how the predators he and the group had encountered had ended up so far from Gangari. Some of them must have survived the crash and set up housekeeping right there.

He frowned. He'd solved the alleged puzzle from twenty-five kilometers away, in the darkness, after barely thirty seconds of study. Were these Trofts really so stupid that they couldn't figure it out, too?

Unless they *had* figured it out, and this was a test to see if Merrick and Anya could do likewise. Or, worse, it was a test to see if they would give the true answer or else feign ignorance in hopes of hiding guilty knowledge.

And there was only one reason Merrick could think of for any such test.

Casually, he took a step backward, pretending he was trying to find a spot where he could see better. Out of the corner of his eye he could see now that both Trofts' radiator membranes were quivering with suppressed excitement.

They knew about the crash, all right. This was a test to see how Merrick reacted to that knowledge.

They were on to him.

His first impulse was to run. To kill the Trofts, grab their aircar, and run. There was a whole forest out there where he could hide. Maybe even a whole planet.

Only he couldn't. He couldn't shoot down a pair of Trofts in cold blood that way, no more than he'd been able to do it back on Qasama. He could stun them, of course, but that would buy him even less time than killing them would.

In fact, as the adrenaline rush faded and his mind started working again he realized that running would be the absolute worst thing he could do. If this was a test to smoke out a possible spy they would surely have backup waiting for him to make his move. He would most likely barely get the aircar off the ground before he would be surrounded and forced down again.

And even if he somehow got clear, what would happen to Anya and Gangari? Henson had warned them not to come back without the two Trofts. Did that mean there were already threats hanging over the village?

He took a second sideways look at the Trofts' radiator membranes. They were still quivering.

But they weren't stretched out the way he would have expected for a pair of aliens facing an enemy Cobra. That suggested they had no idea who he actually was.

In fact, as he studied the membranes and the Trofts' infrared facial patterns more closely, he realized it wasn't even clear that they knew for a fact he and Anya were spies.

Which made sense. The theft of the food bars aboard the slave ship might have been noticed without the aliens having any idea which human or humans had been responsible. These two Trofts might be nothing more than the first-pass investigators, sent here to poke around and see if there were any slaves they could definitely cross off the suspect list.

[The male human slave, he will look at it,] the first Troft said, taking the scope from Anya and thrusting it toward Merrick.

Merrick took a careful breath. *Steady . . .* Taking a step closer to the trees, deliberately putting the Trofts at his back like a slave with nothing to fear, he keyed off his opticals and pressed the scope to his eye.

The first decision had been made: he wasn't going to run. Now for the second, equally crucial question: what exactly would a totally innocent, non-spy slave make of the gap in the woods? Especially a slave who had no idea that the Trofts had been importing razorarms onto Muninn?

Once again, the question turned out to have a straightforward answer. The Trofts' nightscope had even better telescopics than Merrick's own opticals, and seen through it, the gash in the foliage was clearly and obviously the result of some cataclysmic event. Only a fool, and a blind fool at that, could conclude otherwise.

And no matter how innocent a slave he was, Merrick decided, he certainly wasn't a foolish one. Handing the scope back to the Troft, he used his hands to pantomime an aircraft plowing through the trees on its way to a fiery crash landing.

[The answer, you are certain of it?] the first Troft asked, eyeing Merrick closely as he rolled the scope gently between his fingers.

Merrick shrugged, holding his hands palm upwards. [The answer, he is not completely certain of it,] Anya translated. [But the answer, it seems reasonable to him.]

For a moment the Trofts looked at each other in silence. Then, to Merrick's cautious relief, their membranes folded back down onto their arms. If it wasn't the exact response they were looking for, it was apparently close enough. [The answer, we will ponder it,] the first Troft said. [Your work, you may return to it.]

[The order, we obey it,] Anya said as she and Merrick both bowed to the aliens.

They returned to the fire pit and knelt down beside it. "I don't understand," Anya murmured as Merrick adjusted the chunks of wood on top of the kindling. "Why did they ask such a question of us?"

"I think one of their ships went down over there," Merrick murmured back. "Looks to me like they wanted to see what we knew about it."

"How could we know anything?" she asked, sounding bewildered. "Such an event would have left smoke and odor lingering in the air for days afterward. Yet we only arrived yesterday. Surely they know that."

"One would certainly assume so," Merrick agreed, casually turning his head. Out of the corner of his eye he saw that the Trofts were working on their aircar, reconfiguring the couches into the flatter mode used for sleeping. Apparently, they were planning to spend the night up here instead of returning to their base and rejoining the winghunt in the morning.

On the plus side, he could see nothing in their movements or the positioning of their radiator membranes to indicate extra stress or excitement. "Even if they're suspicious of us, I doubt they'll do anything until they see how we do at winghunting tomorrow," he went on. "That'll be the real test of whether we're who we say we are."

Anya was silent a moment. "Only, you aren't," she said.

"Not yet," Merrick admitted. "But hopefully, I will be by morning. Or at least good enough to fake it."

"Without getting yourself killed?"

Merrick swallowed. "Definitely," he agreed, still studying the Trofts. Everything *seemed* to have settled down.

But something still wasn't right.

"Is there trouble?" Anya asked.

"I don't know," Merrick said, trying to chase down the troubled feeling whispering through him. "So there was a crash, and they wanted to see our reaction to it. But why? Usually there's nothing all that noteworthy about a crash—equipment fails, the weather goes crazy when they're trying to land, or the pilot just makes a mistake."

"Yet this crash seems important to them," Anya said slowly. "Could it have been something other than an accident?"

"You mean sabotage?"

"Sabotage from within, or destruction from without," she said. "Perhaps it was attacked, either from the sky or from the ground."

Merrick shivered. A successful attack deep in their territory would definitely get the Drims to stand up and notice.

And how and from where that attack had come was a bit of information that could end up being crucial. To the Trofts, but also to Merrick. "I need to get a look at the crash site," he said, running the numbers through his mind. From the previous night's encampment he knew the darkness would last about ten hours. Getting back down the mountain, a twenty-five-kilometer jog down the road, through the forest to the crash site, then reverse the process . . .

"No," Anya said, her hand snaking out to grab his wrist. "Not now. Please. If they catch you—"

"Hey, relax," Merrick said, reaching over to pull her hand off his arm.

"No," she said, her grip tightening. "You can't do this."

"It's all right, Anya," Merrick soothed, wincing a little. He'd known she was strong, but she had some serious reserves in those slender fingers. "I'm not going anywhere. Not tonight. I'll wait until we're off the mountain and the Trofts have left. Okay?"

She stared into his eyes, though how much she could see of his expression in the dim starlight he couldn't guess. Then, slowly, the grip on his wrist eased and she took her hand away. "The dark memory the master spoke of earlier," she said, her voice full of old and distant pain. "I don't want my village to go through that again. Ever."

"I understand," Merrick said, wishing he actually did. Maybe it was just as well that he didn't.

Abruptly, Anya stood up. "Finish the fire," she ordered, pulling a knife from beneath her jacket. "I'll go find us some food."

"You want me to come with you?" Merrick asked, starting to also stand up.

"No," she said tartly, her hand pressing down on his shoulder.

"You sure?" Merrick asked, eyeing her closely.

Her shoulders sagged a bit. "I'm sure," she said again, more quietly this time. "I would like to have time alone."

"Sure," Merrick said, lowering himself back into a crouch as he keyed his infrareds. Once again, her face was a tangle of unreadable emotions. "If there's any trouble, just give me a shout."

"I will," she promised. "Have the fire ready." She shifted her eyes across the clearing to the Trofts. "After we eat, we'll begin your instruction."

Merrick felt his stomach tighten. Hanging beneath a piece of cloth hundreds of meters above the ground... "Sounds good," he said. "Don't worry. It'll be all right."

"Yes," she murmured. "It will."

CHAPTER SIXTEEN

The news filtered in slowly from Archway, in bits and pieces, half of them genuine news, the other half unfounded rumors. The fact that the comm connections between Bitter Creek and the rest of DeVegas province were running a fitful on-again-off-again pattern didn't help.

But gradually the horrifying picture became clear.

Lorne was out in the forest, hunting spine-leopard way stations, when the news of the mob action at Yates Fabrications came through. He was taking a short, restless nap when the factory's sabotage was reported.

He was in Mayor McDougal's store, reporting that the last way station had been cleared out, when he learned about the slaughter.

"I'm so sorry," McDougal said quietly as Lorne stared at the report on the mayor's comboard. "I'm so very sorry."

Lorne nodded mechanically, his eyes frozen to the short list of names.

Bates. Jankos. Harper. Men he'd known. Men he'd worked and fought beside. Men with whom he'd shared meals, drinks, laughter, danger, and curses. Three Cobras dead.

Three Cobras murdered.

"Do we know what happened?" he asked, his voice sounding like a stranger's in his ears. "I mean, what *really* happened?"

"Not really," McDougal said, the anger in her voice a match for the fury roiling through Lorne's gut. "And I doubt we will anytime soon. You can see the Dominion wrote that piece and just slapped it in under Harry's name. They didn't even bother to match his style. They're in charge of all news. Probably all comm and radio activity, too."

"First rule of conquest," Lorne murmured, still staring at the names.

The deaths were bad enough. But what was worse were the two names that *weren't* in the report.

Because they should have been. His parents had been on the outskirts of Archway when he last talked to them, heading in to check on the supposed riot that Sergeant Khahar had talked about, and neither of them was the sort to stay in the background when there was danger or trouble. An article that took the time to name all the so-called ringleaders of the so-called mob should certainly have included Paul or Jasmine Broom in that roster. The deliberate lack of such a mention could only mean one thing.

Reivaro had taken them.

In fact, the more Lorne thought about it, the more he wondered if the entire confrontation had been staged deliberately to draw his parents into a situation where the Dominion could manufacture an excuse for a grab.

But maybe it wasn't too late for him to get them back.

"I have to go," he said, looking up. "I have to get to Archway."

"No," McDougal said flatly.

Lorne stared at her. "What the hell is *that* supposed to mean? *No?*"

"It means you can't help them," McDougal said. "Your parents aren't in Archway anymore."

"And you know this how?"

"I know because the Dominion may be many things, but they're not stupid," McDougal said, nodding at the comboard. "Look at the time-stamp. It's been hours since the riot. If this was an excuse to declare martial law and grab your parents, they've long since done it."

"We don't know that," Lorne persisted. "And don't forget Chintawa. He'll be fighting this, fighting the whole martial law thing, at least fighting for jurisdiction over my parents. There's a fair chance they're still in limbo while Santores and the Dome thrash it out. If they are, I have to get down there."

McDougal shook her head. "You're not going."

A red haze seemed to settle in between Lorne and the woman. "How are you going to stop me?"

"Hopefully, with reason," McDougal said, the anger in her voice and face turned into something hard and cold. "First reason: as mayor of your assigned town, I'm still officially in charge of you. If I say you stay, you stay. Second reason—" A muscle in her jaw tightened. "I think that's exactly what they're hoping you'll do."

Lorne frowned. "What are you talking about?"

"Think about it," McDougal said. "The report comes in late and doesn't mention your parents. That provides the illusion that you still have a window in which to act. At the same time, it makes that window so small you have to act immediately, without taking time to think, or you risk losing your chance." She shook her head. "No, whatever it is they want your parents for, they want you, too."

Lorne's mind flashed back to the family's last dinner-table conversation. "I can't just sit here."

"I know you don't want to," McDougal said. "But it really is your best option. You saw what happened when they tried to come and get you. They're probably not anxious to go that route again. I say we make them. We make them choose between coming here in person, or giving up and leaving you alone." She looked through the window at the open area in front of the store. "And we make sure that if they *do* come back, we're ready and waiting."

Lorne looked down at the comboard, a dozen conflicting emotions swirling through his brain. The thought of just abandoning his parents was tearing him apart. But down deep, he knew McDougal was right.

Or at least she was half right. "No," he said.

"No what?" McDougal asked warily.

"We'll let them come for me," he said, looking up again. "But the people of Bitter Creek have already stuck their necks out far enough. From now on, I'll handle it myself."

For a moment McDougal eyed him measuringly. Then, she gave a soft snort. "You got sand, Broom—I'll give you that," she said. "But it's pretty stupid sand."

"Runs in my family," Lorne said, trying to force

humor he didn't feel. "If I don't see you again, thanks for everything—"

"Wait a second." McDougal pursed her lips tightly, a pained expression on her face. "Look, I don't know if I should say anything about this. But... okay, look. During the Troft occupation, the Cobras who weren't pinned down used to run raids against their encampments. I don't know much about it—we were too far away from Archway to give them much help, and the whole thing was a deep black secret. But I do know that their rendezvous point was somewhere at or near Braided Falls. You know that area?"

"Well enough," Lorne said. "Badj Werle used to talk about a little cave or something right behind the falls where he and his friends sometimes hung out when they were in school."

"It's more like an extra-deep indentation than an actual cave," McDougal said. "And I don't know if they met there or somewhere nearby—there might be other caves in that bluff that I don't know about. Regardless, if any other Cobras got away, that's probably where they'll gather. Think of it as a compromise between being an easy target in Archway or a lone duck in Bitter Creek."

"I'll keep it in mind," Lorne said. "But for now, this is where they'll be looking for me. It'd be a shame to disappoint them."

"Don't be an idiot," McDougal snapped, a flash of anger cracking through her calm exterior. "You don't even know what you're up against. Their weapons, their people—Broom, they're way beyond us in everything they've got. Be smart, go down to the Falls, and take the time to think this through."

"I have," Lorne said. In fact, to his own mild surprise a plan was already forming in the back of his mind. "And just for the record, Dill De Portola and I got a pretty good first approximation of their weapons systems yesterday morning. I think I can take them down."

"What, all by yourself?"

"Hardly." Lorne forced a smile. "Reivaro has his Marines. I have Aventine."

"I thought you didn't want our help."

"Not the people," Lorne corrected. "The planet." He peered out the window. "It's not Caelian. But I think it'll do."

The plan was simple enough in concept. The execution turned out to be much harder.

First there was the location to scout. Lorne spent a solid half hour trudging along Stony Creek before he found what he was looking for: a section of ground between a rotting log and the creek where years of spring overflows had washed out a narrow but relatively deep hollow. Equally important was the thick-trunked arrowcrest tree standing just behind the log with a set of branches stretching outward fifteen meters above the ground.

Finding the proper-sized rock was next. That part was much easier. As McDougal had pointed out earlier, the naming of Stony Creek hadn't required an abundance of imagination. A little hunting yielded a nice hard stone, which he tucked under a tuft of grass at the end of the hollow.

Capturing a spine leopard was next, and wasn't nearly so straightforward. Lorne had killed uncounted numbers of the predators during his years of Cobra service, but never before had he had to take one alive and unharmed.

It proved considerably trickier than he would ever have guessed. More than once during the stalking and chasing he wished he had Jody and her animal-physiology and management degrees with him. The trap she'd constructed for capturing predators on Caelian would have been even more useful.

Finally, with persistence and patience, he managed to corner a good-sized male and knock it out with a pair of shots from his stunner. He tied its legs together with the medical tape from his field pack and hauled it back to his hollow, securing it to the log with more tape to make doubly sure it didn't get away. A little experimentation showed that a low-level fingertip laser burst at close range would almost completely vaporize the tape.

And after that came the hardest part of all.

The waiting.

He spent the rest of the afternoon patrolling the forest. Not so much to protect anyone—the townspeople had either retreated indoors or were out in the relatively safe fields south and east of town doing last-minute crop work—but more to keep himself too busy to second-guess his decision. If McDougal was wrong about Archway being a trap, staying in Bitter Creek would probably lose him his only chance of freeing his parents.

On the other hand, by now it was probably too late for him to do anything no matter what had actually gone down at Yates Fabrications. He wasn't sure if that made him feel better or worse.

Evening had come and gone, and the first stars

were peeking through the darkening sky, when they finally came for him.

There were two of them, judging from the noise they made as they strode through the forest undergrowth. They seemed to be making no attempt to keep their presence secret, any more than they'd tried to hide the approach of the aircar they'd arrived in.

Though he suspected the aircar's wide, lazy circle had been driven less by showmanship than by the tactical necessity of mapping out the infrared signatures of all the townspeople before they came in for a landing. If that was true, they must surely have spotted Lorne out here in the forest. Hopefully, that meant they hadn't stopped in town first to browbeat Mayor McDougal.

Still, professional pride alone should have dictated a more stealthy approach toward their prey. Maybe their slaughter of the three Archway Cobras had convinced them of the superiority and strength of their weapons.

With a little luck on Lorne's part, they would learn that the race wasn't necessarily to the swift, nor the battle always to the strong.

He tracked their movements as they came deeper into the woods. Every so often he fired off a finger-tip laser as if he was still taking out spine leopards or other predators, giving the hunters glimpses of distant light that should continue to draw them in. The one glimpse he got of the pursuers through the trees showed that their Marine combat suits had been supplemented by close-fitting helmets and visors, the latter probably including nightscope capabilities.

After that look Lorne made sure to stay completely out of their sight, relying on his audio enhancers to keep track of their movements.

The hunt had been going on for about twenty minutes when their patience finally ran out. "Broom?" Sergeant Khahar's voice boomed through the trees. "Come on, Broom, this is ridiculous. We know you're here, and you know you can't hide forever. Come out and make it easy on all of us, okay?"

"We promise we won't kill you," Chimm added. "Our orders are to bring you in alive."

Lorne glanced around, giving himself a quick orientation. The Marines were probably thirty meters away; the trussed spine leopard no more than five. Time to make his move. "Go away!" he called back, using the cover of his voice to move quickly through the leaves and grass to the ambush point. "I'm busy."

The spine leopard glared up at him as he came around the arrowcrest tree, its mouth half open, its extended forearm spines showing its anger and frustration. Lorne stepped up to it, a sudden and unexpected qualm rippling through him. Normally, spine leopards were killed in the heat of combat, in self defense or defense of others. The thought of killing a helpless animal—of any sort—was unpleasant and more than a little heart-rending.

But he had no choice. Steeling himself, he raised his right hand and fired three shots through the predator's kill points.

It dropped without a sound, its spines relaxing in death. Quickly, trying not to think about what he'd just done, Lorne fired three more bursts into the predator's tether and the tape around its legs, leaving no obvious indications of its recent captivity. Lifting up the carcass, he lowered himself into the hollow and laid the dead animal on top of him. He pushed up the edge of the body just enough with his left hand to allow him a narrow view slit beneath it, looking out toward the creek. With his right hand, he picked up the rock.

He'd been in position for exactly fourteen seconds when there was a faint crackling sound near the edge of his vision and the two Marines stepped into view.

"Damn him, anyway," Chimm muttered, swinging his head and torso back and forth, his voice just barely audible even through Lorne's enhancers. "Where the *hell's* he gotten to?"

"He can't be far," Khahar muttered as they came to a stop three meters away from the spine leopard Lorne was hiding beneath. "That's a fresh kill—probably the one he was just shooting at. Freeze."

Both men stiffened into statues. Lorne held his breath, wondering if they'd somehow spotted him beneath the spine leopard's heat signature.

"Nothing," Chimm said, looking around again. "He's gone to ground, all right."

"Or to sky," Khahar said, peering up at the branches of the arrowcrest towering above him and then doing a quick scan of the surrounding trees. "Probably hoping we'll get close enough for a quick two-shot."

Chimm snorted. "Lot of good *that'll* do him."

"I'd shelve the strut if I were you," Khahar warned. "I've seen the specs, and those antiarmor lasers are nothing to sniff at. If that Cobra in Archway had been able to get off a second shot, and if Rivelon had taken the first in the heart instead of the stomach, he'd be very dead right now."

There was a moment of silence as Chimm digested that. "So what do we do?"

"We flank him," Khahar said, giving the trees one final sweep and then starting an equally methodical ground-level survey. "Antiarmor's in the leg—limits how fast he can shoot in opposite directions."

"Good plan," Chimm said. "One problem: how in hell do we flank him when we don't know where he is?"

"Oh, I know exactly where he is," Khahar said with malicious satisfaction. "Right up there, off that little bend in the creek. See it?"

"You mean that eddy pool?"

"That's the one," Khahar said. "Why did you think I pointed it out to you on our way in? It's the perfect spot for an ambush: he's invisible, his IR profile is blocked by cold water, and he'll even be able to hear us when we start splashing water toward him." He did another slow circle. "And he's nowhere else. He's there, all right."

"If you say so," Chimm said, clearly not convinced. "You want me to cross over?"

"I'll go," Khahar said. "There's a spot about thirty meters back where I can cross without touching the water. Even if he's listening, he won't hear me. Wait until I'm on your nine, then we'll head toward him together." He pointed again toward the pool. "And keep an eye on those reeds along the edge—he's probably breathing through one of them. One of them moves, mark it and we'll know exactly where he is."

"Got it," Chimm said, giving the area around him a quick look. "Just make it snappy. This place gives me the creeps."

"If I see any birdies, I'll tell them not to warble too loud," Khahar said sarcastically. "Watch out for the trees—they're pretty scary, too."

He backed out of Lorne's view, disappearing into the woods. Chimm muttered a curse under his breath, took a final look around, then settled himself to watch the eddy pool as he'd been ordered.

It would take about thirty seconds, Lorne knew, for Khahar to reach the narrow spot in the creek that he assumed the Marine was heading for. The optimal timing would be to give him just long enough to get there, but not enough to start across. Twenty-five seconds, he decided, and it would be time.

He fingered the rock in his right hand, freshly aware of the awful risk he was taking with Chimm's life. The stone was twice the size of Lorne's fist: heavy, relatively smooth, and extensively marbled with different types of rock. His theory in choosing it was that under the sudden heat stress of a laser blast it would shatter into a dozen good-sized fragments.

Lorne had seen how Dominion Marine parrot guns functioned against relatively large targets like spine leopards. The crucial question was how well they would do against something the size of the rock. If they worked as Lorne hoped, Chimm would end up merely unconscious, probably with only minimal physical damage.

If they didn't, the Marine would end up dead.

Fifteen seconds. Lorne set his teeth together, trying to shift his focus from Chimm's life to the deaths of the three Cobras in Archway. Whether or not Chimm or Khahar had been directly involved in that incident, they were part of the Dominion and they shared its guilt. He would do his best to preserve their lives, but he would give no guarantees.

Five seconds. Lorne tightened his grip on the stone and eased his left hand along the spine leopard's underside to rest against its lower torso, right at its center of mass. Taking a deep breath, his mind flashing back to his memories of the war on Qasama, he settled his mind into combat mode.

The timer hit zero. Bracing himself against the damp ground, he convulsively straightened his left elbow, throwing all the power of his arm, chest, and hip servos into the effort, and lobbed the carcass in a high arc straight at Chimm's back.

The darkness of the forest exploded into a brilliant strobe-light display of blue light as the parrot guns' defensive programming kicked into full gear, blasting every laser in the Marine's epaulets at the incoming threat.

And as the already dead animal began to disintegrate into a cloud of smoke and blackened skin, Lorne threw the rock as hard as he could at Chimm's head.

The parrot guns tried their best, spotting the new threat and retasking some of the lasers to deal with it. But too many of them were already engaged, and the rock had a much higher heat capacity than living tissue, and there simply wasn't enough time. The stone shattered into fragments under the barrage, just as Lorne had anticipated, and those fragments slammed with devastating force into the back and side of Chimm's helmet.

The helmet was strong enough to take the impact without serious damage. Chimm's skull wasn't. Without a sound, he toppled to the ground, the charred spine leopard carcass landing with a second muffled thud across him. Scrambling to his feet, Lorne bent his knees and jumped.

He was crouched on a branch in the arrowcrest tree directly above Chimm when Khahar burst into view.

If Khahar had had another few seconds he might have suspected a trap. With a few seconds more, he might have noticed that the dead spine leopard he'd seen beside the log earlier was missing. But he didn't have any of those seconds. His partner was on the ground, there was a predator lying across him, and in that first instant there would be no doubt whatsoever in his mind as to what had happened. Sprinting through the last few clumps of bushes, glancing reflexively around him as he ran, he reached Chimm's side.

And as he started to crouch down into a crouch beside the unconscious Marine, Lorne dropped out of the tree.

Once again, the defense system did its best. But the Marines were ground forces, and their parrot guns had clearly been designed to deal with threats coming mainly from ground level. The lasers once again blazed into action, sizzling out a V-shaped wedge of fire as Lorne dropped toward his target. But they couldn't shoot straight up, and the design and width of the epaulets meant that even the sharpest angles of fire were too wide to deal with the threat coming from the sky.

The lasers were still firing uselessly when Lorne's boots crashed down onto Khahar's shoulders, crushing his epaulets and parrot guns and slamming the Marine to the ground beside Chimm and the spine leopard.

The parrot guns cut off, and darkness flowed back into the forest. Blinking a couple of times against the afterimages, keying in his opticals to take up the slack while his eyes adjusted, Lorne stepped off Khahar and knelt beside the two Marines. If he'd miscalculated with either of his attacks...

To his relief, he hadn't. Both men were still breathing, their heart rates slow but steady. Chimm would likely awake to a severe headache and probably a mild concussion, and Khahar would awake to some broken bones and maybe a concussion of his own. But they *would* awake.

And with that, Lorne had another decision to make.

He straightened up, his body trembling with adrenaline reaction as he gazed down at the unconscious Marines. By now, his parents were long gone from Archway—that was pretty much a given. As far as he knew, the Dominion shuttles were only landing in Capitalia, and there was still a chance the prisoners were on hold somewhere in the Dome while Chintawa and Santores thrashed out jurisdiction. If Lorne was fast enough, there was a chance he could get there before any final decisions were made.

But it was a slim chance. Legal limbo or not, his parents would certainly be under the watch of more Dominion Marines. Lorne had been able to set the stage here in the DeVegas forest, and he'd been lucky. He couldn't count on having either of those advantages the next time.

The alternative was to go into hiding. That one had a much higher chance of success. He knew DeVegas province far better than Reivaro did, not just its geography but also its people. Even under martial law, there would probably be some who would be willing to hide him while he figured out his next move.

Finally, there was the Braided Falls thing McDougal had mentioned. If there were still supplies and equipment there, and if he could find them, he might be able to get by for awhile without having to involve the locals at all.

He looked down at the two Marines. The smart move, he knew, would be to go to ground.

But then, no one had ever accused him of being smart.

Half an hour later he was in the Marines' aircar, burning through the night sky. With luck, Khahar's failure to capture him wouldn't be reported until he'd reached his destination.

If it was ... well, he'd face that bridge when he got to it.

CHAPTER SEVENTEEN

Jody was in the middle of a restless dream about being caught in one of her own animal traps when she was startled awake by a sudden thud against her door.

She stared into the darkness, her heart pounding, trying to sort out the dream from reality. The thud had sounded like a knock, but up until now none of the Dominion people had ever bothered to request permission before entering her cell.

Could it have been something from the ship's engines? That was an even more terrifying thought than her dream. If Tamu was starting up the *Squire's* engines it either meant he'd succeeded in getting Omnathi aboard or else had given up and decided to settle for the half-loaf that was Jody herself.

And then, across the room, the door slid open to reveal the figure of a man silhouetted against the corridor light.

Or rather, two men. One was standing, the other was crumpled in a heap on the floor.

"Jody Moreau?" a voice murmured.

"Yes," Jody said, throwing off the blankets and jumping out of bed, a trickle of cautious relief whispering through her. There was only one group of people who habitually and stubbornly emphasized the Moreau side of her family. "Djinni Ghushtre?"

"Yes," Ghushtre confirmed. "Come—we must hurry."

"Right," Jody said, already pulling on her silliweave tunic and trousers. Grabbing her shoes, she padded quickly to the door. "Ready—"

From somewhere in the near distance came a high-pitched sound, more felt than heard, and suddenly the universe twisted violently around on its ear. Jody grabbed for the door jamb, missed, and was heading face-first toward the floor when Ghushtre caught her arm and steadied her. "Careful," he warned, his attention on something down the corridor.

"I'm okay," Jody said, focusing on Ghushtre's chest as the world slowly straightened out again. She tried again for the door jamb, made it this time, then leaned close to Ghushtre and looked past him down the corridor.

Just in time to see one of the other Qasamans a few doors down fire a burst of current from his hand into one of the room locks. The door slid open in response, and there was another disorienting jolt as the Qasaman fired a sonic burst into the room. He paused for a moment, possibly assessing the situation, then moved briskly toward the next door in line.

Jody caught her breath. The Qasaman had fired that lightning bolt from his hand. Not from a Djinn combat-suit glove, but from his bare hand.

Ghushtre and his companion weren't Djinn. They were Cobras.

She turned her eyes back to Ghushtre. "Indeed," he confirmed, an edge of grim amusement in his voice as he helped her the rest of the way through the doorway and pointed toward the ship's bow. "We must leave while Kaza clears the rest of the sleeping soldiers from our backtrail."

"Right," Jody said as they headed down the corridor. "Remember that there will probably be a couple more Marines in full combat gear by the hatchway."

"That's as expected," Ghushtre said. "If we can take them by surprise we'll be all right."

Jody nodded, bracing herself as another burst of sonic came from behind them. From what she'd seen of the Marine combat suits she wasn't at all sure taking them by surprise would even be possible. But Ghushtre seemed to know what he was doing, and this was no time to stop and discuss it.

In fact, maybe the third Qasaman, Nisti, was already on it. From what she'd seen of Qasamans, she wouldn't be at all surprised to find the sentries already sprawled unconscious on the ground outside the ship.

She and Ghushtre were within ten meters of the hatchway when the question suddenly became moot. Two Marines suddenly appeared around the corner from the short entryway corridor, still very much conscious. They stopped in the center of the corridor, their parrot gun epaulets gleaming in the corridor light, their stance practically dripping with arrogance and challenge.

Ghushtre braked to a halt, pulling Jody back and then pushing her another meter behind him. Again she fought for balance as a Cobra sonic echoed off the walls and ceiling.

But the off-duty Marines and crewers that Kaza was stunning behind her weren't wearing combat suits. This pair was, and the sonic washed over them without any noticeable effect. Ghushtre fired a second burst, then began backing away, his grip on Jody's arm giving her no choice but to retreat with him.

If he was expecting the Marines to just stand there and watch, that hope didn't last very long. "Halt!" one of the Marines ordered, and in unison they strode forward toward the retreating prisoners.

"No!" Ghushtre called back, increasing his pace.

"Wait," Jody protested, trying to free her arm from Ghushtre's grip. Backing away from the Marines did nothing but move them further from the hatch and freedom. They needed to stand their ground, maybe duck into one of the rooms and fight from there. Anything except retreat. The Dominion wanted Jody alive—maybe she and Ghushtre could use that fact to advance on the Marines with Jody in front. If she could prevent them from using their parrot guns until Ghushtre was close enough to bring one of his other weapons into play, they might still have a chance. She opened her mouth to suggest it—

Without warning, Ghushtre screamed.

Jody jerked with surprise and shock at the completely unexpected sound. Her whole body twitched, her feet stumbling and threatening to tangle with each other. The Marines, as unaffected by the scream as they had been by the sonics, merely kept coming.

They'd made it three more steps when the plate over the storage bin they were crossing exploded upward, carrying both Marines with it and slamming them with bone-breaking force into the low ceiling.

There was a muffled grunt from one of them, and then men and plate clattered to the floor and lay still.

It was only then, as Nisti hopped calmly out of the open bin, that Jody belatedly realized what had just happened. "Take them by surprise," she said.

"A weapon that cannot fire downward begs to be turned against its owner," Ghushtre said calmly as he reversed direction and again pulled her along with him toward the hatchway. Nisti was already on his way, and out of the corner of her eye Jody saw that Kaza was sprinting up behind them. "Quickly, now, before reinforcements can be brought against us."

They reached the hatch without encountering any further trouble. The heavy door was closed, but the instructions for opening it were printed on its surface in white letters. Nisti headed for the control board and keyed in the printed opening sequence. Ghushtre strode past him to the door itself, grabbed the wheel in the center, and tried to turn it.

The wheel didn't budge. "Again," Ghushtre murmured.

Nisti was already rekeying the command. "Try now," he said.

But the wheel still wouldn't turn. "We blast it," Ghushtre decided, taking a couple of steps back and giving Jody a shove that sent her three quick steps farther than that. He shifted his weight onto his right leg and lifted his left, aiming his antiarmor laser at the hatch's edge.

"Don't bother," a voice came from a speaker over the control board. "That's forty centimeters of solid hullmetal. It would take you hours to burn a hole through it."

Jody frowned. It was Lieutenant Commander Tamu, but his voice was so stiff and tense that for that first moment it was almost unrecognizable.

"Very clever," Tamu continued in that same taut voice. "Come in pretending to be Qasaman Djinn, only you're actually Qasaman Cobras. I can see why Nissa Gendreves and the others are so upset that Paul Broom gave Isis to you."

Ghushtre made a series of quick hand gestures. Kaza and Nisti nodded and headed silently up the stairway. "If you know of Isis, you know what we are capable of," Ghushtre called toward the speaker. "I also do not believe it will take more than an hour for us to open the hatch. Shall we make a test of it?"

"You open fire on that hatch, and you'll live to regret it," Tamu warned. "This isn't a freighter or pleasure vessel, Ghushtre. It's a ship of war."

"I thought it was a courier," Jody murmured.

"Even couriers of the Dominion Fleet are ships of war," Tamu countered. "We have two gunbays, fully armed and armored. Both are manned, and both are locked off and inaccessible to you. In addition, there are still four combat-suited Dominion Marines inside Stronghold. If you take any further action against me, I'll order retribution against the people of Caelian."

"Have a care, Commander Tamu," Ghushtre said, his voice dark. "Action against unarmed civilians would bring more destruction upon you than you can dream of."

"There's no need for violence," Jody put in quickly. Qasamans had a low threshold for threats, and she had no desire to learn where Ghushtre's trigger point was. "All we want is for you to go away and leave us alone. Open the hatch and let us out, and we can be done with this."

"You know I can't do that," Tamu said. "Commodore Santores needs to see you."

"I thought I was just a small fish."

"I'd be happy to trade you for something bigger," Tamu said. "Counter-offer: if you and your companions surrender now, I promise there will be no repercussions for your actions of the past few minutes."

"There will be no surrender," Ghushtre said flatly. "But you speak of a trade. Let me offer a different such bargain: your life for ours."

The speaker hissed with Tamu's snort. "Clearly, you're unfamiliar with Dominion warships," he said. "Just as the gunbays are sealed, so are CoNCH and engineering. You can't get in, not even with Cobra weaponry, any more than you can blast your way out through the hatch."

Frowning, Jody peered back down the corridor. Sure enough, the door she'd seen yesterday leading into the engineering section was closed.

And though it was hard to tell at this distance, it looked to be the same material as the hatchway and the *Squire*'s hull.

"So we have a stalemate," Ghushtre said.

"Not for long," Tamu said. "The Marines in Stronghold are preparing to move on the Government Building. Their orders are to take Uy and Omnathi into custody and bring them here."

"They will not succeed," Ghushtre warned. "Not four men. Not against a world full of Cobras and Djinn."

"I think they will," Tamu said. "Shall we make a test of it?"

Jody frowned. Suddenly, something that had been nagging at the back of her mind came into focus.

The ship was quiet. *Extremely* quiet, with only the soft whooshing of the air system to fill the gaps in the threat-filled conversation.

Only it shouldn't be. Tamu was under attack from within and was facing the possibility of threat from without. Even more telling, he'd threatened in turn to open fire on the people of Stronghold.

A definite and serious threat, assuming Tamu wasn't lying about the gunbays . . . except that the *Squire* wasn't in any position to carry it out. It was sitting here in the landing area, hundreds of meters from the city itself. The only way for Tamu to bring his guns to bear—on anyone—would be to physically raise his ship and fly it over there.

So why hadn't he started his engines? There was only one reason Jody could think of.

And if she was right . . .

"This is ridiculous," she spoke up, cutting off whatever threat or counter-threat Ghushtre had been starting to make. "Shahni Omnathi doesn't have any idea where Qasama is, so if that's what you're going for you're out of luck. But if Commodore Santores really just wants to talk to him—as an equal—then I say let's do it and get it over with."

Ghushtre was staring at her in disbelief. Jody shook her head quickly, lifted a finger to her lips. His eyes narrowed, but he nodded.

"What do you suggest?" Tamu asked cautiously, apparently just as surprised as Ghushtre.

"We bring His Excellency and his entourage aboard and fly them to Aventine," Jody said. "He and Santores have a chat, and when they're done you bring him back. Nice, neat, and no one gets hurt."

"If he refuses?"

"I think I can persuade him," Jody said. "He doesn't want bloodshed any more than the rest of us do. Get me an open channel to the Government Building and let me talk to him."

There was a short pause. "One moment," Tamu said.

Abruptly, an odd hum filled the air. "What are you doing?" Ghushtre murmured.

Jody frowned; and then the humming sound clicked. It was the special Cobra sonic frequency designed for suppressing bugs and other listening and recording devices. Ghushtre was making sure Tamu wouldn't be eavesdropping on their conversation. "Tamu's threatened to starting shooting at Stronghold," she murmured back. "But he hasn't fired up his engines—if he had, we'd hear them. The only explanation for why he hasn't is that he can't."

"We've done no damage to any major equipment," Ghushtre said, frowning.

"I think the equipment is fine," Jody said. "It's the *people* who aren't in position. Tamu may have gotten himself and his gunners behind locked doors, but either the pilots or the engine room crew didn't make it to their stations before he locked everything down."

Ghushtre peered down the corridor toward the engine room door. "You suggest we stunned them when we were neutralizing the personnel on this deck?"

"Or else Tamu panicked and locked the doors before they could get there," Jody said. "Were you poking around upstairs earlier?"

Ghushtre nodded. "We retrieved our combat suits

immediately after escaping our cell. Commander Tamu wasn't in his cabin at the time."

"Then that's probably what happened," Jody said, nodding. "He returned to his cabin after you got the suits, realized you were loose, ducked into whatever this CoNCH thing is—probably the command room—and hit the panic button. Maybe literally."

"And he can't open it again because he fears an ambush."

"Because he doesn't know exactly where all of you are," Jody confirmed. "If I'm right, we should be able to use all this against him. Did your combat suits include the usual sleep-gas canisters?"

"Yes," Ghushtre said. "But if the control and engine doors are properly sealed, the gas won't be able to enter."

"We don't need it to," Jody said. "I'm hoping I can get Tamu to open up the door."

Ghushtre's eyes were steady on her. "Using His Excellency as bait?"

Jody's mouth suddenly felt dry. Qasaman loyalty was right up there with Qasaman ingenuity and dedication, and even suggesting the idea of a hint of betrayal could be an extremely unhealthy thing for her to do. "I think it's the only way, Ifrit Ghushtre," she said as calmly as she could. "You have to trust me."

"I trust you with my life, Jody Moreau," Ghushtre said. "I'm not sure I trust you with His Excellency's life."

There was click from the speaker. "Broom? Are you still there?"

The hum of Ghushtre's sonic disappeared. "I'm here, Commander," Jody said. "You have a connection?"

There was another click— "Ms. Broom, this is Governor Uy," Uy said, his heavy formal tone showing he knew Tamu was listening in. "I understand you have a proposal for us?"

"I'm just trying to avoid bloodshed," Jody said, acutely aware of Ghushtre standing close behind her. "I thought that if Shahni Omnathi and his people were willing to go to Aventine and talk with Commodore Santores, this whole standoff thing could end here and now."

There was a short pause. "You really think that's a good idea?" Uy asked.

"I think it's the only way," Jody said. "Commander Tamu has everything locked up tight, and he's threatening to fly over Stronghold and take potshots at anything that moves."

"Is he, now?" Uy said, and Jody could sense fresh interest beneath the formal tone. "Do I have to remind him that such action would constitute an act of war?"

"There's no such thing as war between member worlds of the Dominion of Man," Tamu put in. "It's a legal impossibility. All the law allows for is rebellion and corrective action."

"My mistake," Uy said stiffly. "Tell me, Commander: if His Excellency agreed to accompany you, what guarantees would you offer for his safe conduct to Aventine and his subsequent safe return?"

Jody felt her heartbeat pick up. The fact that Uy was even suggesting he might hand over Omnathi was proof that he'd caught her hint, confirmed the *Squire*'s lack of engine emissions, and had come to the same conclusion she had.

"As a foreign head of state, he's entitled to full diplomatic protection," Tamu said, so sincerely that Jody almost believed him. "I also give you my personal pledge that he'll be returned safely to Caelian, or anywhere else he wishes to go."

"Such as Qasama?"

"Anywhere he wishes to go," Tamu repeated. "The *Squire* is completely at his disposal."

"Good to hear," Uy said. "And Jody Broom?"

"She can accompany Shahni Omnathi to Aventine or stay here on Caelian," Tamu said. "Her choice."

There was another moment of silence. Uy consulting with Harli and the other Cobras? Possibly with Omnathi himself? "If His Excellency was willing, what procedure would you wish to follow?" Uy asked.

"I have four Marines still in Stronghold," Tamu said. "They could meet Shahni Omnathi and his entourage at the door of the Government Building and escort them here to the *Squire*. Once they're aboard, Ms. Broom will be allowed to leave if she chooses."

"I presume that by *escort him here* you mean they would fly together in an aircar?"

"I could certainly send an aircar for him," Tamu agreed. "I don't trust my Marines in one of yours, of course. Confined spaces, limited fields of fire—I'm sure you understand."

"I understand only that I have no intention of letting His Excellency simply disappear into an aircar niche inside your ship before Ms. Broom has the opportunity to leave," Uy countered. "You can send your aircar, but it will stop at least fifty meters from your ramp, and Ms. Broom and Shahni Omnathi will emerge into the open at the same time. They'll cross in plain sight of all of us, and then she can choose whether or not to return to the ship and travel with him to Aventine."

Jody clenched her teeth. Uy and Omnathi had deduced her plan, all right.

Except they'd only deduced half of it. They'd figured out that she was planning to use the sleep-gas canisters on Omnathi and the Marines, but they were assuming she herself would be the one to set them off.

And that half by itself would be disastrous. Gassing everyone that far away from the *Squire*'s hatch would undoubtedly leave the party still in range of the ship's gunbays. With Ghushtre and his companions still on the loose inside the ship, the situation would once again settle into a stalemate.

Except that the stalemate would now include Omnathi lying helpless in Tamu's sights.

And she couldn't warn Uy about the gunbays. Not without tipping off Tamu that she had something devious in mind.

"That would be acceptable," Tamu was saying. "I presume Cobra Ghushtre and his men will wish to remain aboard."

"That will be a decision for His Excellency."

"Of course," Tamu said. "I merely mention that because if they remain aboard there will have to be safeguards against mischief on their part. But the details can be discussed once Shahni Omnathi is aboard."

"His Excellency is, as you say, a foreign dignitary," Uy said. "How large an entourage would you be prepared to host?"

"As large as he wishes to bring," Tamu said. "It's only a day's journey to Aventine, after all. Of course, any additional Djinn or Cobras would have to submit to the same safeguards I've already mentioned."

"Such safeguards including constant surveillance by your Marines?"

"That's one option," Tamu said. "But again, it's only a single day's journey. Surely men trained to war will be able to put up with a few minor inconveniences for so short a time."

"Very well," Uy said. "Give me a moment to discuss this with His Excellency. I'll return shortly with his reply."

And almost too late, Jody had the answer. Maybe. "And please remind His Excellency that he needs to bring his translator along," she spoke up as casually as she could. "There may be subtleties of Anglic during his conversations that he'll miss but that she'll catch."

She held her breath, feeling Ghushtre's frown on the back of her neck. As far as she knew, Rashida Vil was the only Qasaman woman on Caelian. If Uy and Omnathi picked up on the hint and were able to follow Jody's logic...

"His Excellency will of course bring her along," Uy said, his voice carrying the patient stiffness of someone who's just been lectured on the obvious. "A moment, if you please."

The speaker went silent, and the hum of Ghushtre's sonic once again tickled at Jody's ears. "What is your plan?" he asked quietly. "Why do you require Rashida Vil?"

Jody felt her stomach tighten, his comment about trusting her with his life flashing to mind. "The only way for Shahni Omnathi to be truly safe is to get him off Caelian and back to Qasama," she said. "That means we need a ship, and this is the only one available."

"You plan to seize control," Ghushtre murmured.

His forehead was wrinkled in thought, but his voice was calm enough.

"Yes," Jody said. "The problem is the gunbays. If they're as secure as Tamu says, we're not going to be able to get in there quickly and knock them out. We'll only be able to get one more group inside before they realize what we're doing and lock down all approaches to the ship. That's why we need Rashida Vil to come aboard now, along with His Excellency."

"Understood," Ghushtre said. "Tell me your plan."

"Tamu's not going to open his command room until he knows exactly where all three of you are," Jody said. "I'm guessing Tamu will try to get all of you to meet the aircar, and that he's already instructed the Marines to signal him when they can see all three of you in the entryway. I'm also guessing that Tamu will want to lift off as soon as possible once His Excellency is aboard."

"Which means he'll open the door for his pilot as soon as he knows it's safe."

"Exactly." Jody gestured above her. "Do we know where this CoNCH place is, by the way?"

"There's a large sealed room in the center of the middle deck past the mess room," Ghushtre said. "It's just past the point where the main corridor splits into a T-junction. The only door that I saw leading it faced toward the rear of the ship."

"Sounds like the place," Jody said. "Okay. Where's—?"

She broke off as the speaker clicked. "His Excellency Shahni Omnathi agrees," Uy announced. "He and his entourage will meet your aircar at the city gate."

"Excellent," Tamu said, and there was no mistaking the relief in his voice. "My Marines will meet him at the Government Building."

"Your Marines will meet him at the city gate." Uy said tartly. "My Cobras will also be accompanying him."

"Sounds a bit crowded," Tamu warned. "But not impossibly so. The aircar is on its way."

"And you *will* treat him with respect," Uy added. "Or I promise that you'll answer for it."

"Have no fear," Tamu said, and Jody could envision the man's condescending smile. "We will treat him with all the respect and honor he deserves."

"Then we shall see you again soon, Commander," Uy said. "Safe travels."

There was a click as Uy cut off his side of the conversation. "Ifrit Ghushtre?" Tamu called. "Are you still there?"

"I am," Ghushtre said.

"Proper Dominion procedure calls for a military honor guard to welcome dignitaries aboard," Tamu said. "Since you've already neutralized the entire onboard Marine contingent, I'd like you and your companions to provide that escort."

"Of course," Ghushtre said stiffly. "We would hardly leave His Excellency to the mercies of your forces. I trust you'll be on hand to greet him personally, as well?"

"Under normal circumstances, I would be honored," Tamu said grimly. "In this case, I'd prefer to wait behind locked doors until my men confirm there's no threat to my ship."

"Such courage you have," Ghushtre said sarcastically. "Now allow me a time of silence. I need to meditate on the proper welcoming greeting."

Jody gestured, and the Cobra activated his sonic again. "Where are your combat suits?" she murmured.

Ghushtre nodded down the corridor. "Back there," he said. "Come."

He led the way to the storage bin where Nisti had launched his ambush against the two Marines. Tied together in a bundle in one corner were the three scaled gray suits. "We planned to clear the guards from the hatchway and then retrieve them," Ghushtre explained as he removed the two gas canisters from one of the suits. He did something to them, then handed them to Jody. "They're keyed for impact trigger," he said. "You need merely throw them against the wall or floor."

"Got it," Jody said, gingerly taking the canisters and putting one in each of her tunic's side pockets. "I'll go try to find a place where I can watch the CoNCH. If someone opens the engine room door, will you be able to get a canister in there if you're all the way up by the forward hatch? The ceiling's too low to get much of an arc on the throw."

"That won't be a problem," Ghushtre assured her, eyeing the engine room door as he removed the other suits' canisters. "I can set them for timed detonation so that bounces won't matter. There's another stairway leading up from just in front of the engineering door that will give you a view of the CoNCH entrance."

Jody craned her neck. There *was* another stairway down there, all right. She hadn't noticed it before. "Perfect. Remember, don't gas Shahni Omnathi and the others until they're all the way inside the ship. If they're anywhere still outside, they'll probably be in range of the gunbays."

"Understood," Ghushtre said. "Good luck."

The massive door sealing off the control room was just where Ghushtre had said it would be. Jody settled into position on the aft stairway, crouching a few steps down with her eyes on a level with the deck. As long as no one tried to use the stairs, she should be mostly undetectable. And if someone *did* start down from the upper deck, the sound of footsteps should give her enough warning to get back down and out of the way.

Pulling the gas canister from her right-hand pocket, setting it onto the top stair in front of her, she rubbed her suddenly sweaty palms on her silliweave trousers and settled in to wait.

And tried to force calm into her mind. Because suddenly, the fate of two worlds were resting on her shoulders.

It hadn't been like that during the Troft invasion. She'd played her part in Caelian's victory, certainly. But the planning and execution had been handled by other people. Experienced people, or at least trained people. She'd been one of hundreds who'd helped, followed orders, and occasionally come up with a useful idea or two.

This time it was different. She was the one who'd first recognized the corner Tamu had backed himself into. She was the one who'd figured out how to exploit that. She was the one crouching here now with a gas canister.

She was the one whose actions over the next few minutes would mean success or failure.

She drew a long, careful breath, pushing back the doubts. She was a Broom, and a Moreau, and her family had a long tradition of standing at the pivot points of history. Her parents, grandparents, and brothers had all played such roles. It was time for her to step up and do the same.

And then, as she wiped her hands one last time,

there was a soft but deep click from in front of her, and the door began to swing ponderously open. As it did, one of the other room doors nearby slid open and two men slipped into the corridor and hurried toward the CoNCH door.

Jody smiled grimly as she picked up the gas canister. She'd guessed right, all the way down the line. Perfect. Rising half to her feet, she lifted the canister over her head.

And as she cocked her arm to throw, a hand closed around hers. "I don't think so," a voice murmured in her ear.

Jody jerked violently, her heart suddenly pounding. She wrenched at the grip, trying to pull her hand free, trying to spin around. Trying to do *something*.

But it was no use. The man behind her had an iron grip, and her efforts didn't even budge him.

"Come on," he said with a grunt, hauling her to her feet and pushing her the rest of the way up the stairs. The two men who'd been running for the open door looked back over their shoulders at the little drama, their expressions part startled, part relieved. Jody's feet reached the deck, and as her captor forced her toward the door his other hand caught her left wrist and pulled it back behind her, twisting it up at the elbow in a hammer-lock hold. "Keep moving," he added, picking up his pace.

She peered back over her shoulder. It was one of the Marines, wearing the same type of fatigues as the other crewmen she'd seen aboard the *Squire*. But over the fatigues he'd thrown on his dress tunic.

Which only made sense. The fatigues didn't have parrot gun epaulets. The dress tunic did.

"Nice try, though," he continued as he hurried her along. "Your Qasaman friends are good, too—together, you almost had us. Not your fault none of you knew about the hidden sentry post behind the stairs."

"So it was a trap," Jody said, a bitter taste in her mouth. "You were there the whole time."

"Hardly," the Marine admitted. "I couldn't come out of hiding and get into the sentry post until we were sure all three Qasamans were at the hatchway. But it's going to work out just fine, thanks to you and your cleverness." He bent her arm up a little harder toward her shoulder blades, forcing her to speed up. "Oh, and I wouldn't count on the gas to knock out the other Marines, either," he added. "The full combat suit includes gas filters."

Jody said nothing, her stomach churning on the edge of being sick. So it was over. The Marines would capture or kill Ghushtre and the others, bring Omnathi and Rashida aboard, and as soon as the pilots got the engines going Omnathi would be on his way to Aventine.

And unlike Omnathi, Rashida *did* know how to find Qasama. In fact, if she'd brought Jody's recorder along, they would have the location without even having to interrogate anyone.

And it was Jody's fault. All of it. "You've got what you want," she managed as the Marine pushed her toward the open door. Maybe she could at least salvage Ghushtre's life out of this. "Let Ghushtre and the others go."

"And you?" Her captor snorted as he shifted his grip on her right hand and took away the gas canister. "Sorry. Commander Tamu's taking you back to Aventine."

Jody took a careful breath. The two pilots were already inside the control room, taking their places at one of the consoles. From behind and beneath her, she could hear the rumble as the engines powered up. Whatever was going to happen at the hatchway was going to happen, and there was nothing in the universe she could do about it.

But it suddenly occurred to her that there was a chance for her to do something here. One last chance.

She waited until they was nearly to the room. Then, bracing herself, she leaned forward at the waist, taking some of the pressure off her arm, and kicked back as hard as she could with her left foot.

The kick went a little wide, her heel slamming into his upper left thigh instead of her intended target. But it was close enough. The man didn't bellow with pain—Dominion Marines were apparently too tough for that—but she had to bite down on a bellow of her own as his fingers dug into her left wrist. She clamped her teeth together and brought her foot back for another try—

With a shove that sent a dazzling stab of agony up her entire left arm, he shoved her hard through the open doorway.

She stumbled forward, trying to get her feet under her. But her upper body was moving too fast, and she toppled forward toward the deck. As she fell, she twisted her torso a few degrees to the side in midair—

"Get in there, you fremping little horker," the Marine snarled.

—and as she slammed to the deck on top of her other gas canister it went off, wrenching her back as the pressure of its eruption twisted her hip back around and filled the control room and corridor around her with a sweet-smelling mist.

Her last memory before the darkness took her was of the Marine's body slamming down onto her legs.

CHAPTER EIGHTEEN

Two hours of instruction, Merrick suspected, was considerably less than the typical winghunter got before setting off into the sky.

Unfortunately, two hours was all he was going to get.

It would have been better if they could have done at least some of the training outside. To spread the wing out all the way, which Anya couldn't do in the confines of the hut, to strap himself into the harness that hung beneath the wing and actually see how the control bar moved—that would have been far more useful than the half-open wing and tentative examination of the bar and the struts and bracing wire. Even more helpful would have been some actual in-flight training.

But both were out of the question. The two Trofts were tucked into their aircar just across the clearing, and anything that looked like instruction between two supposedly skilled winghunters would only increase their suspicions.

What the effect on those suspicions would be when Merrick fell out of the sky like a rock tomorrow morning was something he really didn't want to contemplate.

But even more disturbing than the sense of his own impending doom was the fact that Anya didn't seem at all worried about it. She was glacially calm, as unruffled as if she was instructing him in a new cooking procedure instead of something that could cost him his life.

She wasn't just putting up a good front, either. An infrared analysis of her face showed that her calm was genuine.

It took him the entire two hours to figure out a way to ask her about her attitude without making it sound like he was accusing her of not caring whether he lived or died. But when he did ask the question all she would say was that she had ultimate faith in him. Whatever that meant.

The hut had only a single bed. Anya insisted Merrick take it, just as she had back in their Qasaman prison cell. For her own part, she wrapped herself in a blanket and stretched out on a pair of woven-leaf mats on the floor.

Merrick didn't sleep much that night. When he did drift off, his dreams were filled with horrific images of him plummeting toward the forest below while Anya calmly watched. In some of the dreams, she laughed as he fell past her.

They woke early, and ate breakfast while it was still dark. The meal consisted of a piece of leftover dinner meat that Anya had tucked away beneath the embers the night before. Merrick had expected to find the slab burned to a crisp, but Anya had buried it just deeply enough for the heat above it to keep it warm without overcooking. The Trofts emerged from their car midway through the meal, and for a tense couple of minutes Merrick thought they were going to commandeer the slaves' food for themselves. But they merely watched the humans eat while munching some kind of field rations of their own.

It seemed uncommonly generous of them, especially since they'd calmly helped themselves to the first cut of the meat the evening before. With the already dark mood Merrick was in, the whole thing felt uncomfortably like he was being granted a condemned man's last meal.

The group set off as soon as it was light enough to see, Anya and Merrick continuing their trudge up the mountain while the Trofts floated behind in their aircar. The terrain was getting stepper, Merrick noted uneasily, and each time they reached a spot that afforded a view downward he felt a fresh surge of acrophobia-tinged trepidation.

But by midmorning, to his mild surprise, the fear had vanished. Either the emotional part of his brain was tired of dealing with it and had shut down, or the logical part had reluctantly realized that a five-hundred-meter fall wouldn't kill him any deader than a fifty-meter one.

It wasn't exactly a comforting thought. But the challenge was looming closer and closer, and he was ready to take anything that would help clear his mind.

It was midafternoon when Anya decided they'd climbed high enough.

[The wings, we shall assemble them there,] she told the Trofts, pointing past a row of short trees to a flat rock outcropping that jutted out from the edge of the cliff. [The rock, it will provide a natural jump-off point.]

[The nets, you have brought them?] the first Troft asked. [The jattorns, I long to feast on them.]

[The nets, we have brought them,] Anya confirmed. [Assistance, we may need it in a moment.]

Both Trofts' radiator membranes fluttered. [Assistance, you will provide it yourselves,] the second Troft said tartly. [The masters, we are they. The slaves, *you* are they.]

[Your pardon, I crave it,] Anya said, bowing to him.

[The hunt, you will begin it,] the second Troft bit out.

[The order, I obey it.]

She turned and strode between the trees onto the rock outcropping, pulling off her pack as she walked. Merrick followed, setting his folded wing beside hers. "If you don't mind, I'll let you go first," he murmured as he gingerly lowered himself to his knees on the rock.

"There's no need for you to assemble your wing," Anya said softly as she knelt down across her pack from him. "You will not be hunting today."

A chill ran up Merrick's back that had nothing to do with the cold mountain air. "What are you talking about?" he asked carefully. For a moment his mind flicked to the Trofts, but his back was to them and without turning around he couldn't tell whether or not they were watching. "Of course I'll be hunting today. I can do this."

She shook her head, a quick, nervous movement. "They'll know," she said, her voice starting to shake. "As soon as you take to wing and sky they'll know you aren't one of us. They'll take you, question you, and kill you. And once you are dead, our chance for freedom will be gone." Her right hand, he noted suddenly, was hovering at the edge of her jacket. "And so, you must not fly."

"Let me guess," Merrick said, consciously relaxing his muscles. He saw now where she was going with this. He could only hope that his programmed reflexes could handle it. "You propose to wreck my wing and then take off as if you're trying to get away from the Trofts. The Trofts chase you, you crash, and they assume you were the spy they were looking for. Problem is, It won't work."

"It *will* work," Anya insisted. "For I will not simply take to wing and sky and leave the masters with time to give chase and capture me." Her eyes flicked over Merrick's shoulder. "First, I will kill them. It will be their fellow masters, those who certainly now watch from afar, who will give chase and drive me to my death."

Another chill ran up Merrick's back. He hadn't realized just how far she was willing to go with this plan. "Does that also mean your plan for putting me out of action won't stop at simply damaging my wing?"

"I'm sorry," Anya said, her face glistening with tears. "Please. Free my world."

Her hand darted beneath the jacket and reappeared with her knife. She hesitated a fraction of a second, then jabbed the tip straight at Merrick's left forearm.

The blade never reached its target. Moving like a blur under his nanocomputer's control, Merrick's left hand snapped up from his side, lightly slapping the back of her hand to deflect the attack, then grabbing her wrist in a lock-fingered grip.

For a second he just knelt there, ignoring her struggles to free her arm, his full attention on her face. Slowly, the twisting and pulling stopped, and the fear and frustration faded from her face. "It won't work," Merrick said when she finally stopped struggling, "because I won't let it."

She shook her head, her throat working. "You must," she said, her voice pleading. "If you don't let me do this, they will kill you."

"I won't let them do that, either," Merrick said. "Neither of us is going to die today."

"But—"

"Neither of us *can* die today," he continued, "because I need you."

She shook her head. "You need no one," she said. "You are powerful beyond my strongest night imagination."

"But I'm a stranger here," Merrick reminded her. "This is your world. These are your people. We do this together, or it doesn't get done." He tried a small smile. "And I don't know about you, but I'm not ready to give up."

For a long moment she stared into his eyes. Then, she lowered her gaze to the knife, and to his hand still gripping her wrist. "I'll go first," she said at last. "Watch how I assemble the wing, and do the same. When we jump, watch how I use my control bar."

"I will," Merrick said, finally releasing her hand. "Don't worry—I'll be fine."

[A problem, is there one?] the first Troft called from behind Merrick.

[A problem, there was a small one,] Anya called back, holding up her knife for the aliens to see before putting it back beneath her jacket. [The problem, it is fixed.]

[The hunt, you will then begin it.]

[The order, I obey it.]

Anya had run Merrick through the assembly method the night before, and though the hut hadn't had enough space for him to actually practice it, the procedure had sounded reasonably straightforward.

In his experience, things in life that promised to be simple seldom were. But in this case, the theory actually matched the reality. If anything, the wing came together even easier than he'd expected.

The jattorn net was only slightly trickier. The flexible ring at the mouth of the long, silky tube was attached to two smaller elastic rings that Anya secured around Merrick's upper thighs. Once in the air, the rings were designed to slide down to his ankles, which would then allow him to control the size of the net's mouth by spreading his legs or bringing them together.

It seemed an unreasonably awkward design, but Anya assured him it was how the nets had always operated. The only way Merrick could rationalize it was if the jattorns were so powerful and aggressive that even with their wings pinioned they could fight their way out of the net unless the hunter kept the mouth closed. He made a mental note to take a close look at the first group of birds Anya managed to snare before he went after any himself.

And with that, it was time to go.

Anya went first, leaping off the end of the cliff like a high-diver hanging beneath a giant arrowhead. For a pair of heart-stopping seconds she fell straight down, the net catching the air and stretching out into a long tube behind her. The drag of the net tugged the anchor rings down to their proper position around her ankles, and only then did she pull up from her dive and settle into horizontal flight.

Merrick swallowed hard. She'd never mentioned *that* as being part of the winghunter technique. For a brief second he considered trying to pull the same maneuver, but common sense quickly intervened. He would go horizontal as quickly as he could and trust that the net would deploy anyway.

[The hunt, you will begin it,] the first Troft called from the aircar hovering behind him.

Taking a deep breath, settling his grip on the control bar, Merrick took a few quick steps to the edge of the cliff and leaped.

A second later, he was soaring through the cool air, gliding like a bird over the forest far below.

"Huh," he breathed, the gasp a mixture of released tension and unexpected exhilaration. He was flying. He was actually, literally flying.

No—he was actually, literally *falling*. Clenching his teeth, he pushed the control bar forward.

Pushed it too far. The wing above him angled up toward the position Anya had warned would put him into a stall. Hastily, he pulled back on the bar, again overcorrected, and eased it a little bit forward. A couple of jerky tries later, he finally got the wing flying smooth and steady.

Blinking against the wind blowing across his face, he took a moment to look around. Anya was paralleling him fifty meters to his right, watching him closely. She raised her eyebrows, and he gave her a quick nod. She nodded back, and pointed ahead and a few degrees below them.

He turned to look, careful not to move the control

bar. About half a kilometer away a large flock of birds was floating lazily through the sky below them. Giving his wing a quick look to make sure he was still flying level, he keyed in his telescopics.

He'd never seen a jattorn before, but the birds definitely fit Anya's description. They were large and majestic, with plumage done up in a complex pattern of blue and white, with hawk-like beaks and V-split tails. Their legs were tucked beneath them out of his sight, but given that Anya had tagged them as raptors, he imagined the feet included impressive sets of talons.

And he was supposed to fly into the middle of the flock, let those things get right up beside his legs, and scoop them into a net?

Apparently so, because that was clearly where Anya was headed. She had dropped the nose of her wing and was heading down toward the flock, pulling ahead of him as she converted her drop in altitude into extra speed. Wincing, Merrick shifted his attention to the control bar. If he pulled it back just a *little* . . .

[The enemy who sent you, who is he?] the first Troft called.

Merrick twisted his head around. The Troft aircar was sitting practically on top of him, pacing him from three meters back and two meters up. The Trofts had lowered their side windows, and the first Troft was leaning out the left-hand window toward him.

The wing jerked as Merrick's movement again shifted the control bar a little too far. He spun back to face forward, fighting to get the fragile aircraft back under control. [The enemy who sent you, who is he?] the Troft called again, more insistently this time.

Merrick turned back again, shaking his head and

taking the risk of lifting one hand off the control bar to give a gesture of confusion at the question, a gesture he could only hope the Trofts understood.

The alien seemed to get the idea. He also clearly didn't believe it. [A lie, do not make it,] he said sternly. [A winghunter, you are not one of them. A spy for our enemies, you are one of them. The enemy who sent you, who is he?]

Merrick again shook his head, trying desperately to try to think of something else he could do to persuade them.

An instant later the wing again jerked as a laser flashed twice from the aircar, gouging out a pair of tears across the center of the wing directly above his head. [A winghunter, you are not one of them. The enemy who sent you, who is he?]

Of course I'm not a winghunter, the protest boiled up through the bubbling panic in Merrick's throat as he fought to bring the damaged wing back to level flight. *We told you that back in Gangari. I'm only a winghunter assistant.*

But he couldn't say that. He couldn't say anything in his defense. He was a mute, and a sudden recovery of his voice would do nothing but confirm to the aliens that he and Anya had been lying to them all along.

And even if he could somehow persuade them to accept such a miracle cure, his accent alone would instantly brand him as an outsider.

Another pair of bolts sizzled through his wing. [The truth, you will give it,] the Troft insisted. [Or death, it will find you.]

They were baiting him, he knew. They weren't out here alone—even Anya had realized they had backup and observers somewhere close at hand. This pair was the bait, pushing the suspected spy to see if and how he would react.

And if he *wasn't* a spy, but merely an innocent slave, they would probably continue to fire and push and fire some more until his wing disintegrated above him and he fell to his death. No great loss, and they would move elsewhere in their search.

Merrick clenched his teeth. Letting them kill him just to maintain his cover would be the ultimate in futility. But revealing his true identity would be equally disastrous. If the Drims realized there was a Cobra loose on Muninn, they would turn the whole planet upside down looking for him, and probably kill untold numbers of innocent slaves in the process.

But maybe there was a small patch of middle ground. If he could reveal that he was a spy, but *not* that he was a Cobra...

Another laser shot cut through his wing, and this time no amount of maneuvering could keep it flying level. Merrick was going down—not too steeply yet, but he was definitely going down.

His final fate was sealed. But the Trofts apparently weren't interested in the gradual approach. Peering back over his shoulder, Merrick saw the aircar move lower, and to his stunned disbelief the Troft on that side began gathering in double handfuls of the net tied to his ankles. [The truth, you will give it,] he shouted. He pantomimed yanking back on the net. [Or the net, I will hang you from the sky from it.]

And with that, Merrick no longer had a choice. Glancing back at the aircar, flicking targeting locks on both Trofts' foreheads, he shifted his grip on the control bar, curling his right hand over the top and pressing his little finger awkwardly along the bar, aiming it toward the bar's outer end.

The Troft was still gathering in the net, but so far hadn't attached it to anything inside the aircar. Wrapping his other fingers around the bar, Merrick settled his thumb against the right ring-finger nail, the trigger for the fingertip laser's highest setting. Taking a deep breath, he twisted the bar violently around to his right, swinging the end toward the aircar, and fired.

The two flashes weren't as bright as the ones that had sliced all those tears in Merrick's wing. But they were more than powerful enough to kill the two aliens where they sat.

At least Merrick hoped they had. His nanocomputer had barely fired off the second shot when the world erupted in a dizzying spiral as his wing went completely berserk.

He twisted back forward and grabbed the bar again, this time in a proper grip. But his ninety-plus-degree turn to line up the control bar with the Trofts had completely wrecked both his stability and his forward momentum. An instant later the spin abruptly became a three-dimensional spiral roll as the now driverless aircar shot past, catching the wing's tip as it arced toward the forest below.

For an eternity of seconds Merrick tried everything he could think of, every maneuver and trick Anya had taught him. Finally, finally, he managed to dampen out the spin and roll.

But it was only a temporary victory. The Trofts' laser shots had damaged the wing far beyond Merrick's ability to compensate. He was falling, and there wasn't a single thing he or his weapons or his fancy Cobra programmed reflexes could do to stop it.

He was still trying to regain some altitude, wondering what it would feel like to die, when he was abruptly jammed into his harness as the wing was jerked upward. Somehow, the nosedive had been halted, or at least slowed.

He looked over his shoulder, expecting to see the aft end of a Troft aircar behind the edge of his tattered wing. To his surprise, what he saw was a trailing jattorn net.

He craned his neck to look straight up. A pair of hands were sticking through the flapping tears in the fabric, holding tightly to the support struts.

A flood of relief flowed through him. There was no way Anya could keep them in the air for long, and any chance of a hunt was completely out of the question. But if she could hold on long enough she should at least be able to bring them to a more or less smooth landing. Certainly a landing that would leave them both alive. "Thank you," he shouted toward her. "Your timing is perf—"

"They're coming," she cut him off, her voice rigid. "There—to the left. They're coming."

Merrick turned to look. To the south, just above the range of mountains, a fast-moving speck had appeared. Snarling under his breath, he keyed in his telescopics.

It was an aircar, all right, the same design as the one he'd just sent on a power dive into the forest. Unlike that one, though, this model came equipped with a pair of hood-mounted weapons. Lasers, or something equally nasty.

His plan to convince them that he was a spy had

worked, all right. And the backup crowd had come loaded for bear.

What in the *Worlds* were the Drims up to on Muninn that the possibility of a lone spy could prompt this kind of violent response?

"Merrick Hopekeeper, what do we do?"

"Take it easy," Merrick said as soothingly as he could as he searched for inspiration. Below them, the forest seemed to stretch forever in all directions, with Gangari and a handful of other villages forming the only sizeable open areas. The main road they'd come in on was visible, as were a network of narrower side roads, some of them running alongside narrow but fast-looking rivers or streams. More mountains were visible in the distance to the north, possibly part of the same chain as the one they'd just jumped from.

"Merrick!"

"I said relax," Merrick snapped. "You'll be all right— they're coming for me, not you."

He frowned. They *were* coming for him, he realized suddenly. *He* was the proven spy, while as far as they knew Anya might be nothing more than a naïve local whom the intruder had conned into helping him.

Which meant that if they could split up, the pursing Trofts' logical choice would be to chase him and leave her alone.

The trick was how to do that without getting himself captured. Or killed.

But at the same time to let the Trofts *think* he'd been killed . . .

"I need a ravine," he shouted up to Anya. "Or a massive cave, or maybe a sinkhole system. Some place close at hand where a body would be hard to find."

"There's the Jendl River ravine," Anya said. "It's there, to the right, about three kilometers away. What are you planning?"

Merrick looked that direction. He'd spotted the river earlier, but hadn't noticed the ravine. But it was there, all right, its contours obscured by the trees. It looked to be about a hundred meters across and maybe four hundred meters long.

A muted flash caught his eye: a piece of forest a kilometer downriver from the ravine had suddenly sprouted a set of smoky yellow flames. The aircar he'd sent crashing into the woods had apparently caught fire.

"Merrick?"

"Here's the plan," Merrick said, throwing a quick look at the incoming aircar. It was closing fast, but by the time he made his move it should still be far enough away for the trick to work. Even better, it was maintaining its altitude, staying high above the gliders, probably in hopes of avoiding whatever weapon Merrick had used on the first vehicle. "In about ten seconds I want you to drop us to treetop level and head toward the ravine," he continued. "And when I say treetop level, I mean I want us—me, anyway— actually skimming between the tops of the trees. Can you do that?"

"Yes, I think so," she said doubtfully. "The steering will be difficult. I may not be able to keep you from hitting the treetops. Are we then going into the ravine?"

"As long as I don't hit anything hard enough to bring you down, that shouldn't be a problem," he assured her. "And no, the only thing going into the ravine will be my wing. Someplace between here and there, I'll drop off. You'll then continue to the ravine, drop my wing into it, then get as far away as you can before you have to come down. With any luck, they'll start the search for me there. Can you do that?"

"I think so," she said again. "But these trees are twenty meters tall. Can you survive a fall from that height?"

"Let me worry about that," Merrick said. Drawing his knees to his chest, he pulled the tether rings off his ankles and started hauling in the net. He hadn't tested the material's tensile strength, but given that the first pair of Trofts had planned to hang him and his wing from it, the stuff ought to be strong enough for what he had in mind. "You worry about finding a safe place for you to land."

"There are many such places," she assured him. "Do you see that stone dome ten kilometers ahead?"

Merrick keyed in his telescopics as he wadded the net against his chest. Just visible over the trees was a rounded chunk of gray-white rock. "Yes."

"I shall meet you there sometime after sundown," she said. "Are you ready?"

Merrick found the two ends of the net and wrapped one securely around each wrist. "Ready," he said. "Take us down."

An instant later, his stomach seemed to leap into his throat as Anya sent them into a sharp dive downward. The trees rushed up at him, and for an awful second he thought she'd miscalculated and was about to send them crashing at full speed into the forest—

And then, just when it seemed too late, he was again yanked in his harness as she leveled off.

He'd asked her to stay at treetop height. She'd taken him at his word, the tops of the highest trees now whipping past at awesomely dangerous speeds. How she was steering with both hands holding his crippled wing he couldn't begin to guess, but somehow she was managing to avoid the taller trees and only occasionally brushing his shins against one of the shorter ones.

But no matter how skillful she was, her luck couldn't last forever. Time for Merrick to find a way off this bus.

There it was, fifty meters ahead: a treetop reaching to within two meters of his stomach, with no other taller trees immediately behind it for at least ten meters. "Hold us straight on this path," he called to Anya. "Here I go."

"Good luck," she called back.

"You too." Glancing up at the straps fastening his harness to the wing support struts, he put target locks on each of them. Almost as an afterthought he freed the control bar from its own straps and tucked it away inside his jacket. He'd gone to a lot of effort to make it look like he had a laser hidden in the bar, and it would be a shame to leave the thing with his wing where a search team might find and examine it. He looked back at his target tree, trying to judge his timing . . .

With about a quarter second to go, he fired his fingertip lasers, simultaneously twisting his shoulders to the side. The lasers sliced cleanly through the straps, and with a lurch he fell free, the last-second shoulder twist giving him just enough rotational momentum to turn him halfway around. Free-falling down and forward, his back now to the wind, he winced as his target treetop slapped across the backs of his thighs and flew past beneath him.

And throwing his arms out, he sent the loop of net fabric flying behind him and dropped it neatly over the top of the tree.

It was like catching a car with a lasso. His body snapped straight out behind him, his wrists and shoulders threatening to pop out of their sockets as the tree did its level best to change his forward momentum from incredibly high to incredibly zero as quickly as possible. In that first agonizing second of multigee deceleration the only thing that saved him from disaster was the combination of his bone and ligament strengtheners, the springiness of the treetop, and the slight elasticity of the net material itself.

The net was never designed for such strain, and within the first second and a half it snapped in two. But by then its job was done. Merrick had slowed himself from bat-out-of-hell to rapid jog, and he'd lived through it.

And with that, all he had to do was get safely down the twenty meters still separating him from the ground.

But that one, at least, *was* in his repertoire of preprogrammed reflexes. Looking over his shoulder, he put a targeting lock on the tree trunk now whooshing up toward him and bent his knees slightly. His feet hit the trunk, and as his knees bent to absorb the remaining momentum he put another target lock on a tree he'd just passed. His body started falling forward, his knees straightened, and he flew across the gap, turning a one-eighty to again hit the second tree feet-first. Again his knees bent and then straightened, and again the nanocomputer launched him across and down.

It was a technique that had been designed for

city maneuvering, to be used with an alley or narrow street to get from rooftop to street level in a hurry. Apparently, it worked just as well with trees.

The nanocomputer choreographed his final bounce, and as he landed at last on the grass and mat of dead leaves it occurred to him that he'd never been so glad to be on solid ground in his life.

But there was no time to pause for relief or self-congratulation. The Trofts would presumably start their search at the ravine where Anya was about to dump his wing, but if they had any brains they would include an infrared sweep of the entire area. Orienting himself, he headed off into the forest, running as fast as the terrain and his Cobra servos would permit.

He'd had some concerns that the aircar he'd sent crashing to the ground might burn hot enough to ignite a full-blown forest fire. To his relief, that didn't look like it would be a problem. The aircar—what was left of it—was still burning when he reached the scene, but while the vegetation immediately around each of the scattered pieces was blackened, the trees and bushes and ferns even as close as twenty meters away seemed untouched.

The exception being the handful of trees that had been in the direct path of the vehicle's final flight. Two of them had been smashed in the process of shredding the aircar into rubble, while another two now showed the same type of scorch marks Merrick had seen at the other more distant wreckage site.

Near the main fire was what appeared to be the twisted remains of one entire side of the aircar, lying at the end of a deep groove it had gouged in the ground. Wrapping the pieces of the torn jattorn net around his hands to protect them, Merrick went over to the smoldering metal and pulled it back a couple of meters, positioning it over the deepest part of the groove. Then, rewrapping the net into a loose protective turban around his head and face, he crawled along the groove and lay down underneath the metal.

It was hot down there, but not unbearably so. As Anya had demonstrated that morning with the leftover meat, most of the heat from the burning metal was flowing upward away from him.

More importantly, all that rising heat should be more than enough to mask his presence from whatever infrared detectors the pursuing Trofts might be using.

So he would lie here for awhile, resting from his ordeal and waiting for the opening that would come between the Trofts' quick survey of the site and the more detailed follow-up team who would come to collect the pieces for closer study. It would be during those minutes or hours that he would be able to slip away and disappear into the forest.

Only then would he find out whether Anya had also survived this first battle for her world's freedom.

But what had happened had happened, and for now there was nothing he could do one way or the other. Closing his eyes, keying his audio enhancers to full power, he settled down to wait.

CHAPTER NINETEEN

It was clear from the moment Colonel Reivaro stormed into Commandant Ishikuma's former office that the man was in a foul mood. He slammed the door behind him, rattling the frosted-glass window to within a millimeter of shattering, and stomped across to the desk. He flicked on the small reading light and dropped into the chair like he was trying his best to accidentally break it. The chair survived anyway. Glancing across the monitors lined up along the desk's edge, he cursed feelingly and reached for the keyboard.

"I know how your comm system works," Lorne said quietly from his hiding place beside the door. "Twitch either eye, and I'll kill you."

For a handful of seconds Reivaro didn't move, his face and body frozen, his eyes still on the keyboard. Then, a small smile curved one corner of his mouth. "I'm impressed," he said calmly. "I truly am. May I ask how you got in here?"

"Of course not," Lorne said, coming out into the muted light and showing the colonel the small device in his hand. "This is a dead-man switch. I presume you highly advanced Dominion people still know what those are?"

"It's hardly a technology likely to go out of style," Reivaro said. "What's it keyed to?"

"The block of explosive I put under your chair," Lorne told him.

A muscle in Reivaro's cheek twitched. "I see," he said. "Are we making this personal, then?"

"That depends," Lorne said. "Right now, I'm just here to get my parents. Where are they?"

The muscle twitched again. "Unfortunately both are currently beyond my reach."

"I didn't ask if you could bring them to me," Lorne said coldly. "I asked where they were."

"Cobra Paul Broom is in Capitalia, being prepped for interrogation," Reivaro said. "Trust me when I tell you he's completely out of your reach."

"I'm sure you think so," Lorne said. "But then, I'm also sure you thought *you* were out of my reach."

Another half-smile. "Point. As to Cobra Jasmine Broom, her whereabouts are currently unknown."

"Of course they are."

"Believe what you will, but for once I'm being completely and totally honest," Reivaro said. "She disappeared right after she sabotaged the Yates Fabrications power system." He raised his eyebrows slightly. "She *did* sabotage the factory, correct?"

"No idea," Lorne said. "I've been in Bitter Creek all day."

"Of course—I'd forgotten. May I ask what's become of Sergeant Khahar and Marine Second Chimm?"

"Both were still alive and reasonably well when I

left them," Lorne assured him. "Cobras don't kill unless absolutely necessary. Unlike others I could name."

"We all have our orders and our missions, Cobra Broom," Reivaro said. "And you must never forget the reality that's driven everything that's happened here."

"The reality that the Dominion of Man likes power?"

"The reality that the Dominion of Man is at war."

"And no doubt fighting for her very survival?"

"I wish I knew," Reivaro said heavily. "We were holding our own when our task force left Asgard. But that was eight months ago. A lot can happen in eight months."

Lorne took a step toward the desk, forcing back the reflexive flicker of sympathy. His infrareds were indicating a reasonable degree of sincerity on Reivaro's part, which was a point in his favor. But even sincerity, fear, and patriotism combined could never justify shooting down three Cobras in cold blood. "I'll ask one more time," he said. "Where is my mother?"

"I don't know," Reivaro said. "Trust me: if I knew, I'd tell you." Another half-smile. "If only because a rescue mission as insane as your incursion here tonight would give us another opportunity to catch you."

"You may still get that chance," Lorne said, stepping backwards toward the door. His numbers were counting rapidly down, and it was time to go. "See you later, Colonel."

A minute later he was slipping through the darkened Archway streets, his opticals on night-vision, his audios primed for the sounds of the inevitable pursuit.

So his hope of finding and freeing his father had been dashed. Still, that had never been more than a faint hope to begin with. The more reasonable goal, the one that had offered the greater long-term possibilities, had been achieved.

He'd slipped into the enemy's stronghold without being detected. He'd gone straight to the top of the command structure, rattled Reivaro's cage, and demonstrated that the colonel and his Marines weren't nearly as invincible and infallible as they thought they were.

It was a bold stratagem, and a risky one. But if Lorne had learned anything from the war on Qasama it was that prodding the enemy into reaction instead of giving him time for careful thought was the first step toward victory.

And a little misdirection never hurt, either.

Yates was waiting at the rendezvous spot when Lorne returned to the river flowing its serene way through the center of town. With him, to Lorne's relief, was Lorne's mother. "One mother, delivered as promised," Yates said, gesturing to her as Lorne came up.

"Thank you," Lorne said, fighting back the impulse to rush to his mother and giver her a hug. With all of them still eyeball-deep in enemy territory, a display of affection didn't seem appropriate. "I owe you."

"Get these people out of my factory and out of Archway and we'll call it even," Yates said tartly. "Good luck."

He brushed past Lorne and disappeared into the darkness. "Over here," Lorne said, taking Jin's arm and leading her to the trash bin where he'd stashed the scuba gear. "Hope you're up for a little swim."

"Sounds refreshing," she said. "Is it just the two of us?"

"For now, anyway," Lorne said, feeling his stomach tighten. Her voice was calm enough, and he could hear the relief and gratitude that he'd come for her.

But there was a grim sadness there, too. A sadness, and a deep weariness of mind and soul. She would do what he told her to do and go where he led, but her mind wasn't up to the task of making decisions.

And Lorne realized that, for possibly the first time in his life, he was the person in charge. Of everything.

It was a strange and vaguely disturbing idea. Throughout his childhood and teen years his parents had been the ones who made the decisions in the family. After that had come the Cobra academy, with senior officers and instructors in command, and then his assignment in DeVegas province under Commandant Ishikuma. Even during the Troft invasion there had always been someone else with strings on him, whether it was Senior Governor Treakness on Aventine, Harli Uy on Caelian, or the Qasaman commanders he'd worked with in Azras.

But those strings had now been cut. Jin was exhausted with age, the lingering aftereffects of brain surgery, the capture of her husband, and just plain too much fighting. There were no seasoned superiors for Lorne to answer to or seek advice from. He was on his own, standing against an enemy that by all rights he should never have had to face at all.

But that was how it was going to be. The Dominion of Man, in its infinite wisdom, had decided that it was time for the Cobra Worlds' century of autonomy and freedom to come to an end.

It was up to Lorne to convince them otherwise.

They finished suiting up in silence. "Where are we going?" Jin asked as Lorne led them around the barrier and over the bank into the river.

"You'll see," he said. "Follow me."

❖   ❖   ❖

The first thing Jody saw as she rose slowly back to consciousness was Kemp's frowning face hanging in the air over her. "Do I look that bad?" she murmured.

He smiled. But the smile only touched his lips, leaving the rest of the frown still in place. "Hardly," he said, trying for a light touch and not coming even close to succeeding. "Never, really. How do you feel?"

Jody hunched her shoulders and experimentally moved her arms and legs. There were some bruises along her side, especially where she'd landed on the gas canister, but otherwise everything seemed in proper working condition. "Fine," she told Kemp. "I gather it worked."

"Oh, it worked, all right," he said, the brief moment of lightness gone without a trace. "We're the masters of the Dominion of Man Courier Ship *Squire*, or however the proper title goes. The rest of the Dominion people have been collected and they're being sent in small groups back to Stronghold." He made a face. "All except the two stashed in the gunbays. So far, they're refusing to come out."

"What are you going to do about them?"

"For now, we're just leaving them there," Kemp said. "Thanks to you, we've got everyone we need already inside, so there aren't going to be any useful targets for them to shoot at. Eventually, I figure they'll get bored enough or hungry enough to come out and surrender."

"Or you could cut your way in."

"If we want to bother," Kemp said. "But the doors are being watched, so they can't come inside and make any trouble. Anyway, Tamu and the rest are going to be housed in Stronghold for a day or two while more permanent quarters are being prepared for them in Aerie." He gestured. "Meanwhile, the two pilots are sitting in the CoNCH under the spell of one of Omnathi's concoctions and they're showing Rashida Vil and Smitty how to fly this bird."

Jody cocked an eyebrow. "*Smitty's* learning how to fly?"

Kemp shrugged. "He says he always wanted to learn. Personally, I think he just likes hanging out with Rashida. Anyway, Omnathi thinks we'll be able to plug in the course codes from your recorder and head out for Qasama by evening."

"Sounds great," Jody said, eyeing him closely. "What's the *bad* news?"

Kemp sighed. "We'd hoped to do this without further bloodshed. Unfortunately, that turned out to be impossible. Specifically, the four Marines who were escorting Omnathi and Rashida to the ship are dead."

A sudden memory flashed to Jody's mind: the Marine who'd captured her casually mentioning that the approaching group would be immune to Qasaman sleep gas. "The gas couldn't stop them," she murmured.

"Right," Kemp said grimly. "Turned out they had filters built into those helmets of theirs. They took down two of Cobras we'd sent as escort, and were on their way to frying Ghushtre and the other Qasamans when we stopped them."

Jody felt her throat tighten as she thought back to the display of firepower the Marines had demonstrated back in the Government Building conference room. "How many more did that cost us?"

"None," Kemp said. "Do you remember Governor Uy mentioning something called Damocles? Basically, it was supposed to be our last-ditch hole card for future trouble. We took a heavy laser off the more-or-less intact Troft ship and loaded it and a power supply into one of our air-transport vans."

"You made yourselves a gunboat," Jody murmured, an eerie feeling running through her. As far as she knew, the Cobra Worlds had never had any kind of serious combat weaponry before. "Sounds a little dangerous."

"Not as much as you'd think," Kemp said reluctantly. "Or, depending on your point of view, a lot more than you'd guess. Because after Tamu picked you up and started trying to strong-arm us into trading you for Shahni Omnathi, we . . . well, we sort of added in a Qasaman targeting system."

Jody frowned. "You mean one of the systems in their combat suits? But I thought those were keyed into the sensors in a Djinni's eye lenses. How did you—?"

She broke off as the sudden awful truth hit her like a gut punch. "You had a *Djinni* firing the laser?"

"Yeah," Kemp said, not sounding any happier about it than Jody felt. "It wasn't like we had much choice. Cobra targeting systems aren't designed to handle external weaponry. Djinn systems are."

"And so now Qasamans have fired directly on Dominion personnel?"

"And you can imagine how Uy's feeling about *that*," Kemp said. "Still, if it comes to a diplomatic crisis, the fact remains that the Marines fired on us first."

"That's not the point," Jody ground out. "We're Cobra Worlds people, which means we're also Dominion people. Whatever happens between us probably comes under internal legal jurisdiction. But the Qasamans aren't Dominion. Firing on Dominion Marines probably constitutes an act of war."

"I know," Kemp said with a sigh. "And I have no idea how Uy's going to cover everyone's butts on this one. But step one is to head for the tall grass of Qasama along with every human being who knows how to find it." He seemed to brace himself. "That means you, too."

"That's okay," Jody said. Her anger was fading, leaving only frustration behind. "I wasn't going anywhere with the gunbays still manned, anyway. And it's not like I was doing anything useful on Caelian. Maybe things will be different on Qasama."

"What are you talking about?" Kemp asked, frowning. "You did great work on this one. If you hadn't been aboard, we'd have had to blast our way into the control room."

"Which I know now you were perfectly capable of doing," Jody countered. "Especially with a Troft laser to play with."

"And how many more people would a frontal assault have cost?" Kemp retorted. "Not to mention giving Tamu time to wreck the ship so that it might never fly again?"

"Maybe," Jody muttered reluctantly.

"I know how you feel," Kemp said. "But we all have our parts to play. Sometimes they don't feel like much, but it often turns out that they're absolutely vital, and they're parts that only we can play. For whatever it's worth." He stood up. "Anyway, I should probably let you get a little more rest. I'm told that Qasaman sleep gas hits a person pretty hard, especially the first time."

"Hopefully, I won't ever have to see what the second time is like," Jody said.

"Agreed," Kemp said. "See you later."

For a long time Jody lay quietly, listening to the

distant rumble of the engines and the occasional footsteps or muffled conversations as people walked past her door. Maybe Kemp was right. Maybe there was a part in this that only she could play.

And maybe, down deep, she knew what that part was.

She found Omnathi in the CoNCH control room, standing behind Rashida and Smitty as they studied the control board they'd spent the past couple of hours learning how to operate. Other men—some Qasaman, others Caelian—were scattered elsewhere around the room, working at other consoles or conversing quietly over comboards or status displays. "Ah—Jody Moreau," Omnathi said, nodding to her in greeting. "I trust you're fully recovered from your ordeal?"

"I am, Your Excellency," she said, making the Qasaman sign of respect.

Omnathi smiled, making the sign back to her. "I'm pleased," he said. "I'm looking forward to introducing you to the world that your family has done so much to save."

"As I'm looking forward to meeting your people," Jody said. "A question, if I may?"

He gestured. "Of course."

"Cobra Kemp tells me that without my help we couldn't have captured the *Squire* intact, which would have left you marooned on Caelian and at the mercy of Commander Tamu and the Dominion," she said. "Do you concur with that opinion?"

"I do," Omnathi said, frowning slightly.

"Then it seems to me that you and Qasama owe me a favor."

"We owe you far more than that," Omnathi agreed. "Speak your request."

The room had gone silent. "I have reason to believe my brother Merrick was taken captive by some of those who invaded our worlds," Jody said. "I also believe I may have the location of the world where he was taken. My request is this." She gestured around her. "Once we've delivered you and your people to Qasama, I would like permission to take this ship and go look for him."

"By yourself?" Omnathi asked calmly.

Jody swallowed, feeling suddenly a bit off-balance. She'd expected to have to argue a lot longer about the ship before they even got to questions of personnel. "Well, no, of course not," she stammered. "I'll at least need a pilot."

"You got one," Smitty spoke up.

"You have two," Rashida corrected. "With your permission, of course, Your Excellency."

"And the rest?" Omnathi asked, his eyes still on Jody.

Jody frowned. "The rest of the crew?"

"The rest of your request," Omnathi said. "There *is* one more part to it, is there not?"

Jody gazed back, a creepy feeling shivering the back of her neck. She'd heard stories about Omnathi's borderline-psychic ability to read the people around him. But until now, she'd never experienced it for herself. "Yes," she said, bracing herself, suddenly conscious that she was standing right on the edge. The options and decisions were still ahead of her. She could still back away.

Only she couldn't. Because she was Merrick's last hope. "Wherever my brother is, he's in danger," she continued. "If I'm going to have any chance of freeing him, I need to be ready to face down that same danger. As ready as I can possibly be."

She straightened up and looked Omnathi straight in the eye. "Your Excellency... I wish to become a Cobra."

The stars were blazing down from overhead by the time Merrick reached the rock dome Anya had pointed out.

He found her waiting beneath the branches of a prickly-looking mushroom-shaped bush. "I'd almost given up hope," she said quietly as he sank to the grass beside her.

"Sorry," he apologized. "I wanted to make sure all the Troft activity was going on somewhere else before I came. You made it down okay, obviously?"

"There were no problems," she said. "An intact wing can be easily landed in a small area."

"At least by someone who knows what they're doing."

"Yes." She paused. "They will suffer for what we did today."

"Gangari?"

"Yes," she said. "The masters will inflict terrible punishment on them."

"It's not right," Merrick murmured. "They did nothing to help us. Hell, most of them never even saw us between the time we came in and the time we left."

"You seek logic and justice," she said tiredly. "You'll find neither on Muninn."

Merrick winced. "I know. I'm sorry."

For another moment they sat together in silence. "Do you remember Henson Hillclimber speaking of dark memories?" she said at last.

"Yes," Merrick said. "I've been wondering what that referred to."

"Many years ago a group of residents attempted to free Gangari from the masters," she said. "The effort failed, of course."

"And the instigators punished, no doubt."

"The instigators were not punished, for they could not be found," Anya said. "They had slipped away into the night. Those who were left behind were thus forced to accept the full force of the masters' reprisals. Many of the young were taken from them that day. Some were sent to the Games. Others were taken across the stars and sold."

"Including you?"

"Yes."

Merrick nodded heavily. And now the instigators of this fresh act of rebellion had likewise disappeared into the forest. The point of Anya's story was painfully clear. "I'm sorry, Anya," he said. "I wish we could help them. But aside from giving up and turning ourselves in, I can't think of anything we can do."

"I know," Anya said. "But that wasn't why I told you the story. I told you because the ones who led the failed rebellion were my parents."

Merrick stared at her. "Your *parents*? You mean—?" He broke off as the kicker suddenly hit him. "They ran off and *left* you there? Knowing full well that the Trofts would take their anger out on you?"

"Yes," Anya said, and Merrick could hear the echoes of old bitterness in her voice. "I don't know why. I've never known why. I know only that the masters will also remember, and that my part in today's events will weigh all the more heavily on their judgment against Gangari."

Abruptly, she got to her feet. "It's time."

"Where are we going?" Merrick said, standing up beside her.

"To a place where the masters will not find us," she said, looking up at the stars and then turning to face southwest. "A place that has proven its ability to stay hidden from their gaze."

"Sounds perfect," Merrick said, nodding.

"Yes," Anya said, striding off into the darkness. "Pray that they will accept us."

"There's someone else living there?" Merrick asked, hurrying to catch up. "Anyone you know?"

"I knew them once," she said. "Or I thought I did." She hissed out a sigh. "Once, they were my parents."

Barrington had estimated that once the *Hermes* was prepped it wouldn't cost them more than ten minutes to break out of hyperspace, drop the courier, and break in again.

In actual fact, the drop took only seven.

"So that's it," he commented to Lieutenant Meekan as he gave the CoNCH displays a final check. The break-out and break-in had both gone perfectly, and the *Dorian* was once again on track toward Qasama.

Or toward wherever it was Commander Ukuthi was sending them.

Meekan was apparently thinking along the same lines. "You think we can trust him, sir?" the aide asked.

"Ukuthi?" Barrington shook his head. "I don't know. A cruiser like the *Dorian* would be a fine catch for one of the demesnes we're fighting. On the other hand, those demesnes can't possibly expect that we'd be any easier to take intact than any other Dominion warship they've tangled with."

"Perhaps Ukuthi is trying to split our forces," Meekan suggested. "Hoping to take us out one at a time instead of having to face the task force as a whole."

"That one's marginally more likely," Barrington said. "But whatever Ukuthi's game, we know there's at least one other player involved. *Someone* thought it was worth the effort of chasing him all the way to the Hoibe'ryi'sarai home world and sitting on him, whether it was this Tua'lanek'zia or someone else. I think it more likely that Ukuthi's looking at the possibilities of having a Dominion warship on his side in whatever tangled politics he's mixed up in."

"And is using Qasama's location as a bargaining chip?" Meekan shrugged. "Yes, that makes sense. The next question is whether he'll deliver that chip as promised or try to hang onto it against future bargaining."

Barrington felt his throat tighten. "I wouldn't put it past him," he said. "On the other hand, stringing a client along carries its own set of risks. Especially when that client has the kind of firepower that we do."

"True," Meekan said. "And there's something Ukuthi doesn't know: it's entirely possible that Commodore Santores will have gotten Qasama's location from one of the Brooms by the time we reach the other end of this trip. If he has, Ukuthi's bargaining power will be gone and we may be able to get some genuine information out of him."

"Possibly," Barrington agreed. "And either way, we'll have Qasama."

"We'll have Qasama," Meekan agreed, looking closely at his captain. "I confess I still don't understand why the commodore is so adamant on finding it."

"It's very simple, Lieutenant," Barrington said, his stomach tightening. In theory, a mere lieutenant shouldn't be privy to such information. In actual practice, senior command aides were usually exempt from such barriers. "Qasama is Commodore Santores's flying bridge."

Meekan blinked. "Excuse me?"

"Do you know why Dominion warships still have flying bridges?" Barrington asked. "Or haven't you ever wondered about that?"

"The latter, I suppose," Meekan admitted. "I've assumed they were there because warships have always had them."

Barrington shook his head. "That's what I used to think, too. It wasn't until after I graduated that I was able to track down the real reason."

He gestured upward, toward the flying bridge riding the hull far above the CoNCH's armored ceiling. "It's a sucker trap, Lieutenant. It holds two men, has control and power circuits in and around it, and looks every bit like a control node or targeting station or *something* of intrinsic military value. The very fact that it's so open and vulnerable makes it a tempting target for any enemy who manages to get that close."

"Only there's nothing really there," Meekan murmured. "Just a repeater station with a water tank behind it."

"Which, if the enemy's shot gets through, will spew a ton of instant-freezing ice crystals straight at him," Barrington said. "Which will in turn generate surprise, confusion, loss of clear targeting, and possible overload of his point defenses. Not a bad return for some wiring, some water, and two lives."

"I see," Meekan said, his voice sounding strange. "And you say Qasama is...?"

Barrington sighed. "Our orders are to lure the Trofts into a trap," he said quietly. "The original plan was to use the Cobra Worlds as bait. Now that we know about Qasama, Commodore Santores feels it will work even better."

Meekan seemed to digest that. "What if the Qasamans don't feel like taking the brunt of another Troft incursion?"

"I don't think the commodore was going to offer them a choice."

"No, I suppose he wasn't," Meekan murmured. "May God have mercy on their souls."

"No," Barrington said, a shiver running through him. Meekan hadn't seen the full transcript of the Brooms' testimony. Barrington had. "May God have mercy on *ours*."

The following is an excerpt from:

TRIAL BY FIRE

VOLUME TWO OF
THE TALES OF THE
TERRAN REPUBLIC

CHARLES E. GANNON

Available from Baen Books
August 2014
trade paperback

Chapter One

The maglev began decelerating. As it did, the light seeping in through the overhead plexiglass panel increased sharply: they were now beyond the safety of the base's tightly patrolled subterranean perimeter. Caine Riordan, newly minted commander in the United States Space Force, glanced at the young ensign beside him. "Are you ready?"

Ensign Marilyn Brahen looked out the even narrower plexiglass panel beside the door, and checked the area into which they were about to deploy. There was blurred, frenetic movement out there. "Were we expecting a lot of—company?" she asked.

"No, Ensign, but it was a possibility." Caine rose. "So we improvise and overcome." She stood beside him as the doors opened—

—and they were hit by torrent of loud, unruly shouts from a crowd beyond the maglev platform. The group swiftly became a tight-packed wall of charging humanity, their outcries building before them like a cacophonic bow-wave.

Ensign Brahen eyed the approaching mob, news people already elbowing their way into the front rank, and swallowed. "Sir, you think those crazies will stay outside the car?"

"Not a chance." *And given the automated two-minute station stop, they'll have us pinned in here before we can leave.*

"I gotta confess, sir," she continued, "this wasn't what I was expecting when they told me I was going on a field assignment with you."

"Well," mused Caine as the reporters closed the last ten meters, "we *are* off-base. And technically, the civilian sector is 'the field.'" Caine smiled at her, at the charade which was to be his one and only "command," and stepped out the door.

The moment his foot touched the maglev platform, an improbably shrill male shriek— "Blasphemer!"—erupted from the center of the approaching crowd, followed by a glass bottle, spinning lazily at Caine.

Behind him, he heard Ensign Brahen inhale sharply, no doubt preparatory to a warning shout—

But recent dojo-acquired reflexes now served Caine better than a warning. Without thinking, he sent the bottle angling off to smash loudly against the side of the passenger car behind him.

As Caine sensed Ensign Brahen moving up to cover his flank, he scanned the rear of the crowd for the presumably fleeing attacker. Instead, he discovered the assailant was standing his ground, right fist raised, left arm and index finger rigidly extended in accusation—

—and which disappeared behind the surge of newspersons that surrounded Caine as a wall of eager faces and outstretched comcorders. Somewhere, behind that palisade of journalists, the attacker shrieked again. "Blasphemer!" But his voice was receding, and then was finally drowned out by the mass of jostling reporters and protestors that threatened to shove Caine and Ensign Brahen back against the maglev car. Their inquiries were shrill, aggressive, and rapid.

"Mr. Riordan, is it true you're the one who found the remains of an alien civilization on Delta Pavonis Three?"

"Caine! Caine, over here! Why wait two years to announce your discoveries?"

"Who decided that you'd announce your findings behind closed doors: the World Confederation, or you, Caine?"

A young man with a bad case of acne and a worse haircut—evidently the boldest jackal in the pack—stuck a palmcom right under Riordan's nose. "Caine, have there been any other attacks like the one we just witnessed, by people who believe that your reports about exosapients are just lies intended to undermine the Bible?" Ironically, that was the moment when one of the protestors waved a placard showing a supposed alien: a long-armed gibbon with an ostrich neck, polygonal head, tendrils instead of fingers. Actually, it was a distressingly good likeness of the beings Caine had encountered on Dee Pee Three, prompting him to wonder, *so who the hell is leaking that information?*

The young reporter evidently did not like having to wait two seconds for an answer. "So Caine, exactly *when* did you decide to start undermining the Bible?"

Caine smiled. "I've never taken part in theological debates, and I have no plans to start doing so."

A very short and immaculately groomed woman extended her palmcom like a rapier; Caine resisted the impulse to parry. "Mr. Riordan, the World Confederation Consuls have declined to confirm rumors that you personally reported the existence of the exosapients of Delta Pavonis Three at this April's Parthenon

Dialogues. However, CoDevCo Vice President R. J. Astor-Smath claims to have evidence that you were the key presenter on the last day of that meeting."

Caine labored to keep the smile on his face. *It would be just like Astor-Smath, or some other megacorporate factotum, to put the press back on my scent. But how the hell did they find me out here at Barnard's Star?* Caine prefaced his reply with a shrug. "I'm sorry. I'm not familiar with Mr. Astor-Smath's comments, so—"

Another reporter pushed forward. "He made these remarks two months ago." The reporter's palmcom crackled as it projected Astor-Smath's voice: composed, suave, faintly contemptuous. "I wish I could share more with you about the Parthenon Dialogues, but the late Admiral Nolan Corcoran prevented any megacorporation—including my own, the Colonial Development Combine—from attending. However, we do have reliable sources who place Mr. Riordan at the second day of the Parthenon Dialogues."

Behind him, Caine heard a warning tone announce the imminent departure of the maglev passenger car. It would be ten minutes before the next would arrive, ten more minutes surrounded by harrying jackals. *No thanks.* "I'm sorry," he said, "but you'll have to excuse me."

So much for my "first command." He started to turn back to the maglev car.

"One last question, Caine. Who's your new girlfriend?"

Ensign Brahen started as if stuck by a pin. Caine turned back around, foregoing the escape via maglev. Instead, he searched for the source of the question, asking, "Besides being grossly unprofessional and misinformed, just why is that a relevant inquiry?"

"Well," explained Mr. Bad-Skin Worse-Hair as he reemerged from the mass of faces and limbs, "we were expecting to see you with Captain Opal Patrone, your personal guard. And, some say, your personal geisha."

Enough is enough. Caine planted his feet, kept his voice level, his diction clipped. "I feel compelled to point out that, in addition to raising a thoroughly inappropriate topic, you didn't even manage to frame it as a question." Caine looked out over the faces ringing him. "If there are any competent journalists here, I'm ready for their inquiries."

The group quieted; the mood had changed. Their quarry had turned and bared teeth. Now, the hunt would be in earnest. The next jackal that jumped in tried to attack a different flank. "Mr. Riordan, is it true that you were present when Admiral Corcoran died after the Parthenon Dialogues?"

Caine pushed away the mixed emotions that Nolan's name summoned. The ex-admiral-turned-clandestine-mastermind had arguably ruined Riordan's life, but had also striven to make amends and forge an almost paternal bond. Caine heard himself reply, "No comment," just as the maglev car rose, sighed away from the platform, and headed off with a down-dopplering hum.

"Mr. Riordan, do you have any insights into how Admiral Corcoran's alleged 'heart attack' occurred?"

"Why do you call it an 'alleged' heart attack?"

"Well, it's a rather strange coincidence, don't you think? First, you were reportedly present for Admiral Corcoran's heart attack in Greece, and then for the similarly fatal heart attack suffered by his Annapolis classmate and crony, Senator Arvid Tarasenko, less than forty-eight hours later in DC. Comment?"

"Firstly, I don't recall any prior assertions that I was near Senator Tarasenko at the time of his death—"

"Well, an anonymous source puts you in his office just before—"

An anonymous source like Astor-Smath, I'll bet. "Madam, until you have verifiable information from verifiable sources, I'm not disposed to comment on my whereabouts at that time. In the more general matter of the heart attacks of

Misters Corcoran and Tarasenko, I cannot see any reasonable explanation *except* coincidence." Which was superficially true; Caine had no other explanation for the heart attacks that had, within the span of two days, removed the two leaders of the shadowy organization which had sent him to Delta Pavonis Three: the Institute of Reconnaissance, Intelligence, and Security, or IRIS. On the other hand, Caine remained convinced that the two deaths had been orchestrated. Somehow. "Timing aside, there's not much surprising in either of these sad events. Admiral Corcoran never fully recovered from the coronary damage he suffered during the mission to intercept the doomsday rock twenty-six years ago. And Senator Tarasenko was not a thin man. His doctors' warnings to watch his weight and cholesterol are a matter of public record."

Tasting no blood, the jackals tried nipping at a different topic. "Mr. Riordan, our research shows that you spent most of the last fourteen years in cold sleep. And that your 'friend' Captain Opal Patrone was cryogenically suspended over fifty years ago. What prompted each of you to abandon the times in which you lived?"

As if choice had anything to do with it. "In the matter of the recently promoted *Major* Patrone, she's the one you should ask her about her reasons." *Hard to do, since Opal's on Earth by now.* "But I can assure you that she did not 'abandon' her time period. She was severely wounded serving her country. In that era, her choice was between cryogenic suspension and death."

"And *your* reason for sleeping into the future?"

"Is none of your business." *And is a* non sequitur, *since it wasn't my choice.* Caine had simply stumbled across IRIS's secret activities, which had earned him an extended nap in a cold-cell. "Next question."

"A follow-up on your long absence from society, sir. Some analysts have speculated that, as a person from another time, you were just the kind of untraceable operative needed for a covert survey and research mission to Dee Pee Three. What would you say in response to that speculation?"

Caine smiled, hoped it didn't look as brittle as it felt. *I'd say it's too damned perceptive.* Aloud: "I'd say they have excellent imaginations, and could probably have wonderful careers writing political thrillers."

Bad-Skin Worse-Hair jumped back into the melee. "Stop evading the questions, Riordan. And stop playing the innocent. You knew that the Parthenon Dialogues were going to be biggest news-splash of the century. So did you also advise the World Confederation on how to shroud the Dialogues in enough secrecy to pump up the media-hype? Which in turn pumped up your consultancy fees?"

Caine stepped toward the young reporter, who hastily stepped back, apparently noticing for the first time that Caine's rangy six-foot frame was two inches taller than his own and decidedly more fit. Riordan kept his voice low, calm. "It's bad enough that you're plying a trade for which you haven't the aptitude or integrity, but you could at least check your conclusions against the facts. Without commenting one way or the other about my alleged involvement with the Parthenon Dialogues, it must be clear to anyone—even you—that the world leaders who attended were grappling with global issues of the utmost importance, and that the secrecy surrounding them was a policy decision, not a PR stunt. In short, whoever brought information to the Parthenon Dialogues may have delivered a sensational story, but not for sensational purposes."

But if that admonishment curbed the jackals momentarily, Caine could already see signs that they would soon regroup and resume their hunt for an inconsistency into which they could sink their collective investigatory teeth. And there were still at least five minutes before the next passenger car arrived. Five minutes in which even these bumbling pseudo-sleuths might begin to realize that the real story was not to be found in the storm and fury of Parthenon itself, but rather, in the surreptitious actions that had been its silent and unnoticed prelude. They might begin asking how the mission to Delta Pavonis had come to be, and—in the necessary nebulousness of Caine's responses—discern the concealed workings, and therefore existence, of some unseen agency. An agency that was unknown even to the world's most extensive intelligence organizations—because its select membership dwelt amongst their very ranks. An agency, in short, like IRIS—

From behind Caine, the maglev rails hummed into life, braking and hushing the approach of a passenger car. Surprised by the early arrival of the train, Caine turned—and saw that this passenger car was a half-sized private model, furnished with tinted one-way windows. The pack of reporters fell silent as the doors hissed open—

—to reveal a shapely blonde woman, sitting at the precise center of the brushed chrome and black vinyl interior. She smiled. It was a familiar smile.

Caine grimaced.

Ensign Brahen looked from the woman to Caine. "Isn't that Heather Kirkwood? Isn't she a reporter? A *real* reporter? On Earth?"

Caine resisted the urge to close his eyes. "She is that. And worse."

"Worse?"

"She's my ex."

"Your—?"

Heather cocked her head, showed a set of perfect teeth that were definitely more appealing—and far more ominous—than those possessed by the half-ring of jackals surrounding them. She crooked an index finger at Caine. "You coming? Or are you enjoying your impromptu press conference too much to leave?"

If possible, Ensign Brahen's incredulous eyes opened even wider. "Do we go with her?"

Caine sighed. "Do we have a choice?" He led the way into the car.

—end excerpt—

from *Trial by Fire*
available in trade paperback,
August 2014, from Baen Books